"...die," she hissed and dropped the bottle over the edge. Fire plummeted past the dangling cage and hit the ground like a bullet. I immediately pulled Fudge back up and out of the way of the flaming carnage—and carnage there was.

The bottle exploded and liquid fire doused the closest poxers. They immediately burst into flames and started squealing. One by one they popped, and burning chunks hit the next wave of undead. So it went, over and over again until almost every dead thing on the street was truly snuffed. Burning piles were strewn everywhere and that attracted more poxers. They were too stupid to realize that fire was bad, so they reached for the embers as though the crackling piles were something yummy to eat.

Several more poxers were offed that way.

"Pure genius," I said. "I can't believe that plan worked."

Dead (A Lot)

by

Howard Odentz

Bell Bridge Books

Bell Bridge Books
PO BOX 300921
Memphis, TN 38130
Print ISBN: 978-1-61194-299-6

Bell Bridge Books is an Imprint of BelleBooks, Inc.

Printed and bound in the United States of America.

We at BelleBooks enjoy hearing from readers.
Visit our websites – www.BelleBooks.com and www.BellBridgeBooks.com.

10 9 8 7 6 5 4 3 2 1

Cover design: Debra Dixon
Interior design: Hank Smith
Photo credits:
Zombie © Yorkberlin | Dreamstime.com

:Lldr:01:

Dedication

For David

1

NO ONE KNOWS what's going to happen. That's the way that life works. We're born, we live, we die, and in between a whole lot of stuff goes down that we can never guess. Not in a million years.

Take me, for example. I never knew my world was going to end. I never really thought about it.

For a while there, life flowed easy. Dad was a doctor. Mom went to Harvard. Me and my twin sister, Trina, lived in a good town—nice house, nice school. We had the prerequisite pedigreed dog, even though she was a poodle and sort of lame. I had friends. I had the Internet.

What else did I need?

Need—now that's an interesting word. For example, just this morning what I really needed was a handgun—something light and easy to use—something that wouldn't kick back and blow my head off because I didn't know what the hell I was doing.

Chuck, my sister's muscle-head of a boyfriend, was on one side of our granite kitchen island, and it was seriously clear that the football king wanted nothing more than to get around that slab so he could eat me.

That's not normal behavior, but the world had very recently exited the normal ramp, and the new normal was like a bazillion light years away from the old normal.

Chuck was dead. That was clear. He had one eyeball hanging out of his head from a stringy-thingy, and he kept gnashing his teeth together and smacking his lips like I was some sort of deep fried yummy treat.

The good news was that death apparently made Chuck slow and stupid, or stupider. The bad news was that I needed his car keys, and I was fairly sure they were in his pocket.

I had to think. So I started walking around the island, keeping a good distance ahead of Chuck and the width of the slab between us. I didn't have to walk too fast. His version of *Dead Man Walking* wasn't exactly speedy.

I didn't need speed. I needed a gun. In most zombie flicks it seems like they die if you blow them away. Too bad the only gun in the house was attached to my gaming station, so that plan was a bust.

In the comics, zombie deaths are caused by that old standby of chopping off their heads. I had knives, but, well, first—gross, and second—all my mom had were butter knives and some doohickey I think she used to core apples.

I couldn't core Chuck to death, and buttering him up was out of the question, but clearly I had to do something.

After a couple minutes, Chuck burped and farted at the same time. This noxious invisible gas filled up the kitchen.

Still he kept on walking.

A couple more minutes and I started breathing through my sleeve because, damn, he smelled nasty. I suppose I could have left, but seriously, I really needed those keys.

Then Sprinkles, our poodle, came in.

Don't blame me for the name. My mom picked it out because she had this thing about ice cream with . . . wait for it . . . sprinkles.

Chuck saw her through his one good, dead eye and forgot about me. Sprinkles took one look at Chuck, clicked her little, painted toe nails right over to him and was still wagging her tail when he scooped her up and bit off her face.

Yup, that's what I said. He bit off her face.

I couldn't help thinking about that face-transplant lady in France whose poodles ate her original one. I didn't think Sprinkles was going to be a face transplant candidate, but I did take her transformation into poodle pie as my cue to run around the kitchen island, reach my hand into Chuck's pocket, and pull out his car keys.

With his keyring jangling in my fist, I ran down the hallway and straight out the front door where Trina was waiting for me in Chuck's car.

Life was always easy for me and that goes for my relationship with Trina, too. We've been tight from day one. I still remember in middle school when I still had a face full of peach fuzz, a pre-steroidal Chuck had pushed me into my locker between gym and lunch. Trina knocked him flat and told him she was going to unscrew his balls and keep them in her pocket because he obviously wasn't deserving of a pair.

I think that's when he probably started to like her.

"Where's Chuck?" she screamed when I got into the car.

"He's dead."

"I know he's dead, Einstein. Where is he?"

"He's eating Sprinkles."

I started the car and just sat there for a moment, enjoying a well-deserved mental break. Trina sat there, too. She leaned back in the seat and looked out the window. After a moment she pressed the automatic door lock.

"Like with ice cream?" she finally asked.

"No," I said. "He's just eating Sprinkles."

I threw the car into reverse. Somehow I didn't think it mattered that neither of us had finished Driver's Ed yet.

2

WHO WOULD HAVE thought that when I woke up that morning my life would change forever?

Mom and Dad had gone up to our lake house in Vermont for the weekend. They left a note that said:

Dear Tripp and Trina,

Here's $200 in case you order out for Chinese or pizza. Or in case you want to go to the movies. Or in case you go to the mall. Or in case you have a party. No Drugs. No Drinking. No Sex.

Love Mom and Dad.

P.S. Don't forget to feed Sprinkles.

Chuck came over shortly after Mom and Dad pulled out of the driveway. He and Trina barricaded themselves in Trina's room for a round of rule-breaking.

I stuffed my ears with a pair of mental ear plugs, threw on a pair of shorts and a t-shirt, and nested in front of the computer.

Mom and Dad never got the whole idea of parental controls on our PC, so I checked out some websites that I probably shouldn't have looked at before getting bored and watching some previews of upcoming movies.

Everything looked totally lame so I downloaded an indie horror flick and lost myself in mummies for a couple of hours.

Around seven or so I realized Chuck and Trina were never coming out of her room, so I nuked myself something out of the freezer and pocketed a twenty, making a mental note to tell Mom and Dad that I had taken their suggestion and had a pizza delivered.

Around eight the alarm on Chuck's car went off.

"What the hell," I heard him scream from upstairs. "Yo, Tripp, Dude, you touch my car?"

"Yo, Chuck, Dude. Don't call me Dude."

I heard him fumbling around upstairs. A minute later, he came down in his t-shirt and jeans, no shoes or socks, and went out the front door.

Trina came down a few minutes later wearing sweat pants and Chuck's shirt. Her blond hair was a little messed up. Even in loser clothes, Trina's pretty. That makes me a guy's version of pretty, right?

"What's for dinner?" she asked.

"Dinner was leftover leftovers. I ate them all."

"That's totally uncool," she said

I hopped up on the counter. "Are you and Chuck doing the nasty? I mean, I'm all for biodiversity, but shouldn't you at least be dating in your genus?"

"Shut up, Tripp. At least I've hit puberty. What are you, anyway, XXY?"

"Nah," I shot back. "I just think shaving's for sissies."

Outside, Chuck's horn kept bleating away. His mommy and daddy had bought him a Hummer, which was both lame and awesome. It was school bus yellow, which was even more lame and more awesome.

The lamest part, however, was that Chuck Peterson had a car at all. The Light twins were still holding permits instead of licenses, and it didn't matter anyway because Dad said something about Hell freezing over when we asked him about a car for our sixteenth-and-a-half birthday.

Little did any of us know that, far from freezing, Hell was heating up with an Indian summer right here on earth, and Chuck's Hummer was parked out on Lucifer Lane.

"What's the deal?" I muttered after a few minutes of his car horn tearing up the night.

"Like I know," said Trina. "I'm hungry." She opened up the fridge and rummaged inside.

I hopped my butt off the kitchen counter and walked over to the front door. I guess Chuck's horn had stirred up the neighborhood. There were a bunch of people milling around his car, which was all lit up and glowing because, A—it was a school bus yellow Hummer, and B—the street light was right at the end of our driveway.

I opened the door and stepped out into the night. Trina followed behind me, shoving a piece of cold chicken into her mouth.

That's the moment when normal first exited, stage right.

"Chuck?" she said, but what it really sounded like was 'Cuff,' because she was chowing down.

"What the . . ." I stopped and stared.

Mrs. Ruddick from next door was standing out on our front lawn in her bra and panties, and Mrs. Ruddick was flannel pajama material at best.

Geez, a kid could go blind seeing something like that.

Old man Levin from across the street was there, too. He was shuffling aimlessly around, bumping into people and growling at them.

Two middle school kids who lived a few doors down were gnawing on what looked like turkey legs from a county fair. I didn't see their little brother anywhere, and since when did turkey legs have fingers?

Dr. Jeffers and his current wife, who mom called Number Three, were both crawling on the ground and grappling for something meaty and wet, like pit bulls fighting over a kitten.

A woman I didn't recognize was teetering around without an arm—just a blood-soaked shirt and a stump. She kept sticking her tongue out and bending her head so she could lap at the blood that was splashing up onto her shoulder.

Chuck was down.

"Um," I said. "Is this where we change the channel on the remote?"

"Don't move," whispered Trina.

"Wasn't planning on it. Am I seeing what I think I'm seeing?"

"Like Halloween but in September?"

"Why is Chuck sitting down?" I asked.

Trina slowly grabbed my arm. "So how shallow would I be if I said I didn't give a crap about Chuck right now and was just worried about you and me?"

"Shallow's a strong word," I said. "I'd go for practical."

"Let's get inside." Trina carefully pulled me backwards while Chuck's horn kept rifling off the same tune. Her nails sunk into my arm, but I'm not sure I cared. When we were both inside, Trina softly closed the door and turned off the light in the foyer. We both crouched down and glued ourselves to the windows on either side of the doorway and watched.

Sprinkles came up beside Trina and wagged her little pom-pom tail as she peered at the spectacle outside. Thank God for puppy daycare. She wasn't a barker.

"So are we talking air-borne disease or the classic 'if-you're-bitten-game's-over' scenario?" I whispered.

"What?"

I couldn't tear my eyes away. My mouth moved on its own. "I mean, I guess I should be more scared, but I've seen way too many zombie movies. What's this one called, Twilight of the Dead?" My words came out faster and faster. "They've already made Night and Dawn and Day. They were kind of campy. The Romero remake of Night was a little more serious. He also did Diary of the Dead and Island of the Dead and that was just . . ."

"*Tripp,*" my sister hissed.

I guess I was babbling.

"What do you mean air-borne?"

The whole conversation was totally surreal.

"Well, it looks like the entire neighborhood is infected," I whispered. "So, did they catch some weirdo disease that the government let loose in a cloud like acid rain?"

"It's not raining, and stop freaking me out any more than I'm already freaked out." Trina came over and knelt down beside me. "What are you saying? This is like some disease you catch on the wind? Are we breathing it now? Are . . . are you going to eat me?"

Outside someone started bellowing. It was Mr. Mic, this really tough, bald guy from down the street. He came running toward the lady who was trying to eat what was left of her arm. He had a baseball bat over his head. The entire neighborhood of the dead turned to look at him as he wound up like an all-star at home plate and swung at her melon.

It flopped sideways, and something gooey dripped out of her ear.

One of the middle school kids dropped what he had been gnawing on, staggered over to Mr. Mic, and took a chunk out of him right around waist level, because that was just about mouth level for the kid.

Mr. Mic started hollering and smashed his baseball bat down on the kid's head maybe three or four times. Finally, the kid let go. Mr. Mic dropped the bat and started running back down the street and disappeared into the dark. Trina made this gulping sound but didn't say anything. A minute later Mr. Mic came stumbling back out of the gloom, but this time he was just like all the rest of them.

"I guess that answers that question," I said.

"Biting," we both whispered in unison.

A few more minutes passed as we watched transfixed behind the glass windows of our foyer. Sprinkles made a little doggy sneeze and clicked away into the guest bathroom. After a moment I heard her lapping water out of the toilet.

Trina finally broke the silence. "What's Chuck doing?" she asked.

I supposed I should have cared more about Chuck, but I wasn't the one playing tongue tango with him, so I was more focused on the rest of the insanity. He was still down, but he was writhing and squirming a little bit. A few seconds later he leaned his head back against his Hummer, and Trina covered her mouth with both hands to stifle a scream that threatened to spill out between her fingers.

His left eye was halfway down his cheek, and I think he picked up what the middle school kid dropped and was getting ready to slurp up some sloppy seconds.

That's when the lights went out.

3

WE SPENT THAT first night in the back of the basement in my father's work room. We called it The Putter Room because all he ever did was putter in there. Every once in a while Dad would emerge with a birdhouse or a bookcase—strictly amateur hour. The Putter Room was filled with gadgets—lots of them.

I used his battery-powered screwdriver to drive about a million screws into the door frame. Trina had gathered a bunch of blankets and pillows from upstairs, bags of chips, and snacks, soda, and a bowl of water for Sprinkles. My mom was a candle freak, so I took about ten jars down with us and lit them all over the room.

It smelled like a mixture of cooking and fruit.

After I screwed us in, Trina confessed she didn't have her cell phone with her, which was monumentally stupid. Mine was down to two bars. I called and texted almost everyone I knew, but no one answered. I even called Mom and Dad, but that was a bust, too.

Thankfully, Sprinkles only whined for a couple minutes before she peed and crapped in the corner. Our unified chorus of 'good girl, good girl' most likely undid every bit of house training she ever had, but these were definitely extenuating circumstances.

A few hours in, I peed in the corner, too. Finally, so did Trina, although she thought that peeing there was about the grossest thing she ever did.

Right around midnight, I got the first and last text from Dad. '*We are ok but can't get home. Get to Aunt Ella's any way you can. Do what you have to do. Please respond.*'

Trina and I stared at the little screen and read the message over and over again. Aunt Ella lived up in the Berkshires near the Vermont border. She had a farm and a lot of land.

"Do you even know what town she lives in?" Trina asked.

"I only know she lives off of the Mohawk Trail. That's about it."

"Me, too," she said. "I remember you go to the coffee shop, turn right, and pass a million apple trees. After that I'm clueless."

I texted Dad back.

'Freaked but ok here. What town?'

We waited for a response, but nothing ever came.

"Why Aunt Ella's?" Trina finally asked.

"I don't know. It's not like we go there a lot. I guess it's because it's about half way between us and where they are in Vermont. Also, there aren't many people around up there. Maybe they think we'll be safe."

"Safe? My boyfriend just turned into a zombie along with everyone else in our neighborhood. For all I know, everyone in town's a corpse, and you've screwed us into our basement. I'm really not feeling the safety here, Tripp." Her voice began to waver.

"Listen," I said, mostly because I was feeling about as unsafe as she was. "I'm really tired. Should we take shifts or something?"

Trina ripped open a bag of chips. "You've got two hours." Trina ate when she got stressed. Even though I wasn't hungry I reached my hand out so she'd toss a few chips over to me before she ate them all.

"Trina," I said. "What are we going to do?"

"Live," she said without skipping a beat, which is exactly what I would have said if she had asked me first.

"Live," I repeated. "I can live with that."

4

TWO HOURS OF dreamless sleep later the pounding started. Trina shook me awake and put her finger to her mouth. Someone or something was pounding rhythmically on the front door upstairs—slowly and methodically—like my guitar teacher's metronome.

"We can't stay here," I whispered.

"We can't go out there."

"We're going to have to go out there."

Trina bit at her lip. "My shift is up," she said. "Let me sleep for a couple hours." She curled up in a blanket but couldn't stop looking at the spot on the edge of the ceiling, just about underneath where the pounding was coming from.

I nodded and crawled to my feet to take my shift.

Trina never slept. Around 3:30 or so, the pounding stopped only to be followed by the sound of breaking glass. Almost immediately I heard someone moving around over our heads. Sprinkles stared at the ceiling and tilted her head from side to side.

"Some watchdog you are," I muttered.

"Crap," Trina whispered.

"Capital C."

"Any bright ideas?"

"Yeah," I said. "We're going to Aunt Ella's to see Mom and Dad and figure everything out from there." I hoisted my dad's electric screwdriver and started working on the screws I used to penny us in The Putter Room. "And we may have to kill a zombie in our house."

"Already dead," she said.

I grimaced and continued unscrewing screws knowing full well the sound was going to attract the thing upstairs.

About a half hour in, whatever was upstairs realized the sound it was hearing was coming from the basement. Trina gasped when she heard the clunk of heavy feet coming down the staircase. I figured it was useless to be quiet and hope that the thing would go away, so I kept on unscrewing the screws, letting them fall to the floor at my feet.

About three quarters of an hour in, something started to bang on the other side of the door. We both jumped. Hell, it's not like we weren't expecting something like that to happen, but when it finally did, we completely slid over into Stephen King land.

"The door's latched right?" Trina stammered. "It's latched. Please say it's latched." She was clutching my dad's crowbar with white knuckled fists.

"How's girl softball been doing?" I asked and motioned for her to stand to the left of the door.

I continued unscrewing until all the screws were out. Carefully, I reached for the latch.

"Are you crazy?" she hissed.

"How the hell else do you think we're going to get out of here? Besides, they're slow. You saw them. They're slow and really stupid." My hand caressed the latch. "So are we cool?"

"Just do it already."

I unlatched the door, grasped the knob, and pulled.

Chuck Peterson fell through the doorway, dangling eyeball and all. As he did, Trina swung the crowbar and struck him square in the shoulder. He went sprawling across The Putter Room, and Trina and I ran out, trailed by our soon-to-be-deceased poodle.

We dashed up the basement stairs and locked the door behind us. I was scared out of my mind. Trina glued herself to me like a shadow while I crept through the house to see if there were any others lurking about. But there weren't. One of the windows next to the front door had shattered. Out front, the sun was rising, and I could see a couple of bodies lying on the street that I doubted would ever be mobile again.

The school bus yellow Hummer glowed in the break of dawn.

"We're taking Chuck's car," I said.

"I don't think he'll mind."

"I don't think he has a mind to mind. Where are his keys?"

Trina looked at me with blank eyes. "In his pocket," she said.

"In his pocket," I repeated. "The one attached to the jeans he's wearing?"

"That would be correct."

"Crap," I said. "Crap, crap, crap, crap, crap."

"He's slow and stupid, remember? I'm going to grab a few things, then we're out of here. You get his keys." She was off and running before I even had a chance to protest.

"That's just great," I muttered. "That's just freaking great."

Less than thirty minutes later, she had two duffle bags filled and crammed into Chuck's Hummer. She also had the crowbar she used to bean him with. We agreed that I would open up the basement door and wait for mindless Chuck to come bumbling up the stairs. Once he did, I would do what I needed to do, with whatever I could find to do it with, to get his keys so we could get out of there.

In retrospect, both of us really did forget about Sprinkles.

When Chuck finally noodled out how to get up the stairs and started staggering after me in a demented game of Duck, Duck, Dead around the kitchen island, I should have done more to save her.

After all, she was family. Operative word: was.

Good dog, Sprinkles. Good dog.

SO THAT'S HOW the zombie apocalypse started, just after dawn on the eighteenth of September, our junior year of high school. Summer hadn't yet worn off, and the chill of a Massachusetts autumn seemed a long way off.

When I started Chuck's Hummer that morning and slowly backed out of the driveway, I saw two things. One was the chewed remains of a little boy's arm lying on our front lawn. The second was Chuck staggering out through the broken window next to our front door.

Trina sniffed and gripped the crowbar just a little bit tighter. I think it's safe to say they broke up.

5

WE SAW NO ONE anywhere—no one alive that is. There were loads of Necropoxers. That's what the guy on the radio called them. We had Necropoxers aplenty, but nobody breathing.

After we pulled out of the driveway and I got used to Chuck's wheels, I drove slowly down the street while Trina turned on the radio. There was nothing but static on our regular stations.

She went all the way through the FM channels twice. There was nothing, so she switched to AM. Somewhere around 760 she landed on someone talking.

I pulled over to the side of the road right outside our development and listened.

The D.J. said his name was Jimmy James, and he sounded tired. He explained that the 'poxers' started popping up all over the place sometime late yesterday afternoon. By the time the electricity failed, they were already out in force.

Jimmy James explained that he had switched the station's power to their back-up generator and would continue broadcasting as long as he could. He didn't know how long that was going to be. He was locked in the sound booth, and the sound booth was surrounded by the evil-dead.

The Necropoxer name came from one of the people who called in to the station. Unlike Trina, Jimmy James had his cell and power cord with him when everything started to happen. He kept urging anyone alive with juice in their cell to call in and report on what they were seeing. He had his phone on speaker so listeners could hear what the callers were saying. In between calls, he repeated what he knew.

The caller wouldn't identify himself which made me think he was a government whistle blower. He called the disease Necropoxy. It was airborne, and less than one percent of the population was genetically immune to the airborne version, but no one was immune to the bite.

Let's hear it for us one percenters—Whoo Hoo!

Necropoxy was actually a parasitic disease. As soon as it found its human host, it went right to the brain and started multiplying at a freakish rate. Within a very short amount of time the host body filled with parasites.

What's worse was that Necropoxers wouldn't decompose and fall apart in a few weeks. They were actually human bags filled with living organisms. They weren't even going to rot as long as the host bodies kept feeding the parasites.

What they fed on was meat.

We were meat.

On the radio, Jimmy James fielded a call. "Where you from?"

"Littleham," she said. "Near Springfield."

"That's here," Trina whispered.

"I know," I whispered back. "Why are we whispering?"

"Shhh. I want to hear."

Jimmy James kept the caller talking. "Are you safe?" he asked.

"Not really," she said, fear infesting her quiet words. "I don't think any of us are safe. I'm in the coffee shop I work in. I was supposed to close up last night. Thank God I had the key to lock the door."

"So where are you now? You must have power if you're reaching me."

"On the floor behind the register," she said. "I found an old battery radio next to the sink, but my cell phone is almost dead. These things keep walking by the window, but I don't think they know I'm here. And I've had like a gallon of coffee."

I pulled Chuck's Hummer out into the street and headed for the Mug N' Muffin in the center of town. That's the coffee shop that she was talking about.

"What's your name?" asked Jimmy. He was trying to keep her calm.

"Prianka," she said. "Prianka Patel."

"Prianka Patel!" I almost drove right off the road. "I hate Prianka Patel."

Okay, it's not like I hated her in that I wanted her to get eaten by zombies for real, but I'm sure in one of the many hate fantasies I had about her, being eaten by zombies had probably crossed my mind.

Year after year, Prianka Patel was in almost every one of my classes, and year after year she made it her personal mission to be just a tiny bit better than me in practically everything. If I got a 95 on a quiz, she got a 96. If I got an A on a paper, she showed off an A plus. What's even worse was that she was pretty—pretty in that exotic, dark haired, foreign sort of way that you can't even make fun of without other guys looking at you like you're crazy. Pretty like . . . ugh . . . what was I thinking? I hated Prianka Patel.

"Hate is just another four letter word for love," said Trina.

"Shut up. She's a self-righteous know-it-all."

"Maybe. But we need some extra smarts right now."

I didn't say anything. Instead I focused my attention on the new world in front of us. The Necropoxers were wandering and eating. Every second or third one that we saw was gnawing on a piece of bloody something. I hoped they were eating each other, but I wasn't sure that was the case.

Another thing I noticed was that they were getting faster.

The Chuck-shuffle that we both saw last night seemed to be replaced by a chaotic stagger. We were watching the parasites infest people right before our eyes. The more the infestation took hold, the faster they were getting, and the faster they were getting, the hungrier they were getting.

We drove down Mountain Road and turned left on Main Street. The Mug N' Muffin was down a block to the left, right across the street from the bank. There were like a dozen poxers wandering back in forth in front of the entrance. A van had turned over in the middle of the road, and there was a bloody smear on the tar.

I pulled out my phone and punched in the phone number to the radio station. Then I turned down the radio and waited for him to answer.

"You've reached WHZZ, and this is Jimmy James. Who are you, and how you holding up?"

"My name's Tripp Light," I said. "I'm with my sister, Trina, in Littleham. If Prianka can hear this, we're coming to get her."

"How cool is that," he said in a voice that was slowly turning to gravel. "Hear that, folks? Chivalry ain't dead, although the white horse our man Tripp's riding in on might be if he's not fast enough."

"My white horse is a Hummer," I said. "It's plenty fast, and right now I think we're all up for a little game of zombie bowling."

"You go, man," said Jimmy James. "You go."

Trina reached over and put on her seatbelt then braced herself with one hand on the dash and the other gripping the handle above the window.

"Prianka friggin Patel," I hissed through clenched teeth and floored the Hummer.

I hit the first poxer square in the chest. She was our age, but I don't think I recognized her from school. She flew straight back like she was being pulled really fast by an invisible rope and landed about thirty feet away and missing some key parts.

The poxers all turned toward us and moved a little too quickly toward our car.

"Back up, back up, back up," Trina screamed in my ear. I did, just slowly enough that they could follow us without losing interest.

When we were about two hundred feet away, I suddenly threw the car in drive and slammed on the pedal. I can't say what I did wasn't pretty sick, because it was. There was dark blood and bodies everywhere, but I didn't care. My eyes were fixed on the front door of the Mug N' Muffin and Prianka Patel, key in hand, waiting behind the glass door.

In seconds we were there. She stuck the key in the lock, opened the door, and made a dash for our Hummer. Out of nowhere, a poxer was on her. This one was a little girl about seven or eight. Without skipping a beat, Prianka whirled around and did some sort of weird, sideways, high kick square in the little poxer's teeth. She went sprawling.

Prianka yanked open the back door and hopped inside.

"Don't tell me, you're a black belt, too," I said, purposefully running over the little poxer as I pulled the Hummer out on to the road. The squashing sound was almost satisfying.

"I have to get home," she blurted out.

"Well, gee. Hi, Tripp. Hi, Trina. Thanks for saving my ass even though I'm a narcissistic know-it-all and . . ."

"Tripp!" Trina snapped and punched me in the arm.

It didn't hurt as much as the sting I felt in the pit of my stomach when Prianka started sobbing in the back seat.

An old lady poxer lurched in front of the Hummer, and I winged her as we sped by. Trina watched apathetically as she pinwheeled off the road and into some bushes. She turned around to face Prianka.

"Pri," she said. "You live on Dwight, right?"

I saw her nod through the rear view mirror. Her makeup was smudged and dripping down her face, and there were serious bags under her eyes.

She didn't say anything more, but that's where we went—Dwight Street.

6

LITTLEHAM, MASSACHUSETTS, population of about 6,200 according to the sign on the road into town, had now, at best, a population hovering somewhere around sixty and dropping by the hour. Of those sixty, my guess was that most of them would be bitten. The ones who didn't get bitten would probably do something really dumb like take pills or accidently crash their cars.

Or fall down wells.

We were essentially on our own.

Dwight Street ran behind the Littleham Country Club. As we slowly drove down the street, I saw some figures way out on one of the greens that were poxers for sure. They were stumbling aimlessly around. I ignored them and pulled into the Patel's driveway.

"That'll be five dollars please. Don't forget the tip."

Trina shot me a shut-up glance. Prianka just sat in the back seat, unable or unwilling to move.

Finally Trina turned around, put her hand on Prianka's knee, and said, "Do you think anyone is still alive?"

Prianka sucked on her lip and fresh tears spilled from her blackened eyes. "My parents are away," she said. "Someone in there is supposed to be watching my brother, Sanjay."

A brother? Ugh. Wasn't it bad enough that there was one Patel in town? There had to be two?

"How old is he?" asked Trina.

"Ten. He's ten," she said. Her hands touched the handle of the door. Through the rearview mirror I could see her stare out the window, mentally calculating how far we were from the car to the house.

"I don't think there are any of those things around." I offered, but she didn't move.

Trina was the one who finally got her going. She opened her door and climbed out of the Hummer, crowbar in hand.

"Fine. Let's go get him," she said.

Prianka, still staring at the front door, pulled the handle and stepped out onto her driveway.

"This sucks," I muttered under my breath but followed them both out into the open. I'm not sure if I was more pissed off that we were stuck in this situation in the first place, or if Trina was slowly trying to emasculate me by getting out of the car first. In either case, you know that adrenaline rush you get when you are just about to be attacked in a video game? Well multiply that by ten, and that's how I felt. I was practically jumping out of my skin.

We trotted to the front door. Prianka stuck her key in the lock and opened it. We stepped inside and closed the door behind us.

"Sanjay?" Prianka hissed, barely above a whisper.

We slowly made our way further into the house. There was nothing. No sound. No shuffling of dead shoes on linoleum. Everything was mausoleum quiet.

Creepy, creepy, was all I could think. The Patels obviously had a passion for the color red, because everything looked as though a giant tick had exploded and doused the whole house in blood. Red carpets, red curtains—there was even a plush, red couch in the middle of the living room. We didn't head that way, though. Instead, Prianka turned toward a long, skinny hallway where I assumed all the bedrooms were.

It seemed to stretch a million miles long.

"Listen," I said. "If there's a poxer here, I want to know now." I started banging at the walls and shouting. "Yo, you dead piece of dirt. Come and get us. We're right here. An all you can eat, multicultural buffet."

Prianka rolled her eyes, as did Trina.

I shrugged. "Cover's blown. Let's get him and get out."

"Sanjay," Prianka screamed. "Sanjay, where are you?"

"Not to be pessimistic and all," I said, "But, you know, he could be one of them."

Prianka whirled around and snapped at me. "The guy on the radio said immunity was genetic. Didn't you learn anything in biology, Tripp? Or don't you listen? If you and Trina are both immune and you're brother and sister, than Sanjay might be immune, too. He might still be here."

Ah, that was the Prianka I knew and totally detested. But I couldn't deny her logic.

"So what about whoever was watching him?" asked Trina.

The door at the end of the hall swung open. Question answered. An old Indian lady wrapped in orange robes fell out. The orange clashed against the red walls. She was definitely infected with both bad taste *and* Necropoxy.

"Way to manifest," I said.

"Gimme that thing," Prianka growled and grabbed the crowbar out of

Trina's hands. She raised it above her head, dashed down the hallway and brought the heavy iron down on the poxer's head.

Again and again and again.

"Where," *thwack*, "is," *thwack*, "my," *thwack*, "brother," *thwack*, "you," *thwack*, "crazy," *thwack*, "old," *thwack*, "witch?"

There was blood and gore everywhere. Trina gagged. I fell in love. Go figure.

Prianka stood over the mass of tissue and body parts that she just created. Her back was to us, heaving up and down. She threw the crowbar to the ground and frantically began opening doors.

"Sanjay?" she screamed. "Sanjay, where are you?" She disappeared through a doorway to the left, and we followed.

"What the . . ." I said when we caught up to her. We were in an empty room with a giant, green, metal tube filling up almost the entire space. It looked like a mini submarine. Up against the wall were a bunch of oxygen tanks, the kind you see creepy clowns use to fill up balloons. The 'submarine' had two portholes on either side. Prianka ran up to one, cupped her hands around her eyes, and peered in.

"Sanjay," she screamed. "Thank God." She bent over, breathing heavily. I thought she was going to pass out.

"What is this?" I asked.

She looked up at us, her dark eyes wet but filled with relief. "It's a hyperbaric chamber," she said. "It's for my brother's treatments."

Trina and I circled around the other side of the chamber and each looked through a porthole. Sanjay Patel, a frail little ten-year-old was sleeping inside on a pillow, his arms wrapped around a ratty stuffed dog. He was wearing an old football helmet.

"Um, what kind of treatments?" I said rather slowly. The whole world just turned zombie on us. For all I knew the Patel's were some weird sort of mad scientist family, and Sanjay was their pet project. Yesterday that would have been a little far-fetched—today, not so much. I mean, really? A hyperbaric submarine tank in your house?

"He's autistic, isn't he?" Trina said.

Look who jumped to the head of the class.

Prianka and I both stared at Trina with surprise.

"We just read about hyperbaric chambers in health," she continued. "There are a whole bunch of studies showing that oxygen therapy is helping kids with autism. This is one of those machines, right? It gives him, like, super oxygen."

"Um, yeah, that's right," said Prianka as if the Lights couldn't possibly be as smart as her.

We all peered into the portholes again.

"Are you sure he's not dead?" I asked.

"I don't think poxers sleep," snapped Trina. "And quit being such a downer. Where's the fun, huh?"

"It died last night with your boyfriend."

"Oh my God, Chuck Peterson's dead?" gasped Prianka. As if, like, everyone wasn't dead.

"Tripp killed him," said Trina. "He was jealous."

"Shut up," I barked. "Prianka, how do you open this thing?"

Prianka moved around to the front of the chamber and turned a big metal wheel. After a moment there was a popping sound, and the door swung open.

Sanjay Patel started screaming like someone was murdering him.

"It's okay, Sanjay. It's okay," said Prianka. Her hands shot out in front of her to try and calm her brother.

Sanjay Patel scrambled to the back of the long tube, hitting his head several times as he went, hence the football helmet. He cowered up against the iron wall. Out of the corner of his eye he saw me and Trina looking at him through the portholes, which caused him to scream even louder and bolt back to the middle of the chamber.

He was like a mouse cornered by a cat.

Finally Prianka started singing a weird, lilting tune, obviously in some Indian dialect.

> *Nini baba nini*
> *Mackhan roti cheene,*
> *Mackhan roti hoa gia,*
> *Soja Baba Soja,*
> *Mera baba soja,*
> *Ninnie Nina baba so gaya, gaya.*

She finished with, "Sleep, baby, sleep."

Sanjay physically calmed down. Then, in a tiny voice, he repeated every word she sang, accenting the end, "Sleep, baby, sleep," just like she did.

Prianka held her arms out, and he shot into them, fiercely hugging her. She unstrapped his helmet and pulled his head free. A mop of unruly black hair, thick and curly, spilled out. She stood, and he wrapped his legs around her waist and put his head on her shoulder.

"Scary," he whispered as he clutched the ratty stuffed dog. "I hid from Mrs. Bhoola with Poopy Puppy."

"Yes you did," she whispered into his ear. "You were very, very smart."

"Poopy Puppy was very, very smart," he said. "Poopy Puppy showed me how to close the door from inside. Mrs. Bhoola got real mad."

Prianka hugged him tightly and once again let loose with the waterworks.

Yuck.

And the whole thing would have been a lot more touching if three poxers weren't staring in at us through the window.

7

"PLEASE TELL ME we locked the front door," I yelled as I raced down the hallway, leaping over what was left of Mrs. Bhoola.

No go. The door was wide open. That meant that, one, we didn't lock the door, and two, we weren't alone.

I slammed the door, turned the lock, and backed up against the smooth surface.

"Zombies in the house," I screamed, half ready to crap my pants.

Trina ran down the gore-stained hall and snatched up her crowbar from where Prianka had dropped it. It was slick with Bhoola juice, but she didn't seem to care. Prianka came up behind her with Sanjay still clinging to her like a monkey.

"Poopy Puppy says kitchen," he whispered to her. "I'm shutting my eyes now."

"You do that, little man," I said. "Prianka, where's the kitchen?" She didn't have to answer me, because I heard a crashing sound coming from somewhere behind where the red couch sat.

As a unit, we quietly slipped through the living room and peered into the kitchen beyond. The side-by-side refrigerator and freezer were wide open, and there was food everywhere. There was a fat guy, without a shirt on, sitting on the floor and gnawing on a piece of frozen steak.

"That's gross," I said.

"Which part?" asked Trina.

"Fat people without their shirts on. I bet he has butt crack showing, too."

The fat poxer looked up at us from where he was sitting amidst the Patel's weekly groceries and let out a long, low snarl.

"Prianka. I don't suppose you have a panic room?" I asked.

She put Sanjay down. The poxer snarled even louder but seemed unwilling or unable to pull himself to his feet and away from the frozen piece of steak.

Sanjay held Poopy Puppy up to the side of this head like a telephone. A moment later he spoke.

"Poopy Puppy says in the 1968 version of *Night of the Living Dead*, running time one hour, thirty-five minutes and seventeen seconds, zombies can be killed by a bullet, a sharp blow to the head, or by fire."

Trina and I stared at each other in that silent way that implied that Sanjay Patel and Poopy Puppy were every bit as weird as the fat zombie in the kitchen. Prianka, however, reached over to a small end table that was positioned against the red couch and yanked open the drawer. She rummaged inside and pulled out a lighter. My mouth dropped open as she picked up one of a set of little plush pillows that were neatly arranged on the couch and lit a tasseled end.

"Sorry, Mom," she whispered to herself.

"Are you kidding me?" I said. "What's that supposed to do?"

"You got a better idea, genius?" Prianka barked.

"The crowbar worked really well on the old lady in orange," offered Trina.

"And I have years of therapy to look forward to for that," said Prianka. "Just let me try something."

By that time, Fatso the frozen steak-eating poxer had gotten to his feet and began moving toward us.

"Here, catch," yelled Prianka just about the time that she would have had to drop the pillow anyway, because, you know, tacky polyester burns really fast. The burning fashion faux-pas hit the poxer square in the chest and dropped to his feet.

It was like someone had doused the guy with gasoline. He went up in flames in a matter of seconds—clothes, skin, blubber, everything. The fire got so big so fast that the flames reached up to the Patel's kitchen ceiling. In the middle of the tower or fire, Zeppo the zaftig zombie began to scream and scream and scream.

Finally he exploded all over everything, and the kitchen was engulfed in flames.

Prainka, Trina, and I turned and looked down at Sanjay Patel and the ratty little stuffed dog that somehow told him how to make a zombie barbeque.

"Poopy Puppy's smart," he said with a big smile. "Poopy Puppy's really smart."

Sure, I thought to myself. Creepy, creepy.

8

WE PUT OUT THE FIRE with a mini fire extinguisher that the Patel's kept in their front hall closet, but their kitchen was trashed. Sanjay sat on the couch, his feet dangling because they didn't reach the floor, with this big smile plastered on his face.

"My parents are going to kill me," Prianka said when the last of the flames were finally put out. The kitchen was a mess, and the whole house stank of too many fast food dinners all wrapped up in a pig's blanket.

"Where are they, anyway?" I asked.

"My parents? They're in India," she said. "For three weeks. Might as well be three hundred thousand years at this point."

Uh oh. I braced myself for the waterworks again, but they never came.

"At least I have Sanjay," she said.

"And Poopy Puppy" he quipped.

Enough with the Poopy Puppy crap already—it was just too weird. Besides, we had bigger things to worry about. Trina had positioned herself by the front window. The poxers that had been staring in at us when we were in the hyperbaric chamber room were now clustered around the front stoop. I think they were deciding if the door was something they could eat or something they could go through.

"What about your parents?" asked Prianka, so I told her about their trip to Vermont, their late night text, and their instructions to meet us at Aunt Ella's house.

"But who even knows if they're still alive," I said. The words felt funny coming out of my mouth, like I was trying them on for size for the very first time. The truth was we really didn't know if they were still alive, or if they had been bitten, or something worse.

"But they might be," said Prianka. "So that's where we'll go."

"We?" I said a little too quickly.

"Yes, we," said Trina. "Anything has to better than this place. Littleham was already Deadsville before yesterday, anyway. We just have to figure out how to get through this little group of trick-or-treaters out front because they're about to . . ."

Bang!

"Figure out how to get inside."

Bang! Bang! Bang!

The gruesome trio had started on the door. Sanjay's hands flew to his ears, and he screwed his face into a grimace of terror. I gathered up the remaining pillows from the couch. Truth be told, they should have been burned a long time ago, anyway.

"Prianka, give me the lighter."

"As if," she spat back at me and pulled it out of her pocket. "My house, my fire."

Ugh. Prianka—control freaking—Patel.

"Whatever. So how do we do this?"

Trina stood at the window and watched the poxers claw at the door. After a moment she quietly flipped the lock and tested to see if she could silently slide it up. She could. Trina pushed the window back down and turned to Prianka.

"Pri," she said. "Light one up for me."

Prianka plucked a particularly ugly pillow from my hands, lit one corner, and turned it upside down as the fire took hold. When the fabric started to burn she handed it to Trina.

"Make it count," she said. Trina pulled up the window, stuck her head out, and yelled at the poxer closest to her.

"Hey, ugly," she screamed. "Hot potato." She winged the burning pillow at the poxer, slid the window down, and flipped the lock.

The doorway immediately lit up like the fourth of July. The poxer she hit burst into flames, and the other two soon followed. Just like with the fat guy in the kitchen, they started screeching so horribly that Sanjay started to screech too. Within seconds we heard a series of loud pops and nothing more.

I ran to the window and peered out with Trina and Prianka. The poxers had exploded all over the walkway. The front lawn looked like the gory floor of a slaughter house.

Unfortunately, the front door was burning, too, as though someone had smeared tar on the wood and lit the place on fire.

"Put it out," I screamed.

"You put it out. I'm not opening the door," Prianka screamed back at me.

"This is your house," I screamed back.

Sanjay just screamed and screamed and screamed.

We both faced each other, our chests puffed out like chickens, until she turned from me and ran over to Sanjay.

"Really, Tripp. You're my hero," muttered Trina. She grabbed the small fire extinguisher and ran back to the window, pulled it open, and climbed out right on top of the Patel's shrubbery. She swore as I heard her stumble through the garden to the front door and start spraying. All the while, Sanjay kept screaming until Prianka, in her practiced way, calmed him down.

Right about the time that he stopped screaming, Trina stopped spraying. A moment later she was back at the window.

"Hate to be a killjoy, but we've got incoming from the golf course, and your roof is on fire. I think we have to leave."

"I need some things," Prianka said. "Tripp, can you please sit with Sanjay. I'll only be a minute."

Sit with him? And do what? Before I had a chance to say anything she disappeared down the bedroom hallway.

"Hurry up, Pri," Trina yelled. "We'll have poxers here any minute, and your roof is smoking."

As for me, I just stared at Sanjay Patel and Poopy Puppy. We were light years apart. Sanjay rocked rapidly back and forth, his tiny shoulders hugging his ears. I had to confess I knew nothing about autism. He looked pretty normal to me. In fact, he had the same features as Prianka, with the same deep, olive skin and dark eyes. I reached over to touch his arm, and he practically jumped out of his skin.

"It's cool, Buddy. I'm not going to hurt you."

He sniffed and stared straight ahead. "Who's Buddy?"

"Ah, um, it's just a nickname."

"What's a nickname?"

I gingerly sat down on the couch, being careful not to get to close and spook him. "It's a name you call someone instead of their real name."

"Why?"

I guess I never thought why, so I said, "You use a nickname when you like someone."

Sanjay turned the stuffed dog over and over in his hands. "Poopy Puppy knows nicknames."

Okay, I had him talking. Babysitting an autistic kid wasn't so hard.

"Really? Like what?"

Sanjay Patel held the stuffed dog up to his ear and knitted his brow. He sucked on his lip for a second and said, "Willy Foo Foo, Mr. Magnificent, Sparky, Mister Googlehead, Dollface, Tons of Fun, Johnny Fanny Gina Head, Captain Awesome, Mr. Fabulous, Porkchop, Emma Bemma Bum Smella, Pissy Missy, Miracle Boy, Danger Dan, Sister Boom Boom, J. Fo, Squirt, Mr. Wonderful, Fatty Fatty Bom Bom, Awesome McAwesome . . ."

My mouth dropped open for a second time as the information poured out of Sanjay's mouth. He kept talking as Prianka rushed back into the living room with a bag in her hand. She scooped her brother up in her arms, stared at the ruined front door, and yelled to Trina.

"We're going out the back. We still clear?"

"For just about a minute," Trina yelled back after checking the area behind her. Then she disappeared from the window.

I followed Prianka through the torched kitchen and out the back door while Sanjay Patel kept rattling away.

"Joe Kickass, Snaggletooth, Pissy Baby, Fingers, Spunky, Ross the Boss, Retarded Jimmy . . ."

"Don't use that word," she snapped as we ran around the side of the house.

"Spanky, Weirdo . . ."

"Or that one," she snapped again.

I made a mental note. Retarded and weirdo were off the table.

"Okay, okay," I said to Sanjay. "You know nicknames."

"Poopy Puppy knows nicknames," he corrected.

Maybe he did. Who knows?

We got to Chuck Peterson's bright yellow Hummer and piled inside. A few hundred yards away a group of poxers were advancing on the house—bloody, frightening, horrible things that were probably living very average lives up until they got infected. They were approaching speedy, or a necropoxer's version of speedy. If I had to clock them, I'd say they weren't going to win any metals at the Special Olympics, but I could really see how someone would have to be going at a pretty brisk walk to stay ahead of them.

We all slipped on our seat belts, because, well, safety first. I started the Hummer and backed out of the driveway. The roof on the Patel's house was really starting to burn.

As we pulled away, Sanjay peered out the window and watched his home light up.

"Bye-bye," he said as we passed by the staggering horde.

I didn't know what we were doing or where we were going, but Sanjay's words seemed pretty fitting.

"Yeah. Bye-bye," I echoed. "Bye-bye."

9

I LOOKED AT THE Hummer's clock. The glowing display read just 10:52 in the morning. How so much could have happened in such a little amount of time was surreal. Still, there was one thing I knew—I was beat. Trina had packed a bunch of food in the duffel bags she had brought from our house, and we all took turns eating out of a box of Frosted Flakes. The sugar did us good, but I think we all still needed sleep, except for probably Sanjay who I guessed slept like a baby all night long in his big green submarine.

"Does anyone know how to get to the highway?" I said. "Those of us of the non-licensed variety don't know directions."

Prianka stared out the window, and Trina said nothing.

"No, really. I'm serious. I don't ever watch where we're going when Mom and Dad are driving. I don't know where to go."

Prianka blew air out through her nose. "When we . . . when we used to go to the movies we went down Main Street all the way to the end and took a left. I think the highway is out that way."

"It's a start," I said and took a left off of Dwight and plowed down Main. Trina reached over, turned on the radio, and dialed to Jimmy James's station.

" . . . bookstores, libraries, and schools," he said in an increasingly more raspy voice. "I repeat—this isn't a movie. It's imperative that you get as much material as you can get your hands on regarding survival skills. The best places to find this information is in bookstores, libraries, or schools. From what we're hearing, it's not pretty out there folks. Be prepared."

I pressed redial on my cell. His phone rang on air, and he answered.

"This is WHZZ, and I'm Jimmy . . . just Jimmy. I could sure use some good news."

"Tripp Light to the rescue," I said.

"Tripp, my man. How did you guys make out?"

"We got her," I said, looking in the rearview mirror at Prianka. Sanjay was huddled up against her, and she was stroking his head.

"Way to go, Dude," said Jimmy James. There wasn't a lot of gusto in his voice. "Where are you now?"

"Still in Littleham," I said.

"Listen up, folks," said Jimmy. "We have to help each other. Tripp here is a first rate example of what we need to do. If we don't help each other, we're no better than . . ." He stopped for a moment. When he started talking again he was slow and purposeful.

"Human beings are odd creatures," he said. "We create weapons to destroy each other by the millions, yet we risk our lives to save just one. So be it. If each one of you out there can save just one, we're twice as strong. If those two each save two, we're four times as strong." He coughed and was silent for a long moment. Finally he said, "It's up to you, folks, because I'm not going to be here much longer."

I remembered what he had said about where he was—in a sound booth, surrounded by Necropoxers.

I looked at Trina, and she looked at me. We didn't need words to know what each other was thinking.

"Hey, Jimmy," I said. "Can you take this call off the air for a sec?"

"No problem," he said. "Be right back y'all. Meanwhile, here's a little tune from our favorite local band, Little Gray Men."

The music started, and I turned down the volume and pressed the speaker button on my phone.

"I'm here," he said.

"Are you still surrounded by poxers?"

"Yeah," he said. "Seven of them and a little boy. Is it really true out there? I feel like I'm losing my mind."

"It's really true," said my sister. "I'm Trina, Tripp's prettier sib. We have Prianka with us and her little brother, Sanjay."

"Unreal," he said. I had to agree. "Listen, I'm in Amherst—only about a half hour from Littleham. Do you . . . do you think maybe you could come and get me?"

"No one has tried to get you?" gasped Prianka. "Unreal is right."

"I know," he said. "I'm just the voice inside the box. No one cares. I guess they figure they'll listen until I just go off. I got to tell you, I'm pretty scared. I don't know how I'm going to get out of this sound booth and past all of them. Have you noticed that they seem to be getting faster?"

We noticed.

"Jimmy, how old are you?" I'm not sure why I asked.

"Nineteen," he said, and we all exchanged glances. "This is my first gig as a D.J. I was getting some work-study credit at the University."

We drove by the Mug N'Muffin where we saved Prianka. The glass on the door had been smashed. A few poxers sat on the front stoop and tilted their heads as we passed. Prianka gave them the finger, which was both weird and funny at the same time.

"You're really just thirty minutes from Littleham?" said Trina.

"Yeah," he said. "Would you really come for me?"

"We need someone older than us who knows things," I said. "My parents texted us right after everything happened and told us to meet them at our aunt's house, but we don't know how to get there."

"Where?" he asked.

"Someplace off the Mohawk Trail."

Prianka leaned forward and dropped something between the two of us on the front seat. It was a road atlas of Massachusetts. "I found this in the door pocket," she said.

"We have a road map. What's your address?"

"I'm not broadcasting from campus," said Jimmy. "I'm on Pleasant Street right next to the sub shop. The number is 610."

"So we come get you, then we go to my aunt's house to get my parents," I said. "You game?"

"I'm sure as hell not playing any other," he said. "But how are you going to get by all the dead people?"

"You leave that one up to us. Keep the lines open. We're on our way."

Prianka took the map back and gave it to Sanjay. He plopped Poopy Puppy down on his lap and opened up the atlas. Then quickly and methodically, he flipped through page after page until he had gone through the whole thing. By the time he was done I was at the end of Main Street and just starting to turn left.

"Right," he said.

"But the highway's left."

"Poopy Puppy says the way to 610 Pleasant Street in Amherst, Massachusetts is right."

There was that Poopy Puppy thing again. Trina flipped down her visor and looked at Sanjay through the mirror.

"Listen to him Tripp," said Prianka. "He knows."

"What do you mean, he knows?" said Trina.

"He just read the map," she said. "So now he knows."

Her words were so matter-of-fact that there was really no room for debate. I shrugged, and without even questioning, I turned right because Prianka Patel's autistic kid brother's creepy stuffed dog told us to.

Hey, good enough for me.

10

"SANJAY'S A SAVANT," said Prianka as we drove down Three Rivers Road and over a green, metal bridge.

"A what?" I said.

"Savant," said Sanjay. "Poopy Puppy says savant syndrome, sometimes referred to as savantism, is a rare condition in which people with developmental disorders have one or more areas of expertise, ability, or brilliance that are in contrast with the individual's overall limitations. Although not a recognized medical diagnosis, researchers say the condition may be either genetic or acquired based on the epidemiology of the disorder."

Mouth drop number three.

"He has both an auditory and a photographic memory," said Prianka. "If he sees it, reads it, or hears it, he remembers."

"So where did he just get that weird little definition from?" I asked. Trina was still staring at him through her mirror visor. I think I would have been, too, if I didn't need my eyes on the road.

"Internet," said Sanjay. "Poopy Puppy likes the Internet."

"And the doctors say that his stuffed animal is like his microphone," said Prianka. "For some reason everything has to come through Poopy Puppy."

"Because Poopy Puppy's smart," said Sanjay.

"Yes he is," I agreed. Creepy, creepy.

Three Rivers Road ended at a stop sign at the bottom of a long, wooded hill. There was a log cabin on the corner. Three necropoxers were wandering on the lawn. When they saw the Hummer, they immediately started moving toward us.

"Which way?"

Sanjay just stared into space. The poxers were half way across the lawn.

"You have to ask him what you want," said Prianka as she eyed the poxers while testing the electric locks on the door. They clicked and clicked again.

"I did," I said.

"Exactly. You have to say what you want—exactly."

"Sanjay," I said with just a teensy bit of hysteria rising in my voice. "There are zombies coming. Which way to 610 Pleasant Street in Amherst, Massachusetts?"

Sanjay took the ratty dog and held him to his ear. We waited. The poxers were ten feet from the car. He nodded and closed his eyes. The poxers were at the windows. God, they were ugly. Their skin was mottled and smeared with dried black gunk. Their eyes were dead eyes, filled with fog.

They started to bang on the windows with their fists. Now was not the time to see how well built a Hummer really was.

I slowly backed the car up, and they followed.

"I know one of them," said Prianka. "That's Ms. Whipple. She's my karate teacher." So Prianka really did have a belt of undetermined color. Knowing her, the belt was black, or at least some sort of dark, dark gray.

"Do you . . . did you like her?" I asked.

"Like in a 'should-you-run-her-over-for-me-in-Chuck-Peterson's-Hummer' kind of way?" she said. "No, I'm good. But thanks for the thought. It was . . . it's nice."

Sure. Murder can be nice—just like wrapping up a bunch of body parts in a bouquet.

The poxers followed the car as I continued to back up the hill.

Finally, Sanjay spoke up. "Poopy Puppy says take a right, go 1.2 miles, then take a left on East Street." He opened his eyes and saw the Necropoxers and started to scream that high-pitched scream of his. I pressed the gas and spun the wheel around the poxers, narrowly missing Ms. Whipple. When I got to the stop sign, I palmed the wheel right.

"You didn't stop," said Trina, mostly out of habit.

Oops. Guess I won't be passing my driving test.

Prianka put a protective arm around Sanjay and began humming the same tune to him that she used back at the house. He stopped screaming pretty quickly.

Precisely 1.2 miles further down the road I took a left on East Street. I tried not to notice the little park we passed with dozens of dead things walking around the seesaws. I kept my eyes on the road. Driving was easier that way.

When I turned, Trina spoke up. "Sanjay," she said. "Which way to 610 Pleasant Street in Amherst, Massachusetts?"

"Straight," he said without skipping a beat. I guess Poopy Puppy must have told him that during their last conversation.

"Straight it is," she said. We went over another bridge and through a neighborhood of older homes. Gradually, the houses faded away to rolling fields. I remembered this road. This was the way that Mom and Dad used to take us when we went pumpkin picking at Jolly O's Fruit Farm.

The sun was shining. The sky was that crisp, blue color that you see in postcards. We had ourselves a perfect day, except for all the incredible imperfectness of it all.

Five minutes further down the road I saw something in front of us.

"What's that?" said Trina.

Prianka leaned forward and squinted.

"Moo," said Sanjay.

Moo was right. There was a herd of dairy cows in the middle of the road. I guess someone forgot to shut the barn door—or they were spooked.

I slowed down until we were about a hundred feet away from them.

"Why aren't they crossing the road?" said Prianka.

"I guess they aren't too anxious to get to the other side," I said. I couldn't resist, but it earned me a punch in the arm from Trina.

"Moo, moo," Sanjay cried out. "Moo, moo." He pointed over to our right and into the field where the cows had probably come from.

There was a crowd of poxers circling a dead cow like vultures. I'm not quite sure what they had in their hands, but I'd lay bets that whatever grossness they were fondling was from poor Bessie. The poxers were all in sturdy work clothes. I guessed this was their farm. Now that meat was number one on the priority list, they'd hit the zombie equivalent of the lottery.

"Don't look, Sanjay," said Prianka and put her hands over his face. "Can we just get out of here?"

The poxers swarmed the poor cow like locusts. I admit, the whole scene was pretty gross, and I had seen my fair share of pretty gross things in the past twenty-four hours.

I gently pressed on the gas and the Hummer crept forward, just enough so that the cows begrudgingly parted for us as we waded through them.

"It reeks," I said as the ripe smell of cow patty hit us.

"It masks the smell of the poxers," said Trina. "And I bet they smell worse."

When we finally got through the cows, I sped up again, and we were on our way. For future reference, when that little arrow on the dashboard is pointing squarely on E, that means E for empty.

No one ever told me that before.

11

"IT'S NOT MY FAULT," sniped Trina.

"Well who was the one who had to date the big, stupid jock with the gas guzzler?" I shot back.

"The Hummer's a bummer," said Sanjay. "The top five reasons not to buy a Hummer are—the gas mileage will kill you, the Hummer receives more complaints than any other car, oil addiction leads to war, soldiers are dying in them, and other people will hate you."

"My dad likes cars," mumbled Prianka, avoiding our glares. "He reads a lot of online stuff to Sanjay."

"That's just great," I said. "Can the walking Internet tell us how to get some gas?"

WE WERE A few miles further down East Street when Chuck's banana-mobile sputtered and stalled. There were a couple of houses around, but not many. They looked a little like someone from the Ozarks had put them together with duct tape.

No poxers anywhere so that was good.

"I know this," said Trina.

"Know what?" I said.

"I know how to get gas." She opened the door and stepped out of the car. "How many stupid, apocalyptic horror movies do you have to watch before you know what to do?" she said and tramped off to the closest house.

"Coming?" I said to Prianka as I opened the door. She rolled her eyes, took Sanjay's hand who, in turn, tightened his grip on Poopy Puppy, and they both got out of the car, too. The whole situation did have lame horror movie written all over it. All we needed was some banjo music, a movie cut-away shot of someone watching us through the trees, and a heavy breathing soundtrack.

"What are you doing?" I yelled after Trina. She ignored me and walked up one of the driveways. The house was tiny and dark with a couple of cars parked on the lawn and a motorcycle with a For Sale sign spelled '4 sail.'

Plenty of brain power living here.

The curtains were drawn, and the house looked empty. If anyone was alive inside, they certainly weren't advertising for survivors.

Trina didn't go to the front door. Instead she went to the garage.

As she bent to twist the metal handle and pull up the door, too many scenarios ran through my mind, like we were breaking and entering, or someone was alive in the house and was going to shoot us for looting, or someone was dead in the house and was really, really hungry.

Or there were poxers behind that door.

"Wait!" I yelped.

"For what?" I caught up to her and pushed her hand away from the handle. She glared at me like she's been glaring at me since the womb. What I wanted to tell her was that if a poxer was behind that door and had its sights set on my sister's throat, the thing would have to come through me first. Something entirely different came out.

"The door looks heavy, and, well, you're just a girl."

She practically bared her teeth at me like a crazed chimp. "So are you," she sneered as she pushed me away and pulled.

Thankfully there was nothing on the other side except what you would expect to be in a garage. "We need a garden hose," she snapped

"To syphon gas?" said Prianka who was suddenly at my side with Sanjay in tow. "Perfect. We can stick one end of a hose in a gas tank and suck on the other end until the gas starts to flow. All we need to do is dump it into our own tank."

I mean, I knew that, but did the Girl Scouts have survivorship pins or badges or something?

"I'm impressed," I said.

Prianka's eyes literally scanned me over from head to toe. "I'm not."

Ouch.

Sanjay pointed to a pile of junk in one corner. "Gas can," he said. "Poopy Puppy says so."

Poopy Puppy was right. Trina grabbed the red plastic jug and continued poking around the garage.

"Hose," said Sanjay and pointed on the wall. A new hose with the price tag still hanging from it hung on a peg-board hook.

"Where's Waldo?" I said to Sanjay, but he didn't respond. That's fine. It was a lame joke anyway. I had to do something to keep my street cred, which was becoming tougher every time the two Amazons traveling with me showed how little they needed a guy around.

Trina grabbed the hose and an axe that was hanging on the peg board, too. Out on the driveway she unrolled the hose and hacked off a piece that was about ten feet long. Next she chose the closest car, which probably hadn't seen a carwash in, well, never, and unscrewed the gas cap.

"You want the honors?" she said, handing me the hose.

I sighed. "Why not? Just one more sucky job in a pretty sucky day." I snaked one end of the hose into the gas tank and sucked hard on the other end. The gas filled my mouth surprisingly fast, and I gagged.

"You're not supposed to drink it, idiot," she said and pulled the hose out of my mouth and transferred the flowing liquid into the gas can.

"Now *I'm* impressed," said Prianka. "That was very, um, impressive."

I spat on the ground to try and get the taste of gas out of my mouth.

"But that wasn't," she said and turned away.

Trina filled up the gas can and trotted back over to the Hummer and poured the contents of the can into the gas tank. She came back and syphoned some more from the car. Prianka, Sanjay and me sat on the front lawn. I was really tired. At this point we had been running on almost no sleep, and I missed my own bed and my own house and my own charmed life.

Sanjay studied the grass for a while, murmured something, and shifted his gaze to the trees. Watching him was a little like watching a living, breathing computer.

"Whatcha looking at, Buddy?" I asked him.

"Buddy's a nickname," he said.

"Yup. We established that."

He looked at the changing colors of one of the trees in front of us. "Four thousand and twenty-seven," he said.

"Four thousand and twenty-seven what?"

"Leaves," he said. A gentle breeze blew our hair, and the sky rained leaves for a moment.

"Three thousand, eight hundred and ninety-two," he said.

I suppose I should have reflected on what he just did, but I was too beat. Prianka sighed and pushed her hair back. She looked tired, too. I couldn't help but think about her parents in India. Was Necropoxy there, too? My guess was yes, which meant that there was virtually no way they were coming back to Massachusetts any time soon.

Hell, who even knew if they were alive, although it was pretty right on of Prianka to notice that immunity was somehow genetic. Up until the last text, my parents hadn't been infected, and for all I knew they were waiting for us less than an hour away at Aunt Ella's.

Prianka's olive skin looked warm and smooth in the sunlight. She closed her eyes and leaned back against her elbows. I watched. Pretty soon Sanjay noticed me watching, so I turned away.

Trina ran back and forth a few more times before checking the gauge on the Hummer.

"I have about a third of a tank," she said. "I don't want to waste any more time." She trotted over to us and held her hand out for Prianka and pulled her to her feet. She left me sitting in the grass.

"Thanks, sis" I said.

"Welcome." She tossed the keys at me, and we begrudgingly filed down the driveway and back into the Hummer.

"Sanjay, which way to 610 Pleasant Street in Amherst, Massachusetts?"

He didn't answer. He just pointed straight ahead. I took a look at the gas gauge and prayed Chuck's fuel hog would get us to Jimmy James and my aunt's house.

As for me, I was running on empty.

12

THE CLOSER WE got to Amherst, the more zombies we saw. The worst batch was in the center of Bellingsfield. The town common was full of them, making everything look like some sort of demented farmer's market, the green was already decorated with scarecrows, pumpkins, and bales of hay. The poxers added that much needed Halloween flavor to the whole scene.

Also, the driving was getting worse because there were car-crashes all over the road. I had to weave in and out of some pretty nasty wreckage and ding a few poxers along the way. I don't know why, but I thought hitting them was a little fun—probably courtesy of too many video games mixed with a healthy dose of adrenaline and lack of sleep.

My phone rang as Sanjay blurted out directions, and we merged on to Route 9. We all jumped.

It was Jimmy James. "Are you still coming for me?" He sounded desperate.

"No worries," I said. "We ran into a little gas glitch along the way, but we're cool."

"That makes one of us," he said. I heard him yell something in the background. He sounded fearful and a little desperate. "Hurry, please. I've got death knocking at the door, and I'm not broadcasting anymore. Not enough juice," he said. "I had to choose between the radio and the lights. I voted for the lights."

He didn't say anything for a moment, but I could hear fear in the silence. I didn't know what to say, so I blurted out, "I think we're not far. Hang tight."

When I hung up I turned to Trina. "He's scared," I said. "He's probably . . ."

"Watch the road," she yelped.

I swerved to avoid a smart car that was playing dumb in the middle of the pavement. We were definitely getting close. Only in a college town like Amherst would there be a smart car, anyway. Driving an anti-environmental gas guzzler like Chuck's ride was practically sacrilegious here. This was the land where granola bars grew on trees and everyone's favorite color was green.

The car wrecks were definitely worse here, and there were a lot of dead hippies staggering around. Prianka told Sanjay to count birch trees, the ones with the Dalmatian bark, to take his mind off of how bad everything really was.

In between his counting, he managed to navigate us directly to 610 Pleasant Street—a low, white building with darkened windows. Thankfully, the radio station was also on the edge of town and away from most of the poxers. Still, when we pulled into the parking lot alongside an old van, a few of them staggered over to us, and they weren't looking for donations to UNICEF.

"Do you think Chuck is going to care about his English Lit book?" said Prianka, as she picked up a paper covered volume off the floor and pulled out her lighter. She ripped off the paper-bag covering. For some reason that made me think of my dad sitting at the dining room table and covering my school books for me. That was our yearly tradition. I guess this year was the last.

Prianka opened the window, crumpled the paper into a ball, lit it, and threw the bag at the closest poxer. She was a girl about our age with braided hair and lots of make-up. In the world of twenty-four hours ago I might have looked at her more than once. But now, the word 'ick' came to mind. Her mouth kept opening and closing like a fish. The paper hit her and stuck to her poncho. Within seconds she was ablaze just the like the necropoxers back at Prianka's house.

Prianka pushed the close button on the window, turned away, and pointed out a couple of birch trees across the street to Sanjay.

The poxer popped with a wet, dull noise and sticky fire hit the car and the other two zombies that were close by. One was an old man who didn't even look like he should be walking. The other was a young guy wearing sandals and a t-shirt that said: *Be careful or you'll end up in my novel.* Funny? Sure. The two of them torching up the parking lot and exploding? Not so much.

The fire was short lived, and pretty soon there was nothing left where the poxers stood but grease marks and, oddly, one Birkenstock.

I stared at the building. Jimmy said there were poxers inside. I wasn't too worried about them, because they turned into ash pretty easily. I was more worried that the building would go up in flames before we could get out.

"Game plan, anybody?"

"Call him," said Trina. "Find out where he is and what we're up against."

When he picked up the phone he sounded half mad. "Please don't say you aren't coming," he cried. "Please. Please."

"We're here. We're outside. I just need to know how to get to you."

"There's a handicapped ramp around the right side of the building," His words came in tattered gasps. "Go through the door. The broadcasting room is down the hall and to the left." He took a deep breath and stifled what I can only assume was a sob. "They're awful. Truly, they're just awful. How are you ever going to get to me?"

"Don't worry about that. Just be ready to run."

Jimmy began to say something else, but I hung up before he had the chance.

13

"THIS ONE'S ON me," I said.

Venom shot out of Trina's eyes. "The hell it is. I'm faster."

"Aw, that's sweet, sis, but like I said before, you're just a girl," I thought her head would explode.

While Trina was working out her feminist issues I turned and took the lighter and Chuck's English Lit book from Prianka. She let me have them without hesitation.

"Good luck," she whispered.

"Good luck, Buddy," echoed Sanjay. He pushed Poopy Puppy into my face and made a smooching sound.

"Lock the doors behind me," I said to Trina. "And here's my phone. You call Jimmy if we're not out of there in ten minutes. If we don't answer, you leave."

"Shut up," she said.

"Shut up yourself," I said and opened the door.

Somehow, I think I would have felt a whole lot better if I had a gun instead of a lighter and a copy of Chuck Peterson's remedial English Lit text. But, as my dad always said, never underestimate the power of the written word.

Around the side of the building was a long low ramp up to a door. As I slowly walked up the ramp, I ripped out about ten pages from Chuck's book and shoved them in my pocket. They were part of a short story called "The Lottery" by Shirley Jackson. Now, I wasn't much for English Lit, but I remember reading that story and liking it, even the creepy stoning-to-death ending which seemed fitting considering what finally ended up happening with Jimmy James.

At the top of the ramp was a door with a small window. I cupped my hands around my eyes and peeked inside. The lights were on, but they were dim. All I could see was a hallway with doors on either side.

I get it, I thought to myself. The station's like a fun house at an amusement park. You walk down the hallway and hope like hell nothing pops out at you from behind one of the doors.

Only in amusement parks, you get to get off the ride.

I took a deep breath, gripped the handle of the door, and pulled. Quietly, very quietly, I stepped inside and let the door close softly behind me.

Twenty, maybe thirty feet to the end of the hallway—that's all. Twenty or thirty feet, turn left, and the broadcast room would be right there—except I couldn't will my feet to move.

I wasn't scared. I knew I could handle this. The poxers lit up like Styrofoam thrown in a campfire, which you're never supposed to do, because burning plastic is bad for the earth but everyone does anyways because it's so cool to watch. No, what I hated was the adrenaline rush—like that feeling you get on a roller coaster right before going down the first hill. This was just like that—a roller coaster ride.

I lit up Shirley Jackson's first few pages and ran down the hall expecting terrible, ugly things to pop out of every doorway.

They didn't.

Seconds later I was at the end, and I had to drop the papers because they were getting preciously close to my fingers. I stamped them out with my feet. No sense in burning up my only exit.

To the left, about ten feet from me was a set of double doors. To the right was a blank wall. I looked back at the gauntlet I had just run. Nothing was following me. Any poxers in this place were probably trying to eat Jimmy James in his sound booth.

With lighter in hand I gingerly walked the last ten feet to the double doors. There were muffled sounds coming from the other side, but I couldn't make them out. I pulled another page of Shirley Jackson out of my pocket and stuck a corner in my mouth. For some reason, I really wanted at least one hand free.

Gently I pushed the door open and looked inside.

The broadcast room was big—bigger than I imagined, with dark walls and a high ceiling. There were several empty desks scattered with paper, overturned soda cans, and someone's dinner in an opened carton, like the ones you get from Chinese food restaurants.

The whole place smelled like death and Pork Lo Mein.

At the far end of the room was a separate booth with a big glass window in the front. The lights blared, which seemed weird compared to the rest of the place. Surrounding the booth, like moths to a flame, was a whole host of uglies that probably occupied the desks and the rooms in the hallway until right after Jimmy James's shift started late yesterday afternoon.

They were banging on the glass windows with open palms—desperately clawing at the see-through pane to get inside at what, I'm guessing, was dinner.

Dinner was Jimmy James.

I could see his shock of red hair inside the booth. His face, I guess pleasant enough to someone as shallow as my sister, was twisted into a horror mask.

With a gentle nudge, I pushed the door further and stuck my head inside. That's when the poxer who was sitting on the floor to my right with her legs straight out in front of her got a whiff of me and let out a snarl.

'In for a dime, in for a dollar,' is what my dad always said. I lit the paper that was sticking out of my mouth, grabbed one end from between my teeth, and dropped the flames on her. Then I slipped completely inside the broadcast room and ran left as far as I could. Within seconds I could feel the heat on my back. By the time I reached the end of the room and got myself behind a desk, I turned to see the poxer engulfed in flames and screeching.

That caught the other poxers' attention, and they all turned. Then she popped.

Not one of the flaming bits of flesh got far enough across the room to hit any of the others.

"Aw, come on."

I counted six in all, most of them probably college or grad students. There was one older guy wearing a bowtie and glasses who reminded me a little of my dad, a black guy with awesome dreads, a couple of non-descript twenty-somethings, and this girl who looked like she was going through a serious rebellious faze. She had plugs, more piercings on her face than I could count, purple streaks in her hair, and several pigtails where pigtails shouldn't be.

I wish I had time for Plan C, which means I would have already had a Plan A and a Plan B, but let's face it, there was just me, a lighter, some old short story, and whatever else flammable I could find. That, and the determination of knowing that whatever happened, Jimmy and I were going to walk out of here alive.

One of the non-descriptoids wearing an untucked oxford shirt staggered toward me.

"Fire's my friend," I mumbled as I lit a piece of paper. When he was close enough, I flicked the flames at him. The burning wad landed on the ground just short of where he was standing. Like the brainless wonder that he had now become, he reached down to make friends.

I heard the 'whoompf' as the flames danced up his arm set him ablaze. Ten seconds later a falsetto scream filled the room, so I ducked below the desk and waited for the pop, which came in record time.

Four others were close enough to him to get hit by the poxer pyrotechnics, and pretty soon they also lit up like dry wood on a hot fire, shrieked, and burst.

There was one left to go—the guy with the bowtie. He watched with dead eyes as his buddies burned up the place—and that was no exaggeration. Wherever poxer goo hit, the walls and the ceiling started to smolder. Finally, bowtie guy turned and began slapping his palms against the glass of the sound booth.

Jimmy James looked crazed. He wouldn't move. He just sat there with his eyes open and his mouth agape.

"We gotta go, Jimmy," I yelled at him, loud enough that he could hear me through the glass. He just pointed at bowtie guy and wildly shook his head. I grabbed the remaining pages I had and gingerly maneuvered through the burning remnants toward the sound booth. When I was close enough, I lit the last few pages off of a burning chunk of something really gross and walked up behind the guy.

"Hey, mister," I said. "Got a light?"

The poxer whirled around to face me, shoulders hunched, with drool dripping out of his mouth. I stuck the burning paper in his face and backpedaled half way across the room to watch him light up like a fourth of July fireworks display.

When he finally popped and burning glop hit the glass window of the sound booth, Jimmy James became just a little unhinged and turned white.

"Suck it up, college dude," I muttered to myself as I made my way back across the room. Smoke was starting to fill up the place, and we had to get out soon. "Jimmy, please. We gotta go."

I saw his head over his equipment sort of half nod. He slapped himself hard in the face a couple of times and looked at me with tears in his eyes. His gaze spoke volumes, and I could only imagine what the past night had been like for him, locked in the sound booth with the dead all around him.

He motioned to the side of the booth, and I went to the door, watching his head and shoulders as he sort of crawled over to let me in.

'He must be in shock,' I thought as I heard the door lock click and watched the handle turn. The door swung open wide, and it was my turn to be in shock.

Jimmy James, D.J. extraordinaire of WHZZ, was in a wheelchair.

14

NOW I'M AS politically correct as the next guy, but . . . are you kidding me? A wheelchair? Everything was going too fast, and I couldn't stop and think about our brave new world filled with zombies and how much of a liability a wheelchair would be. I supposed I could have left him there and told the others that Jimmy just didn't make it, but I couldn't do it.

Besides, I think Poopy Puppy would have known I lied. So I said, "Hurry, before we're fricasseed."

"I don't know how I can thank you."

"I'm sure I'll figure something out. Do you need me to push you?"

Jimmy James gave me a look that made me feel like a very small, amusing child. "Ah . . . I think I can manage," he said.

I suppose he was right. Wheelchair or not, the guy's arms were thicker than my legs. He had leather gloves on his hands, and his wheelchair was tricked out like a racing bike. He grabbed a backpack off the ground and slung it over his shoulders.

"When we're out of here you'll have to teach me your little pyro routine," he said and popped a wheelie. "Let's go."

The smoke in the room was definitely getting thicker, and the ceiling was already on fire. Jimmy rolled straight through the carnage, letting his wheels leave tread marks all over what remained of the poxers.

I followed closely behind him, his back muscles flexing as he palmed the chair forward. Geez, he must have worked out ever since he was old enough for training wheels. When we got to the double doors he stopped me from opening them and pushed through himself.

Just like that we were out of the broadcasting room and safe from what might have been a grim fate for our man on the airways.

SEVEN OF THEM, he had said. He was surrounded by seven of them—and a little boy.

The boy was waiting for us around the corner.

I think I let out an involuntary yelp, not because I was scared of a pint-sized zombie, but because I had come straight down the very same hallway just minutes ago, and the kid hadn't been there before. This hallway was supposed to be safe!

He was about the same age as Sanjay, with light brown hair and freckles. He looked like someone's kid brother, anybody's kid brother, which is exactly what he probably was less than twenty-four hours ago. Now, he was a mindless monster, albeit a little one. A little one just like him bit Mr. Mic last night and infected him on the spot.

I pulled out the lighter and reached into my other pocket for what was left of 'The Lottery,' but the pages were all gone. I had used them inside the broadcast room.

"Quick, in here," I said and pushed Jimmy into a room to our right. I didn't even have time to check for oogie boogies. I closed the door behind us and turned to look for something to burn. My bad. A middle aged woman was sitting behind a desk with her head on the ink blotter. The desk was slanted against the far wall.

At first I thought she was dead, dead. Like really dead.

I was wrong. She lifted her face up, and a large portion came off and lay on the desk in front of her.

Jimmy's wheelchair flew out of my hands. In a second, he was across the small office. He reached down with both his hands, found the lip of the desk, lifted with his freakishly bulging biceps, and pinned the poxer to the wall.

Everything on her desk—her computer, pictures of family, little memorabilia from vacations past—all fell on the floor with a crash.

The poxer snarled and gnashed her teeth but couldn't free herself.

"Now what do we do?" he said to me. "And don't push my wheelchair. I can do it myself."

"We burn it," I said. "And duly noted."

I flicked the lighter and nothing happened.

"No."

"No what?"

"No," I said again as I flicked and flicked and flicked. Nothing happened.

That's when I got mad. I mean really mad. Mad that everyone turned zombie on us. Mad that my parents were gone. Mad that Sprinkles died and I was driving around in Chuck Peterson's stupid gas guzzling Hummer. Mad that I had to endure Prianka Patel and Sanjay the human robot and Poopy Puppy. Mad that the one guy I thought would be able to help us was a human cart on steroids.

Mad that the stupid lighter failed just when I needed fire the most.

Hatter mad.

Yes siree. I was officially mad enough to do just about anything.

I reached down and grabbed a chunk of rock that fell off the lady poxer's desk. Someone had written something on it in Spanish—words that didn't mean a hill of beans to me, because I was too mad to see them through the red haze in front of my eyes, much less read them.

"We're leaving now," I said. "Stay or come. Your choice, man." I opened the door and stepped into the hallway. The little boy was still there, drool dripping from his mouth.

"Move," I said.

He didn't.

"Well then. I don't ask twice." With that, I fast-balled the rock as hard as I could right in the middle of his head, and he dropped.

The thing didn't even have a chance to get up, because I picked up the rock and slammed it down on his head again. Okay, maybe more than once. I kicked the body to the side of the hall, letting loose with a whole bunch of pent up anger the whole time. I'm not exactly sure what I said, but as Jimmy wheeled past me he looked at me but didn't say a word.

At the exit, he pushed open the doors and wheeled down the ramp. I followed him around to the front of the building.

I've thought about that rock a lot since that happened. What were the odds that it was there, right when I needed it most?

One thing was for damn sure. When you got poxers to deal with there ain't nothing that feels better than a good old fashioned stoning. Don't ya think?

15

JIMMY HAULED himself into the back seat next to Prianka and Sanjay, and we threw his chair into the way back with the rest of our belongings. The chair folded up pretty neatly so there was still room.

Both Prianka and Trina shot off a whirlwind of questions. Was he scared? How could he be so brave around all those zombies? How many times a day did he work out? Did he have a tattoo, because college guys always have tattoos? Did he have a girlfriend?

Hello, Trina. Chuck just keeled less than twenty-four hours ago. Down girl, down.

Poor Mr. Muscle in the tragic chair was soaking up the attention like a sponge. Vulnerable guys are chick magnets, or that's what my dad always said. You know—guys with puppies or babies—or apparently, wheelchairs.

As we pulled out of the parking lot Jimmy said, "So what's the deal with fire?"

"The necropoxers are combustible," said Prianka. I looked in the rearview mirror to see if she was mooning over Jimmy as much as Trina.

Her dark eyes were brimming with excitement. Life sucks.

"Combustible?"

"Combustible," repeated Sanjay. "Combustible. Capable of igniting and burning. Alternate definition, easily aroused or excited."

That shut the girls up for a moment. I snickered. Sanjay added his signature flourish to the announcement as he showed Jimmy his stuffed mouthpiece. "Poopy Puppy says so."

"You're a regular Einstein, aren't you?" said Jimmy and reached over to ruffle Sanjay's hair, but Sanjay shrank away from him.

"He doesn't like to be touched by strangers," I said.

"Oh. Hey, I'm sorry Buddy. No harm no foul?"

Sanjay leaned over to Prianka. "Why does everyone call me Buddy? It's not my name."

Jimmy caught my eye in the mirror. He looked perplexed.

"He's autistic," I said. "Got a problem with that?"

"No, man," he said. "I'm cool."

I suppose he was, so we explained everything to him. Actually, we gave him a blow by blow of what happened since Chuck's car alarm went off the night before. There was a lot of yawning while we talked, so when Jimmy offered his place as a crash pad for a couple of hours before we went on to Aunt Ella's, Trina and Prianka were quick to agree. I wasn't so easily swayed until he told us he had lighters and food. I guess the caveman with the supplies wins.

He guided us down a few side streets until we were in a quiet part of town with trees overhanging the road and white picket fences.

We ended up in the driveway of a little, one story bungalow.

"Pad, sweet pad," he said. None of us moved. "Come on."

"There could be poxers," said Trina. "I can't deal with any more poxers right now."

"And Tripp broke my lighter," added Prianka. "We don't have any fire."

"I didn't break your stupid lighter."

"Well I guess it just broke itself."

"Maybe it did," I snapped.

"Maybe it did," she snapped back.

"Whoa, whoa," said Jimmy. "How long have you guys been going out?"

Sanjay barked out a laugh and that was enough to get Prianka moving. She opened the door, took Sanjay by the hand and got out of the car. Jimmy reached around to the back of the Hummer with one thick arm. He grabbed his chair, opened his door, set the wheels on the ground, and maneuvered himself into the seat like a gymnast on a pummel horse. Trina and I didn't even look at each other. We just sat there for about ten seconds before both reaching for the door handles at the same time, and got out of the car. Weird twin thing, I guess.

We followed Jimmy up to the front stoop. There were three brick steps there, with moss eating through the cracks. They led up to a small porch.

"No handicapped ramp?" I said.

"Who's handicapped?" said Jimmy as he turned his chair around, popped a wheelie, and literally hopped the chair up the stairs backwards on two wheels like some sort of freakish circus act.

Just shoot me now.

"You know, I think there're some old phone books lying around," he said as he rummaged in his backpack for his keys. "Maybe you can look up where your aunt lives."

"I never thought about using a phone book," said Trina. "Aren't they just for old people?"

"Yeah, but some folks still swear by them, so they keep getting printed.

You'd think they'd have gone green by now. Everything else has."

Jimmy dug deep and finally produced his keys. He examined them for a second before pulling out the one for the front door.

"What if there're zombies inside," I said.

"I live alone."

"But what if they got in the house?"

In answer to my question, a small voice from inside said, "Hello."

Trina and I bolted off the porch in one leap.

Jimmy rolled his eyes and just stared at us. Prianka picked up Sanjay, and he wrapped his legs around her waist.

"Hello," the voice said again—high and lilting.

Jimmy unlocked and opened the door. "Hello?" he said into the emptiness.

A black shape flew out of the doorway, and Prianka screamed like a little girl. It was a crow. The bird flapped its wings and settled on Jimmy's shoulder then cocked its head and looked around at all of us as though we were new and interesting toys.

"Hello," the crow said.

"And hello to you," said Jimmy. "How's my pretty bird?"

"Pretty bird," repeated the crow.

"You have a talking crow?" I said.

Jimmy kissed the bird on the beak and stroked its back feathers. "Everyone, this is Andrew. Andrew, these are my new friends. Can you show them some respect please?" On cue, Andrew the crow bowed his head like I've seen parrots do on TV shows about stupid animal tricks.

Sanjay stared at the crow, fascinated.

"I missed you," said Jimmy to the bird. "Sorry that I didn't come home last night, but I got into a little bit of a jam."

"Got lucky," said Andrew and Jimmy turned a color of red that looked funny against his hair.

"You're a dirty bird," he said," But yeah, I guess I did get lucky or you would have been locked up here for good." Andrew clucked and bobbed his head. "Come on in everyone," said Jimmy. "If there are poxers around, let's not advertise that we're here."

That got us all moving. We followed Jimmy James and Andrew into the house, closing and locking the doors behind us.

Without electricity, the interior was gloomy. Jimmy, with Andrew on his shoulder, quickly wheeled through the house and did a quick inspection of all the windows. He went in and out of each room to make sure everything was locked. After he checked each window he pulled the shade.

We parked ourselves in the room to the left. There was a futon couch, an old coffee table, and a bunch of pillows on the floor. In the far corner was a computer desk. Sanjay climbed down from Prianka and went over to the computer and just stared at the blank screen.

There were some men's fitness magazines on the futon. I caught myself wondering how flammable they were. Trina picked them up and dropped them on the coffee table, then, without a sound, Prianka, Trina, and I all collapsed on the overstuffed mattress.

Exhaustion rolled over us like the numbing waves of a winter sea.

16

IT WAS DARK WHEN I woke up, and my arm was fast asleep because Prianka Patel was lying on top of it. Trina was sleeping against Prianka. We all must have looked like a weird game of pig pile.

There was a candle lit on the coffee table, but there was barely enough light to see anything.

I disentangled myself from Prianka and got up, leaving her and Trina to sleep. My mouth tasted like cotton, and I really had to pee. There was another small candle by the doorway, sitting on a stack of telephone books. Down the hallway was another candle on the floor. I felt my way in the dim candlelight and was thankful that the first door on the right was to a small bathroom.

Leaving the door cracked so I could get a little bit of light from the candle, I did what I needed to do.

When I was done, I gingerly lifted the window shade and looked outside. The night was clear, and there were stars everywhere.

We weren't alone. The street wasn't swarming with zombies, but there were a few shambling back and forth. Maybe they had lived in the neighborhood before they died. Maybe they smelled life somewhere close. Who knows? But for the moment, they didn't seem to be targeting the house, so I wasn't too worried.

Out of the bathroom and a little further down the hallway was another, slightly ajar door. Through the crack I could see candlelight flickering.

When I peeked in, a shirtless Jimmy, wearing only blue jeans and socks, lifted up his head from his pillow and gave me a short wave.

"What time is it?" I said.

"Somewhere a little before dawn, I think. We all crashed. It took me a bit to get the little guy to go to sleep, but we came to an understanding."

"What do you mean?" said Prianka who was now standing behind me.

"Come on, I'll show you." Jimmy sat up and stretched then lifted himself over into his wheelchair. Yup, college guys do have tattoos, and I couldn't help noticing Prianka noticing the band etched around Jimmy's arm.

He grabbed a t-shirt that was rolled up at the bottom of his bed and slipped it over his head. Prianka and I parted as he wheeled past us.

Across the hall was another room with the door almost closed. Jimmy put his finger to his lips before softly cracking it open. A flavored jar candle sat on the floor in the middle of the room that made everything smell like cinnamon buns. I couldn't help but think of my mom. In the far right corner sat a weight bench and a bunch of dumb bells on a rack. The weights went higher than I could lift. Hell, they went higher than Chuck Peterson could ever dream of lifting.

"Where is he?" she whispered.

"Sleeping in my makeshift hyperbaric chamber," he said and tilted his head toward an upturned, red, plastic kayak that stretched along the back wall. Andrew was perched on top of the boat with his head tucked under his wing. "We had a little difference of opinion about the color because he kept insisting his chamber had to be green."

Prianka smiled and nodded approvingly—just enough to annoy me. Score another point for the man in the chair.

"He's usually so uncomfortable with strangers," she said as she quickly glanced over at me. "Or the other way around." There it was, the proverbial knife slipping quietly into my gut. "But most people don't understand how special he is." Yup, that was the sound of the knife being twisted.

"Listen," said Jimmy. "When you grow up differently abled you get lumped in with a lot of other kids who don't quite fit the norm. You learn how to talk to them in ways they understand. He's a genius, your brother. He told me exactly what he needed, and I filled in the blanks. I even gave him an old football helmet to wear. He hasn't stirred while we've been talking. My guess is he's out cold."

Okay. So Jimmy was a little impressive. I'd give him that.

"And Andrew is totally into him. I've never seen that flying chicken bond so quickly with anyone." The crow ruffled his feathers when he heard his name.

The three of us backed out of the room and gently closed the door. We followed Jimmy down the hallway and turned right into a small kitchen.

"You kids drink coffee?" he asked as he produced a match and lit the gas stove. A blue ring of flame appeared in a circle. He opened the dead fridge and pulled out a lukewarm jug of water and filled up an old pot and stuck it on the flames. Jimmy was so adept in his chair, it's as though he wasn't even in one.

"Yes," Prianka and I both said in unison.

"Me, three," added Trina, who had just woken up and joined us in the kitchen. "What time is it?" She stretched and yawned.

"Almost sun-up," I said.

"I had the strangest dream. The world turned all zombie on us, and we had to leave Littleham to go find Mom and Dad. We were with this girl from school, her autistic little brother, and a wheelchair bound D.J. with a pet crow. Weird, huh?"

"True that," said Jimmy as he rummaged around in a cabinet for a jar of instant coffee. "You left out the part about not being able to wake up."

"Yeah," she said. "Maybe I'm still dreaming." All of a sudden she went rigid and terror ran across her face. "Where's Sanjay?"

"Chill," I said. "He's fine."

"It's all good. He's sleeping," answered Jimmy as he pulled out four coffee mugs, a jar of instant coffee, and some nondairy creamer. "No sugar, guys. Sorry."

That was just fine with me. Coffee tastes like tar anyway, and no amount of sugar can help. What I really needed was a pop tart or something.

"Got any food?" I asked.

"My larder *es su* larder," he said and pointed over to a cabinet next to the sink. What I found inside was pretty grim. He had a half a jar of organic peanut butter, some seaweed treats, bran, and a couple cans of bamboo shoots.

"Jimmy, Jimmy, Jimmy," I said. "Your parents must have raised you better than this."

"Ah, foster child," he said. "Never made the real family cut—they weren't wheelchair accessible." I suddenly felt about two inches tall. "But speaking of parents, what about going and finding yours. I left a bunch of phone books out near the door just in case one of them was for the town where your aunt lives. Maybe we can find the address."

The water on the stove began to boil, and Jimmy filled up four mugs. I went and got the phone books and brought the stack back into the kitchen and plopped them down on the counter.

Prianka picked up one of the books and looked at the towns listed on the cover. "Would you know the name of the town if you heard it?"

"Not sure," both Trina and I said in unison.

"My dad and his sister weren't exactly close," Trina explained. "So we didn't see Aunt Ella and Uncle Don much—maybe once a year. Dad used to call them hippy freaks, and Mom didn't like us hanging around them. She said they were a bad influence."

"Sounds like my kind of people," said Jimmy.

"Aunt Ella would have a field day with all this poxer crap," I said. "She was always talking about how the government had things hidden up its sleeve and that someday someone was going to mess up really bad. She was one of those people who believed in everything. No conspiracy theory left unturned, you know? Bigfoot, the Loch Ness Monster, ghosts, UFOs, secret government labs—who would have ever guessed she was right?"

"I saw Bigfoot once," said Jimmy as he sipped his coffee. "I was in Maine and . . ."

"Hippy freak," said Trina, and we all laughed. It felt good to laugh—just for a moment—because laughing seemed like one of those things that we weren't going to be able to do anymore, like playing video games or surfing the Internet. The laughter was short lived, and soon we were all quiet again, sipping our coffee and lost in our own thoughts, which, for me at least, were sort of frightening.

After a while, I put down my cup and wiped my hands through my greasy hair. "So, um, yeah. We have to figure out where Aunt Ella lives. We know she's up off the Mohawk Trail."

"That's Route 2" said Jimmy. "I know how to get there."

Trina said, "We know there's a coffee shop or something on the corner of the street we turn on to get to her house."

Prianka picked up one of the telephone books. "This one says Greenfield. I think Route 2 runs through there. A bunch of other towns are listed, too."

"Like what," I said.

"Greenfield, Lakeville, Niantic, Cummington, Turners Falls and Monta . . . Monta something."

"Montague," said Jimmy. "Yeah, I know all those places. They do run up Route 2."

I turned to Trina. "Cummington sounds familiar, don't you think."

"I don't know," she said. "Pri, her name is Ella Light. See if she's listed. Oh and my Uncle is Don Dark."

"You're joking," said Prianka and Jimmy at the same time.

"Aunt Ella always said they were two halves of a whole, like soul mates, so when they got married she kept the Light name, and he changed his last name to Dark. So they're Light and Dark."

"No wonder your parents kept you away from them," said Prianka as she began thumbing through the pages. She flipped through the Ds but found nothing. Then she went to the Ls and hit pay dirt. "Ella Light, 8 Captain Logan Way, Cummington."

"Let's roll," I said.

Jimmy backed his wheels up and turned to face us. "Listen, you guys. I gotta thank you for getting me out of that jam yesterday. There aren't a lot of people who would have done that for someone."

"That's because there aren't a lot of people," I said.

He smiled grimly. "Point taken. Anyway, I really appreciate everything you've done but . . . um . . ."

Prianka was the first one to speak. "Yes," she said.

Trina agreed, and I reluctantly gave a thumbs up.

"Yes, what?" said Jimmy.

"Yes you can come with us," she said. "That's what you were going to say, right?"

Jimmy smiled like someone who just got a reprieve from a death sentence. "I wasn't sure," he said. "I mean, once you saw that I was in a wheelchair I didn't think I was going to get the sympathy vote."

"What wheelchair?" said Trina as she got up and went over to the window and peeked out. A shaft of light from the morning sunrise made her face glow a little. She touched her hair the way she used to do when she first starting dating Chuck, and kept looking outside.

Jimmy couldn't stop staring at her.

17

NONDAIRY CREAMER mixed with water for milk sounds pretty gross, but Sanjay didn't care. Neither did he care about eating the last of our Frosted Flakes. He sat at the kitchen table with Andrew close by. Every so often, Andrew would hop over and dip his beak into Sanjay's bowl and hop away with a soggy flake.

Sanjay was fascinated. He took another spoonful of his cereal, swallowed, and said, "Poopy Puppy says Corvus brachyrhynchos."

I sat across the table from him eating out of the bag of potato chips that Trina had shoved in her duffle bag. "Say what?"

"Poopy Puppy says Corvus brachyrhynchos," he repeated and plopped the grimy toy on the table next to his bowl. "The American crow is a large passerine bird species of the family Corvidae. It is a common bird found throughout much of North America. It is one of several species of corvid that are entirely black, though it can be distinguished from the Common Raven by size and behavior and from the Fish Crow by call."

"If only we could harness your brain power for electricity," I said.

"His name's Andrew," said Sanjay as he slurped at the last of his cereal. "He talks."

Andrew hopped over to Sanjay again and looked at the empty bowl. He squawked and flapped his wings before hopping on the boy's shoulder. Sanjay didn't mind one bit.

Prianka and Trina came in the kitchen with a box they filled with junk from the basement. "So we got batteries," she said. "Some tools, matches, a lighter, a couple of flashlights, um . . . can you think of anything else?"

"What else was down there?" said Jimmy, who was on his third cup of coffee. I've never been in the basement. I told my landlord I wasn't going to need the space, so he used it for storage."

Prianka and Trina shared a wicked glance.

"What?" I said.

"What?" Jimmy echoed.

Trina chewed at her lip. "Well there is something else that we thought might help." She motioned for me to follow her and Prianka to the basement. I looked back at Jimmy and shrugged. I had no choice but to follow them.

Storage was an understatement. The basement was a flea marketer's dream. There were boxes upon boxes of everything laid out neatly in rows with labels on them.

"A little anal retentive, don't you think?"

Trina just kept that wicked smile of hers plastered on her face and motioned for me to follow to the back of the room. There was an old couch there, and a couple of coffee tables, some boxes labeled 'Grammy's china," and a tall glass-fronted cabinet with a padlock.

"Ta da," she said and pointed her flashlight through the glass.

"Am I looking at what I think I'm looking at?"

"That depends on what you think you're looking at," said Prianka.

Illuminated by the beam of the flashlight was a series of hunting rifles. They gleamed beneath the light. The wood was shiny, and the barrels were mint.

"A gun cabinet? No way. His landlord must have been a hunter."

"That's not the best part," said Prianka and bent down in front of the cabinet. There was a drawer on the bottom with a brass handle. She pulled it open, stepped back, and put her hands on her hips. "So what do you think of that?"

My eyes turned into big, round saucers. "That would be bullets," I said staring at row after row of neat white boxes. "That would be one boat load of bullets."

Trina put the flashlight down on the coffee table so it was still shining on the cabinet. She slipped through the pile of boxes and came back with an axe in her hand.

Prianka stuck out her hand. "I'm having rage issues this morning," she said.

"Aw come on," whined Trina. "How often do we get a chance to break things?"

"My rage issues trump your glee at breaking things. Gimme."

Prianka wouldn't budge, so Trina handed the axe over to her. We both took five steps back and covered our faces with our elbows. Prianka held the axe handle tightly between her fists and tested the blade against the lock.

She managed to whack the lock once. but nothing happened. She hit it a second time. The third time around, she didn't even bother. She just smashed the glass with the axe head and let it shatter all over the floor.

"Feeling better now?" asked Trina.

"We'll see," she answered.

There were four rifles there. I knew a little about shooting. My dad used to take me to the annual Turkey Shoot over in Hanover every year.

Shooting turkeys isn't as heartless as you think. The contest winner is the guy who can hit the paper turkey target as many times as humanly possible. The winner gets a huge Thanksgiving turkey from Brimmer's Turkey Farm, which is a local town fixture in Littleham. We never won, but I always had a blast.

Prianka picked up one of the rifles and tested its heft like those tough guys do in the movies. She held the shaft out straight and studied the barrel with one eye closed.

"Don't tell me. You know how to use that thing, too?"

"I will soon enough," she said.

"All of us will," said Trina as she unloaded the guns from their cabinet and stooped to take out the boxes of bullets. Over near the old couch was a stack of milk crates. I grabbed one and stacked the boxes of bullets neatly inside.

After a quick look around, the three of us left Jimmy James' basement for the last time, guns and ammo in hand.

18

TRINA AND I decided that we'd be the ones to do it because if anything happened to Prianka, Sanjay would be totally lost—and as mucho macho as Jimmy was, he was still in that damn chair.

We stuck the paddle inside the kayak, and Jimmy made us take his life vest and shove it way down in the nose of the boat. He said, "It might come in handy."

I took the phone book with Aunt Ella's address, ripped out the page, and put it in my back pocket. I also ripped out a hunk of paper and handed a bunch to Trina along with a lighter. I shoved the rest of the pages down the front of my shirt so they'd be easy to get to.

Jimmy was at the window.

"Okay. Mrs. Demetrion's out in front of her house just sitting on her stairs and twitching every once in a while. There're some girls who live down a couple houses. I can see three of them. They're doing that wandering back and forth thing. I hate that."

"Can you see to either side of us?" I asked.

"Double checking." Jimmy craned his neck and pressed his face against the glass, first one way than the other. "Nothing," he said.

We were all packed and ready to go. Sanjay sat on the futon in the living room clutching Poopy Puppy. Prianka stood by the door. At her feet were the few boxes that we had packed along with the milk crate of bullets and all the guns.

Andrew soared out of the kitchen and landed next to Sanjay. He delicately stepped on to his shoulder. I didn't need to ask. The bird was coming, too.

"So my guess is we're going to draw a lot of attention as soon as we start moving," I said to Jimmy and Prianka. "We'll try to be as quick as we can, but if you see something we don't, scream. As far as I'm concerned every one of those things can pop and burn, but if any of that goo gets on my car . . ."

"Your car?" said Trina.

"You know what I mean. If any of that black crap gets on *the* car, it's like freaking molten tar. I don't care about the paint job. I care that we don't have fried wheels."

Jimmy rubbed his thighs with the palms of his hands. "You sure you don't want me to do this, man? Putting the kayak up on a car is cake. I've done it a million times."

"It's not a car, it's a truck," I snapped. "And this isn't a contest."

Thankfully, Trina backed me up, even though she should have throttled back just an eensy bit. "This isn't a game of who can do more pushups."

Ouch.

Jimmy looked away and didn't say anything.

Sanjay held his stuffed dog to his ear and said, "The world record for the most number of non-stop pushups is 10,507 by Minoru Yoshida of Japan, which was achieved in October 1980."

We were all quiet. Trina crossed her arms over her chest and stared at the floor. Prianka bent and pretended to tie her laces.

"I get it," said Jimmy and went back to looking out the window. "I get it." He blew out a gust of air. "Let's just get this done."

The kayak was laid out in a straight shot to the front door. There were handles on the bow and the stern, and it was incredibly light. I picked up the front end and Trina picked up the rear. When we were ready, I nodded to Prianka, and she quietly unlocked the door and swung it open.

Just like that Trina and I were out in the open. Seconds later, we were at the Hummer and heaving the kayak on top.

"Upside down," hissed Trina. "It has to be upside down."

She jumped on the hood, I grabbed the end, and we turned the boat over. Surprisingly, our movements aren't what got the poxers moving. Instead, the clank of the paddle inside the plastic shell is what alerted Mrs. Demetrion that there was fresh meat in town.

I saw her out of the corner of my eye as I struggled to thread the straps underneath the roof rack and over to Trina. Mrs. Demetrion hunkered down on her steps and let her arms hang down below her like some sort of demented ape. Seconds later she stood straight up and started toward us.

"Trina, hurry."

"I am. I am," she cried.

"We've got a lady poxer incoming, and she's not looking pretty."

Jimmy was already through the door and out on the porch. "Burn her," he yelled. "Light her up." I know he was just trying to help, but when he yelled, the three girls down the street heard him and started toward us too.

Prianka ran out past Jimmy and jumped the few steps to the ground. She already had a lighter and paper in her hands. She looked at the girls heading toward us and then at Mrs. Demetrion. Mrs. D. was closer.

"I can't get the stupid clip in," yelled Trina.

I made sure that both clips on my side were fastened tight before running around the Hummer to her. I didn't need to see Prianka light up the poxer behind us, but I heard the screaming as the thing burst into flames. In seconds, Prianka was at our side. She reached through our octopus of hands and deftly slipped the clip into place.

"I was going to go to Harvard," she cried with a mouthful of venom. She headed toward the poxer girls. "I was going to go to Harvard, and I was going to get a scholarship," she shrieked at them. "I was going to get a scholarship to Harvard, and I was going to be famous. Do you hear me through your ugly, dead heads? I was going to be famous."

We didn't need to look. The rage machine was pumping full steam in Prianka, and I knew that she could handle the poxers no problem. Trina and I ran for the door, bolted past Jimmy who wanted nothing more than to get up out of his chair and help Prianka, and grabbed the guns, the ammo, and everything else.

When the girls started to burn and squeal, poor Sanjay put his hands over his ears and started wailing, too. Andrew flew off of his shoulder, out the front doorway and landed on Jimmy's head.

"Time to fly, Buddy," he said to the bird as I ran past him with an armful of rifles. I remember thinking there was no way he was going to get down those stairs in that chair without becoming sidewalk pizza, but after I threw the guns in the back seat of the car and turned around, I knew I'd never underestimate Jimmy's determination again.

Jimmy was already out of the chair and sitting on the porch. He grabbed a wheel with one hand and heaved the chair down to the ground then scooted down the three steps on his butt and hoisted himself back into his seat. He did it all in just about the time I would have taken to walk down the steps on two legs.

Prianka didn't even wait for the girls to pop before she was back in the house and kneeling in front of Sanjay trying desperately to calm him down.

"Poopy Puppy said it's time for all of us to go," she said. "Really, Sanjay. He said it's time for all of us to go."

Sanjay relaxed a little and rocked nervously back and forth. "But where's Andrew?" he said. "Where's Corvus brachyrhynchos."

Prianka held out her hand to her brother. "He's coming with us," she said. "You, me, Tripp, Trina, Jimmy, and Andrew."

Fresh tears leaped from her brother's eyes. "What about Poopy Puppy?"

"And Poopy Puppy, too."

Sanjay got up, the dog hanging from one arm at his side. "That makes seven," he said. "Like dwarves or Double O."

"You're right," she said. "That makes seven." She took Sanjay's hand.

Trina and Jimmy were already in the car. Andrew was sitting on the roof. When Sanjay appeared in the doorway, Andrew flew to him and landed on his head. In the middle of the street I could see the fires burning. Was this what it was going to be like from now on? Were we just going to burn them all?

I got in the front seat and looked at Trina. There was fear in her eyes—that and determination. Maybe she was scared of the poxers, or maybe she was scared that we weren't going to find Mom and Dad.

Maybe she was just scared, like me, that this really was what it was going to be like from now on.

This, and nothing else.

19

I WAS STARVING. All I had eaten in the past two days were potato chips, frosted flakes, and some mediocre coffee. We all agreed we needed real food, and we needed to find some in a place where there weren't any poxers. Jimmy first suggested raiding Mrs. Demetrion's house because, well, she was dead, but ultimately we just wanted to get out of the neighborhood and to a place where lots of corpses weren't staggering around.

Jimmy volunteered a back way out of town that passed by a service station and a convenience store. We could stock up on food. After, if we were lucky, we could get to Aunt Ella's in a couple of hours.

The plan sounded easy enough, but nothing ever goes smoothly. Amherst is a college town, and during the school year, the population swells. The dead were everywhere, and it freaked us out.

All along the route there were poxers—poxers in the streets—poxers on the lawns—poxers gorging themselves on bloody things that I didn't even want to speculate about.

On the far side of town, up behind the University campus, we spotted an old white sedan moving in the opposite direction. I slowed the Hummer down and the other driver slowed, as well. When we reached each other, we stopped in the middle of the road with driver side windows facing.

I lowered our window, and he lowered his. He stared at me first before his gaze passed me and found Trina.

"Um, hi," I said.

"Who's that with you?" he barked at me. He was old. Like really old.

"Just my sister," I said. That was all. I remember once my father telling me that if you want to get someone else to talk, just stare at them and don't speak. They'll get uncomfortable, and they start to babble.

"Who else?" he growled. "In the back. Who else you got?"

Prianka lowered her window and glared at the man. "Listen, we don't want any trouble," she said. "We're just looking for some food."

"I don't have any," he said.

"That's fine. We're thinking we might find a convenience store."

"They're all closed."

"We understand that," I said. "We don't think anyone will mind."

"You're looters, aren't you?" he spat out. "The lot of you. You're all damn looters. Well you can't have my lunch, no siree Bob. It's my lunch, and you can't have any." Before I could say anything he pointed a little pistol right at me.

The first living person we find since yesterday and he had to be a nut job? For the moment, I was speechless. Thankfully Jimmy took over the conversation.

"Excuse me, sir," he said. "I don't think there's any reason for that."

"Says you."

"We have a little boy with us. You don't want to frighten him, do you?"

"I don't give a crap about your little boy," the old guy said. "I don't give a good God damn about any of you. I'm probably dead, anyway, and this is some sort of purgatory."

He lowered the gun a little and let it rest on the side of his car door. My heart was thumping a mile a minute. Other than paintball once when I was eleven, no one had ever seriously pointed a gun at me. Being on the muzzle end of a pistol was a 'make you pee in your pants' moment for sure. Thankfully, I didn't.

The old man pulled the gun back into his car and looked straight ahead with an odd sort of smile. "I'm going to Maine," he said. "I've always wanted a beach house on the coast of Maine, but I could never afford one."

"I don't think that's an issue anymore," said Jimmy from the back seat.

"I think I'm going to find the nicest, cleanest one I can with whitewashed floors and big open windows. Then I'm going to shoot myself in the head and make a mess of the whole thing." He laughed and held up the handgun and pointed it at us again like he was going to pull the trigger.

"Wanna join me?"

"Stop that," cried Prianka. "You're scaring my brother."

The old man snorted and put his gun down. "I'm scaring your brother? *I'm scaring your brother?* I'm not even one of the scary ones," he cackled. "But you'll see. You'll all see soon enough."

Then he just closed his window and left.

"Freak," I whispered under my breath as I watched through my side window as the white car faded in the distance.

"It's going to be like that from now on," said Jimmy. "People are going to be crazy or shell shocked or are just plain not going to trust each other."

"So the living are going to turn into monsters just like the dead?" I said as I started down the road again. "That's just great."

"Who knows?" said Jimmy. "After all, we're all just dumb animals, anyway. We're all just dumb animals that ruin everything we touch."

"Enough," said Trina. "Really. Things are already about a b'zillion times worse than our worst nightmares. We don't need you two adding more fuel to the fire."

"Yes, ma'am," said Jimmy, mostly because he knew she was right.

"Sorry," I muttered. "I just want some food."

Jimmy directed us down a few side streets and out on to a main road that was mostly rural. Off in the distance I saw the gas station and convenience store. The road was blessedly free of poxers, and in a minute we were in the parking lot.

The convenience store said North Amherst Sundries on the sign. There were a few other cars in the parking lot, but they all had 'for sale' signs on them, which made us think that there was no one around.

"Food first," said Trina. She had a one track mind. "After that, a little bit of gas syphoning is in order." The Hummer's gauge hadn't budged much from when we had to steal gas yesterday morning, but we were going to need to fuel up soon.

The memory of gasoline mouth from yesterday made me grip the steering wheel until my knuckles turned white. "The hose is in the back. Be my guest."

"You syphon gas?" said Jimmy. "Who taught you that?"

"Poopy Puppy says you stick one end of a hose in a gas tank and suck on the other end until the gas starts to flow out. Then you fill up a gas can and dump it into your own tank," said Sanjay, which was exactly how Prianka had described it yesterday.

Jimmy laughed.

"What?" said Trina.

"You're like some rich kid's gang," he said. "Like the Littleham Marauders or maybe the Little Looters of Littleham."

"Yeah, that's us," I said as I opened the door. "We're the Little Looters of Littleham. We're the Triple L gang. You help us loot, or you get the boot."

I walked cautiously up to the storefront. There weren't any poxers around. I tested the door and thankfully found it was unlocked. Everyone else got out of the car, including Andrew, who had made a comfortable new home on Sanjay's shoulder.

Together, we went inside North Amherst Sundries and found paradise.

20

YEAH, I KNOW we were looking for real food, but there was so much junk food I couldn't ignore it.

Sadly, we found the cashier behind the counter. He was dead. A lot. Dead, like in the half eaten sort of way, so we made sure to steer Sanjay clear of him.

Each of us grabbed one of those little, red handheld baskets and started filling them up with what we determined were essentials.

Trina was all about the potato chips. Jimmy was all over anything organic in the case next to the register. You know, the pretend junk food that tastes a little too much like hay? He was really psyched about the fruit juice and the carob flavored cookies.

Ever the practical one, Prianka took two baskets and filled them with loaves of bread, peanut butter, and jelly.

I zeroed in on the chocolate, because, well chocolate is awesome. Sanjay stuck with me. I made sure to grab a bunch of little packs of sunflower seeds and nuts from the peanut rack for the bird. It's not that I was getting fond of the flying rat or anything like that, but, well, whatever.

We loaded our loot into the back of the car. After that, we went back and took as much bottled water as we could fit.

Since the gas pumps weren't working, I took the hose and the gas can out of the back of the car, but this time Prianka snatched them out of my hands. Trina didn't object. We all watched as she expertly syphoned gas out of an old Volvo, followed by a pickup truck that had definitely seen better days. Only after the gas gauge was on the F for full did we allow ourselves the chance to take a break and eat.

"Where do you suppose the poxer is who got the cashier?" I said to no one in particular as I shoved a powdered doughnut into my mouth.

"You're disgusting when you eat," said Trina, so I smiled at her with a pie hole full of powder.

"Wandered off," said Jimmy. "Who cares as long as it isn't here?"

"Poxer," said Andrew, and flapped his wings a few times. Sanjay held out his palm, and Andrew delicately picked roasted sunflower seeds out of it.

"Andrew learned a new word," said Sanjay and stroked the crow's feathers.

"He's a smart bird," said Jimmy. "Been my best bud for four years now."

"Yeah, about that," said Trina. "What's with the pet crow?" She guzzled an energy drink and tore into a bag of pizza flavored chips. She might have prom queen looks, but my sister could never be called dainty.

"Andrew? His nest blew down in a rain storm in front of my foster home. He wasn't even old enough to fly. There were three of them all together. My foster mom at the time, Mrs. Emrick, was pretty cool, and she helped me set up a box with a heat lamp for them. We went to the library and read about how to take care of young birds, and we just sort of, you know, raised them."

"What happened to the other two?" I asked.

"Flew the coop," said Jimmy. "Andrew here decided he liked the easy life and stayed."

I never even thought about foster kids before. For that matter I never even knew someone in a wheelchair before. I barely even knew what autism was and pet crows were what wizards had in fantasy books. Throw in Prianka Patel who vacillated between mega bitch, teen genius, and, well whatever, and we were a pretty odd group.

"Poxer," Andrew squawked again, and I was just about to tell him to shut his beak when I saw a zombie coming around the corner of the building. He was a young guy about Jimmy's age with a University of Massachusetts sweatshirt on that was covered in dark, bloody splotches. He made a beeline right for the Hummer.

"Now I guess we know who got the cashier," I said and turned on the ignition.

"Poxer," repeated Andrew.

"Poxer," said Sanjay as he held up Poopy Puppy in front of his face. "Poopy Puppy says Poxer, too."

"I think that's our cue to leave," I said and backed out of the North Amherst Sundries parking lot. Jimmy pointed to the right, so I palmed the wheel and pulled the Hummer onto the road.

The poxer watched us go. I bet he had been hungry, too.

21

CAN SOMETHING suck so badly that the light from normal sucking would take a million light years to reach this new level of sucking? Yes.

Jimmy directed us down the road and told us that there was an exit to Route 116 coming up on the left. If we went down 116, we would eventually find a ramp to the highway up to Greenfield and on to the Mohawk Trail.

Piece of cake, right?

There were a few cars on the exit to Route 116 and one accident that I had to maneuver around. When we got up to the main road my jaw dropped.

"Are you serious?" said Trina. It's doesn't happen often, but my sister covered her eyes with her hands because she knew she was going to cry.

"*Tatti*," whispered Prianka under her breathe and Sanjay stared at her like she had just said the worst word ever.

Well, I later found out that *tatti* was Hindi for what I was thinking, too.

Sprawled out in front of us as far as we could see were cars. Some were still lightly smoking because they had been in accidents. Some were turned sideways. Some were even on top of each other.

"They must have been leaving the University," said Jimmy softly. "They must have been leaving the University when everything hit. Route 116 goes to the highway, and the highway goes north."

"Don't we have to go north?" I asked.

"Right now, we have to go back," he answered. "Look."

All along the grassy sides of Route 116 were poxers—literally thousands of them. They were in groups and pairs, and some singles, staggering back and forth, probably looking for scraps.

There were more here than we had seen anywhere, and they were definitely aroused by the movement of our car, because they were acting as though someone had just rung the dinner bell. They all started marching toward us, if you could call what they were doing a march. Old ones, young ones, hippy freaks and professor types—all dead, all ravenous, all infected with Necropoxy.

Their faces were riddled with bite marks. I think they were so hungry that they were taking bites out of each other. That was the grossest part. Clotted blood and bits of flesh hung off of them like victims of piranha attacks who refused to lie down and admit they were dead.

Open bone and muscle spilled out of them because there was no skin to hold it back.

The one I remember most—the one that is burned into my mind—was a guy with a red flannel shirt and a baseball cap that said "Mechanics do it with grease". He staggered toward us with both hands up and his shirt wide open. Beneath his tattooed chest was an angry, jagged cavity, and out of it, in loopy sausage rolls, came his intestines. They were wrapped around one of his arms, and he was eating them.

Trina squawked, "Go back," but the fear had knocked reason temporarily out of my head. "Tripp, go back," she shrieked again and jabbed me in the arm.

"Ow, quit it," I said as the nightmare procession-without-end descended on us.

"We have to go back, man," said Jimmy.

"Poxer," chirped Andrew, and I snapped out of it. High five to the bird. I threw the Hummer in reverse and navigated back down the ramp and around the accident as best as I could.

My shoulder ached, and my head swam with hideous images. That's when I saw her out of the corner of my eye. There was a woman, maybe my mom's age, locked inside one of the cars in the traffic jam. She kept popping up in the window, waving frantically at us, then popping out of sight again so she wouldn't arouse the interest of any of the poxers.

It was already too late. Some of them divided off from the pack and began climbing over her car and clawing at the windshield.

Trina saw her, too, and she looked at me hard. I knew what she was thinking. This time . . . this time she was right.

Trina looked the other way and began to chew her nails.

I twisted my neck around and navigated the rest of the way down the ramp. When we got to the bottom, I turned on to the back road and just kept driving.

"Do you know where this takes us?" I asked Jimmy, choking back the frog that was rising in my throat.

"I'm pretty sure all roads just lead north."

"Okay," I sighed and pressed hard on the gas. "North." Even now, I still remember the look of horror on that woman's face when she realized we weren't going to help her. There was nothing we could have done. There were scores of poxers all around her, and we just weren't prepared.

I silently prayed for her as I drove through the autumn colors. Trina said nothing. After about five minutes I felt a hand on my shoulder. It was Prianka's. She just stared at me through the rearview mirror and managed a sad smile on her stone face.

She said, "It was the right thing to do," and nothing more. After a moment she removed her hand and placed them both in her lap.

It didn't help at all.

22

THE NEXT TOWN past North Amherst was Sunderland. I only knew that because of the incorporation sign we passed as we entered. The signpost was decorated with dried corn stalks and a few pumpkins. Leaf-peeping season was just around the corner, and this was just one more staunch, New England example of how seriously we take our Fall.

Town center was virtually nonexistent. There was a minimart, a gas station, a post office, and a fruit stand—each on a corner. That's all. A huge mountain with a bald top loomed over us from across a river that snaked its way through the valley.

"Mount Sugarloaf," said Jimmy as we all looked up. "There's an observatory on top. From there you can see for miles. You can probably see all the way back to Littleham from this side. I know you can see Vermont and a tiny bit of New Hampshire from the other side."

We crossed the bridge that spanned the river, zigzagging around a few cars and narrowly missing a poxer that looked like he escaped from a nursing home. On the other side of the river we all stared at the mountain growing before our eyes.

"Great make-out spot," Jimmy said under his breath. Trina blushed. I didn't even know that blushing was part of my sister's repertoire.

As we passed by the entrance to Mount Sugarloaf State Park I noticed that the gate was open. Maybe no one had a chance to close up before everything hit. That's when what Jimmy had just said about the make-out spot registered.

"How far did you say you could see?"

"Pretty far." Jimmy only took a second for him to latch on to what I was thinking. "At least far enough to see if the highway is as bad as Route 116."

"What's the dif?" said Trina. We'll know when we get there, won't we?"

"Or we'll be in the middle of another poxer fest," I said. "Not really anxious to push our luck if we don't have to."

I stopped the car and backed up to the entrance and pulled in. I admit, the trees were beautiful. I could really see why people were so drawn to

Massachusetts in the fall. I never used to notice things like that, but now I was beginning to see how precious and fragile and beautiful everything was.

We climbed up the steep, winding road that led to the top of the mountain. There were a couple of really sharp, hairpin turns, and half way up the mountain, a rock wall flanked us on one side for a while and a sheer drop on the other. A couple of juvenile offenders had left their marks on the rock. One said 'Go Lancers' and another paint-scrawled message read 'Kris and Gary forever.' I wondered if when Kris and Gary were defacing public property they knew that forever wasn't quite as long as they thought.

When we reached the top we found an empty parking lot and a pathway up to the observatory. I parked the Hummer, and we all got out, including Jimmy. "I love this place," he said as he pumped his wheels with his muscular arms. "Race you to the top." He was off and rolling before any of us had a chance to respond.

Andrew took flight and followed Jimmy, circling above him. After a moment, he came right back to Sanjay's shoulder. Prianka was wary, looking everywhere for signs of dead movement. I suppose Trina and I were doing the same thing, but Prianka looked like she was engaged in taking a midterm exam—like life and death and Harvard depended on it.

Well, I guess it did, except for the Harvard part. Who could blame her?

Mount Sugarloaf's observatory was on a large plateau, maybe 200 feet across. The tower itself was a three-story wood structure with a steep, metal, spiral, staircase running up through its middle. Thank God the path was paved, or Jimmy wouldn't have gotten very far.

He easily beat us all to the top. Around the plateau were park signs with information describing what observers were seeing. Directly below us was Route 116 winding its way through the valley. I could even see the traffic jam of cars that trailed off into the distance.

Off to the left was the University. There was enough smoke rising from one of the buildings to confirm it was burning to the ground. All I could imagine was that some survivors unluckier than us figured out that poxers burn like paper but didn't get out of the way fast enough and fried their hideout.

To the right of us were low hills that gave way to layer after layer of mountain ranges. The foliage was amazing. Puffy clouds in the sky made me feel like I was looking at a painting instead of the real thing.

"Wow," I murmured under my breath.

Jimmy wheeled up to me. "Pretty awesome, right?"

"You could say that."

He pointed to the mountains slightly off to the left. "That's where your Aunt Ella lives. I'm guessing that's about thirty miles from here." Then he pointed down to Route 116 and off in the distance to where it met the highway. "And that answers the question of the day."

My eyes followed to where he was pointing. The highway was jammed with cars, too.

I got really frustrated. "I don't get it. Who goes to Vermont?"

Jimmy shrugged. "Leaf peepers, dead heads, people who want to be as far away from a city as possible. I'm thinking that if this all went down and I had a car, I would have headed north, too. South is Hartford, New Haven, and New York City. North? There's nothing's north but Vermont and Canada. That means lots of wide open space and not a lot of people."

I heard a commotion behind us. "Sanjay—NO," Prianka scolded from near the observatory. He was already scrambling up the stairs with Poopy Puppy in one hand. Andrew flapped off his shoulder and climbed into the air. Prianka and Trina dashed after Sanjay.

I was ninety-nine percent sure there was nobody up there, but that one percent tugged at the corner of my brain.

"Crap," I said to Jimmy. "Come on."

At the foot of the spiral stair case, Jimmy lowered himself out of his wheelchair and grabbed on to the metal railing. He swiftly pulled himself up the stairs with ease. He was pretty amazing. As I followed after him, I noticed a tiny toad sitting on the edge of one of the iron treads. It regarded me with beady, alien eyes. I couldn't figure out how the toad had gotten there to begin with, but when I gently stooped to pick it up, it jumped.

If I was cornered, would I jump? If I had nowhere else to turn, would I take that final, fatal leap?

The thought of that toad jumping still stuck on my mind as I reached the top. There weren't any poxers there or anyone else but us for that matter. Trina, Prinaka, and Sanjay were at the railing looking off into the distance. The view was amazing. How could three stories make so much difference? The whole of New England was laid out before me.

From here I could guess where Littleham was.

From here I could see across the valley for miles. One way was the distant mountains of Vermont, and a small edge of New Hampshire. The other way was the University. In front of us was village after village, and every once in a while a thin pillar of smoke.

"At least people are fighting back," said Prianka as she lifted her chin toward the smoke.

"Power to the people," said Jimmy.

One of the smoke trails withered to nothing and disappeared. "Peace out," I said.

That was when Trina totally lost it.

23

I HATE WHEN people cry. It's awkward. I don't know what to do. Their faces screw up in these freakish masks and sometimes they even get red. Every bit of inner frustration or anger or hurt leaks out of their pores all at once.

Trina crumbled to the ground like someone had unpinned her. Maybe all the tension of the past two days finally caught up to her, like Chuck or our missing parents or the rest of the world turning poxer. Maybe she just needed to vent. I don't know.

But there was one thing I did know. When my sister cries, the last thing she wants is for me to be anywhere near her. She thinks she is supposed to be the strong one—the one who is supposed to take care of me. Not the other way around.

Sanjay ignored her and kept looking out across the valley. After a moment, Prianka guided him away from the view and back down the stairs.

Jimmy looked back at me, and I looked back at him, and somewhere in that silent communication I gave him permission to take this one on, mostly because I wasn't willing to extend a helping hand to Trina and pull back a stump.

He crawled over to her and she turned away from him, so he leaned up against the edge of the deck and just sat there. Jimmy gave me the thumbs up, so I left, silently following Prianka down the spiral stair case and out of the observation tower.

I looked around for the toad when I got to the bottom of the stairs, but it was nowhere to be found. It got away. Somehow, it took a leap of faith and got away.

"I never took Trina Light for a girl who cries," said Prianka. She sat down on a stone bench and watched as Sanjay went to the edge of the plateau.

"She usually doesn't," I said. "But everyone has their moments, I guess."

Prianka stared off in the distance, and I stared at my feet. Andrew leaped off Sanjay's shoulder and flew out over the sheer drop, sweeping into a wide arc then floating on the air. Sanjay clapped his hands together and held Poopy Puppy up high over his head, presumably so the grimy little bag of cotton fluff could see, too.

In another world, it would have been a Kodak moment.

"Thanks," said Prianka after a while.

"Thanks for what?"

"Just . . . thanks," she said.

"Um, okay." My dad said I would never really be able to figure girls out. He was right—Prianka was a complete mystery to me.

She ran her hands through her thick, black hair and absentmindedly brushed some strands behind her ear.

"You could have left me at the Mug N' Muffin," she said.

"No I couldn't."

She shook her head. "You could have dumped me as soon as you saw Sanjay."

"Nope on that, too."

She was quiet for a moment. Could I possibly have just made the great Prianka Patel speechless? No such luck.

"I'm not sure I would have done the same for you," she said.

I snorted and looked directly ahead. Andrew looped back over the plateau and rode a light breeze to the top of the observation tower.

"Yes you would have," I said.

"How do you know?"

How did I know? I didn't know, but that's how I would have wanted her to be.

"Because you're always right," I said. "And if I had been stuck at the Mug N' Muffin instead of you, you would have come to get me because that would have been the right thing to do."

Prianka sat quietly. Andrew cawed from up above and swooped down to land on Sanjay's shoulder. That kid was going to be a big responsibility for her. He probably always had been and that made my opinion of Prianka slowly creep up just one notch, but only one. That's about as generous as I felt at the moment.

We didn't say anything more to each other. About five minutes later, Trina and Jimmy came down the stairs. Her eyes were puffy, but she had stopped crying. Jimmy pulled himself up into his chair and checked his watch.

"Not even noon," he mused.

Wow, a lifetime ago we had left his house in Amherst.

"We should go," said Prianka.

I thought about the highway. "Go how?"

"Back roads, I guess," said Jimmy. "You got from Littleham to Amherst, and we managed to get here. How hard can it be?"

Really hard.

24

JIMMY WAS FLOORED the first time we used our human navigator. Sanjay was filled to the gills with junk food and had absolutely no interest in sleeping. He sat on Prianka's lap in the back seat and stuck his head out the open window like a faithful hound dog.

Andrew sat on the headrest between her and Jimmy. He obviously enjoyed the fall breeze, too. Every once in a while, he spread his wings and let the air rush through his feathers.

We slowly inched our way down Sugarloaf Mountain. The road was a little less freaky than the one coming up. We had to hope we didn't encounter any cars along the way, because there would have been no place to pass. We'd have to go back the way we had come.

When we got to the bottom, I stopped the car and turned around.

"Sanjay?" I said. "Hey, Buddy?" He blushed and tucked himself down into Prianka's lap as though he could hide from me. "Listen, Buddy. We're all going to need your help again like you did yesterday. We have a new address, and we're hoping that you can help us find the way to get there."

"What are you talking about?" said Jimmy.

I ignored him. "Do you think you and Poopy Puppy can help us? Well, because, you know, Poopy Puppy is smart."

Sanjay nodded his head in agreement. "Poopy Puppy's smart," he said. "Poopy Puppy's very smart."

Jimmy started to ask again, but Prianka just put her hand on his and shook her head.

I reached into my back pocket and pulled out the piece of paper that I had torn out of the phone book. "We're going to see a really nice lady named Ella Light," I said. "She's my aunt. She's Trina's aunt, too. I bet when we get there she'll be really happy to meet you and Poopy Puppy and Andrew."

Sanjay didn't say anything, so I continued.

"But we have a little problem. We can't go on any highways, and we can't go on Route 116. Do you think you can get us there by just going on regular roads?"

Again, he didn't respond so I opened up the piece of paper and read the address out loud. "We're going to see Ella Light at 8 Captain Logan Way in Cummington, Massachusetts." I repeated the address. "8 Captain Logan Way in Cummington, Massachusetts. Do you know which way we should go?"

Sanjay pulled Poopy Puppy close to him, closed his eyes, and said, "'A total of 48 sheep were seized along with 13 goats from a small farm in Cummington.'"

Trina gagged on the bottle of water she was drinking.

"'I have rescue groups lined up that want to take these animals and give them the care that they need, said Sherrie Gilbert, Community Liaison, Cummington County Animal Care Services.

"A judge approved the seizure Thursday, deeming the conditions the animals were living in at the farm of Ella Light and Don Dark questionable.

"While Gilbert said samples taken from the farm were being tested for certain livestock related diseases, Ms. Light and Mr. Dark insisted the seemingly poor conditions were caused by recent extremes in weather.

"It was noted that all animals were well fed and hydrated at the time of the seizure. The county attorney is expected to file animal cruelty charges against the couple this coming week.'"

We all fell silent. I felt the red spread up my neck and across my cheeks. Trina sucked in her lips and made this weird little whistling sound.

Jimmy just stared at Sanjay in utter amazement. He was too stunned to speak.

"Really?" Prianka barked. "Your aunt and uncle are like, like felons?"

"I can't believe he dredged that up," I stammered. "That was years ago. Aunt Ella says one of their neighbors reported them because he didn't like them."

"What just happened?" asked Jimmy, his mouth still agape.

"That's just great," Prianka went on. "That's just peachy."

Trina started giggling a little. "You can choose your friends, but you can't choose your family," she offered but none of us laughed.

"Is Sanjay . . . is Sanjay an idiot savant?" said Jimmy like he just found out aliens landed on the White House lawn.

"Don't say that word," Prianka snapped.

"Yeah, Dude. We're not down with the putdowns," I said.

He shook his head in disbelief with this stunned, amazed look on his face. "I knew people like him existed, but, I never thought . . . I mean, I never . . ."

Prianka sighed and gave him the quick rundown on Sanjay.

While Jimmy's head was still reeling I asked Sanjay again. "Do you think you can get us there, Buddy?"

Sanjay consulted with the dirty dog for a moment before nodding his head once. "Go straight," he said. "Poopy Puppy says all roads lead north."

Jimmy laughed. "I said that, didn't I? I mean I said that just this morning, and he repeated it word for word. That's wild. That's really wild."

"Yes, we know," I said.

Trina turned to Jimmy and sort of shook her head a little. That was enough for him to stop talking.

"Straight it is," I said, and we all motored out of the entrance of Sugarloaf State Park and one step closer to my mom and dad.

25

MY MOM USED to tell us a story about the people in the hill towns. This was the part of Massachusetts that nobody ever visited—kind of north of the University but not north enough to be in Vermont, and kind of west toward the Berkshires but not west enough to be part of the Berkshires.

It was no man's land. Oh, sure, there were towns there with weird names like Lucifer's Knoll, and Black Water, and Devil's Pulpit, but they were so small that most Bay Staters never even heard of them.

My mom said there were some weird things that went on in some of those towns—things that people never talked about. Supposedly, that's where all the witches from Salem eventually settled back in the sixteen hundreds, or at least the ones who didn't get burned. Also, tons of people from the state mental hospitals went there when they were closed down for lack of funding.

There were even legends of a whole group of people called the Big Headed Clan that lived deep in the woods. Supposedly, their heads were huge—like the size of watermelons. Mom said they were all inbred—like having kids with your sister, or your uncle, or your cousin once removed. From time to time, she would tell us that she heard talk about the Big Headed Clan, but no one ever really saw them. Even kids in my school would joke about them every once in a while, which scared the crap out of me because I was convinced that my mom had made the whole thing up.

Just the same, my mom would tell us that if we were bad, she'd take us up to one of those towns like Lilliput or Covered Bridge and leave us there for the Big Headed Clan. They'd know what to do with kids who misbehaved. They'd know what to do and how.

As I meandered down the road, weaving past stalled cars or the lone poxer here and there, I couldn't help but think about the big headed people. Were they real? Did we have more things to contend with than just poxers? For a few miles there, I really spooked myself out. I kept scanning the woods for people with heads too big for their bodies. What if there were big headed poxers now, too? Did they eat more? Did they take bigger bites out of you because their mouths were as disproportionately large as their heads? Were they smarter than the average poxer?

Chill, I told myself. All this nonsense is the byproduct of three candy bars, a bottle of coke, and something so processed and gross and good at the same time that I shoved the whole thing into my mouth before catching the name on the wrapper. All the sugar was playing tricks with my head.

That—or maybe the revelation that, as of two days ago, monsters were real after all.

Thankfully, by the time five miles had passed, the heebie jeebies had simmered a bit. We came to the end of the road we were on. Without asking, Sanjay pointed to the right.

"That's away from the highway," said Jimmy.

"Away from the highway is just fine with me," I said as I turned the wheel.

Another few minutes of silence and Prianka spoke up, "So whatever happened to all the animals?"

"My aunt and uncle's animals? They got them back. Like I said, that was a couple of years ago, and the whole story was all a big misunderstanding, anyway. I mean, don't get me wrong. Their farm is kind of gross, but it's no glue factory."

"It's gross," said Trina. "Every time we come home from there I have to take an hour long shower."

"What a girl," I said, and simultaneously Trina punched me in the arm while Jimmy and Prianka both flicked the back of my head.

"Quit it," I yelped. A nanosecond later I was slamming my foot hard on the breaks.

There was a kid standing in the middle of the road with a bow and arrow in his hand pointed directly at us.

"Crap," said Jimmy.

"What do I do?"

"Run him over," said Trina, the ever so practical one.

"I have a better idea," said Prianka and reached in the back for one of the rifles. She passed it forward to Trina and took another one for herself.

"Watch Sanjay," she said to Jimmy. "Trina, time for acting 101." She opened the door, and my sister followed.

"Get out of the car," the kid barked. He couldn't have been more than eleven or twelve.

"We're getting out of the car," said Prianka rather nonchalantly. Once her feet were firmly planted on the ground she lifted the rifle and pointed it directly at the boy. "The point is—what are you going to do about it?"

Trina lifted her rifle too and took a step forward. "Yeah," she said. "What the hell are you going to do?"

I gripped the wheel tightly. Who did they think they were, anyway?

Bonnie and . . . well . . . Bonnie? They didn't even have bullets. My sister never shouldered a gun in her life, and I don't care how perfect Prianka Patel thought she was, I'd lay odds that she never had either.

"Not good, not good, not good, not good," Jimmy kept saying over and over from the back seat.

"Go ahead and shoot me," challenged Prianka. "My friend here will drop you before I hit the ground and vice versa."

"Try me," said my sister, repositioning the rifle on her shoulder and cocking her head like she was figuring out the best line of fire.

The boy's face turned white. Trina was scary enough, but Prianka Patel? Yikes! The bow and arrow he was holding began to shake so badly that I though he was going to let the arrow fly by accident. Trina stood her ground, and Prianka's face was a mask of menace.

A few seconds later, a wet stain began to spread across the kid's crotch. He dropped the bow and arrow and ran down the embankment to our right and off into the woods.

We all watched him go. I probably even felt bad for him—but not for long. Trina casually slung the rifle over her shoulder, high fived Prianka, and together they climbed back into the Hummer.

"What a girl I am," she said as she passed the rifle back to Prianka.

I never made that mistake again.

26

"DON'T YOU THINK we should go back for him?" said Jimmy. He craned his neck to see if he could catch a glimpse of the kid in the woods

"No," I said a little too quickly, but no one jumped down my throat. "Listen, Trina and I haven't heard from my parents since Friday night. We just want to get to my Aunt Ella's house. We can save the world tomorrow."

"He's just one kid," said Jimmy.

"Yeah, a stupid one," I snapped. "What the hell does he think this is anyway, cowboys and Indians?"

Prianka muttered something under her breath.

"What? You have something to say, too?"

"I said we don't have any room."

"Yeah," I said. "We don't have any room."

That, in fact, was the truth. With all our stuff and the food from the store and the wheelchair and the bird, we were packed tight. I stepped on the gas and continued down the road. There were fewer cars here. Every once in a while we saw a poxer ambling along the median, but other than that, it was relatively quiet.

After what seemed like an eternity but was probably only a minute, Jimmy said, "We're going to have to do a lot of bad things. Hopefully we'll forget them or maybe the good things will outweigh the bad."

None of us responded, because we all knew he was right. Now more than ever I wished that I could go back three days and have a do-over. Not that it would have mattered anyway. I wasn't the one who created Necropoxy or somehow let the disease loose. I didn't kill the world. Still, I felt crummy. I could only hope that the crummy feeling would disappear after a while.

I could only hope.

I can't understand why I used to watch all those movies about zombies and the apocalypse. Maybe because they were really cool from the outside looking in, just like watching people hike the Grand Canyon or camp out on the frozen tundra. Adventure looks so neat and exciting on TV, but when you're living it, it's hard and scary.

I never thought I'd have to deal with zombies. Zombie movies were fantasy. Zombies were the things that were totally made-up. Not like a government-created super-flu that kills almost everyone or a natural disaster wiping out the world. Zombies fell into the same category with vampires and werewolves.

Until now. This was real life and poxers were upon us.

Out of habit, I picked up my cell phone, charged courtesy of the Hummer, and punched in my dad's phone number. I got nothing. No busy signal or anything.

"What?" said Trina as she studied my face.

"I don't know. I thought that Mom and Dad might answer."

"The towers are dead," said Jimmy.

"What do you mean?"

"The cell phone towers. If the towers don't have power, all cell phones are shot, too."

"Well how are we supposed to talk?"

"With your mouth," said Prianka. "You don't seem to have too much of a problem with that."

I started to say something but stopped myself. There was no point. Up ahead there was a big sign for Butterfly Kingdom. The sign felt sort of random, like seeing a sign for Sea World in the middle of Ohio. I had heard of this place before—a big, tropical room filled with thousands of plants and butterflies. For a few bucks, you were allowed to walk through and let the butterflies dance around your head. Talk about torture! If I wanted to be swarmed by bugs, there were plenty of woods around. Who would pay for the privilege?

Still, I wondered what was going to happen to all the butterflies. I mean, up until Friday night someone had the job of feeding them kibble or butterfly chow or whatever butterflies eat. What about all the pets in pet stores? Who was feeding the puppies and the fish? Were they just going to starve to death? For that matter what about all the animals caged up in zoos or on farms or in people's houses?

Jimmy spoke from behind me, interrupting the 'oh so happy' thoughts that were filling my mind.

"What?" I said.

"Up here. The road curves to the left. It's the back way into Greenfield. It's going to start getting residential soon. Be careful."

The road slowly curved, and I followed it. Jimmy was right. Houses started popping up on both sides of the road, and with them came the poxers.

There were a lot, like in Bellingsfield and Amherst. Most of them were

milling around on front lawns and sidewalks. They took notice of the
Hummer as we drove by, and some started to follow the sound. There
weren't any sizeable groups of poxers. Nothing that could challenge us in
the Hummer, but the roads were bad here. Not as bad as Route 116 or the
highway. I was able to maneuver around the car wrecks and pile-ups and the
occasional poxer posse.

What a mess.

Just two days ago, all of these people were alive. They had lives. They
had jobs. The kids went to school, and the old people did whatever old
people do. Now, they were all just mindless, disease ridden bags of death.

Up ahead was a sign that said Greenfield Center with an arrow
pointing left. Underneath was a smaller sign with the number 2.

"That's Route 2," said Jimmy. "The Mohawk Trail starts right on the
other side of Greenfield."

I went up a hill and took a left. Main Street lay before us like a creepy
picture postcard of a creepy New England town. There were a lot of cars
and a lot of poxers. I was just about to ask Sanjay if there was another way
to go that was a little more remote when the Hummer lurched to the right.

Andrew flapped his wings and cawed.

"What was that?" said Trina.

"Oh, no," said Jimmy.

"Oh no what?" said Prianka. "Oh no what?"

In my gut I knew what he was going to say. I closed my eyes and shook
my head.

"That, my friends, was a flat tire."

27

RIGHT HERE? Right now? Really? If we were out in the country or on one of the back roads, a flat wouldn't have been so bad, but we were right at the top of Main Street and there were zombies everywhere.

"I can still drive on a flat, right?"

"If you want to ruin the tire for good, you can," said Jimmy. We'll be riding on the rim before we get out of town."

"So now what do we do?"

He didn't answer me. He was staring at a poxer looking at us from across the street.

"Look, a clown," cried Sanjay, his smile curling up to touch his ears.

Yup. As if zombies weren't creepy enough, we'd found a zombie clown across the street. He had bright orange hair and big pull-up overalls with oversized autumn colored leaves painted on them. His shirt was pumpkin orange.

I made what my parents called my 'what the hell' face. For once, I was stunned into silence. Trina pointed to a banner that stretched across the street that read, 'Greenfield Fall Fest, Sept. 17-19.' It was decorated with the same sort of leaves that were on the clown. "You gotta be kidding me," I said.

The clown stood there quietly watching us. All of a sudden, it snapped its head to one side. Everyone in the car, except Sanjay, yelped.

When the clown took a step off the curb, we all yelped again.

"Sharks and clowns," cried Prianka. "Only sharks and clowns. I can deal with snakes. I can deal with spiders. I can deal with poxers. I can even deal with you, Tripp Light." Her voice began to rise. "But the two things I absolutely, positively, can never, ever, ever handle are sharks and clowns."

"What about clowns who bite?" Total bad timing for a joke.

Sanjay said, "Clowns are comical performers stereotypically characterized by the image of a circus clown replete with a grotesque appearance, colored wig, stylistic makeup, outlandish costume, unusually large footwear, and red nose. Although some find clowns to be scary, their aim is to entertain people."

"Red nose," repeated Andrew, and Sanjay clapped his hands together in delight.

I shifted the Hummer in reverse, but something was drastically wrong. Now we weren't moving at all, and the more that I pressed on the gas, the louder the engine revved, and the more the engine revved, the more poxers noticed us as being uncharacteristically alive in their very dead world.

The clown was closing the gap between us. Prianka gripped the back of my seat like a terrified cat.

With time running out, I opened the door and got out to see what was wrong.

Not only was the tire flat, it had totally burst. What's worse, the reason we were no longer moving was that underneath the tire and almost fully wrapped around the rim was a dead guy, guts and clotted blood dripping out of him, grappling to get untangled.

"Get out of the car," I ordered. "We're footing it." No one moved, so I threw open the back door. "We run, or we die," I yelled. "There's a poxer wrapped around the wheel."

That was enough to get them moving. Jimmy grabbed his chair. Prianka grabbed Sanjay. Trina grabbed a hair brush, don't ask me why, and we were all out on the pavement in seconds.

"Watch out," Prianka cried and tossed my dad's crowbar at me. I barely even looked as I swung it wide and hit the clown in the head with the sharp end. He crumbled to the ground, and I swiveled to yank the crowbar back out. The clown's maw was still chomping away as he lashed out with one dead claw and succeeded in grabbing my foot, at which point I brought the crowbar down and through his hand.

The clown let go.

Another poxer, this one about fifteen or so and frankly so androgynous that I didn't know if it was a boy or a girl, was right on the heels of the clown. I didn't have a chance to get the crowbar out and up fast enough. The androgynous zombie was on me in seconds. The thing's hands were cold and hard with breath like the very worst part of a sewer.

I dropped the crowbar and pushed as hard as I could. The poxer fell back a foot or so before coming at me again. That was when a black shape shot out of nowhere and engulfed the poxer's face in a mass of movement. It was Andrew. He scratched and clawed and pecked at the poxer, giving me just enough time to grab the crowbar and run after everyone else.

"Andrew, to me," yelled Jimmy as he pumped the wheels on his wheelchair without looking back.

I ran after everyone. They were headed for a storefront on the left hand side of the street. Jimmy jumped the curb with ease. By the time they all got to the door, I had caught up with them and Andrew was sitting on Jimmy's shoulder, his beak a little bit bloodier than usual.

Trina pulled the double doors open, and we all ran inside.

28

"ARE YOU BIT?" screamed Prianka, pawing at me like a terrified, overprotective, psycho mother.

"First—I would have turned poxer on you already. And second—if you wanted to cop a feel, you could have just asked. But if you're enjoying yourself, feel free."

She kneed me in the groin, and I dropped.

I barely heard Jimmy yell for everyone to help drag whatever they could get their hands on in front of the door. As for me, I was getting the full, unedited version of what it meant to see stars. I think I did a fair bit of groaning and writhing around before I was finally able to open my eyes. Sanjay was standing over me with Poopy Puppy dangling from his hand.

"Hi, Buddy," he said. "You use a nickname when you like someone."

I managed a weak smile and rolled over to look at the front of the store. My gooey crowbar was stuck between the two handles of the double door. Trina and Prianka were dragging a heavy desk in front of the glass. Jimmy had abandoned his chair and had already found the long, metal rod that fit into the gear system for the storefront's mesh security gate. As he rapidly turned the bent handle the gate descended in front of the door, effectively cutting off the poxers that were already gathering for the buffet.

Once the gate completely lowered to the ground, everyone stopped. Trina sank to her knees along with Prianka. Jimmy fell back against the wall, his chest heaving up and down.

"Not to be a killjoy or anything," I said, "But are we alone in here?" I got to my knees and slowly stood, the pain in my nether regions subsiding to a dull ache. Trina and Prianka both shot to their feet, and Jimmy was immediately on alert.

Facing us was row after row of cramped book cases. We had locked ourselves inside a used bookstore.

"Bookstores, libraries, and schools," said Sanjay. "I repeat—this isn't a movie. It's imperative that you get as much material as you can get your hands on regarding survival skills. The best places to find this information is in bookstores, libraries, or schools. From what we're hearing, it's not pretty out there folks. Be prepared. Poopy Puppy says so."

"I said that on the radio, didn't I?" said Jimmy.

"Word for word," said Trina. "Word for word."

"Tripp's right," said Prianka. "We don't know if we're alone." She grabbed the closest paperback book and pulled a new pack of matches out her pocket.

And I thought she was smart. "Whoa, Pyro Patel. We're in a bookstore. *A bookstore.* Like paper and stuff that burns as easy as the poxers do. What the hell do you think you're going to do with that in here? One of those things explodes, and we're toast—literally."

She gritted her teeth. I could almost hear them grind together.

"And I don't care if you are a girl. Kick me like that again, and I'll punch you in the head." She didn't say anything, which was just fine by me.

The bookstore was packed. The shelves went back into the shadows. Not good. Not good all.

"We have to fan out," I said. "And we have to find something we can hit them with."

Trina walked over and knelt down in front of Jimmy. "You have to watch Sanjay, okay? We need you to do this." Jimmy started to open his mouth, but she put one finger to his lips, and he stopped.

"Whatever," he muttered and shook his head. "Hey, Sanjay," he said. "Why don't you, Poopy Puppy, and Andrew come over here, and we can read a book?"

"Thanks," said Trina. I saw the next thing coming from light years away. She leaned over and softly brushed her lips against his red stubble. I think I threw up a little bit in my mouth.

Sanjay went over and sat down beside Jimmy, and together they turned their backs to the horde that was massing in front of the store.

Trina stood and took the security gate handle from Jimmy. Prianka and I each grabbed a hard cover book to use as a club. The three of us each chose an aisle and slowly began walking through the stacks.

"Keep talking," I said. "If they're here, they'll come to us."

"Why don't you keep talking for us," said Prianka from somewhere to my right.

"Ah, I see you found the bitchy feminist books."

With that, a hardcover sailed over the shelves and landed in front of me. "Missed. Want to go for two?"

"You're not worth the paper."

"Oh, I think I'm worth a ream or two."

The bookstore got dimmer the further we wandered through the stacks. At the end of the first set of rows, the three of us met up. From here to the back of the store the rows ran horizontally. Walking down the middle aisle allowed us to look both ways. Easy. We didn't find poxers or people.

Toward the end of the aisle was a black spiral staircase with a sign next to it that read 'reading loft' with an arrow pointing up.

Above us the floor gently creaked.

"Damn," whispered Trina.

"Yeah," I said. "Where's Buffy when you need her?"

The three of us stared at each other. Finally I took the gate handle from Trina and grabbed the bannister.

"Hello?" I yelled up the stairs, but no one answered. The floor creaked again.

"Fat mice?" I offered hopefully. Prianka frowned at me.

I took another few steps up the spiral staircase and shouted again. Who was I kidding? Poxers don't yell back. I looked at my sister and Prianka and shrugged, so I continued up the spiral staircase, gripping the gate handle with both hands. The reading loft was dark—like really dark. I couldn't see anything.

"Prianka, I need a match."

"But you said . . ."

"Not for that. I can't see." She came up the staircase behind me and pressed the book of matches into my hand.

"It's creepy up here," she said.

"It's creepy everywhere."

I lit the match and held it up. The reading loft wasn't much bigger than my bedroom back home. Bookshelves lined the walls. In the center of the room were two oversized well-worn couches and an old trunk. I could see behind one of the couches. The other one was facing us.

"Light another match," I whispered, pointing to the couch I couldn't see behind. Whatever was up here was hiding there. I gripped the gate handle with both hands and raised it high over my head. Together, Prianka and I quietly tiptoed over to the couch.

Huddled behind the oversized love seat, we found Stella Rathbone, owner of the now defunct Wordsmith Used Book Emporium.

Thankfully, she was very much alive.

29

"DON'T HURT ME," she screamed and threw her hands up over her face.
"I don't want to die." Prianka and I stood over a heavyset woman probably
about the age of death's mother. I had the gate handle raised over my head
like I was going to plunge it into her skull, right down through her body,
and into the floor.

"We're not going to hurt you," I screamed back, mostly because she
was screaming at me.

"Stop screaming," screamed Prianka as she lit another match.

"I'm not screaming," I screamed back at her then realized that I was,
so I notched it down a few decibels. "I'm not screaming."

"Put the rod down you idiot," Prianka said. She pushed me aside and
offered her hand to the old woman. Stella shook her head fiercely. "We're
friends," Prianka said calmly. "Really—we're okay."

I lowered the gate handle just in time to hear Trina run up the stairs.

"What's happening?"

"Survivor," I said. "We'll be down in a minute."

I sighed and tossed her the metal rod, making sure I was very obvious
about removing it from the situation. Trina took it with her and slowly went
back down the staircase. On the old trunk was a jar candle. Prianka quickly
lit the wick.

The candlelight illuminated the face of terror that was Stella Rathbone.
I guess calling her older than death's mother was a little harsh. Maybe
death's wife or spinster sister would have been more appropriate. She was
wearing a man's plaid shirt, heavy pants, and work boots. Her gray hair was
knotted into long braids that fell halfway down her back, and her thick
glasses made her eyes look a little too big for her head.

"We're friends," Prianka said again and knelt down beside her. Stella
adjusted her glasses on her round face and studied Prianka. All of a sudden,
she engulfed her in a bear hug and began sobbing hysterically.

Not my area of expertise. Not by a longshot.

"I'll be downstairs with everyone else." Prianka nodded and waved her
hand dismissively while continuing to let Stella cry herself a river roughly
the size of the Ganges.

When I got to the front of the store, Jimmy was already back in his chair. Trina was sitting on his lap.

"Um, that's my sister," I said.

"Yeah, I know. Cool, huh?"

For the second time in not so many minutes, I felt the bile climbing up my throat. Sanjay was sitting on the floor next to the two of them, leafing through a picture book. Andrew sat on his shoulder and watched the colorful drawings pass by.

"So who is she?" Jimmy asked.

"I don't know. She looks like someone who hangs out in used bookstores."

"And?"

"And she's old," I said. "I don't think she's grandmother old. I just think she's sort of old, old."

"Happens to the best of us," said Jimmy.

"Unless we get eaten by zombies because our crew rolls off to safety without so much as turning around." I glared at him. "At least you saved the bird—and my sister."

Jimmy gulped. "Hey, Dude. I thought you were bitten."

"What if I were?" I snapped.

"Then you wouldn't have been you anymore, and we'd do what we have to do."

He was right. I wouldn't be me anymore.

"Whoa—the two of you—stand down," Trina begged as she balanced on his lap.

"He can't stand," I snapped and folded my arms.

I suppose we could have volleyed insults back and forth for a few more rounds, but instead, Jimmy snorted and started giggling. "Good one," he chuckled. "That was a good one."

I just rolled my eyes and let the tension dissolve in the air. Arguing wasn't going to change anything. Besides, I was clean out of one-liners.

We heard movement from behind us and turned to see Prianka leading Stella through the stacks. I have to say I was a little at a loss for words. Our little band of under twenty-somethings had been doing just fine. Adding a real live adult into the mix seemed to suck the mojo out of us, like I was expecting her to hit my hand with a ruler if I said something bad.

"My word," Stella gasped when she saw us all. "How did you ever manage to get here?"

"We had a Hummer," I said. "Now they have it." I pointed my thumb over my shoulder at the teeming horde of poxers massing at the window.

Stella stared at them for a long time, shaking her head back and forth.

"I know some of these people," she said. "You live in a place all your life thinking you're safe. Look where it gets you."

"Well you're alive," said Prianka. "That's got to count for something."

The ancient one turned and faced us. "I'm Stella Rathbone," she said. "This is my shop."

Jimmy gasped and almost fell out of his chair. "*The* Stella Rathbone," he said. You're really the real Stella Rathbone?" Stella pursed her lips just a little, which I guess meant it was true. "I don't believe it. Guys do you know who this is?"

"Stella Rathbone?" I guessed.

"No, really—I mean—oh my gosh. Can I shake your hand?" Jimmy cast Trina off his lap like she was a raggedy cat. He rolled over to Stella with his palm outstretched and pumped her hand enthusiastically.

"I've read your book so many times that the binding is going."

"You're too kind," said Stella and put her hand over his to calm his exuberance.

Jimmy wheeled around to face us. "Stella, I mean Ms. Rathbone . . ."

"Stella's fine," she said.

"Wow. I have goose pimples. Stella's the author of *Urban Green.*"

We all sat there with bored expressions on our faces. I scratched my head. "*Urban Green*—isn't that what they make into people?"

"That would be Soylent Green," said Stella with a hint of humor in her eyes. "*Urban Green* is about how one can be self-sustaining in an urban environment."

"It's iconic," said Jimmy. "It's amazing."

"It's a serendipitous coincidence, is what it is," said Stella as we all stood there in the gloom of The Wordsmith Used Book Emporium.

"*Urban Green,*" said Andrew and readjusted himself on Sanjay's shoulder.

"That's right," said Stella. "Come. I'll show you."

30

"WOW," SAID TRINA when we finally reached the top floor of the building. I carried Jimmy's chair, and Jimmy pulled himself along at a pretty impressive clip—up the spiral staircase to the reading loft and up another set of stairs to this.

Wow was right. Stella's home was amazing. She lived on the third floor of the building—the *enitre* building. Not only did she occupy the space above her bookstore, her home spanned the whole block of stores. Her place was gigantic.

What's more, Stella had electricity. Hanging from high ceilings were dozens of fans slowly churning the air. Along one wall was an entire bank of potted plants under grow lights. Running along the back of the building was a series of sliding glass doors that opened on to a deck. The deck was planted with vegetables—enough for an army.

There were several stationery bicycles strategically positioned throughout the space. Each one was attached to different contraption.

"How do you have lights?" asked Prianka. "The electricity went out along with everything else."

Stella smiled from ear to ear. "I have solar energy," she said. "And a lot of things that I use run on people power."

"What's people power?" I asked.

She walked over to one of the bikes that sat next to a big comfy chair and a lamp. She got on and pedaled for a moment, and the lamp slowly began to glow. "Now I'd have to do this for a good half hour or so to give me enough power for a night of reading, but it's free, and it's on my terms. Besides, I make my own candles."

"This is the essence of your book," cried Jimmy. "Sustainable living in an urban setting. You're living a self-sufficient, low impact, green life right in the middle of downtown Greenfield. What do you do for heat?"

"Wood burning stoves," she said. "Thank heavens I've already stored my wood for the year, and my water is from rain water that I collect with rain barrels." Stella pointed to the far end of the deck. There were several large barrels out there. "I've never had a problem getting enough water for me and the plants."

Jimmy was like a kid in a candy store. "Mind if I look around?" he asked as he reached for his wheelchair. I popped his ride open and watched him effortlessly climb aboard.

Andrew jumped off of Sanjay's shoulder and glided across the room. Stella's place was truly huge, and he seemed more than happy to stretch his wings and get a little exercise. Jimmy set off in the same general direction. I couldn't help but think of Willy Wonka's chocolate room. All she needed was a bunch of orange Oompa Loompas and some marshmallow mushrooms, and she'd be all set.

Sanjay saw a bookshelf full of books. He went over and pulled one out at random and began leafing through the pages in an orderly fashion.

Prianka, her arms crossed over her chest, began to inspect the stationery bikes and the things that were attached to them like she was a judge at a grade school science fair.

Trina just had to pee.

"Out on the deck," said Stella. "I have a composting toilet. That's how I get such great plants."

I made a mental note not to eat any of her vegetables, because the thought of what she just said almost made me dry heave. I just stood there with Stella Rathbone in the middle of her enormous carbon footprint with my hands shoved in my pockets.

After an uncomfortably long time she put her hand on my shoulder and guided me over to her reading chair. I sunk into the cushion but was too tense to let it envelop me. She disappeared for a moment and came back with a napkin and a couple of cookies.

"They're carob," she said. I didn't know what carob was, but I took one anyway. Carob, or at least Stella's carob, tasted a little like dirty chocolate prunes, but I managed to chew and swallow a bite. That was the polite thing to do.

"So . . ." I said.

"Yes?"

"Can those things get in here?"

She shook her head. "I don't think so. The door is blocked, the gate is down, and we're locked inside."

Fair enough, I thought. She was probably right. I bet the crowd of poxers stopped milling around the front of the bookstore the minute we disappeared from sight.

"So . . ." I began again.

"Yes?"

"You live alone?" I guess that was rude to ask, but this was the part in most horror films where you find out the nice, little, old lady is keeping a pet poxer or five for company, and they're getting hungrier by the minute.

"From time to time," she said. Frankly I didn't know what that meant, and I didn't want to ask. "Enough about me. Tell me how the five of you managed to find yourself in my store."

That was easy. I spilled my guts. I told her everything from the beginning

"The highways are really that bad?" she asked when I was finished. She shook her head. "I always knew something was going to happen. Frankly, the way human beings mistreat the Earth, it's amazing that something hasn't happened sooner."

She took one of her carob cookies and nibbled on a corner. "I just always assumed the earth would fight back with a super storm or a famine—but zombies? Zombies seem to fall into the realm of fiction." She glanced over at Sanjay and sighed. "They always say the meek will inherit the earth."

"Have you met my sister and Prianka? I'm not sure that meek is a word I would use to describe either of them."

"I bet you're grateful to have them both," Stella said. She wasn't asking a question—she was making a simple statement.

"Yeah," I said. "I suppose I am."

One of the sliders opened, and Trina stepped through the door.

"From the end of your deck you can see a small park and a little of Main Street." she said. "There are poxers everywhere."

"Is that what you call them?" asked Stella. "Poxers?"

Jimmy rolled back toward us. He explained about the caller at the radio station who told anyone who was listening about Necropoxy.

"We just started calling them poxers," I said. "Somehow the word zombie sounds unreal, and even though this whole thing is unreal, not using the word somehow makes accepting that they're here a little easier."

Stella stood and checked her watch. The time was a little after two in the afternoon. Less than forty-eight hours ago, Trina, Prianka, and I were sitting in high school on a lazy Friday afternoon waiting for the final bell to ring. Sanjay was probably devouring the Internet with Mrs. Bhoola while Jimmy had been getting ready for his stint on WHZZ.

A crow named Andrew had been staring out the window at the other birds, perfectly content to be domesticated. My mom and dad were putting the final touches on that note to the two of us and laying out way too much weekend cash on the kitchen counter. A small white poodle was blissfully unaware that she would inadvertently give her own life to save mine and my sister's.

Less than forty-eight hours ago—that was before the whole world went to hell.

31

WE ALL SAT AROUND a huge table that Stella had made out of broken odds and ends she found in the alley behind her building and a few old doors that were in the basement when she bought the place.

Her handiwork was pretty cool—like art gallery cool.

She laid out a spread for us with homemade bread, jam, egg-salad, and a few things from her garden. A plate of carob cookies sat in the middle of the table daring anyone adventurous enough to try one.

Stella explained that with the proceeds of *Urban Green* she had been able to buy the entire building and set up her home along with The Wordsmith Used Book Emporium. She made sure that the other stores on her block were all to her liking, which meant a health food store, a used clothing outlet, and an agricultural cooperative.

As the owner and landlord, she naturally had access to each one of them through various stairs and hallways throughout her kingdom.

"I never have to leave my building," she said. "And with the agricultural cooperative, I even have a ready supply of organic food for the chickens."

"Chickens?" we all said in unison.

"I draw the line at eating beef, but eggs and poultry? That I can handle."

"Where do you keep chickens?" asked Jimmy. He was completely in his element. It was weird to think that this woman was almost totally self-sufficient while, up until recently, most of the rest of the world's biggest worry was how to get their next fast food fix. I could see how Jimmy would think Stella's way of life was cool, except for the part about everything tasting a little too much like rabbit food.

"I have a chicken coop," she said and pointed to her deck. There was a red shed in one corner with a slanted metal roof and white trim. I had noticed the shed before, but it was filled with potting supplies for the garden. "I'm fifteen strong right now."

"Do you eat them?" said Trina

"Occasionally," she said and leaned forward with a mischievous grin on her face. "If they're bad."

Mental note to self: don't be bad.

"What I really use them for are their eggs—and—not to be crude, but their poop makes wonderful fertilizer."

I stopped chewing because the notion of poop, fertilizer, and egg salad all in one thought made my stomach do a flip-flop. I put the sandwich down after I managed to swallow the last bit that was in my mouth.

"Um," I began. "Stella, we really appreciate everything and the lunch is great, but we still have to somehow get to my Aunt's house."

"With a flat tire," said Trina.

"And a wall of poxers between us and your boyfriend's Hummer," added Prianka.

Jimmy looked down at his plate but didn't say anything.

"Ex-boyfriend," said Trina. "Chuck's dead."

I can't fault the guy at all, but Jimmy smiled just a little when Trina said that. Yeah, gross. I know.

Stella quietly picked up our plates and began clearing the table. She neatly stacked the dirty ones by the sink and scraped the excess food into a bowl on the worn wooden counter. After a moment she cleared her throat.

"You know," she began. "I've created my whole life around solitude. I made sure that I had everything I needed, and even the things I didn't need I didn't have to go far to get. All I wanted to do was read books and tend my garden and lead a simple life. Up until two days ago, I thought I had reached my goal. I thought that this was it—that I had everything I set out to get."

Stella turned to face the rest of us. I knew what was coming next. I think we all did.

"Now the world is gone, and I don't know how long any of us have." She rubbed her hand across her eyes. I don't think it's because she had dirt in them. "Don't you think . . . don't you think you would be better off if you stayed here for a while?"

I was about to say something when Prianka opened her mouth first. Her words came out slow and strong.

"Stella," she said. "We have someplace to go. If it hadn't been for Tripp and Trina we would all probably be dead by now. I think we owe it to them to get to their aunt and uncle's house. If immunity is genetic I'm thinking at least their aunt is still alive. Their mom and dad might be there, too. We don't know, but we have to try."

"But out there?" Stella stammered. "You have to go out there? You've seen what the world has become out there. You all have." Her voice began to tremble a little. "You have a child with you. You have a responsibility."

"Yes, we know," said Prianka. "We have a responsibility to Tripp and Trina, too."

Suddenly it hit me. More than that, it slammed into me like a freight train. Stella *never* left the world she'd built around her—not before Necropoxy and not now. She was one of those shut-ins—one of those people afraid to leave her own home.

I think we all figured it out in unison because Sanjay got off his chair with Andrew still on his shoulder and walked over to Stella. His dark eyes found her face.

"Agoraphobia," he whispered, as he held Poopy Puppy to his ear.

Stella looked away and stared out the window to her garden.

"Agoraphobia is an anxiety disorder that arises from the fear of being in a setting from which one cannot escape. Sufferers avoid large, open spaces where there are few places to hide. In its worst form, agoraphobics confine themselves to their homes and are unable to travel from its perceived safety."

Stella's eyes moistened. We were all quiet except for Sanjay.

"Poopy Puppy says so," he said and nothing more.

32

"THREE YEARS," said Stella.

It took time to process that. Three years was a lifetime. Three years ago I was in eighth grade. Three years ago Chuck Peterson had pushed me into my locker. Three years ago I was as hairless as a naked mole rat.

"Three years?" repeated Jimmy.

"Ever since *Urban Green* became a bestseller. At first there were the crowds at book signings and then just the people. All that attention was too much for me. I finally had to set things up so I didn't have to be bothered unless I wanted to be bothered." Stella wiped the tears from her eyes and looked away from us. "I guess my dream became my jail."

Prianka and Trina were out on the deck with Sanjay. They had investigated the chickens and now were walking through the rows of vegetables that were just about ripe enough to harvest. There really was everything here. Why would Stella want to leave? She could keep out the poxers by making sure the security gates were shut in front of all the storefronts. She could manage here for a good long while.

It's just that we couldn't.

"I wish you would come with us," I said to her.

"I wish I could, too. But I can't. Besides it's safe here for me."

I couldn't argue with that. The hordes of the undead outside would soon forget that there was anything in this building worth eating and would leave it alone. Stella had enough food to last her at least the winter. During the spring and summer she could grow vegetables again, and next year, if she ran out of wood to burn, I guess she had plenty of books to throw on the fire.

"I wish you would stay," she said. "I don't have hopes of seeing my sister and her children again. It's nice to have voices around me."

"Were they in town?"

"Oregon," she said. "About as far away from here as you can get without hitting the Pacific."

It would have been useless to say something like 'I'm sorry' or 'maybe they're alright' because the words would have just come out wrong.

Another thought tugged at my conscience. I didn't want to let it creep into my mind any further, but it already had.

Jimmy, Prianka, and Sanjay could stay here.

They would be safe.

Just because Trina and I were heading to my aunt's house didn't mean they had to come with us. I appreciated that they wanted to, but was that really the best decision for them?

Stella was right. Prianka had Sanjay to think about. Then there was Jimmy. I didn't care how tough he was or whatever budding romance was kindling between him and my sister—a guy in a wheelchair would eventually be a liability out there. In here, he was safe, too.

The girls came in from the deck with Sanjay and Andrew. The bird flew over to the kitchen counter and inspected the bowl that Stella had filled with our leftovers.

Trina took one look at us and knew immediately what happened.

"You're not coming?" she said to Stella.

Stella only smiled weakly. "Maybe someday I'll have to, but for now, I'm safe behind my own four walls. If I don't think too hard about it, it's like nothing's changed except for a lot fewer customers in the bookstore."

I stared hard at Trina and let whatever twin synergy we had do its work. She knew what I was thinking, and I knew she knew because her face suddenly hardened and she crossed her arms over her chest.

"Guys . . ." I said.

"We're girls," said Prianka. "Actually bright, intelligent, young women."

"People . . ." I began again. "Trina and I have to get to our aunt's house. We have a shot at finding our parents. But you guys? It's safe here. Jimmy, this is your thing, man. You love this earthy, crunchy crap. And Prianka? Stella's right. You have Sanjay to think about."

Trina shifted her feet but didn't say anything. She couldn't or wouldn't look at Jimmy. Prianka, on the other hand, looked like her eyes were about to pop out of her head, and her hair suddenly took on a Medusa-type quality. I almost turned away from her for fear of being transformed into stone.

"Excuse us for a moment," she seethed and grabbed my arm hard and dragged me across the room and behind a partition that divided the kitchen area from a seating area in Stella's living space.

"Ow," I cried. "You're hurting me."

"Good," she hissed.

"Let go."

"No," she said as she whirled me around so we were face to face. The venomous stare was still there. I didn't know what to do. I thought she might actually knee me in the crotch again, but I wasn't sure why.

Instead, she did the last thing that I could have ever imagined. She did what two days ago would have been about the most ludicrous, preposterous, unimaginable thing ever.

Prianka Patel, my nemesis, kissed me.

Hard.

I dated for a couple months when I was in ninth grade. My friends thought I was cool and Karen Comitsky was pretty in that very suburban, pampered, blonde sort of way. She insisted on holding my hand when we walked down the hallway at school or at lunch, which made it really hard to eat with only one free hand.

We kissed a lot but nothing much past that. When we kissed, it was soft and nice and totally, unbelievably boring. I asked Trina about that once, which was a big mistake because I had to listen to a barrage of ribbing before she told me that the reason she dumped Duke Posnick was because he was a lousy kisser.

I didn't think Karen Comitsky was a lousy kisser. She just didn't have any life in her lips. Kissing her was like kissing a mannequin—or my pillow.

This was totally different. When Prianka kissed me there was life there. So much life, in fact, that I almost forgot we were surrounded by death. I kissed her back, and we stood there kissing for almost a minute in ways that I never kissed Karen Comitsky.

"Are you okay?" yelled Trina from the other side of the partition.

Prianka pushed away from me.

"We're fine," she yelled back.

We stood there staring at each other. I wasn't quite sure what I was supposed to say. Honestly, I was a little in shock. Finally she put her evil Prianka mask back on and said, "You're a dense idiot, Tripp." She stomped away from me and back to everyone else.

I followed a moment later.

"We're leaving, Stella," said Prianka. "All of us."

Stella chuckled a little and tilted her head towards me. "He just figure that out?" she asked.

"No," said Prianka. "I've always been the smarter one."

I thought I was being nice by telling them to stay. I thought I was thinking of someone else besides myself for once. I guess I wasn't. With one stupid kiss, Prianka knocked over my carefully constructed house of cards, and now I had to build it again in a new and different way.

The only thing I knew for sure was that Stella Rathbone had no intention of leaving her home, and the rest of us had no intention of staying. Nothing I could say or do could change any of that.

I didn't even try.

33

"WE HAVE TO make sure that Stella's safe here," said Jimmy when we were back sitting around her funky kitchen table. "That means we have to shut the security gates in front of the health food store, the used clothing outlet, and the agricultural cooperative."

"Are there any other entrances or exits?" Prianka asked Stella.

Stella sat with her hands tightly folded in front of her. "There are the doors to the alley," she said. "There's the basement, too."

Jimmy continued. "Once we know the building is secured, we have to figure out how to get the car running again."

"The Hummer?" I gasped. "I don't know about you, but I don't think any of us are in the position to change a tire all wrapped up nice and pretty with a poxer-bow while there're literally hundreds of those things outside."

"Fine. We'll take another car," said Trina. "We have plenty to choose from."

She was right. It wasn't like we were stealing. There was no one left who minded.

"What about our supplies?" I said "We have guns and Sanjay needs his kayak to sleep."

Stella murmured something, but we were all too pumped to listen.

"We'll just have to pick a big car," said Prianka. "Or a truck."

"Yeah," Jimmy said. "A truck would be awesome."

"Maybe even something bigger" I said "Like an eighteen wheeler. With one of those, we could just roll over the suckers."

Stella slammed her knotted fists down on the table, and we all stopped.

"Can you hear yourselves?" she cried. "You have guns? You're all babies. What are you doing with guns?"

We were all silent. Finally, Trina said, "We don't know how to use them yet." Stella was clearly upset. Her hands were shaking. "Stella, we're going to have to learn. Besides fire, we don't even know what else slows the poxers down. For all we know a gunshot to the head does nothing."

Stella pursed her lips. "What if one of you gets hurt?"

"We don't get hurt," said Trina. A lifetime ago when we were screwed into my dad's Putter Room, Trina said the only thing we had to do was live.

She was right. Our job was to live any way we could.

Stella," I began. "We all appreciate your concern, but sooner or later, and I'm thinking sooner, we have to get ourselves out of here and out of this town. Either you can help us or not."

She sighed and rubbed her forehead. Her face scrunched up the same way my mom's did the few times I saw her cry. Thankfully, Stella didn't cry. Instead, she reached into her pocket and pulled out a key-ring full of keys. Each one was meticulously marked as to what door it opened. She tossed them in the middle of the table.

Andrew hopped off Sanjay's shoulder and landed in front of the keys. He pecked at them as if they were a new, bright, shiny, toy.

"We'll close the security gates first," said Jimmy. "If we find any poxers inside, we'll torch them and put out the flames with fire extinguishers. The last thing we want to do is burn down the building. After that, we'll lock the alley doors and check the basement."

"Sounds like a plan," I said.

"Agreed," said Prianka.

"Me, too," said Trina. "But, Jimmy. You're not coming."

Jimmy clenched his fists and flared his nostrils. "I can do things, you know."

"Yes, I know," she said as she leaned into him. "I want you to be around to try."

Barf.

I quickly recovered. "Jimmy—you and Stella check out the situation from the deck and windows up here. See if you can scout out some transportation for us."

"And watch Sanjay?" he sighed.

"That would be great," said Prianka.

"Yeah, great," he echoed.

Frankly I was getting a little tired of his pity party. Yo, Dude. You're in a wheelchair and have testosterone issues. We all get it. We really get it. Be satisfied that one of the only two girls around, not counting Stella, is into you.

I reached for Stella's keys and endured an indignant squawk from Andrew. Bird-brain gave me a crow's version of a dirty look when I lifted them off the table. He hopped back over to Sanjay who was sitting quietly flipping through a copy of *Urban Green*.

Good, I thought. That might come in handy someday.

Stella reluctantly explained to us where the main doors were throughout the building. We were on the third floor. Like the bookstore, each of the other three stores had ceilings that were two stories high with lofts on the second floor. Each of the lofts had a metal door for which Stella held the key. Each of those doors led up to her living space.

There were fire extinguishers at the bottom of each stair case, at the front of each store, and at the back doors to the alley.

Each of the stores also had access to a common basement near the alley doors.

I weighed the keys in my hand. Not only were they labeled, they were color coated. Red was for the used clothing store.

We went there first.

34

"GROSS," YELLED Prianka as she doused burning poxer chunks with a fire extinguisher. We had found three zombies in the used clothing store. Two of them appeared to be a mother and daughter combo pack. Mom was on the young side and definitely beaten with the ugly stick. Sissy was equally blessed in the looks department. It didn't help that she was wearing knee-highs, a party dress, and pigtails.

They were in a dressing room in the middle of the store. Between the two of them, there wasn't enough brain wattage to figure out how to use the door handle. Instead, they had amused themselves over the past few days by taking bites out of each other.

I held the flashlight. Trina torched. Prianka extinguished.

The third poxer was a woman who looked like my health teacher, Ms. Dealey. Even in death, she still had that smug, superior expression on her face and a pair of librarian glasses perched on her nose.

She seemed enthralled with a mannequin dressed way too preppy even for New England. No wonder the poxer wanted to bite its head off.

Trina lit her up, and we all waited for the high pitched squeal and the pop. Too bad she fell back into a rack of clothes and exploded. Everything in a ten foot radius that wasn't flame retardant went up pretty fast. Putting everything out took the rest of the fire extinguisher and part of another one. The smell of burnt plastic lingered in the air.

Amidst the smoldering heap of hand-me-downs and OshKosh B'gosh, we made our way to the front of the store, checked and locked the entrance and closed the security gate.

Outside I could see the Hummer—so close yet a million miles away. The streets were filled with poxers—not like Times Square on New Year's Eve, but definitely overwhelming. I didn't even want to think about how we were going to get out of there. I just focused on securing the building.

After we locked the back door and the basement door we made our way up the stairs and back down into the health food store. We were lucky. There was a sign on the front door that said 'Closing at 4 for Fall Fest.' The place was empty, and locking all the doors was a piece of cake.

It was at the Agricultural Cooperative where things got dicey.

At first we thought we were going to be lucky again. There didn't seem to be anyone in front. We locked the door and shut the gate. I guess Stella forgot to mention the back room. This is where they did all their loading and unloading. There was a big bay door that was wide open. There were also five poxers, all dressed in overalls, and all focused on us. What's worse was that we were all surround by bags of grain, farmers' supplies, and about a hundred bales of straw.

Straw burns. I learned that from the Wizard of Oz when the Wicked Witch of the West gave a little to the scarecrow. Fire was out of the question.

"We have to shut the bay door," said Trina.

"Do you think it's electric?" That's the last thing we needed.

"Better hope like hell it's not," she said and made a mad dash through the Red Rover poxer line. One of the dead made a goofy grab at her with both arms as she passed. I supposed I could have laughed if the whole situation wasn't so freaking scary.

Next to the bay door was a ladder. At the top of the ladder was a rope-pull used to open and close the door. Very farmy, don't you think? Trina sprinted up the ladder just in time. The poxers had turned and surrounded her, but not one of them could figure out how to make one foot go in front of the other to climb up after her.

Next to Prianka was a row of wheel barrows, all bright and shiny and ready to be sold.

"I have an idea," I said and grabbed the one closest to me. I threw a bag of horse grain in the blue plastic to weigh down the wheel barrow before running full steam ahead and ramming the closest poxer closer to the bay door. He growled and turned to me, so I backed up and rammed him again until he fell backwards out of the bay and down the five-foot drop to the ground.

Prianka got with the program, too, and pretty soon we were chasing after the poxers and herding them toward the big opening. One by one they dropped out the door until we got all five of them. Trina dropped the counter weight on the rope-pull and the bay door came crashing down.

Of course, we had to be all gross in the process. One of the poxers had his hand on the cool cement, trying in vain to pull itself back up through the bay door.

The hand separated neatly from the body with barely a sound.

"That's disgusting," Trina said as she pointed at the writhing thing.

"Not for long," said Prianka and threw a match on the wriggling fingers. The hand lit up pretty quickly, so she blasted the whole thing with the fire extinguisher before we had to deal with another explosion.

Together, we all twisted the huge manual handle on the bay door and pulled the lock into place.

"That was easy enough," I said as we all leaned our backs against the door, breathing heavily.

"No. That was dangerous," said Prianka.

"Okay. Dangerous and easy. I'll even throw a little scary in there."

Trina kicked the burnt hand, sending the severed palm spinning into the middle of the floor. "I'm not scared of them anymore," she said. "I'm just really, really annoyed."

Hell hath no fury like my sister annoyed, which was a useful emotion to have. Still, when we came to securing the basement, we all lost our nerve.

The basement door of the Greenfield Agricultural Cooperative was wide open. Steep, wooden steps led down into darkness, and who knows what could be lurking down there? We told Stella we would secure the building, and that's exactly what we did. I pushed the door closed, stuck the key in the tumbler, and twisted the lock. Tada! Whatever was down there could rot for all I care.

Just like that, we were done with our clean sweep.

The three of us made our way back up to the third story and Stella's place. Stella and Jimmy were sitting at her kitchen table, and Sanjay was lying on the floor with a pile of books in front of him. Poopy Puppy was at his side. Andrew was perched on his back

"Did you find any . . . were there any of those things in the building?" Stella asked.

"Not anymore," said Trina and blew on the edge of the lighter she was carrying as if she just let loose with a barrage of bullets from a six shooter. "We didn't risk the basement, though," she explained. "It's off limits to you, okay."

"I never went down there anyway," Stella said. "Spiders, you know." Great—she was agoraphobic *and* arachnophobic.

"Don't worry," I said. "What's down there isn't going anywhere. Those are heavy duty doors. Nothing can get through them." I had to hope I was right. Of course I was right.

I'm sure I was right.

"How many in the shops?" asked Jimmy.

"Three in the used clothing store and five in the agricultural cooperative," said Trina. "They all went bye-bye." She walked over and nestled into his lap again. This was seriously going to take eons of getting used to. I turned away and focused my attention on the plate of carob cookies that were still set out for us. Frankly, I couldn't think which was grosser—my sister and Jimmy or the prospect of eating another one of

Stella's organic confections.

"What about you guys?" I asked without making eye contact. "Any ideas on how we're going to get some wheels and get out of here?"

Stella and Jimmy exchanged glances.

"Well, we might have an option, that is, if Stella agrees," he said. "There're no guarantees that what we're thinking will even work, but we can try."

"Try what?" said Prianka.

"The chickens," explained Stella. "Maybe what we're thinking will work. But remember, I can't afford to lose even one of my hens."

I was getting confused. "Maybe you're thinking *what* will work?"

Jimmy said, "Here goes," and explained their plan.

35

"IT'S JUST CRAZY enough to do the trick," said Trina and hugged Jimmy hard.

I shook my head in utter disbelief. "So let me get this straight. You want us to tie a rope to a chicken and lower her over the roof in front of the bookstore like some demented form of zombie fishing? Then, when the poxers come you want to dump hot coals on them and watch them burn?"

"Essentially . . . yes," said Stella.

"The whole building could go up in flames," said Prianka.

"No, dear," said Stella. "Not when we're made of bricks."

She had a point. Everything inside was flammable. Outside? Not so much. I guess we were in the right little pig's house.

Still, what I couldn't figure out was how to tie a rope to a chicken

While my thoughts were focused on various knots and how to tie up a hen, Sanjay, who had been quiet for quite some time said, "Early thermal weapons were used in warfare during the classical and medieval eras, particularly during sieges. Sometimes, substances were boiled or heated to inflict damage by scalding or burning. The simplest and most common weapons were poured over attackers. Then smoke was used to confuse or drive them off."

I shook my head at Prianka. "Does he know everything? What did he do all day long—read the Internet?"

Sanjay didn't move. He lifted the book he was reading over his head. The cover was dark and brooding with big read letters that said *Medieval Warfare.*

Jimmy shrugged. "We thought we would put him to work while you guys were out zombie hunting."

"That book is part of my personal library," added Stella. "One can never be too prepared."

Sanjay put the book back down and continued flipping through the pages. Prianka bent down and looked at the rest of the pile stacked next to her little brother. On the top was *Survival for Dummies.* The next one down was the *2008 Boy Scouts of America Handbook.* The rest of them were more of the same.

I thought Prianka was going to explode. Instead, she came back to the table and sat down and muttered, "I wish I had thought of that."

I looked at Stella's clock. It was just past four. There was no way we were going to get to my aunt's house today. Even if we were able to get out of the building and find suitable wheels without getting bitten, I wasn't willing to risk the dead roads at night.

"About this chicken and rope trick," I began. "How exactly would that work?"

Stella straightened her back and folded her hands in front of her.

"Well, to be perfectly honest, I was thinking of using one of the roosters instead. You see, I have two of them, and one of them, well, one of them I don't like very much."

I never really thought in terms of likes or dislikes when talking about chickens other than what flavored sauce I wanted to go with my nuggets at the drive-thru.

"He's a Cuckoo Maran," she said.

"A cuckoo moron?"

"Cuckoo Maran," said Sanjay without tearing his eyes away from the book he was devouring. "Known as chocolate egg layers for their very dark brown eggs, the breed was developed in France in the mid eighteen hundreds. The Cuckoo variety displays feathers that are crossed with irregular slate colored bars. It is a dual purpose bird for both eggs and meat. Poopy Puppy says so."

I glanced over at Prianka. She just shrugged and very bravely reached over to take one of Stella's cookies.

Stella smiled. "Your brother is really rather remarkable."

"Yes he is," said Prianka as her eyes grew wide and round. "Wow, these cookies are great."

I didn't even know what to say to that. Great was about the last word I would use to describe Stella's cookies. Maybe I just had junk food taste buds.

"So this moron bird—what's your beef with him?"

Stella cleared her throat. "Too much testosterone, I suspect. I don't like the way he treats my hens." She pursed her lips. "Frankly, he could do with a little dose of humility."

"So we thought we could use him as bait," added Jimmy.

"In a cage, of course," said Stella. "There are plenty of them down in the agricultural cooperative."

Of course there were, along with rope, chains, and probably anything else we might need to lower the cuckoo bird to his probable death.

"I don't want him hurt, mind you," said Stella. "I have a feeling that I am going to be in this building for quite some time, and two roosters are better than one if I have a chance of hatching a replacement flock."

"Ooh, chicks," gasped Trina. "I love chicks."

Jimmy opened his mouth to agree but caught my 'don't say it, man' glare, so he shut his trap.

"We'll need fire," I said.

Prianka swallowed the rest of the cookie and said, "Lighter fluid."

"What?"

"You know, lighter fluid like you use for a barbeque. You do know what a barbeque is, don't you?"

Well, yeah, I knew what a barbeque was, but I thought you just pushed a button and the flames started up. I didn't know that you had to use special fluid. Trina and I exchanged befuddled glances.

Prianka licked the last crumbs off her lips. "There was a fall special in the front of the agricultural store with a bunch of grills. There was also a display of lighter fluid. I thought about stocking up on some before we left."

There we had it—our basic plan. The only thing left to figure out was how we were going to get a new ride.

"What about wheels?" I said. "We still need a car."

Again, Jimmy looked at Stella. She smiled weakly. He gently pushed Trina from his lap and rolled forward until his own clasped hands were sitting on the table.

"Yeah, um, about that," he began.

With that, he proceeded to ruin the rest of my day.

36

"A MINIVAN?" I cried and threw my hands up in the air. "You want us to drive a minivan?" Even though the Hummer had its fallbacks, Chuck's big, yellow, gas guzzler was pretty beast as far as transportation goes—but a minivan? You got to be kidding me.

"Obviously, I don't drive," said Stella. "Even if I did, the last thing I would be driving is a minivan. I would be driving a hybrid of some sort. Be that as it may, I own a minivan that belonged to my late mother. She left it to me in her will as a joke. Now, said joke has been sitting in my garage, unused, for over two years."

Prianka tensed. "You have a garage?" she said. "Did we miss your garage in our sweep of the building?"

Stella shook her head. "No, Dear. The garage is in the alley, and I have the key. She picked up the key ring we used when we went through the building. There were two identical keys marked 'van' and two more that read 'garage.'

"Don't worry," she said. "Mr. Embry, who owns the health food store, starts her up for me weekly and makes sure she's fed and watered, or whatever one does to an automobile. Mother's minivan should be in good working order with a full tank of gas."

Everyone was quiet. I wanted more than anything to close my eyes and not be hyped up on adrenaline for a couple minutes, but I didn't think that was likely to happen. When I opened my eyes, I found everyone staring at me.

"So, are you in, Dude?" asked Jimmy. I saw each of their faces—Trina, Jimmy, Prianka, and Stella. Sanjay, however, was in his own little world absorbing SAT knowledge like a sponge. Why were they waiting for me to give the thumbs up? Who died and made me leader of our happy little band?

Oh yeah. Everyone died.

"This is whacked," I began. Trina rolled her eyes and curled her lip at me. "But it's the best we've got so, yeah, I'm in."

"No alternative," said Prianka, which was probably true. The next thing I knew, Pri and I were downstairs in the agricultural cooperative picking out a small, square cage that looked about rooster-sized, along with some heavy duty rope and as many bottles of lighter fluid as we could carry. We dumped everything by the stairs to Stella's place before sneaking back up to the front of the store.

"Don't let them see you," I whispered.

"Yeah, duh," she said. We crouched behind the checkout counter and watched the dead lurch by.

"Do you believe this?" I said.

"Which part?"

"All of this. Who would have ever thought zombies could be real? Who would have even thought there would be a woman like Stella living not far from us, shut into her own little world like some reclusive celebrity?"

"She *is* a reclusive celebrity."

"Oh, yeah," I said.

"Besides," said Prianka. "I thought you were talking about our kiss."

Way to catch me off guard. I nervously cleared my throat and concentrated on two middle-aged poxers obviously having a beef with each other. One was snarling, and the other one was posturing like something out of a nature documentary. The whole thing was surreal—just like the bombshell Prianka dropped on my head.

"Yeah, well, that was pretty hard to believe, too," I said.

"Why? Was I that bad?" she snapped.

"That's not what I meant," I said. "I mean it was unbelievable." I was going for the quick save but not doing a very good job.

"What was so unbelievable?"

"I . . . um . . . ugh . . . that you kissed me at all?"

Prianka stood and stormed off toward the back of the store.

Great. Just great. No pun intended, but this was virgin territory for me. Why did she have to be so confusing? So Prianka was sort of hot. So I sort of despised her. So she was kind of annoying. She was still sort of cool to have around. Someone really needed to hand me a road map because I was lost, big time.

I stood and followed her to the back of the store but she had already stormed upstairs with some of the supplies. Of course she left the lion's share for me.

I guess I was being punished. I just wasn't sure for what.

37

NO WONDER STELLA chose the bird she did. The rooster was a bastard and a half. Not like the white one, which was totally friendly. She could pick that one up and tuck him under her arm, and he remained perfectly content.

But the one she wanted us to use? Let's just say making direct eye contact wasn't a good idea. We finally manhandled him into the cage, ruffled feathers flying everywhere, and locked him down tight.

Andrew didn't know quite what to make of the whole spectacle. He kept twisting his head from side to side and hopping back and forth from Jimmy to Sanjay. He even landed on my shoulder once before realizing he was on the wrong perch, which made him leap off like he'd been burned.

On Stella's deck there was a fire escape which led to the roof. We decided our first order of business was to clear all four sides of the building. If we could get that done, we had a chance at getting to the minivan and, after, to Chuck's Hummer for the rest of our supplies.

None of us said so, but we all knew we didn't really need most of the things in the Hummer. We could have made due with packing up on groceries from the health food store. What we really needed were the guns. Even though none of us could shoot, without those guns, who knew how vulnerable we would be out there? I did notice, as disapproving as Stella was about the whole kids and firearms scenario, she added a book on basic firearms safety to Sanjay's pile.

We also needed the kayak or the kid would likely pitch a fit come bedtime.

I took the fire escape first. Prianka handed the rooster up to me along with three bottles of lighter fluid and the rope. Then she climbed up followed by Trina, who was holding a shopping bag full of supplies.

We carried everything to the front of the building and laid it all out in front of us.

"Let's see," said Trina as she surveyed her booty. "We've got some empty bottles, a box of matches, and some old tie-dyed t-shirts I think may be pre-Woodstock."

"Aren't those worth money on eBay?" I asked.

"Not anymore," she said.

I patted the cage with the rooster. "I've got the bait."

Prianka picked up the coil of rope. "I guess that makes me rope girl." She took one end and carefully threaded the rope over and under the mesh wire from one end of the cage to the other. In the middle of her work, the rooster let out a crow, and we all jumped. "Let's hope that means 'Here I am—come eat me,'" she said as she pulled about a two foot length through the other end of the cage and knotted it tightly to the rest of the rope.

"If you're rope girl, I'm cocktail girl," said Trina as she filled an empty bottle about three quarters of the way full with lighter fluid. She rolled up one of the tie-dyed shirts and stuck an end all the way down into the bottle. The other end she let hang out. "Molotov cocktail, that is." She soaked the end that was hanging out with lighter fluid.

We all looked over the side of the building. There must have been at least a hundred poxers close enough to come running when the dinner bell rang.

I lifted the cage up and over the edge.

"Wait," said Trina. "Maybe we should name her."

"Seriously?" I said.

Prianka looked the other way and tried not to let my sister see her roll her eyes.

"Yeah. I think if she doesn't survive unscorched, she should have a name so we can all remember her." Trina thought for a moment. "Didn't Sanjay say this kind of bird lays chocolate colored eggs?"

"This kind of bird's a boy," said Prianka.

"Well I think *she's* pretty," said Trina.

"Then how about Cuckoo," snapped Prianka.

Hormonal much? I stood there watching my sister and Prianka having a little hissy fit over a chicken. I can't say I wasn't mildly amused. I needed a little bit of levity right about now.

"I'm not calling her Cuckoo," she huffed. "I don't care if she's a cuckoo moron or whatever Stella said she was." Trina thought for a moment. "I know! I hereby name you Fudge on account of your chocolate colored eggs."

Prianka sighed, and I sort of snorted. "Fudge it is," I said and began lowering the cage down over the side of the building.

About half way to the ground, Fudge crowed again, but none of the poxers seemed to notice. I kept letting the rope out, hand over hand, until the cage hit the ground.

Nothing happened.

The dead kept meandering back and forth in aimless circles. None of them seemed to notice that a nice, juicy, bloody, dinner was being served up fresh and raw. Since the bird was just a teensy weensy bit of a dick and was probably going to be a poxer snack anyway, I pulled the cage up about five feet and dropped the rope. This resulted in two things. First, the cage made a reasonably loud clatter when hitting the ground. Second, Fudge crowed.

Every poxer in earshot took the bait like they were all on remote control. In unison, their heads whipped around toward the cage sitting on the sidewalk in front of The Wordsmith Used Book Emporium.

At first they didn't start moving.

"What are they doing?" said Trina.

"I'm not sure—maybe waiting for an invitation to dinner?" I pulled up the cage and dropped the rope again. Fudge screeched when the cage hit the ground.

This time, they heard the dinner bell and came running.

38

"SEVENTY-THREE," said Prianka. "No wait a minute. Seventy-four." Her hair covered her face as she bent over the side of the building. "Pull the cage up. The last thing we need is for them to get Fudge."

I chuckled and pulled up on the rope.

"What's so funny?" she snapped.

"You called the chicken, Fudge."

"Grow up, Tripp."

"I'm just saying."

Trina held the Molotov cocktail in one hand and the matches in another. She was looking for a spot to drop the bottle so the home-made bomb wouldn't just clunk a poxer on the head. She wanted the cocktail to hit the pavement and explode.

"There's no clear spot," she whined. "It's just one big mass of dead."

The zombies crowded around the cage, reaching up with their grubby mitts. I'm sure Fudge dropped a little fudge on them once or twice, but they probably didn't notice.

"Wait," I said. "I have an idea." I slowly began to shift the rope left to right, and the cage started swaying. The mass of poxers followed the swinging rooster like a beacon. First they all shuffled left, then they all shuffled right.

"That's good," said Trina. "Keep doing that."

I could see her calculating where exactly the bottle would hit pavement close enough to light the poxers on fire. She followed the mob with her eyes as they all moved back and forth, back and forth.

"The damn rooster's going to puke," said Prianka.

I snorted. "I'm sure the damn rooster thinks he's at an amusement park."

"Okay," Trina said as she struck a match and lit the t-shirt soaked with lighter fluid. Flames burst into life.

"One, one zombie, two, one zombie, three, one zombie . . . die," she hissed and dropped the bottle over the edge. Fire plummeted past the dangling cage and hit the ground like a bullet. I immediately pulled Fudge back up and out of the way of the flaming carnage—and carnage there was.

The bottle exploded and liquid fire doused the closest poxers. They immediately burst into flames and started squealing. One by one they popped, and burning chunks hit the next wave of undead. So it went, over and over again until almost every dead thing on the street was truly snuffed. Burning piles were strewn everywhere and that attracted more poxers. They were too stupid to realize that fire was bad, so they reached for the embers as though the crackling piles were something yummy to eat.

Several more poxers were offed that way.

"Pure genius," I said. "I can't believe that plan worked."

"One side down, three to go," said Trina and eagerly filled up another bottle with lighter fluid.

I went to pull Fudge back up to see if he was fried, but he crowed, so I didn't bother. Instead I just dragged the rope around to the left hand side of the building. There was a small park there, carved out of a spot where a building must have been demolished. The park only had a few benches and a fountain. Some tents had been set up for Fall Fest, and there was another healthy poxer population in sight.

This time around, the poxers noticed the cage immediately—maybe because I clanked Fudge against the side of the building when I turned the corner.

Once again, I used the swinging rooster technique to get them all in a tight group. Trina lit the bottle, I pulled Fudge up, and she rained fire down upon them like some twisted demi-goddess with Zeus envy.

Still, things don't ever go smoothly, do they? One of the burning dead tumbled into the side of a tent before exploding, and the tent went up in flames, too. That one caught another tent on fire, as well as a third, which buckled sideways and fell into an awning on the side of the building across the little park.

That building belonged to the little pig who built his house with sticks.

The awning went up in flames fast. Before we really understood what was happening, the whole doorway was on fire. We watched the wood burn, unblinkingly, not knowing if we just did something very, very wrong or something very, very right.

"Well that should keep them busy for a while," said Prianka with her hands on her hips.

"Yeah, but what if that place goes up in flames, or falls this way." I pulled on the rope, hand over hand, until the cage was up and over the side of the building. Fudge the rooster blinked at me with his little, beady eyes but looked no worse for wear.

"Built of bricks," said Trina as she worked on preparing another fire bomb. However, when we went to the right side of the building, we found that most of the poxers were attracted to the smoke and flames in the park and were headed in that direction.

That just left the alley. We carefully gathered our supplies together and climbed down the fire escape. Jimmy and Stella were on the deck nervously staring at the burning building next door.

"Worked like a charm," I chirped. Stella just stared at the flames next door as they rose higher and higher.

"That's an historic building," she said to the wind, her eyes focused on the flames. "Did you know that?"

Tears streamed down her face as she stared unblinkingly as the wooden building burned. Jimmy took her hand as the flames grew. They licked at the second story windows, and pretty soon smoke started pouring out of the top floor.

The poxers that were still mobile in the park grabbed at the fire and burst into flames one after another. With every squeal, Stella shuddered.

"The Lord is a jealous God, filled with vengeance and wrath," she whispered as she surveyed the chaos. "He takes revenge on all who oppose Him and furiously destroys His enemies."

She pulled her hand away from Jimmy's and turned to us.

"He displays His power in the whirlwind and the storm. The billowing clouds are the dust beneath His feet. His rage blazes forth like fire, and the mountains crumble to dust in His presence." Stella wiped tears from her swollen eyes. None of us said anything, maybe because there was nothing to say. Stella sniffed. "Yeah, well, I never took much stock in the bible, anyway." She turned to watch the building burn. "Besides, God didn't do this," she said. "It was man. It was man who did all this."

39

WE ENDED UP staying the night. I really didn't want to and neither did Trina, but we both knew that we couldn't just torch a building then leave Stella there by herself. Besides, we were all exhausted. We turned a lot of poxers into toast. I doubted the ones left were bright enough to regroup by morning.

Besides, if my parents were at Aunt Ella's, we were sure they'd wait for us.

Prianka and I went back down to the agricultural cooperative and brought up one of the bright, plastic wheelbarrows. We figured Sanjay would be cool with sleeping underneath it.

The whole time we were down there, not a word was shared between us.

Later, as the sun sank in the sky, we all sat on Stella's deck and watched quietly as the wooden building next door crumbled in flames. Every once in a while, we heard a poxer squeal and pop, which was totally eerie. Still, I think we all felt comforted knowing there was one less of those things in the world.

We didn't talk much. Everyone was spent. I found myself staring at Prianka more than a few times, and she actually caught me once. My faced turn red. Trina sat right next to Jimmy, leaning up against him. Finally, he stretched, yawned, and when his arms came back down, one draped over my sister's shoulder.

Sanjay lay with Poopy Puppy on the floor, perusing the same stack of books that Stella had given him. I couldn't imagine the size of the brain that was storing all that knowledge, but I was grateful he could.

Andrew perched on the top of Sanjay's back with his head tucked underneath his wing. I guess I was glad that he was with us, too.

We ended up going to bed early. Prianka had surprisingly little trouble convincing Sanjay to sack out underneath the wheelbarrow. Stella brought out a bunch of blankets and pillows and apologized for not having beds for us to use. We were grateful for what she had. For some reason, each of us hugged her goodnight like she was our mom or something.

When we finally did fall asleep, I dreamt about school and Spanish class. The teacher, Mr. Santos, was talking so fast that I couldn't understand anything he was saying—and I was pretty good at Spanish. He kept talking faster and faster until he finally started yelping. After that, his head exploded.

I woke with a start. Trina was cuddled against Jimmy. Prianka was up and standing by the window, staring out at the darkness. I stood and went over to her.

"Hey," I whispered. "Can't sleep?"

"I don't think I'll ever sleep again."

"Me, too," I said. "Bad dreams." I looked past her into the night. "What are you looking at?"

"I'm just looking," she said. "I can't believe we burned down a building."

"I can't believe ninety-nine percent of the past three days."

She sighed but stayed quiet. After a couple minutes I turned to go back to bed. Prianka reached out her arm and stopped me.

"Thanks," she said—again. Prianka Patel was being appreciative all over the place.

"For what?"

There's a whole lot of things she could have said like 'thanks for saving me and my brother,' or 'thanks for helping with the wheelbarrow,' but what she ended up saying caught me by surprise.

"Thanks for staring at me," she said. "Just . . . thanks."

THE NEXT MORNING, I woke up because I smelled something really good. Stella was in the kitchen cooking. "What smells amazing?" I asked her

"What smells amazing is pumpkin muffins with cinnamon, scrambled eggs courtesy of the chickens out on the deck, and apple pancakes," Jimmy chimed in. Everyone else was already up and eating.

Who knew when we were going to be able to eat like that again, so we polished off everything.

After, we readied ourselves to leave. Our first order of business was to open the blinds, go out on the deck, and check to see what the poxer situation looked like below. The building next door was still smoldering. Black smoke rose out of the pile of ashes and sailed off into a perfect sky.

Prianka climbed up on the roof. A minute later she came back down and reported that the zombie numbers were more or less under control. Sure, there were a bunch of them still around, but they seemed to be further down the street toward the center of town. We all looked over the back of the deck and made sure that the alley was empty. Thankfully it was.

We had the green light to leave.

With a little less trouble than the last time around, we stuffed Fudge back into the cage and delivered him to Stella. She agreed to watch out for us from the roof as we sneaked out the backdoor of the used clothing store, which was the closest exit to her garage. Once we were safely in her minivan, she would make sure to keep any wayward poxers distracted while we got what we needed from Chuck Peterson's Hummer.

That was the plan.

Saying goodbye to Stella was hard. I couldn't help feeling like we were never going to see her again. Even though Aunt Ella's house was supposedly only a little ways up Route 2, we all felt like we were abandoning her and going to another country. She put the pile of books she gave Sanjay into a sack. I could tell she wanted to hug him goodbye, but she settled for giving Poopy Puppy a big hug and a kiss instead.

"Thank you," said Prianka. "We *will* see you again. All of us."

"Is that a promise?" said Stella.

"Pinky swear," said Prianka. They hooked their pinkies together, but Prianka crumbled and squeezed Stella so tightly I thought her glasses were going to pop off her head.

Finally, we did the most important thing before we left. We sat Sanjay down and asked him one more time how to get to my Aunt Ella's house.

"Sanjay," I said. "We're at 311 Main Street in Greenfield, Massachusetts. We need to get to 8 Captain Logan Way in Cummington, Massachusetts. Can you tell us how to get there?"

He sat on a kitchen chair with his feet dangling. His eyes looked far off to a point on the wall where there was nothing. After a moment, he consulted with Poopy Puppy. When he was done he said, "Route 2 north for 8.2 miles. Winchendon Road for 7.3 miles. Blackstone Street for .4 miles. Captain Logan Way for .1 mile. Poopy Puppy says so."

Prianka wrote the directions down and handed me the paper. Jimmy shook his head in amazement. Stella smiled like she was doting over a favored grandchild. Trina calculated the math and announced to the rest of us that we only had 16 miles to go.

We said our goodbyes all over again. Then we took Stella's extra set of keys which included a master key to the building, made sure that I had the Hummer's keys at the ready, and were off to the used clothing store to get out of Dodge as quickly and quietly as we could.

40

MR. EMBRY, WHO owned the health food store and took care of Stella Rathbone's minivan, must have been stuck in her garage since everything happened last Friday. I knew he was only one poxer, but none of us expected him to be there after we snuck out into the alley and quietly pulled up her garage door.

We all had lighters and paper ready, except for Sanjay, but the grandfatherly dude with the earring in his ear and the graying ponytail lunged at us as soon as the door opened.

"Mr. Embry," screamed Stella from her perch three stories high, as he went straight for Trina. She wasn't prepared, and he nearly bit her, but Jimmy thought fast and rammed into him from the side with his wheelchair. The old guy went sprawling, which gave us all enough time to torch up our wads and throw them at him. We all backed up as far as we could and watched him light up the alleyway before exploding.

Stella's face disappeared from the rooftop. A moment later she was back.

"There are more in the park," she yelled down to us. "I think they heard." She held up the cage with Fudge. "I'll keep them busy with the rooster. You all be safe."

Then she was gone again.

The minivan was an ugly dark blue with Pennsylvania license plates. We piled in easily enough then shut and locked the doors. For some reason, Andrew insisted on sitting on the coffee cup holder that sat between the driver's and passenger's seats. The bird bugged me. I don't know why. Maybe I didn't like those deep black eyes or the fact that his brain was about the size of my little toenail, yet he still knew how to talk.

He just freaked me out, is all. Creepy creepy, you know?

I pulled the van out of the garage and turned right. We went to the end of the alley, hooked a left, and pretty soon we were around the building. There were black, tarry puddles of slime everywhere. That had to be our handiwork—the first time we took on a horde of poxers and won—rooster style.

I rolled up in front of Chuck's Hummer, and we all hopped out of the car and surveyed the street. There were poxers past where we nuked the building. They had already eyeballed us and started heading our way. Up the street there were more.

"I figure we have just about a minute," I told everyone as I pressed the open button on Chuck's key ring, and we all started unloading the Hummer.

The girls focused on the kayak while I tossed bag after bag to Jimmy, and he threw them into the back of the minivan.

"Forty seconds," yelled Trina, "I can't get the ties undone".

"Start a countdown," Prianka ordered, and we all did.

"Thirty-nine, thirty-eight, thirty-seven, thirty-six . . ." At about twenty-two, Trina was in tears. Prianka kicked the side of the Hummer and told her to forget the damn boat. After all, Sanjay slept just fine underneath a wheelbarrow. He'd just have to learn to adjust. We all did.

Jimmy and I had the guns, our bags, and the food loaded into the minivan.

The poxers were closing in.

"Fourteen, thirteen, twelve . . ." We almost had it made until Prianka shrieked loud enough to make even the poxers stop for a second.

Sanjay was standing in the middle of the street.

He was dangling Poopy Puppy by one hand and waving at the advancing monsters with the other.

"Sanjay!" she pleaded, but it was too late. Within the space of those last twelve seconds they were practically on him.

My head swam with a thousand thoughts at once. How could he have gotten out of the minivan? Why did we let him get out of the minivan? What the hell was he thinking? None of those things mattered. We were going to lose him, the most vulnerable member of our little group, and there was nothing we could do. We were a million miles away from him, and the poxers were too close.

When they were near enough for Sanjay to realize that they weren't people at all, he began to cry.

Andrew, who was also supposed to stay in the car, flew in front of the closest poxer to Sanjay and flapped his wings wildly. The rest of us ran into the crowd, tackling the poxers and dropping them to their knees while staying out of the way of gnashing teeth.

Our efforts bought us scant seconds.

Jimmy, flex-master that he was, literally picked up a poxer kid and threw him at a dude with plugs in his ears, which, by the way, is a totally poor fashion choice. The two fell to the ground in a pile of tangled limbs.

Trina had my dad's crowbar in her hands. She swung the shaft wildly around like she was playing whack-a-mole.

Prianka was showing off her ninja moves like she did way back at the Mug N' Muffin. *I kissed that girl*, I thought. Sometimes stray ideas like that can creep into your brain at the worst possible times. This was one of those times.

Out of the corner of my eye I saw the girl—the one that was going to get to Sanjay—the one that was going to end his brief existence and turn him into a mindless thing. She was only a yard or two away—a hipster with long tangled hair and a peacock colored top. She reached for Sanjay just as I got to him.

I grabbed for his arm, and so did she, but her hands missed. Instead they found Poopy Puppy, and she yanked the dirty, stuffed toy out of Sanjay's clutches and brought it to her mouth like she hadn't eaten in years.

I heaved Sanjay off the ground and tossed him over my shoulder, whipping his legs around and knocking another poxer off his feet.

Something sailed past my head, hit the ground, and tumbled.

It was Fudge the Rooster, without a cage and with no way to get back home to the hen house. He landed on the pavement and immediately puffed up the feathers around his neck and started cock-fighting with anything that moved, which included us.

"Woot woot," we heard Stella holler from the rooftop. "Am I a good shot or what?"

Prianka kicked the rooster toward her closest attacker, and Fudge clawed him in the groin with his talons.

Trina and Jimmy had already started back to the car with Andrew following after them. I pulled Sanjay away, narrowly missing two more poxers that reached for us. He squirmed violently in my arms.

"Poopy Puppy," he screamed. "Poopy Puppy, Poopy Puppy."

We were too late. There was nothing to do but scramble into the minivan.

I struggled to put Sanjay into the back seat. Prianka held on to him as he howled and wailed.

Safely locked inside, we all turned and watched in horror. The poxers had surrounded Fudge, snapping at each other and chasing after him like he was the last portion of the best thing on the menu.

Meanwhile the hipster chick tore Poopy Puppy apart in a vain attempt to find the part of the dog that was meat.

Sanjay kept on weeping then abruptly stopped and went completely mute. When I turned around, I saw that his eyes were glazed over and his face was frozen.

"Is he bitten," I screamed. "Did he get bit?"

Prianka checked every inch of him. The boy who normally didn't like to be touched did nothing as she examined him from head to foot.

He was fine—but he wasn't.

He sat frozen, like he was a statue in a wax museum. No matter what any of us said—no matter what we did—he didn't move.

He stayed like that for a long, long time.

41

WE FOLLOWED BACK streets that paralleled the main road to get out of the center of town. There were poxers everywhere, although not as many as we thought there would be. Jimmy was finally the one who came up with the idea that maybe a lot of them were too stupid to figure out how to get outside.

Just like the mother and daughter in the used closing store, they probably didn't have the brains for door knobs, and unless there was meat to eat on the other side, smashing windows was past their intellectual capabilities, too.

"We really got to be careful when we go inside places," he said. "There's always a chance that we'll run into the hungry dead."

I thought about it for a moment. "Well, if they don't have anything to eat, won't they eventually just waste away?"

"Great," said Prianka. "Anorexic zombies." She sat in the middle seat with her hands in her lap, peering out the window as we drove past a particularly tacky house decorated early for Halloween. Sanjay stared into space, his eyes glazed. Andrew had chosen to leave the front of the minivan and now sat on his shoulder. He gently rubbed his head against Sanjay's cheek like a dutiful dog.

It was selfish of me, but I couldn't help thinking that we were lucky we got the directions to Aunt Ella's house from Sanjay before everything happened. I could understand a little kid being upset about losing a stuffed animal, but Poopy Puppy was far more than just a toy to Sanjay. Like Prianka said, Poopy Puppy was Sanjay's mouthpiece. Without him, he was mute, and none of us knew for how long.

I drove a few more blocks before taking a right and joining up with Main Street again. Finally, we were out of the center of town and away from Fall Fest.

"I know where we are," said Jimmy. "I've been up this way before." He directed us down a hill, which was a little harrowing considering there were a few pileups along the way. At the bottom, we passed a Chinese food place and a big white church.

Off in the distance, I could see the highway. An endless stretch of cars still marred the landscape in both directions, and there was movement everywhere, which meant that there were poxers.

My mind drifted back to the lady who was stuck in her car on Route 116. I bet when she woke up last Friday morning, the last thing she could have guessed was how the rest of her life would be. The look of horror on her face when she realized we weren't going to save her will always be with me, like a piece of movie popcorn stuck in my teeth.

I frowned. Let's not forget the movies. They were gone, too.

As we approached the underpass directly below the traffic jam, dozens of poxers on the highway above twirled their heads around and tracked the minivan with their dead eyes. There were more on the side of the road and in the underpass. When we went through, two of them shambled out right in front of us, and I hit them.

I didn't even slow down.

Black blood splattered the windshield, so I turned on the wipers and pressed the button for the windshield wiper fluid.

"That's gross," said Trina as gore spread across her field of vision. "I can't see."

I flipped my hand. "What's to see? It's dead out there."

No one laughed.

On the other side of the underpass was the entrance to a supermarket—one of those huge ones that had a salad bar and served pizza.

"A supermarket—that's good to know," said Jimmy. He was sitting behind Trina, so he reached forward and massaged her shoulder. "It's just a little blood," he whispered to her. She put her hand on his. I still wasn't getting used to the whole idea of the two of them together.

Next to the supermarket was a shoe store, a pet mart and a coffee shop. A little hint of sadness swept over me as I thought about the animals in the pet place. I know, I know. What a softy, right? At least it wasn't the kind of store that had puppies and kittens. Instead, they had what my parents always called 'disposable pets' like mice and gerbils and guppies—the kind adults give their kids when they're five to teach them about responsibility.

What was worse? Starving to death in a cage with your friends or being tortured to death by a giant toddler. I think I'd pick starving.

"Ooh, shoes," purred my sister.

"Yeah," I said. "A nice set of practical pumps is exactly what you need right now."

"Bite me, Tripp. And can we stop for a sec and wipe off the

windshield? There's gunk everywhere."

I pressed the button for the windshield washing fluid again, but all it managed to do was make the ick a little wetter as it smeared across our field of vision.

"Just spritz the windshield a couple more times," Jimmy said. "It should be fine."

The dark stains eventually faded before disappearing. There was still some crusty junk left along the edges of the window. The first good rain would take care of that.

Past the supermarket, the road curved to the right, and buildings gave way to tall pine trees. As the road began to steadily climb, we passed a big, carved, wooden Indian head with a sign that said, 'Welcome to the Mohawk Trail.'

I remembered the Indian from trips we had taken to see my aunt and uncle. It had a hard, totem pole face with a craggy nose and deep set eyes. Below the carving, a welcome sign said, 'The Mohawk Trail, part of Massachusetts Route 2, was created as one of the United States' first scenic highways. It passes close to Vermont on one side and the Mohawk Trail State Forest on the other. It was added to the National Register of Historic Places in 1973.'

Surprisingly, there were relatively few cars on the road. I supposed that unless you lived off the Trail, you wouldn't have thought to head north this way.

"I remember the Indian," I said. "We're not far."

"We're looking for a coffee shop," said Trina. "That's where we make the right."

We followed the Trail as the road snaked up the mountain. About two miles further there was a little store advertising chocolate and Indian items. There was a lookout tower there, too. I remembered stopping there several times with my parents to get ice cream on the way back from Aunt Ella's house. Ice cream was our reward for enduring the time we spent visiting them. Not that they were all that bad. Aunt Ella and Uncle Don were okay enough. They were just weird.

I peeked in the rearview window at Sanjay. For the most part, Prianka stayed mute, along with her brother. I can't imagine what was going through her head, but the subtext was probably all about how I was the one who let Poopy Puppy got shredded to pieces and that her brother was now a real live zombie instead of a dead one.

I replayed the moment in my mind, when the stuffed dog was snatched away from him. There was nothing I could have done. We were in crisis mode, and Sanjay was about to get torn apart along with Poopy Puppy. Still,

I should have tried harder. I should have been faster. At least that's what I told myself Prianka was thinking.

I turned the rearview mirror slightly and caught her gaze in mine. It was steely and cold. She turned away and kept staring out the window.

Yup. I should have done a lot of things.

42

THERE WAS AN eighteen wheeler turned over in front of the entrance to Winchendon Road. The driver, who had probably been thrown from the cab, was smeared across Route 2 in a couple of pieces.

Thankfully, they didn't move.

The coffee shop parking lot had a few poxers milling about. They watched us slow down and immediately started heading our way. A cute little house with a manicured lawn sat across the street from the coffee shop. The cab of the eighteen wheeler had fallen on a display of corn stalks, pumpkins, and gourds that sat on the edge of the property. They were mashed into the ground, and a couple of crows were pecking at the seeds.

Andrew stared at them with his black eyes and repositioned himself on Sanjay's shoulder. He was just fine staying with us.

I pulled the van into the house's little driveway, drove over the lawn and around the hobbled truck. Within seconds we were on the final leg of our journey.

"Welcome to apple tree world," I said as we began passing the orchards.

I never used to notice things like apple orchards before, but now that everything was different, I was amazed how beautiful the world really was. The multicolored hills gently sloped down toward the road on both sides. The orchards were filled with apples. In another reality, the countryside would have been teeming with leaf peepers, or at least that's what my parents called them. They were the people who visited up north purely to see the brightly colored foliage and tell their friends back home about tasting real apple cider.

Of course, my mind flipped to the fact that all the beautiful foliage was really trees in the process of spectacularly dying.

Morbid much?

There were poxers in the orchards but not a lot. Maybe they were the people who worked there when Necropoxy hit, or maybe they were just wanderers looking for anything living to eat. In either case, when everything happened late Friday afternoon, the orchards were probably gearing up for a killer weekend.

They sure got that one right.

The ride almost seemed a little scary, like something out of a horror movie—a group of teens taking a picturesque ride in the country only to be set upon by a pack of blood thirsty zombies?

I've seen that flick before.

When the orchards thinned out, we passed an antique store that seemed to specialize in old, dirty things, or that's at least what was displayed out front. After that were more trees, which gave way to corn fields on our right and a river to our left.

"Awesome," yelled Jimmy from the back seat. "Kayaking here I come."

"We left the kayak," mumbled Trina miserably.

"Yeah," I grimaced. "Besides, that's Dead Man's Creek." I motioned across the river. There were a couple tents set up on the river bank and a half dozen poxers who didn't have the sense to know how to cross the water. Whoever they were, they had probably been getting their last bit of camping in for the season before the chill set in.

"Never mind," Jimmy said and squeezed my sister's shoulder.

Another mile up the road and near where we had to turn, Trina spied a small graveyard on our right. The rocky terrain was dotted with those really old headstones that had words on them like 'thee' and 'thou.' We had walked through the cemetery once when we were much younger and tried to spook each other with, well, zombie tales of the crypt.

"Turn here," she said, and I palmed the wheel right.

We drove down a steep hill with trees hanging over each side like gargoyles warning us to stay away. Their bark curved and twisted into grotesque shapes. They went perfectly with the whole graveyard vibe.

Halfway down the hill, the trees opened up to a picture perfect view of a valley. I pulled the minivan over to the side of the road and stopped.

"There's my aunt's place," I said. "And we only took four days to get here."

Nestled in the valley below us was Ella Light and Don Dark's farm. A huge, red barn towered over a two story white house with a wraparound porch and a stone chimney.

There were animals in the pastures, but for the life of me, I couldn't tell what they were. Aunt Ella always had something new and interesting living on her property. She went through emus for a while because she said their oil was healthy. Frankly, I wasn't quite sure how you got oil out of an emu, and I didn't think I wanted to know. After the emus, she raised rabbits for meat, which put a whole new damper on the cute and fluffy thing. For a while she had sheep for wool, and one year we all got scarves and mittens and hats that she had knitted herself. There were flecks of hay in them, and they really itched. I think my mom ended up putting all my aunt's gifts in a box and shoving them to the back of a closet.

One year she was all about bee hives because my aunt was convinced that honey was nature's cure for everything. My mom said nature's cure for everything was chocolate and refused to go and visit until my aunt got the bee thing out of her system.

"What kind of animals are those?" asked Prianka.

"It's a crap shoot," I said. "Aunt Ella goes through phases."

Trina leaned forward and narrowed her eyes—so did I. There was a figure moving among the animals. They seemed to give whoever was there a wide berth.

"I guess someone's still alive," I said.

Trina didn't look at me. She sucked on her lower lip. "Do you think they're here?" she asked me.

She meant my parents. I mean, it would be cool and all if Aunt Ella and Uncle Don had survived the nightmare of last Friday night, but what we both really wanted was to see our parents—plain and simple.

"I hope so." I started up the minivan and drove the rest of the way down the hill.

When we reached the bottom, I turned right. We drove alongside one of the pastures with the animals.

"No, really," said Prianka. "What *are* those?"

The animals were bizarre, like something out of a Dr. Seuss dog show. They were huge, fluffy things with long necks and multicolored coats.

"Those would be llamas," said Jimmy. "I guess your aunt and uncle have a llama farm."

"This year," Trina and I both said in unison.

We pulled into the top of the long driveway. There was a metal gate left ajar, and I nudged it open with the nose of Stella's minivan. Once we pulled inside, I stopped and looked over into the field.

"Poxer," said Andrew.

The llamas were grazing but were wary of the person in the field that struggled after them in a futile attempt to grab on to one. Yeah, good luck with that.

"Poxer," Andrew quipped again and ruffled his feathers.

He was right.

There was a poxer.

His name was Uncle Don.

43

I DIDN'T EXPECT that Uncle Dom would have been spared the wrath of Necropoxy. That would have been a sucker's bet. He wasn't genetically related to us. Only Aunt Ella was blood because she was my dad's sister.

I just didn't expect to be mad about what happened to him.

"Tatti," I hissed.

Prianka flinched. "What did you say?"

"You heard me. Tatti, tatti, tatti, tatti, tatti on a shingle."

"What's wrong? It's just another poxer."

"*He's* not just another poxer. He's my Uncle Don."

Jimmy's mouth dropped open. "Seriously?"

Prianka shifted in her seat. "I . . . I'm sorry," she whispered, but her words didn't matter. Just like when Trina had a meltdown when we were up on top of Mount Sugarloaf, it was my turn. I pushed open the door and got out. I didn't know what I was doing. I just knew that I had to do something because the thought of my Uncle Don as one of those monsters infuriated me beyond belief.

How stupid. How pointless. Some lab geek, somewhere, sat on his fat butt and grew this stupid disease in a petri dish for who knows what reason.

Then he decimated the world.

I reached into my pocket and pulled out a lighter along with the directions we had gotten from Sanjay before we left Stella's house.

"Don't you dare," sobbed Trina as she got out of the car.

"It's not him anymore, Trina. Don't you see? It's not him anymore. He's a bag of flesh filled with death, and that's all."

"But that's Uncle Don."

"He . . . it's not Uncle Don. Uncle Don is dead. He's not coming back." I ran over to the side of the fence, grabbing a small rock along the way. With my pitching arm, I wound up and threw the rock as hard as I could at the poxer that used to be Don Dark.

The rock hit him in the arm, and he whipped around and saw me. His face was bloody. His eyes were dead—but there was something more. There were bite marks all over his face.

Either llamas have teeth, even though I always thought they were like big cows, or he had been in one colossal zombie fight. Either way, the poxer that used to be Uncle Don lost interest in the llamas around him and started toward us.

Trina's eyes welled up with fresh tears. Jimmy opened the door, dropped his wheelchair to the ground, and flipped himself into the seat

Prianka opened her door and stepped out, too.

"Do it," Trina said in a hushed voice that sounded as though the wind had been knocked out of her. "That's not Uncle Don anymore. That thing won't ever be Uncle Don again."

Salty droplets started streaming down my face. I couldn't be crying. I hadn't cried in years. I didn't know what they were. Soon, I felt someone next to me. It was Prianka. She put her hand over mine and quietly slipped the lighter out of my hand. I let her—I don't know why. She looked into my eyes, unspeaking, and gently took the wadded up piece of paper that represented her brother's last words, besides his desperate pleas to be reunited with Poopy Puppy. Without hesitating, she lit a corner and turned the paper upside down to make sure the fire swelled.

By that time, Uncle Don had reached the fence. Tears poured down Trina's face. He looked horrible—maybe because we knew him or maybe because he really did look worse than most of the other poxers we had run into.

Prianka flicked the burning paper at him, and he went up in flames just like every other poxer we had torched. The llamas in the field all moved off into the distance with their heads held high and their eyes alert.

Trina took my hand and squeezed tightly as she pulled me back toward the minivan. Prianka stepped back, too, and we all watched as Uncle Don began to shriek the shriek we had heard dozens of times over the past four days.

Finally he popped, and flaming bits of blackened flesh littered the pasture in a ten foot circle.

I don't know why, but I couldn't do anything with all the water that was leaking out of my eyes. I refused to wipe my face with my sleeve.

Somehow doing that just seemed wrong.

44

WE CHECKED the house. We checked the fields. No one was home. Trina and I really had hoped to find my parents or at least a sign they had passed through – maybe even on their way back to Littleham.

Aunt Ella, dead or alive, was missing, too.

The dinner table had been set for two, and there was a batch of chocolate and peanut butter brownies sitting on the counter. They looked like they were freshly made, which made them only four days old. They were a little crunchy, but we all indulged, except for Sanjay. He was completely nonresponsive.

Prianka sat him down on an old, tan couch in the living room directly across from the unlit fireplaces. Andrew settled on the couch next to him. I always loved my aunt's living room. There were huge picture windows on two sides. In past years, fluffy sheep grazed right outside. This year her pasture was filled with llamas. They were so odd looking with their hairy ears and huge, doe-eyes, I felt like we were in a fantasy.

Well that and the zombies.

"There's a lot of space here," said Jimmy as he scuttled down the center stairs on his butt and pulled himself back into his chair.

"Good," I said. "Because I'm not leaving until my parents show up."

Prianka walked passed me and flicked my ear so hard that the lobe throbbed.

"Ow!"

"There's no 'I' in 'we,' Nimrod."

"She's right," said Jimmy. "We've made it this far without killing each other. If it's all the same to you, I think we'll hang tight."

I was thankful. Of course I was thankful. I just didn't know what to say, so I didn't say anything. Trina helped herself to another brownie, and I did, too. We sat at the kitchen table and stared out the window.

From where we were sitting we could see almost the entire property. The grounds were fenced, which was good, and gated, which was even better. I doubted any of the fencing or the gate would keep out a hungry poxer for long, but I couldn't think about that at the moment. All I could think about was Uncle Don going up in flames.

"When did they get so many animals?" Trina asked as she bit into her brownie. At a quick count, there was something like twenty-five llamas. The pasture surrounding the house and barn climbed up a gentle slope to the back of the property. In the front pasture, where Uncle Don had been, there was a small pond with six or seven ducks paddling about. Next to the barn was a pen with about a dozen turkeys.

"Who knows? But I do know one thing. I think we have to feed them all. It's been days."

My sister's lip curled in disgust. "Ugh," she huffed. "I have to shovel tatti, too?" Trina stared out at the bizarre menagerie. "Don't they just eat the lawn?"

I rolled my eyes. "Suck it up, Princess."

Jimmy glided up to us. "I'm usually sort of the veggie type myself, but I gotta tell you, that's a lot of meat on the hoof out there."

My stomach churned.

"There's a supermarket back at the bottom of the Trail. I'm sure there's enough processed crap in there that would last us a lifetime, because if you think I'm eating a llama, you'd be thinking wrong."

Next to the kitchen was a long hallway lined with bookcases. Prianka gently browsed the titles, occasionally looking a little bewildered. She crouched down and slid her hand along the bottom shelf before quickly pulling a book out, like the volume was exactly what she had been looking for. She turned the hardcover over in her hands and glanced at the back jacket.

"Jackpot," she said as she got up and walked into the kitchen, plopping the book down on the table in front of us. I craned my neck to look at the title.

"You're kidding, right?" The book was called 'Raising Llamas for Fun and Profit.'

"Here's everything we need to know about llamas. So let's find the section on feeding and watering and see what we need to do."

"I'm game if you guys are," said Jimmy.

Trina and I were less than motivated.

THE NEXT THING we knew, all of us were standing out in the midday sun looking at Aunt Ella's barn. The two story building had big double doors that slid open. I knew that because Trina and I occasionally went up into the hay loft and hung out there when we were bored to death with listening to the adults visit. The barn also had a lower level that you could get to through an inside staircase. The stairs led to the bottom floor which opened to the pastures, so that the animals could meander in and out.

"They can use the pond for a water source," said Prianka, who had guided Sanjay out to the front porch and sat him down. I could tell she was worried about her brother, and I wished there was something that I could say or do to make everything better, or at least as good as things were before Poopy Puppy got destroyed.

There wasn't, so I figured the least I could do was try and cooperate.

She went on. "So now we have to find hay. The book says that llamas eat grain, too. Where do you suppose that would be?"

Trina leaned up against one of my uncle's old pickup trucks parked in front of the barn. Jimmy sat next to her. Finally, she sighed. "I think she keeps bags of grain inside."

Prianka marched up to the barn door and put both hands on the handle. "So let's do this thing." She pulled back hard and slid the barn door open.

What was inside was on her before she even had a chance to scream.

45

"NEWFIE!" I SHOUTED. "We forgot about Newfie!" The mammoth dog had bowled Prianka over and was now bathing her in huge, slobbering kisses.

"Get it off me. Get it off me," she screamed as she tried to cover her face with her arms, but Newfie's huge tongue lapped at her like she was a rawhide treat. He whined and yipped and wagged his tail as his hairy, one hundred and fifty pound body pinned her to the ground.

"Oh. Yeah. Right," said Trina like she was bored out of her mind. "We forgot."

"That's one big pooch," admired Jimmy as he appraised the gigantic, black Newfoundland. "Newfie, huh? Original."

I trotted over to Newfie and wrapped my arms around his barrel chest. The next thing I knew, he had me knocked over on the ground, too, and my face was washed clean of every bit of dirt from the last four days.

"You must be starving, boy," I said as I scratched his huge head.

"Or maybe not," said Jimmy and gestured inside the barn.

I pulled myself out from under Newfie and patted his head. Then, without really thinking about it, I stuck my hand out and pulled Prianka to her feet. She wiped her mouth with the back of her hand. Slobber came away and dribbled to the ground. I was tempted to ask if my kiss had been better, but I stopped myself. I had to put a padlock on my rapier wit.

That was a tall order, especially for me.

We stood in the entrance to the barn and peered inside. To the left was a wall of hay, neatly stacked in squares. There was also a ladder that went up to the loft. I could see from where we were, the loft was filled with hay, too. I guess Aunt Ella and Uncle Don had stocked up for the winter.

To the right was an equally high wall built with sacks of grain.

On the floor was an old bathtub filled with dog chow. I only knew it was dog chow because there was a big sign in front, hastily painted, that said 'Newfie's Dog Food.' There were also signs on the stacks of grain. Most of them said 'Llama Food,' and the rest said 'For the Birds.'

Newfie, his tail wagging a mile a minute, trotted into the barn and stuck his massive head in the windfall of kibble.

There was a big, manila envelope taped to the front of the tub. The words 'Please read' were written across it in bold, black magic market. I felt like I was in *Alice in Wonderland*, except that I was a dude. Maybe somewhere around was a little bottle that said 'Drink Me' and a piece of cake that said 'Eat Me,' or better yet, maybe there was a plate of leftovers from last Friday night with a note on them that said 'Wake Up.'

Newfie looked at us, his tail still wagging, and stuck his bowling ball sized head back into the giant dog bowl.

Jimmy rolled over to the envelope and pulled it off the tub. "You want to do the honors?" he asked and offered it to me.

"No, man. I'm cool."

"Let me see," said Trina and took the envelope from Jimmy. She slid her finger underneath the top, opened, and pulled out a single sheet of paper.

This is what is said:

If you are reading this note it's because I have left to find anyone else who has survived. Today is Sunday, September nineteenth.

I will be back.

The dog's name is Newfie. He has plenty of food and will drink out of the pond. Please leave him penned in with the llamas and the dead man. He is a good watch dog.

The dead man was my husband. Newfie bit him several times while protecting me.

The man on the radio station called this plague Necropoxy. So far I am immune

The llamas and turkeys have enough food in their pens for a week. If I am not back in seven days, please let all the animals free.

Thank you and blessed be.

Ella Light

Jimmy scratched his head. "I don't understand. Why lock Newfie up? What if no one ever showed up and she never came back?"

Trina turned the page over. "There's a p.s.," she said.

P.S. Please do not think me cruel. If I don't come back, Newfie has plenty of food in the llama pen. If I do come back, he will have protected my animals.

Prianka grimaced. "By 'plenty of food' does she mean the llamas?"

Trina covered her mouth with her hand. "Oh, gross," she gulped.

"But kind of smart," said Jimmy. "Sounds like someone I'd want to know."

Newfie woofed, turned around, and trotted to the center of the room. There was an opening in the floor there, and he disappeared down a flight of stairs. We all went over and stared down into the opening. Looking back up at us were half a dozen llamas, all lazily chewing hay.

Seconds later, I heard Newfie barking outside. He was inside the pasture, racing up the hill toward the back fence. The llamas paid no attention to him. I guess he was doing what he did best—guarding the property.

I suppose I should have felt safe with Newfie being there. Who wouldn't feel safe with a mammoth dog patrolling for poxers and anything else that might slip on to the property?

I didn't, though. I didn't feel safe at all. What's worse, I had a nagging feeling in the pit of my stomach I would never really know what safe felt like ever again.

I really hoped I was wrong.

46

THAT AFTERNOON, we all decided that we needed to clean ourselves up. Four long days since any of us had taken a shower made for a group of pretty grimy kids. Even though we had the opportunity to lather up when we were at Stella's, none of us, even the girls, did.

Teenagers—we're gross, aren't we?

Anyway, since there was no electricity to run the water pumps, a hot shower wasn't an option. I figured we were going to have to resort to using the pond. Trina was totally skeeved by the idea.

"It's gushy," she said.

Now it was my turn to roll my eyes.

"What's gushy?" asked Jimmy.

"She's talking about the bottom of the pond," I explained. "She doesn't like the feeling when the slime squeezes between her toes."

"Doesn't bother me," said Jimmy as he pulled off his shirt. "I can't feel my toes."

We brought shampoo and towels and changes of clothing out to the pond. The llamas trotted to the other side of the pasture. That was fine by me. I had no interest in stepping in llama poo. We sat on the ground at the edge of the water. Prianka brought Sanjay with her and was quietly explaining to him that she had to take his clothes off and wash his hair. He just stared into the air and didn't respond. I felt horrible.

Newfie was with us, too. There was a tense moment when we thought he was going to lunge at Andrew, or maybe the other way around, but miraculously, they seemed to sort of like each other. At first, Andrew flew to Jimmy while Newfie inspected every inch of Sanjay. When the giant dog was through sniffing and licking, Andrew bravely flew back to Sanjay, landed on his mop, and cawed at the dog.

Newfie woofed and laid down next to Sanjay with his head on his paws. Andrew cackled and clucked a few more times, bobbing his head up and down. That was their introduction. Somehow they had formed an understanding that we were all part of a pack or a flock or a group of kids—but whatever we were, we were a team.

The weirdest thing was how Newfie glued himself to Sanjay just like

Andrew did. The kid was an animal magnet. Maybe Newfie and Andrew somehow sensed that he was special or he needed them more than the rest of us. Whatever the reason, Sanjay now had two animal protectors, and I knew that Prianka felt better knowing they were there.

Jimmy stripped down to his tighty-whities and grabbed a bar of soap and shampoo. He was in the water before he even had a chance to test how cold it was.

"Yowza!" he screamed. "The water's freezing."

"Perfect," muttered Prianka as she pulled her shirt over her head and unbuttoned her jeans. Yeah, I knew her underwear was just like a bathing suit, but somehow, I just didn't think of her bra and panties that way. I felt my face burning and turning progressive shades of red. Jimmy treaded water and watched me. When he caught my eye, he winked.

Trina stripped down to her underwear, too. After that, she helped Prianka undress Sanjay.

I reluctantly pulled down my jeans and slipped my shirt over my head. I felt like a little kid next to Jimmy, the muscle man—the big, tough, college dude with the tattoo and the ripped body next to the puny junior with a knack for sarcasm.

Of course, I caught Prianka sneaking a peek at me in my boxers. Great—just great. She probably thought I looked prepubescent.

Trina and Prianka held Sanjay's hands and together waded into the cold water. He didn't flinch, but my sister did a fair amount of complaining.

"Nasty," she squealed, as her feet sank into the mushy bottom. "That better not be llama crap."

"That bad, huh?" said Jimmy as he treaded water over to her. "You just got to count to three and dunk yourself. That's the only way you'll get used to the cold."

Prianka didn't wait for a count. Without warning she dove headfirst into the icy water, came up, and swam about twenty feet into the pond. She turned around and swam back and sat, waist deep, next to Sanjay. Gently, she began rubbing water over his body so he would get used to the cold.

Even the chill didn't rouse him. Wherever he was inside his head, he was far, far away. I tried not to think about it too much, because every time I did, I just felt guilty.

As for me, I stood ankle deep in the water, waiting for the frigid shock to go away. For some reason, the cold made me think of being dead. I wondered if this is what the poxers felt like—chilled and a little slimy.

"Oh what the hell," I said and flopped into the pond. Whatever splash I generated drenched my sister from head to toe.

"Tripp!" she wailed and kicked a spray of water at me.

"Bad move, Trina." I devilishly grinned and palmed a huge wave of water in her direction.

Within seconds all of us except for Sanjay were in an all-out splash war. Jimmy was splashing Trina, I was splashing Prianka, and the girls were splashing back even harder. Of course, Newfie had to get into the action and drenched everyone as he barreled into the pond, barking and wagging his tail.

If anyone had been watching, they would have seen a bunch of normal kids having a last bit of summer fun before the calendar permanently tipped over into autumn.

It felt good—it felt right—but in my gut I knew it was only temporary.

47

LATER, I WENT upstairs and found a watch sitting on the dresser in my aunt and uncle's bedroom. At first I felt sort of weird going in there, like any moment I would be caught and scolded for going through an adult's private things, but the weird feeling quickly passed. I picked up the watch and read the time. It was just past three in the afternoon.

Jimmy and Trina had gone into the basement to take stock of how much food Aunt Ella had stored down there. When we did a sweep of the house earlier that day, Jimmy had commented that my aunt and uncle seemed pretty well stocked for the winter.

"You bet," I said. "Doomsday preppers. They probably were planning on digging their heels in during an alien invasion or something."

Still, I found myself being thankful my aunt and uncle were as nutty as they were.

Besides, I didn't think that Jimmy and Trina were in the basement strictly counting cans of peas and sacks of rice.

I took my uncle's watch and slipped it on. The band was a little big, and I had to notch it back a hole, but that was okay. The watch felt right on my hand.

Back on the first floor I found Prianka sitting on the couch.

"We need candles," she said. "It's going to be dark in a couple hours."

"Do you want me to run out to the candle store?"

She glared at me.

"Sorry," I said. "Yeah, I suppose we need some candles." Sanjay was lying in the corner of the couch with his head against the pillow. Andrew sat above him watching the llamas graze in the pasture. We had left Newfie out there to dry off from our fun in the pond. He was chasing dead leaves rolling across the grass. I stood there, crossed my arms, and stared at the floor.

"So where?" she said.

"I don't know. I feel weird rifling through their stuff."

"I don't," she said, stood up, and walked across the room to the fireplace. There were cabinets on either side of the rough stone. She opened one up and began rummaging through the contents. Her face grimaced.

"What?"

"They have a lot of really weird things, you know that?"

"Like what?"

She pulled out a Ouija board and some gothic looking wine glasses. "Like this," she said.

"What's weird about a Ouija board? It's a game."

"I don't play games."

Um, I beg to differ. She'd been playing some sort of girl game that I couldn't possibly understand, ever since everything started. For all I knew she'd been playing the same game for years. Actually, I always thought that Prianka Patel had a vendetta against me ever since first grade. Stupid me. I guess it's not just the boy who pulls the girl's hair if he likes her.

"That settles that. We're playing tonight."

"Sure," she sniped. "Let's just make everything that much creepier. Can you help me find some candles or not?"

"Fine," I muttered. For the next half hour we ransacked my aunt and uncle's house. My mother, who was the candle queen, had a whole cupboard full of scented jars, but my aunt and uncle didn't strike me as the smelly candle type. Finally, we found a drawer full of beeswax tapers and several boxes of wooden matches in the kitchen.

"Cool beans," I said when I found them.

"Score a point for Tripp Light."

I rolled my eyes. "Wasn't keeping score. Besides, I thought you didn't like games?

Prianka scowled but didn't say anything. She kept opening up drawers and cabinets and seeing what else she could find.

After an uncomfortably long while, Trina and Jimmy came up from the basement. They had a pad of paper with a whole list of supplies they found down there. Apparently, they accomplished more than fun and games, after all. We all went back into the living room where Sanjay was lying on the couch. Jimmy rolled over to Andrew and held his hand out. The crow gingerly hopped onto his wrist.

"You leaving me for Sanjay?" he asked the bird. Andrew turned his head to the side and gently nibbled at the stubble growing on Jimmy's face. Jimmy smiled and put the bird down on top of the couch. "That's cool by me, Bro," he said. "I can share."

Trina plopped down on the couch next to Prianka. Sanjay didn't move. "How is he?" she asked softly.

Prianka crossed her arms over her chest and let out a big sigh. "I don't know," she said. "I wish my parents were here."

Trina put an arm around her, and they sat quietly. Jimmy and I both watched them until I realized that we were staring, so I mumbled something about checking around outside, and Jimmy hastily agreed.

As we both left the living room, I turned back and saw that Prianka's eyes were moist. All she did was make me want to be someplace else even faster. Before we knew it, Jimmy and I were outside in front of the barn.

I sat down on the grass and Jimmy rolled up to me. We both watched Newfie off in the distance.

"I don't know what to do," I said after a couple minutes of silence.

Jimmy folded his hands together like he was a shrink and I was a patient on a couch.

"About which thing? You don't know what to do about Sanjay? You don't know what to do because your parents and your aunt are incommunicado? Or, you don't know what to do about the world going to hell in a hand-basket all around you?"

I stared at the ground and didn't say anything.

"Oh," he said. "Girl stuff."

Newfie barked a couple times.

"Why can't she just say what she wants?" I blurted out.

Jimmy flung his head backwards and laughed from his belly. "When you figure out how to speak 'girl' you let me know," he said. "I suck at foreign languages."

"I know, right? First she hates me, then she kisses me, then she hates me because I don't bring up the fact that she kissed me. And when I try to be nice, she turns into an icicle. I'm so confused. I'm amazed that I haven't gotten dizzy and hurled by now."

"You kissed her? Where was I?"

"Busy getting busy with my sister." I picked up a dead dandelion and blew puffy, white seeds into the wind. Newfie barked some more in the distance. "And for the record, I didn't kiss her. She kissed me—yesterday—when we were at Stella's."

"Cool," said Jimmy. He leaned in toward me. "How was she?"

"What do you mean, how was she? I don't know. Nice, I guess. She sort of took me by surprise."

"Wow," he whistled. "Besides, it doesn't hurt that Prianka's smokin'."

The cloud of dandelion seeds blew across the driveway. "Yeah, I guess." Who was I kidding? Of course she was. I just needed a decoder ring to figure out her special brand of communication.

Newfie's barks started getting louder and deeper. Both Jimmy and I tracked him with our eyes as he ran to the fence in the far corner of the property.

"Hey," said Jimmy. "You order cookies?"

"Huh?"

"You know—cookies. I sure as hell didn't order any. It's not the season."

Newfie stopped at the edge of the property, his head down low.

Jimmy pointed at what Newfie was freaking out about. Season or no season, we had a troop of girl scouts on our hands.

48

"LIGHTER, PLEASE," I yelled as I dashed into the house. Trina jumped off the couch and Prianka turned to look out the window. Her face turned white. "Now that's not even funny," she said. Newfie was at the mesh wire fence, running back and forth and barking his head off at the little troop of dead girls.

For their part, the pixie poxers were doing everything they could to tear through the wire and get at the big Newfoundland and the llama buffet that grazed behind him.

"You need help?" Trina asked in that way that I knew she really didn't expect to lift a finger.

"Nah. You guys chill and watch cable or something. Want popcorn?"

Trina smirked and tossed me a lighter. In the kitchen, I pulled a handful of paper towels off a roll and ran back outside.

Jimmy had pulled his wheelchair back through the entrance of the barn and was quietly sitting in the shadows by the turkey pen.

"Wait," he said. "Don't you want to see what Newfie's going to do?"

"Not especially. If Poxer Spice and the deadettes get through that fence we're going to have trouble.

"Aw," Jimmy whined. "I wanted to see Newfie take 'em out."

"Next time," I said and ran into the barn. The easiest way to get into the pen was through the staircase that Newfie used. I hopped down the old wooden stairs and landed right in the middle of a bunch of llamas munching on a gargantuan pile of hay Aunt Ella had left for them. They looked at me with their big, dumb eyes. I ran out their entrance into the pasture and all the way around the house.

Newfie was up at the front of the fence, barking his head off like crazy. The tiny poxers were pulling at the wire mesh with their chubby little hands. By the time I got half way to them, the wire buckled and popped off one of the fence posts. The dead girls pushed through and trampled into the pasture.

"Newfie, STOP!" I screamed, but he completely ignored me. He jumped on one of them in seconds. She was a little blond thing with a single braid going down her back. He bit her arms more than a few times before taking a good sized chunk out of her cheek. The other poxers grabbed at him as he whirled furiously around, snapping and snarling.

I stopped twenty feet away.

"Hey, ladies," I yelled. "Want a piece of this?" I lit a piece of paper towel and waved it in the air. They came running. When it was almost too late, I threw the flames at the closest one and she lit up like fireworks on the fourth of July.

Another one grabbed at me, and I kicked her over. She went sprawling into a small pile of llama pellets, which was more than a little funny. I dropped another flaming square of paper towel on her then dashed between the two while lighting another piece on fire. Newfie was growling and drooling, but he had backed away from the little monsters.

They stood in a tight group. I supposed torching one was as good as another. I chose a chubby, squat, red headed girl standing in the dead center of the group. Without waiting to watch her light up and pop, I grabbed Newfie's big, red collar and pulled as hard as I could. That's when I discovered that trying to move a hundred and fifty pound dog who didn't want to be moved was about as easy as trying to get Prianka to smile.

I tried a second time, grabbing on to his collar with both hands and heaving with everything I got. He came that time, a little too easily. Maybe he sensed they were going to blow. I don't know. In any case, I got him a safe distance away just in time for the midget zombie to go up in a blaze of glory, pop, and wipe out her partners in crime.

In less than a minute, all that was left were flaming piles of goo burning dirty smudge marks into the pasture. Newfie jumped up on me and thoroughly drenched my face with dog slobber.

"Good boy, Newfie. Good boy," I said as I scratched his massive head. I heard Jimmy whooping and hollering in the distance—my own personal cheering squad. After a few more huge licks, Newfie calmed down and went to sniff at the pools of black tar. A group of four or five llamas also came up and sniffed at what was left of Troop Dead.

My eyes fell on the spot where the poxers had broken through the fence. There was a ten foot stretch between two poles knocked down into a pile of twisted wire.

Jimmy had said that the llamas were a lot of meat on the hoof. I really hoped we would never have to resort to a llama-luau. Still, the last thing we needed was all of them taking a hike on us.

Besides, Aunt Ella would flip a biscuit—if she was still alive.

49

THE SUN WAS sinking fast by the time Jimmy and I finished cobbling the fence back together. He was pretty handy with a hammer and nails, and together, we got the fence looking half way safe—but just barely.

Trina and Prianka put dinner together. I can't say their cooking was anything like Stella's, but at least we had food.

Dinner was peanut butter and honey sandwiches with potato chips and warm juice. Sanjay ate, so that was progress. He gripped his sandwich stiffly in his hands and silently chewed while the rest of us talked. Andrew sat on his shoulder and watched intently as Sanjay repeatedly lifted the sandwich to his mouth, took a bite, and brought it back to the table. When he was almost done, Sanjay stopped and let a little crust of bread sit between his fingers. After a moment, Andrew hopped down and delicately plucked the remaining bits from his hand.

"Bird brain ate his sandwich," I said as I popped a potato chip in my mouth.

"Maybe he wanted him to," said Prianka. "I just wish he'd say something. I've never seen him like this before."

"He'll come around," said Jimmy.

My sister nodded in agreement. Prianka half-smiled, but I could tell she was worried. She stared at her brother with scared, lonely eyes.

AFTER DINNER Prianka and I lit candles while Jimmy and Trina closed all the shades. I went outside and ran up to the top of the driveway and turned around. The house looked dark from the road, which was a good thing. We didn't want to attract any more dead things.

Newfie, who was stretched out in the entrance to the barn, silently watched me climb the porch steps on my way back inside.

"You coming?" I asked. He just watched me with those big, dark eyes and his tongue lolling out of his mouth. "I'm only offering once." Newfie put his head down on his paws and didn't budge. "Your choice," I said as I reached for the knob. I let myself inside and closed and locked the door behind me.

I suppose I was a little more comfortable knowing he was out there.

He could take care of a few poxers. He proved that with the girl scouts.

I found Trina in the kitchen emptying trash from dinner into a big plastic bag.

"What are you doing?"

"Cleaning up. What does it look like I'm doing?"

"I don't know. It's . . . well . . . I don't think I've ever seen you do that before."

She groaned. "Not in the mood, Tripp." She opened up the pantry door and found one bin that said recycling and another that said compost. "Not likely," she muttered and dropped the bag on the floor and pushed the door closed. She stood with her back up against the wall and her arms folded over her chest. "I wish Mom and Dad were here," she said.

I sat down at the kitchen table and reached my hand into the bag of potato chips. My fingers came out covered in grease and salt. I wished my parents were here, too. Doing all this on our own was exhausting. Who knew surviving the apocalypse without adult supervision would be so hard. Besides, I missed them. There was an empty hole inside of me. They had always been there to fill it—and now they weren't.

"I'm sure they just got stuck," I said reassuringly. I didn't know if I really believed what I was saying, but the lame reassurance was what my sister needed to hear. "I mean, seriously. They were up at the lake house. It's all highways from there to here, and you saw what the highways looked like. Mom and Dad are probably crawling their way through the back roads of Vermont to get here."

"Or they got eaten by poxers."

"Well that's just lovely thinking."

Trina plopped herself down next to me and reached into the bag of chips. "I can't help worrying," she said.

"Just think. It took us four days to get here. They're probably finding travel as hard as we did. You can't panic yet."

"I'm not panicking. I'm just worried is all, and I'm really, REALLY, sick of eating potato chips."

Prianka and Sanjay came into the kitchen followed by Jimmy. She was carrying the Ouija board we found earlier that day. "Your idea," she said and tossed the box down on the kitchen table.

Jimmy shook his head and laughed nervously. "I don't like these things," he said. "I was always told not to play around with stuff like that."

"Stuff like what?" asked Trina.

"You know—the occult."

I spit out a mouth full of potato chips and almost choked. "I don't think we can get any more 'occult' than we already are. In case you haven't noticed, we're living in Poxer World, and you have a pet crow. Maybe if we're lucky, we'll even contact the ghost of Edgar Allen Poe."

Jimmy shrugged. "I can't argue with that. Okay. I'm game if you are."

Prianka sat Sanjay next to her. Jimmy pulled his wheelchair up to the table. I opened the box and pulled out the board. It was decorated with the alphabet and numbers one through ten, along with a big 'yes' and a big 'no.' Inside the box was a squat, plastic triangle on tiny supports with little, round, felt bottoms. According to the directions, the triangle was called a planchette. We were all supposed to put the planchette in the middle of the Ouija board, place our fingers lightly around the triangle, and ask questions.

Supposedly, ghosts would spell out the answers for us.

How hokey can you get?

All of us, except Sanjay, balanced the tips of our fingers lightly on the planchette. "Okay," I said to Prianka. "Ask away."

She stared at the board for a moment, lightly running her tongue along her teeth. "Okay, I know," she said, "Is Necropoxy everywhere?"

I knew she was thinking about her parents in India. My throat tightened as I imagined my parents on the other side of the world instead of possibly showing up any moment. What if the situation were reversed and my family was reduced to just me, and Trina was like Sanjay? I would have probably cracked by now.

Not Prianka. Whatever hard, competitive thing was inside of her that made her so freaking annoying was probably helping her cope. I admired her for that.

"Good question," I said and repeated her words to the board. "Is Necropoxy everywhere?"

At first nothing happened.

"This is stupid," whispered Trina. Then she sucked her breath in. The planchette slowly started to glide across the surface of the board.

"Come on, you guys," laughed Jimmy. "Who's moving?"

"Not me," I said because I wasn't. Prianka and Trina said they weren't either. The planchette began to pick up speed. Within seconds, our hands were being dragged around and around the board in a wide circle. Finally, the tip of the triangle landed on the word 'yes' and hovered there for a second before sliding to the word 'no.'

"Well that's specific," I said. "Yes *and* No? What's that supposed to mean?"

"It means he doesn't know," said Prianka, like she thought the Ouija was real.

"Who?" I said. "Who doesn't know?"

She shrugged. "I don't know. Let's ask." She straightened her back and cleared her throat. "Is anybody there?" Again the planchette sat for a moment before slowly coming to life and sliding over to the word 'yes.'

"This is creepy," said Trina and pulled her hands away. We all did. "I don't like this."

"It's just a game," I said. "Come on. There's nothing good on TV."

Jimmy leaned over and gave her a quick peck on the cheek. She smirked.

"Fine," she said. "Whatever."

We all put our hands back on the planchette. The candles flickered as Andrew swept into the room and landed on Sanjay's head. His glazed expression didn't falter.

"Okay. Let's try this again," said Prianka. "Is anybody there?"

When the loud knock assaulted the front door I think we all screamed.

50

"IT'S MOM AND DAD," exclaimed Trina and toppled her chair over as she dashed out of the kitchen and down the hallway to the front door.

"TRINA," yelled Jimmy after her, but she was already gone.

Prianka and I were too stunned to say anything. It all happened so fast. My heart was still pounding because of the stupid Ouija board. Prianka folded herself around her brother.

"Is it your parents?" she whispered.

"I don't know," I gasped. "Newfie's outside. He didn't even bark."

Jimmy wiped sweat from his brow, wheeled his chair around, and went after my sister.

"Damn," I hissed as I got up and went after them, too.

Trina easily got to the door before the rest of us. She turned the lock and swung the heavy wood open on its hinges. The moon was near full, so light spilled into the hallway.

"You!" she exclaimed.

"You!" said an unfamiliar voice.

"Now that's a twist," said Jimmy when he saw who was there.

I stood in the doorway with my sister. Prianka came up behind Jimmy. Her eyes flew open. "No way," she said.

"I . . . I . . ." stammered our visitor.

"Chill," I said. "We're cool—really."

Standing in the doorway was bow and arrow boy. How he found us was a complete mystery. Two days and twenty miles ago we watched him sprint off into the woods with his crotch soaking wet and his pride probably more than a little hurt.

"I . . . I . . ." he babbled again. Then he started to cry—and not just a little bit. His face screwed up into a knot and a flood poured out of him. Trina didn't know what to do at first. Frankly, none of us did. Finally, my sister stepped forward and tentatively put her arms around him. He buried his sobbing face into her shoulder and hugged her fiercely. That's when his legs turned to jelly, and he almost collapsed right there on the porch.

Newfie suddenly appeared, climbing the steps to stand next to him like a furry, rigid support.

"Everyone's gone," he sobbed. "Everyone—everywhere. My mom, my dad, my little sisters, the baby—they're all just gone." Trina turned to look at me, both our faces a mask of confusion. "My dad did it," he cried. "I don't know why. We were all okay except for him. I saw what he did to them—what he did to baby Katie. She didn't . . . she didn't even cry."

Jimmy wheeled forward and put a hand on the boy's shoulder. He was younger than us—maybe twelve or thirteen at most. He had his bow slung over his shoulder, the kind with an attached battery of arrows that serious hunters use to go after deer. He also had a backpack.

After what seemed like a decade, the boy pulled free from my sister and wiped the tears from eyes.

"I didn't run away," he said. "Back when I first met you, I didn't run away. I followed you. You weren't driving that fast, and I had my mom's Vespa scooter hidden in the woods." He dropped his bow from his shoulder. His backpack slipped to the ground. "I saw you get attacked in Greenfield and run into the bookstore. I ended up down the street in a pizza shop."

"You were there the whole time?" Trina gasped.

"I couldn't get out. There were dead people everywhere. I got attacked by a big, fat guy in the pizza place, but I managed to lock him in the freezer. Besides," he said, pointing at Prianka. "She threatened me with a gun."

"You had a bow and arrow pointed at us," she snipped. "What did you expect us to do?"

He looked so helpless and innocent. I could tell as soon as Prianka said what she did, she felt bad. She bit her lip and stared at me like I should take over the conversation.

"How did you find us?" I asked. "We're like miles away from Greenfield."

He wiped his face again. Tears still dribbled down his checks. "Stella sent me," he said.

We were all speechless.

"After you left Greenfield this morning, she hung a sheet out her window that said 'Survivor.' You burned up most of the dead people, so I went into the street and beeped the horn on the scooter. She saw me and let me in."

"No way," said Jimmy.

"Uh huh," said the boy, and he pulled a piece of paper from his pocket. It was a duplicate of the directions that Sanjay had given us right before we left. He held it out like an admission ticket to the movies. Trina didn't take it. Neither did Jimmy. He offered the paper to Prianka and me, too, but we didn't move, either. "She said I could help you."

Help us? What was she thinking? The kid piddled under pressure.

Newfie woofed as if to say, 'I'm outta here.' He turned, trotted down the stairs and back over to his lookout spot in the entrance to the barn.

"Well, I'm not quite sure how you can help us, but any friend of Stella Rathbone's is a friend of ours," said Jimmy. "Come on in. Let's get you something to eat."

"Thanks," said bow and arrow boy. He grabbed his backpack and bow and stepped inside. Trina stuck her head out into the night, did a quick look around, and closed and locked the door behind him. He leaned his backpack up against the wall but was hesitant about dropping his weapon.

"You can leave that here," Prianka said. "I won't shoot."

He gave her a wary glance, so she did her best to smile back at him. She didn't get a smile in response, but at least there weren't any waterworks—from his eyes or any place else that might leak.

"I'm Prianka," she said. "What's your name?"

"Ryan," he mumbled as he tentatively rested the mega-bow next to his backpack. "But no one ever calls me that."

"What do they call you?"

He eyed the bow lovingly. "I started bow hunting with my dad when I was seven," he explained. "Ever since then, everyone just calls me Bullseye."

51

SITTING AROUND THE table in the candlelit kitchen, we got the down and dirty version of what happened to our new guest since last Friday night.

Ryan "Bullseye" McCormick was a sixth grader at Deer Meadow Elementary School. This was supposed to be his last year there. I think he thought we needed to know he was going to be in middle school next year and not a little kid anymore.

No dice, Bro—still an ankle biter.

Anyway, his father was overtaken by Necropoxy at some point during a dinner of Chinese takeout. At first, his mom thought his dad was having some sort of fit and tried to calm him down. He ended up biting her on the arm. His sisters, ages nine and seven, were also bitten in all the confusion.

The baby wasn't so lucky. Neither was Bullseye as he witnessed the worst before grabbing his mother's scooter keys and leaving for help.

Unfortunately, there was no help to be found—only dead people. That first night was the hardest for him. He hid in a tree house that he and his friend, Gunther Davidson, had built over the summer. I gathered he was high off the ground but not very comfy-cozy. He was scared out of his mind and freezing.

The next morning, he did what any red-blooded American kid would do. He went to the Deer Meadow Police Department where Officer McPoxer Pants and Deputy Dead tried to eat him.

I guess that idea bit the dust.

For the rest of that day, he was chased, attacked, cornered, and generally freaked by anything that moved. That second night he holed up in a sporting goods store with another survivor—an old guy named Mr. Choy.

Mr. Choy had the same idea as Ryan for going to the sporting goods store—to get something to defend himself. They hid in the back storage room that night where Mr. Choy proceeded to go bonkers. He kept yelling at Ryan in Korean and calling him Lion instead of Ryan because the guy had a really thick accent and had a hard time with his Rs.

When Ryan woke up the next morning, he found Mr. Choy in the sports equipment section. He had hung himself with a jump rope underneath a basketball hoop. He was stone cold dead, but Bullseye was so freaked that Mr. Choy was going to come back as a zombie, he got up the nerve and shot him in the head with a handgun he found on display in the hunting section near the fishing poles and tackle.

After almost going cuckoo himself, he got it together enough to steal the fancy bow and arrow combo as well as the backpack. He filled the pouch with anything useful he could think of. Useful meant five-hour energy drinks, power bars, the handgun, some ammo, and a set of new hand grips for his new bow.

He was so juiced on energy drinks by the time he ran into us, he didn't know which end was up. To be honest, I give the kid a lot of credit for not having a complete meltdown when Prianka and Trina threatened him with their guns. If wetting himself in front of total strangers was the worst thing that happened to him, he got off easy.

After he piddled a little, he ran off into the woods, and we left, so he followed us into Greenfield to see if maybe he could make nicey-nice.

The rest, well, we knew the rest, except the part about Stella sending him to help us.

"So why did Stella send you?" I said with a confused look on my face.

"My dad was really into the forest," explained Bullseye. "From as far back as I can remember, we went camping and fishing, even hunting. He taught me how to use a bow and arrow, but I guess what's more important to you guys is he taught me all about guns."

Prianka leaned forward. "You know how to shoot?"

He backed into his chair, probably still a little scared of her. "I know how to shoot. I know how to load. I know how to assemble, disassemble, clean, and respect firearms."

"Stella's got our back," laughed Jimmy. "You know, she totally disapproved of us having guns at all."

"I know," said Bullseye. "She lectured me about that, but I think when everything happened with, um, what's his name again?"

"Sanjay," we all said in unison.

"When everything happened with Sanjay, I guess she figured you needed to know how to use them."

"So she sent you?" I said.

Bullseye nodded his head. "Yup. She told me to teach you all how to shoot responsibly."

"I can dig it," said Jimmy. The rest of us agreed. Sanjay stared at a candle, his eyes glazed over in the dim light.

"There's just one problem," said Bullseye.

"What would that be?" I asked.

"I shot three different, um, what do you call them?"

"Poxers," said Trina.

"Poxers—right. I shot three different poxers since I had the handgun—all of them right in the head."

"We've torched dozens," I said. "And . . ."

Ryan looked out the dark window, his face a mask of worry. "The thing is, I shot three of those things right in the head at almost point blank range." His eyes started to well up. "They just got right back up," he sniffed. "They just got right back up."

52

OKAY, SO THE movies had their mythology all wrong. Zombies didn't need their brains to function, or at least poxers didn't. Shooting them in the head didn't do anything. For now, the only thing we knew for sure was that they burned like tissue paper.

Since we lost the kayak back in Greenfield, Trina and Prianka went out to the barn to find a wheelbarrow for Sanjay to sleep under. I put the Ouija board back in the box, mostly because I thought the whole thing was way too freaky for words. Me, Jimmy, Bullseye, and Sanjay went back to the living room where the little guy curled up again on the couch. He folded himself into a tight ball with his face buried into a corner.

Bullseye sat by the fireplace staring at Sanjay.

"My cousin's autistic," he blurted out a little too quickly. His face turned red. "Um, but Stella says Sanjay's really special."

"Yeah, he's been a lifesaver," said Jimmy. "I hope he snaps out of this funk, soon."

Andrew parked himself over Sanjay like a permanent shadow. "Lifesaver," he chirped in an unreal child's voice

Bullseye jumped.

I smiled. "Chill, man. The bird can speak."

"I thought only parrots did that."

"Apparently not," I said. "If Sanjay was in a more talkative mood, I'm sure he'd tell you all about Andrew and what he can do."

Unfortunately, Sanjay wasn't talking, and my stomach was tied in knots. We sat there in the candle light, each lost in our own thoughts. My sister and Prianka came in after a while and set up a relatively clean wheelbarrow upside down on the floor. We pretty much understood that none of us had any intention of sleeping in separate rooms. Everything was too new, too raw. We all felt a lot more comfortable camping out in the living room.

Every once in a while we heard Newfie bark outside. Sometimes he was near the house, and sometimes he was way off near the tree line. I imagined Sprinkles patrolling the fence and couldn't help but chuckle to myself. The chuckle, however, caught in my throat.

Sprinkles was gone.

Everyone was gone.

Jimmy lowered himself to the floor and leaned back against the couch. Trina snuggled into him, and he put his arms around her. Prianka sat on the couch by her brother. I joined Bullseye by the fireplace.

"I've been thinking," Jimmy said. "I don't get why they burn so easily."

"Who knows," I sighed. "Just be thankful they do. My mind's still blown that a bullet to the noggin doesn't do squat."

Bullseye nodded his head. "I know—and I'm a good shot."

"That doesn't mean we can't hurt them," whispered Prianka. She sat in the gloom, not looking at anyone or anything.

"What do you mean?" I asked.

Her voice was like frost in the air. "They're still flesh and blood or whatever that black gunk is. We can still shoot one in the leg or shoot their eyes out." Her words sounded so cold and matter-of-fact, she gave me the chills.

"Okay—scary," I muttered and wrapped my arms around my knees.

"No, seriously," she said. "Just because we can't kill them without a match doesn't mean we can't cripple them. I don't know about the rest of you, but I don't think of them as people anymore." She looked right at me. "It's either us or them, and I choose us."

"I second that," said Trina as she leaned further into her Jimmy pillow. Seeing my sister so comfortable with Jimmy made me wonder if Prianka wanted me to be like that. Did she want me to put my arms around her or make her feel safe? True, I didn't have the pythons that Jimmy had, but I was still a dude and all indications were that Prianka sort of liked me. Or she did until I let Poopy Puppy get torn apart. I'm sure she blamed me. Maybe if I put my arms around Prianka Patel, I would very quickly be in a world of pain.

Still I wondered. Did I even want to be next to her on the couch? I think I did, but I wasn't sure. I have to admit, that kiss back at Stella's was like nothing I had ever experienced before.

The wind blew outside, and Newfie barked again in the distance. I rocked back and forth, lost in my own confused thoughts. After another long bout of silence, Bullseye said he was cold. I was, too, so we took a flashlight and went scavenging upstairs for blankets and pillows. We took everything we found and brought them back to the living room, spread blankets out on the floor, and divvied up the pillows.

"You want help setting up Sanjay underneath the wheelbarrow?" I asked Prianka.

She stared at me, probably just as confused about us as I was. "That would be nice," she said. Together we fashioned a little sleeping area for him. Prianka gently guided her brother inside and lowered the upturned dome over him. She just sat there, her hands resting on the scratched, plastic top, her eyes shut.

I looked at Jimmy and Trina. My sister was staring intently at one of the candles. Jimmy was watching me. He nodded his head and half-smiled encouragingly.

Bullseye had curled up with a blanket and pillow and was already asleep.

Almost before I knew it, I gently put my hand on Prianka's shoulder. She didn't flinch, which was a good thing. She sat there for a moment longer before slowly rising to her feet. My breath caught in my throat when she took my hand and entwined my fingers in hers. Together, we slipped out of the living room to the hallway.

We didn't say anything. We were both comfortable in our silence. I backed against the wall and pulled Prianka to me. I thought we were going to kiss again, but instead, her head found my shoulder. My arms wrapped around her, and the sweet fragrance of her hair wafted into my nostrils.

"I'm sorry about Sanjay," I whispered. "I wish I could have protected him more. I wish I could have saved Poopy Puppy." The words sounded funny coming out of my mouth, but Poopy Puppy was practically one of us, and I didn't save him. I couldn't save him.

"It wasn't your fault," she sniffed. "None of this is. This is all some mad scientist's idea of a bad joke to create Necropoxy in the first place. That's all."

"But I could have done more," I said.

"You've done everything," she whispered and crushed up against me. I stood there for a long time, relishing the warmth of her. Suddenly it hit me. I did want to protect her. I did want to engulf her and keep her safe. I even wanted to listen to her insult me or just be plain, old Prianka, because there was something about her that just felt good and right and real.

As if she sensed what I was thinking, she tilted her head up and looked at me in the dim light.

We kissed—even better than the first time.

In that moment, I felt safe and protected, too. Maybe this is what Trina and Jimmy felt. Who knows? The feeling was great amidst a world in chaos.

I didn't want to ever let her go.

53

WE ALL SLEPT well that night. None of us got up to blow the candles out before we finally fell asleep. They just dwindled down to nothing. Once, during the middle of the night, I woke up and listened to the quiet of the house—so strange without the clicking of a clock or the quiet hum of a refrigerator.

I fell back to sleep thinking about Prianka. When I woke up the next morning I quietly disentangled myself from the spider web of blankets and pillows and tip-toed off to the bathroom to stick a finger full of toothpaste in my mouth.

If I got the chance for another kiss, I wanted to be minty fresh.

Andrew followed me into the bathroom. I jumped when he flew through the doorway and landed on the toilet.

"What do you want, seed head?"

He just stared at me before hopping up on the counter and tapping the faucet with his beak.

"Sorry. It doesn't work." He continued to eyeball me with those creepy black orbs. "Fine—come on." We both must have been in a good mood, because I stuck my hand out, and Andrew tentatively hopped onboard. I padded out of the bathroom and down the hallway to the kitchen.

While Jimmy and I mended the fence yesterday, the girls had unpacked all the food from the car and set our bounty on the counter. We had some jugs of bottled water, so I rummaged around the cabinets until I found an empty jar with a screw-top lid. I unscrewed the cap, set it down on the kitchen table, and poured Andrew a capful of water.

He was more than grateful. I poured a little for myself, too, swished around to rinse my mouth out, and was about to spit into the sink when I realized there was no tap water to wash my morning spittle down the drain. I rolled my eyes and walked quietly down the hallway to the front door and turned the lock.

I squinted as I swung the door open and light poured in, so I put my hands over my eyes as I stepped out on the porch to spit over the railing.

It was cold, like October cold. I could see my breath as my eyes adjusted to the morning light. Newfie was sleeping on his side in the entrance to the barn, his big, black coat heaving up and down. I saw him shake his paws a little like he was chasing a dream poxer.

"You get him, boy." I said. "You tear him to pieces."

The llamas were already grazing in the pasture. The turkeys weren't awake yet, or I think I would have heard them. How long would we last before we singled out one of them for dinner? More importantly, which one of us was going to do the deed? Killing a poxer was one thing, but ending something that was living? That somehow seemed wrong.

There was something interesting and philosophical about that thought, but I wasn't feeling either interesting or philosophical at the moment. I was pretty much just feeling cold.

I went back inside and closed the door behind me. The house was dark and gloomy with all the shades drawn. The thing was, I was sick of the darkness and the things that hid in the shadows. I went around the house, starting on the second floor, and pulled the shades up everywhere. Back down in the living room, I lifted the shades there, too, and in minutes everyone was awake.

Trina yawned and stretched. She had spent the night wrapped in Jimmy's arms, and he was reluctant to let her go.

"What time is it?" she croaked.

"Does it matter?"

"Yeah," she said. "I'll miss World History. Oh, crap, I forgot. There is no more world. History's dead."

"I'm cold," shivered Bullseye.

"Yeah, I'm pretty chilly, too," agreed Jimmy. He propped himself up on his shoulders and reached for Trina. "Hey, I need your body warmth."

"And I need some food that's not potato chips," she said as she got to her feet.

Prianka lay on the couch, her hands cradling her head. She stared at me with dark eyes that spoke volumes about how last night never happened and if I said anything to anyone she'd staple my tongue to the roof of my mouth.

That's how I read it at least.

I threw her a sideways smile, which was one of my cuter looks, if I do say so myself, and motioned my head toward the upturned wheelbarrow. She nodded and got up. Together we lifted it to get at Sanjay.

He wasn't there.

"Where's Sanjay?" Prianka gasped.

"Not far, I'm sure." I knew yesterday was a long day, and we were all zonked when we crashed, but I'd like to think we weren't that far gone to let him slip away without someone noticing.

Prianka stormed out of the living room and started canvasing the first floor. I knew he wasn't on the second floor, because I had just come from there. I could feel a rush of adrenaline wash through my body. I guess there's nothing like a kid disappearing to get the blood pumping first thing in the morning.

Jimmy pulled himself into his chair. "Amber alert," he yawned.

"Got him," I heard Prianka yell from the back of the house.

We filed down the hallway to a room that my aunt and uncle called the library. They had an old computer on an even older desk. There were piles of papers and magazines everywhere, and the walls were lines with books that Aunt Ella probably scavenged from Salvation Army or Goodwill. She always told me that a good book could never go bad. Without TV and the Internet to distract me, I bet we were all going to have a chance to test that theory.

Sanjay was sitting in the middle of the floor with Andrew, who once again eyed me warily, which meant he had already forgotten our little bonding experience. Sanjay was surrounded by books and was once again methodically flipping through them, page after page.

"What is all this?" demanded Prianka as she looked from my face to Trina's and back to me.

"What is all what?" I stooped and picked up one of the books. Immediately that creepy creepy feeling washed over me. I dropped the book and picked up another. Not good. Not good at all. I looked at Trina with that 'help me out' expression on my face.

"Let me see," she said and grabbed the book I was holding out of my hands. She read the cover out loud. "Summoning Spirits," she said.

I handed her another title.

"The Black Arts," she read. A third one was called, 'The Complete Tarot.'

Prianka gently pulled the book Sanjay was flipping through out of his hands. Like a robot, he reached out and hooked on another one, placed it in his lap, and started leafing through the pages. She turned the book over and read the spine.

"Oh, that's just great," she said. "1001 Spells and Formulas."

Jimmy burst out laughing. "I'm, I'm sorry," he said, but the giggles just spilled out of him. They were infectious. I tried really hard not to catch them, but it wasn't easy. Trina's shoulders started to shake up and down, then a raspberry of guffaws burst between her lips.

I looked up at Prianka. "Hey, reading's fundamental, right?"

She shook her head and turned away from all of us.

"Prianka, come on," said Trina between another bout of the sillies. "We told you our aunt and uncle were a little different."

"A little different?" she snapped, her voice beginning to rise. "A LITTLE DIFFERENT? What is this place, Hogwarts?"

That's all she had to say. We all burst out laughing, even Bullseye. Andrew cackled and crowed. Finally, whatever made us all laugh, caught up with Prianka. She tried to contain the smile that was forcing her mouth into a curve, but she couldn't. She snorted, and all of us, including Prianka, laughed so hard we almost cried.

All the while, mute or not, Sanjay was absorbing every book and every detail like a sponge.

54

THE DATE WAS Tuesday, September twenty-first. If Uncle Don's watch was right, the time was just around 7 a.m. Counting backwards to 7 p.m. last Friday night, which was close enough to when this nightmare started, we had been in the land of the dead for just about eighty-four hours.

A lot could happen in eighty-four hours. You could hook up with your arch nemesis. Your sister could get tight with a paraplegic on steroids. Fire could become one of the most important tools in your tool box. You could kill a whole lot of zombies—AND—you could be traveling with a crow with an attitude.

But I was more interested in now than the past. The only decent meals we had eaten in the last eighty-four hours had been at Stella's, and our own stockpile of readily edible food was looking pretty grim. When we were back at North Amherst Sundries, we had been all about the potato chips, chocolate, peanut butter and jelly, bread and water. Trina had grabbed a bunch of junk food from home when we first left, but our original stash only amounted to a couple six packs of cola, cookies, and a bag of apples.

Everything downstairs in Aunt Ella's larder had to be cooked. Unless we were going to go all *Little House on the Prairie* and make breakfast in the fireplace in the living room, we were stuck with peanut butter sandwiches.

Again.

"Or we can use that," Jimmy said and pointed to the deck off the kitchen. There was a gas grill sitting there, a little rusty, attached to a propane tank.

"Um, I don't cook," said Trina. She had already made a conscious choice to eat a bar of chocolate smeared with peanut butter.

"You're going to get zits," I said as I eyed her breakfast.

"I already got you," she smiled as chocolate oozed through her teeth.

"We have a grill . . . um . . . we had a grill at home," said Prianka. "How about I boil some water, and we can at least have coffee."

We all raised our hands in a silent vote of yes. Prianka busied herself with filling a pot with water, turning on the grill, and searching my aunt's cabinets for coffee.

In less than twenty minutes, we were all drinking fresh ground mocha java because that's the only flavor Aunt Ella had. I guess we didn't care that Sanjay and Bullseye were riding the caffeine train right along with us. Maybe a little bit of the jitters was just what Sanjay needed to rattle him out of his funk.

Prianka also toasted some bread for us right on the grill and sprinkled sugar and cinnamon on top. Trina ate two pieces. With the whole world sliding toward the grave, she was coping by binging. If she didn't learn to cope without chowing down, Jimmy was going to be labeled a chubby chaser.

I helped Prianka clean up because I guess that's what I was supposed to do. Everyone else had gone outside. I held a plastic bag as she threw away the remains of breakfast. At one point, I purposely brushed her hand with mine. She stopped and looked at me with that stare that I couldn't quite figure out. Was I going to get whipped with her 'oh so rapier wit,' or was I going to get a little action.

"Don't," she said. "Everyone will see."

"For real?" I gasped. "In case you haven't noticed, everyone's dead."

"You know what I mean."

"No, actually I don't know what you mean."

"Maybe I don't know what I mean."

"Maybe I'm just too sexy for you."

"No. I'm sure that's not it."

"Nice." I said. "Peachy." I stood there with the trash in my hands. Prianka tilted her head sideways and inspected me like I was something she was thinking about buying. "You want me to turn around?"

"What?"

"Never mind. You know what?" I dropped the bag at our feet and grabbed her hands and pulled her to me. "Just shut up and let everyone see."

I kissed her.

No wonder there was a bounce to my step as we joined everyone outside.

TARGET PRACTICE was first on the agenda. We set up apple crates at the end of the driveway and perched empty soda cans on them. Bullseye laid out all our guns on the porch and methodically inspected each one, exactly how his father had taught him.

He looked at our ammunition and matched bullets to guns as though he was a little kid playing that game where you try and fit the right shape into the right hole before the buzzer goes off.

"We're going to need more ammunition," he said when he was finally done. He stood with his hands on his hips, standing over the guns we had taken from Jimmy's landlord. "My father used to stock up at a place somewhere up here. I think maybe in Purgatory Chasm, but I'm not sure."

"Purgatory Chasm?" said Prianka with a weird look on her face. "Seriously? There's a place called Purgatory Chasm?"

I looked at my sister. "Big headed people," I whispered, and we shared a secret smile.

"There's always Greenfield," said Jimmy.

Trina snorted. "Not on a bet."

"No gun shop, anyway," said Bullseye. "Not in Greenfield."

"Yeah," said Jimmy. "Probably not hick enough."

I laughed. "But Purgatory Chasm sounds just hick enough, right?" The name fit right in with Bellows Falls, Darkmeadow, and Satan's Kingdom, all of which were other towns off the Trail.

What were our forefathers thinking? Names didn't scare off people. Poxers scared off people.

Prianka watched intently as Bullseye showed us how to load the rifles, shoulder the butts of the guns, aim, and shoot. His first shot knocked one of the cans right off an apple crate. It spun in the air and landed next to a dying clump of grass surrounded by autumn leaves.

"Sweet," I whistled.

"Can I try?" Prianka asked. Bullseye handed her the rifle and went over all the pointers again. She shouldered the gun and closed one eye as she took aim. She fired, but nothing happened, which meant that the bullet either ended up in the dirt or lodged in a tree somewhere across the street.

"One more try," she said. This time, she hit one of the apple crates but not the can. That was still pretty awesome, and we all clapped. Newfie, who had come up on the porch to join us, watched her with a bored look on his face. As far as guns were concerned, I bet this wasn't his first rodeo. Maybe Aunt Ella had a couple stashed upstairs somewhere. I made a mental note to look under her mattress.

All of us took turns. Jimmy chose the handgun that Bullseye had taken from the sporting goods store. Somehow, I felt funny using it, because of Mr. Choy and what had happened, but Jimmy took to shooting like he was born with a gun in his hand.

"Lots and lots of video games," he explained. "Lots and lots and lots of video games."

Out of everyone, I was the least good at the whole gun thing. I mean, I understood how to use one, and I made a pretty good attempt at one of the cans, but I wasn't naturally comfortable with firearms. If I had to, I could be okay with one. Still, I definitely needed loads of practice. We didn't have the bullets for that.

Trina was a born natural, just like Jimmy. She tried both the handgun and one of the rifles that Bullseye said was mint. Before too long, she was hitting cans with ease.

While the girls were taking turns shooting, I sat down on the front steps with Newfie on one side of me and Bullseye and Sanjay on the other. Bullseye had taken a shine to Sanjay just like the animals had. Even mute, Sanjay was something special. I felt it in the pit of my stomach. I'm sure Bullseye did, too, He softly stroked Andrew's back while the crow sat on Sanjay's shoulder and quietly talked to both of them about everything—his family, his sisters, his parents, his school. I was pretty grateful, actually. He fit in naturally with the rest of us, just like a new little brother. He was a great addition to our family—if that's what we were becoming.

Jimmy wheeled up to me and spun around so he was facing the girls.

"You have something you want to tell me?" he said, leaning forward in his chair, his hands folded together.

"No."

"Okay. You have something, but you don't want to tell me?"

"That sounds good," I said. "Let's go with that."

He smiled and popped his chair back so the front wheels were dangling off the ground. "It's all copasetic," he said.

"Copa what?" I had no idea what he meant. For the first time that day, I thought about what happened when we left Stella's place. Poopy Puppy would have known what copasetic meant. He was smart, after all. Poopy Puppy was really, really smart.

"It's cool," he said. "Five by five."

I shrugged. "Listen, it's no big deal. I guess we're sort of working things out."

"Hey, man. I don't need to know."

"Obviously you do. You asked."

"Just looking out for you, Bro."

"I'm fine—really—everything's copa-cabana, or whatever you just said."

We both watched the girls. Really, Jimmy? Just looking out for me? Who was looking out for Trina? After all, who was this Jimmy James character, anyway? A few days ago he didn't even exist to me. So what if we saved him? Now, he's just some poser in a wheelchair, hell bent on feeling up my sister any chance he gets. True—Trina wasn't complaining, but still, the Light twins watch out for each other.

I leaned forward so I was right alongside his auburn-stubbled face. "If you hurt my sister in any way," I whispered, "I'll drive you down the Trail and drop you by the highway in Greenfield."

Jimmy turned and stared at me—his eyes wide and his mouth opened. He was genuinely speechless. Hey, that's the way we roll in the Light household.

Prianka shot a hole right into a can. I whistled and clapped.

"Good one," I yelled. "That's the way it's done."

After a moment, Jimmy began to clap, too. That's how we left things—one big, fat, happy, clapping family.

55

"BULLSEYE HAS to come," I said. "Not only does he know what bullets we need, he knows how to get to Purgatory Chasm."

"So why do you have to go?" said Prianka.

"I'm driving."

"I know how to drive."

"You have Sanjay." That made her stop arguing.

My sister was sitting on Jimmy's lap again with her arms around his neck. "I'm going, too," she said.

He almost dropped her. "No, you're not."

"Yes I am."

"But . . ."

"But what?" she said. "But-freaking-what?"

I looked at Jimmy, shrugged, and shook my head.

"She can take you," I said. "Muscle head or no, is this the hill you want to die on?" I loved that saying. My mother used to say the same thing whenever I was being pigheaded.

"Fine," he pouted and crossed his arms over his chest. "See if there's an organic place in town. I want something healthy to eat."

"Aye, aye," said Trina and saluted him. I could tell she really did like Jimmy. He wasn't a Chuck Peterson. Jimmy James was the closest thing she had ever come to the real deal. I was happy for her.

We made a short list of things we needed and hoped to find in Purgatory Chasm, including propane tanks. Prianki promised if we could find them, she wouldn't mind making some hot meals on the grill.

Jimmy kissed Trina goodbye in a way-too-gross public display of affection. I was a little more discreet and pulled Prianka into the bathroom for a couple minutes. I didn't know who I thought I was hiding from.

"They know, you know," I told her as I ran my hand through her hair.

"I know," she said. "Trina asked."

"So did Jimmy."

"What did you tell him?"

"I told him if he hurt my sister I would drive him down to the bottom of the Trail and leave him there."

Prianka laughed.

"Trina told me if I messed with your head she'd shave mine while I was sleeping."

"Hey. Us Lights stick together."

Prianka gave me one last kiss. "Please, please, please be careful." She said. "There are poxers everywhere."

"I know. I know. We have Bullseye, and we have lots of fire. Don't worry about us. Purgatory Chasm can't be more than ten minutes up the road. Besides, we're in Hicksville. I'm sure that we can handle whatever poxers we come across."

"Don't burn down the whole town while you're at it," she said. "Who knows what kind of supplies we'll need from there in the future." Back in the kitchen Prianka said, "You know, I'm way happier with the thought of you guys going to the boonies instead of back down to Greenfield. Too many dead things there."

I agreed. "Let's just hope there are a lot less dead things where we're going."

Sanjay sat at the kitchen table with Andrew. He watched the llamas out in the pasture with that vacant Poopy-Puppy-less expression. More than anything, I wished I could get that stupid, dirty toy back for him and for Prianka, too. I just wished I could fix everything.

Ten minutes later, Prianka and Jimmy stood on the porch with Newfie as we backed Stella's minivan out of the driveway. I felt a little weird about splitting up, but the last thing we needed right now was to put all of us in danger. We had guns, and we had a short agenda. There's no way we wouldn't be back in a few hours.

Funny how things never work out the way you plan.

56

THE POXERS WERE definitely getting mangy. Four days with no shower can make anyone rank, but open sores, bite marks, gangrene, and who knows what else were really making them look pretty gross.

Geez—take a sponge bath or something.

We passed several poxers along the road by the orchards on our way back to the Trail. Their hair was matted and tangled. Their clothes were bloodied and torn.

"Hey—slow down," said Bullseye as we came up along a lady in her underwear, staggering along the side of the road. "I want you guys to see what happens when they get shot."

"That's just wrong," said Trina.

I wrinkled my nose. "Shooting one or the fact that she's only in her underwear? What's the deal with that, anyway?"

Bullseye rolled down his window and stuck a rifle out. The poxer lady turned and gurgled at us. There was something stringy between her teeth. I really didn't want to know what her last meal had been. She made a lame attempt to lunge at the minivan. Bullseye waited until she was close—maybe a little too close. Then he shot her in the head.

I wasn't ready to see gray matter explode everywhere. Thankfully, her head didn't bust open. Instead, she stood there dazed for a few seconds before dropping to her knees and falling backwards like she was about to do the Limbo.

"Now watch," said Bullseye. "This is the freaky part."

The poxer lay there for a moment, twitching, before slowly pushing herself back up with her palms flat against the gritty tar. She crawled to her knees and eventually got back up on her feet. The bullet hole was clean, but black goo oozed down her face and landed on her open tongue. She smacked her lips and swallowed the grossness back down.

She growled again, a little more menacingly than the first time, and reached her arms out toward us.

"See—a head shot's no good. But like Prianka said, if you shoot one in the leg, you can stop them in their tracks." Bullseye pointed the barrel of the gun at her knee and pulled the trigger. The whole side of her leg splattered onto the side of the road, and she went down like a ton of bricks—and that was one ton of bricks that was never going to get up again.

"Seen enough," I said. "Thanks for the freak show." I sped up and left Bullet Hole Betty in the dust.

"Weird, huh?" said Bullseye and leaned back in his seat. He was definitely too young for all this. Yeah, sure, they were dead and all, but he just shot a woman in the head and the leg, and Trina and I sat there and watched. I might as well have had a box of buttered popcorn with me.

I could feel waves of tension starting to wash over me. My hands gripped the wheel just a little too tightly, and Trina started biting her nails.

"I hate this," she said.

"We all hate this."

We came around a curve and down a small dip in the road. Before long, we were where the tractor trailer was laying like a dead dinosaur across our path. I took the same route—around—over the lawn—and out to the Trail. I totally ignored the poxers that were still milling around the parking lot across the street.

"How far from here?" I asked.

"Not far," said Bullseye. "I'm sure I'll know the turn when I see it."

We drove with the windows open. The air wasn't quite nippy, but it was definitely crisp and cool in that way that made you think of hay rides and apple cider.

Just like before, there weren't many cars on the Trail. Anyone heading north would have stuck to the highway on a Friday night. Occasionally, we passed a wreck on the road or a poxer or two, but for the most part we were climbing a lonely mountain up to Purgatory Chasm.

Before long, Bullseye started prepping us.

"It's going to be soon," he said. "I recognize that gift shop," he said. "See the fake, plastic buffalo. I remember my dad taking a picture of me sitting on its back," he said.

I'm still not quite clear why there was a fake, plastic buffalo anywhere in Massachusetts, but I guess the thing probably meant something to someone.

Coming up on our left we saw a big sign with two double hearts that said 'Welcome to the Romance Rendezvous' with an arrow pointing down.

"There," cried Bullseye. "Purgatory Chasm's down there." He pointed his arm out the window and past where a big, white restaurant stood called the Romance Rendezvous.

Trina snorted. "Nice place to take Prianka."

"Oh—you are so not going there."

"Going where?"

"Just don't start, okay. I'm wigging out enough without any crap from you."

"It would have been nice if you had told me."

"I didn't think I had to."

"What are you guys talking about?" asked Bullseye.

"Nothing," we both said in unison.

With Bullseye still in the dark, I palmed the wheel to the left, and we headed past the restaurant and down a steep hill toward the center of Purgatory Chasm, Massachusetts.

57

THE FIRST WORDS out of Trina's mouth were, "Where are all the poxers?"

She was right. We were in a small town, slowly driving down a gentle hill with sidewalks on both sides of the road and big, old homes painted all sorts of funky colors. They looked half way between amusement park rides and haunted houses.

Half way down the hill, the road curved to the left and opened up into a town center. Purgatory Chasm was nothing to write home about. There was really nothing there accept two blocks of stores on both sides of the street. There was also a bank and a restaurant advertising a blue plate special of meatloaf and fries along with something called an Awful-Awful, featuring a picture of a milk shake.

"What's a blue plate special?" asked Bullseye.

"You really want to know?" I asked. "They tell you right there it's awful, awful."

Trina lowered her window and let the fall air rush in. "Really, where are all the poxers?"

There were definitely pile-ups in town. One, which looked like two pickups had a monster mash-up, was particularly nasty. As far as people, though—dead, poxified, or otherwise, there was nobody.

I pulled in front of the bank and parked Stella's minivan.

"What are you doing," Trina blurted out.

"Getting bullets and supplies," I said. "That's the plan, right?"

"But aren't you creeped out?"

"I'm creeped out," offered Bullseye from the backseat. "Not that I want to be attacked by poxers or anything, but no poxers is creepier than some poxers, right?"

Trina nodded her head. "That's what I'm talking about. Unless everyone in town is at some spooky intervention for the dead, this isn't right."

Stupid me, I was counting ourselves lucky. Quick in and quick out—isn't that what we wanted to accomplish here? Okay, I guess it was a little odd that there were no poxers around, but we were in the middle of

the hill towns, population like three. How many people did she expect there
to be?

"Maybe when everything happened, everyone was down in Greenfield
for Fall Fest," I offered. "This place doesn't look like a thriving metropolis
to begin with."

Trina and Bullseye weren't convinced.

Those little waves of tension began to lap at my feet like I was standing
on the edge of an incredibly large and scary lake—safe, as long as I didn't so
much as stick my pinky toe in the water.

"Okay, um, what are we doing here?" I asked them both.

Trina stared straight ahead like she was mentally trying to figure out
why things were so deadsville in Deadsville. Bullseye waited for her to say
something. When he finally realized she wasn't going to, he pointed across
the street and down a little bit. "There's the gun shop," he said. "Shouldn't
we go there?"

"I'm telling you, there's something's wrong," she said but shrugged
and opened the minivan door, so I took that as my cue to follow. I had a
lighter and an old magazine with me. Trina had matches and some
computer paper. Bullseye deliberated for a moment before leaving his rifle
in the car in favor of the small handgun he had taken after his encounter
with Mr. Choy. He shoved the barrel down the front of his pants, untucked
his shirt, and draped the cloth over the butt of the gun.

"Very gangsta," I said. He beamed. "Who you hiding it from? There's
nobody here."

"But there was," gulped Trina as she took a few steps and pointed
down the sidewalk in front of us.

There were black, tarlike puddles everywhere. I don't know why we
didn't notice them when we first drove into town, but now, outside of the
van, they seemed to dot the sidewalks and the street.

"Someone was here before us." I said, stating the obvious. I scanned
the center of town. There wasn't movement anywhere, but you could tell
that there had been dozens and dozens of people who had been getting
their last bit of Friday night shopping in when the tatti hit the fan.

Greasy, oily slicks reflected the early afternoon sunlight. There were
splatters on a few of the cars and even on some of the storefront windows
and doors.

"Good," snorted Trina. "One less thing to worry about." She started
across the street toward the Purgatory Chasm Gun Shoppe. Shoppe was
spelled in that funny way that's supposed to make the store sound quaint.

Sure, guns could be quaint—if you lived in bizzaro-world.

Bullseye and I followed her.

"She's kind of scary, isn't she?" he whispered to me when she was about ten feet in front of us.

"I can hear you," she yelled over her shoulder, and I was fairly certain Bullseye would have peed in his pants again if I wasn't there.

"She has her moments," I said.

THE GUN SHOPPE was sandwiched in between a handmade country furniture store and a realtor's office. You could buy a place, decorate it, and shoot yourself a turkey dinner, all in one fell swoop.

Trina stomped up a couple cement stairs and reached for the gun shoppe's doorknob.

"Careful," I cautioned her. "Remember what Jimmy said? Just because there aren't any poxers out here doesn't mean there aren't any inside that are too stupid to figure out how to use the door."

Trina hesitated for a moment, took out her lighter, sucked in a deep breath, and turned the knob.

"Anybody home?" she screamed into the dimly lit store. If we learned nothing else in the past few days, it was to always announce ourselves when going into a building. The poxers weren't big on hiding and pouncing. If you rang the dinner bell, they came running.

Nothing was inside—and I mean nothing.

Not only was Purgatory Chasm Gun Shoppe poxer free, the store had been completely and totally ransacked.

That's when we heard gun shots off in the distance.

58

"PEOPLE," EXCLAIMED Bullseye. "There're people." He started to dash down the steps toward the sound of the gunfire. Both Trina and I grabbed the back of his shirt, hauled him inside the gun shoppe, and closed the door.

"Yeah," I said. "Real live people who shoot real live bullets and torch up real dead towns to the last poxer."

"But . . ." he wailed and really started crying. "I just want to see people," he sniffed. "I . . . I just want everything to be back the way it was. Why can't things just be like that?" He started hitting himself in the head with his fist. "Why can't I wake up? Why can't I be sitting with Mom and Dad and my sisters and the baby, eating Chinese food?"

Everyone's entitled to a meltdown. It's too bad they always came at exactly the wrong time.

Trina pulled him close, and we receded into the gun shop. Bullseye calmed down to a slow sniffle. We crouched behind a glass counter with a wooden lower half so we could peer through the glass to the window and beyond, but no one could see us.

The place had been radically picked over. There were still some guns left and some ammo, but it looked like a tornado had torn through the store, taken the choicest and most deadly weapons available, and whisked them all away.

We heard gun shots again, this time a little closer. The rapid rat-a-tat-tat-tat-tat-tat-tat-tat made me think I was hearing a machine gun. The only time I had ever heard one for real was in one of my video games or in a movie.

Who am I kidding? Those weren't even real.

"Is that a machine gun?" whispered Trina. Her arms were folded around Bullseye, and his head was buried into her shoulder.

My face said yes. Who would be firing a machine gun out here, and at what?

For some reason, all I could think of was Prianka back at my aunt's house. Here I was, cowering behind a gun counter in east cupcake, middle-of-nowhere. She was probably figuring out the exact best way to bake bread on a gas grill.

I missed her.

The gun shots became louder and louder, and along with them, we heard a car.

The last time we ran into another living being with a gun was in Amherst. That weirdo told us he was going to pick out the perfect spot in Maine to kill himself. Who knew what kind of lunatic was behind the trigger this time? Was it some crazed, scary, backwoods freak shooting at anything that moved—dead or alive? Maybe the shooter was just another kid like us. Either way, I wasn't taking any chances. As we heard the car come closer, I put a finger to my lips and made sure that both Trina and Bullseye understood.

The car motor stopped, and we heard voices. They were loud and clear like they were right out in front of the store.

" . . . said we can't take any chances," said a guy.

"What does she know, anyway?" said another. "Just because she's the big cheese, it don't mean diddly."

"Yeah, you say that to her face. I dare ya."

"I ain't stupid."

"No, just ig-nint."

The voices had a southern accent. Whoever they were, they were seriously from not around here. Bullseye clutched Trina even tighter and squeezed his eyes shut.

"I didn't sign up for this, ya know. Y'all think she's all that, but I ain't seen nothing special."

"Well she do look mighty fine in a suit—for a Grammy."

"You know what else looks mighty fine? A lady praying mantis—until she has her way with her beau before eating its head."

Both voices laughed. The laughter got closer and closer as though whomever they belonged to was right in front of the gun shoppe.

Then they abruptly stopped.

"Where did that come from?" said one voice.

I had a sinking suspicion I knew what they were talking about.

"Dang," said the other voice. "Ain't no way that was there before. We parked right there when we did our first round of burning. Ain't no van here then. Ain't, fo sure."

Bullseye twisted around in Trina's arms. He looked scared out of his mind.

The voices trailed off into the distance. No doubt they were going to check out Stella's minivan. I made a mental picture and tried to recall if there was anything we left inside that could lead them either back to my aunt's house or to Stella. The last thing I wanted was to turn the trigger happy twosome loose on the farm or the quiet tranquility of the Wordsmith Used Book Emporium and Stella Rathbone.

"Stay here," I whispered. "I just want to see who they are."

Trina nodded. Bullseye just looked freaked.

I crawled on my hand and knees to the front of the store and lifted my head cautiously over the window sill. There was a jeep parked in front of the shoppe—green—like the one that came with my toy soldiers when I was little.

Off in the distance, inspecting Stella's minivan, were two older guys, well older than us, anyway. They were both jarheads and both wearing fatigues.

Army. They were Army.

59

"I DON'T CARE WHO they are," hissed Trina as we crouched by the window. Bullseye stayed huddled behind the counter while we watched the two soldiers methodically rip through Stella's minivan. "I don't trust them."

"Why? They're just surviving like we are?"

"No. They were talking about someone else. Someone they reported to."

"Maybe a group of them survived. I don't know."

"They said she was scary."

"All adults are scary."

Trina glared at me and rudely pinched my arm like she used to do when we were in fifth grade. "Jimmy's an adult. He's not scary," she said

"Don't get me started, and, OW, that hurt."

The soldiers stood by Stella's minivan, scratching their heads. One of them was holding a big gun, bigger than anything that the Purgatory Chasm Gun Shoppe would have ever carried. The barrel looked like it could pack a serious punch. Maybe that's what was responsible for the rapid fire that we heard.

The soldiers seemed to be in a serious conversation. Then they pointed right at us and headed back across the street.

Trina and I scrambled behind the counter. Bullseye's face was as white as a sheet. Whatever prepubescent freckles he had looked more like chicken pox or measles.

"Chill," I said. "Just be absolutely quiet."

The soldiers' voices became more distinct, and soon we could make out what they were saying.

"Now that's what I'm talking about," said one of them. "Good ole country fried steak and biscuits—none of this meatloaf and french fries crap. Tell me again why the North won the war?"

The other one laughed.

"Seriously, though. Diana said to bring back survivors. I ain't leaving until we find who be driving that van."

"What if they make a fuss like last time?"

I didn't hear the answer. I could only imagine that one of them was drawing a line across his neck with his finger. The tension waves lapped at my feet again, but before I could even shudder, the unexpected happened. The door opened and the two men stepped inside the gun shoppe.

"Cal, aren't we done in here?"

"I just wanna take another looksee. Don't want to miss anything."

"Diana's going to be happy with all the guns and the ammo," said Cal.

"She'd be happier with survivors. Don't know what she's planning."

"Luke, my friend. It ain't our job to ask. For all I know she's dissecting each and every one of them to see why they don't get sick like everyone else. Just be thankful she hasn't turned on us."

Bullseye's lips buttoned together so tightly that I could see tiny lines all around his mouth. He covered both his eyes with his hands and stuck his fingers in his ears, like if he couldn't see them and couldn't hear them they would go away.

I could hardly breathe. The two soldiers rummaged through the mess they had left behind when they ransacked the place the first time. At any moment they would come close enough to the counter to see us, and what would happen then? They'd take us—that's what would happen—probably someplace tucked far away and safe from poxers—someplace that seemed all nice and normal but really wasn't.

Trina and I stared hard at each other. She put one hand on the ground next to mind, and I put mine over hers. I could feel her shaking. Who knew if she was afraid or angry? Sometimes with Trina I couldn't tell the difference.

The soldiers moved to the other side of the store, and Trina quietly pushed Bullseye toward me and shifted into a crouching position. I furrowed my brow. What was she doing? My eyes searched her face. She just looked determined.

No. I knew that look. I pressed down harder on her hand, but she pulled away.

"You see them suckers pop when we fired 'em up?"

"Yeah. Just like a roll of fire crackers. It's weird they do that."

"Nah. Diana says they burn because of the gasses the bugs are farting out."

"Sounds like a bunch of hogwash to me. So we done in here or what? We gotta find whatever yahoo owns that van and hope they don't give us the same sort of trouble that the doc and his wife did."

The doc and his wife? Mom and Dad? Were they talking about Mom and Dad? No wonder they never showed up at Aunt Ella's. Did they have a run in with Cal and Luke? No. No. No. No. No.

Trina and I looked frantically into each other's eyes. She was thinking the same thing as me. I knew she was.

Her cheeks flushed. She looked at the ground and shook her head back and forth, and her whole body tensed. I didn't know what she was doing. When she finally moved, I didn't even have a chance to stop her. She shot to her feet like a freaking jack-in-the-box.

"Hiya," she said cheerfully, and that's all she had time to say.

The gun blast was deafening.

60

"WHAT THE HELL are you doing?" shouted one of the soldiers as the wall exploded behind Trina's head.

"I . . . I . . ."stammered the other.

"Yeah," shouted Trina as she used her foot to slide open the wooden paneled door on the back lower half of the glass counter." What the hell, you ignorant idiot?"

Before I even knew what I was doing, I pushed Bullseye inside the lower half of the cabinet as quickly and quietly as I could. Trina kept her tirade going to cover any noise we might be making.

"You're supposed to serve and protect, you dumb hick," she screamed. "I'm a civilian. Can you spell it? C–I–V–I–L–I–A–N. You almost took my head off."

"I'm, I'm sorry," I heard one of the soldiers say.

"You better believe you're sorry. What are you using a stupid gun for anyway? You can't kill them with bullets, you know, or haven't you figured that out yet?"

"Just hold on one damn minute," barked the other soldier. "And put your damn gun down, already," he snapped to his partner.

"Yeah," shouted Trina. "Get that thing out of my face."

"Shut up, blondie. You're pretty loudmouthed for a kid."

"Oh, yeah?" Trina said. "You haven't heard me loud. This is my library voice."

"Where did you come from? Me and Luke scoured every inch of this place. That your van out there?"

Trina leaned over with her elbows on the countertop, her chin perched in her hands.

"Who wants to know?"

"Gimme that," he barked at his partner. I heard a clicking sound, and Trina's legs stiffened.

"The one pointing a gun at your pretty little head wants to know, little sister."

"What? You going to shoot me now?"

"If you don't answer my questions, I just might."

"Cal. Stop it, Dude. She's just a kid. Probably not even old enough to drive."

Trina was dancing on the edge of a knife. "The hell I'm not, soldier boy."

I heard loud stomping, and the next thing I knew, one of the soldiers, probably Cal, was mouth breathing right into Trina's face.

"I said, is that your van?" he growled.

"Get out of my face, you ugly G.I. Joe."

Crack. He backhanded her hard, and I squeezed my nails into my palm so tightly I almost drew blood. I bit my lip and prayed Trina hadn't gone too far. This was a dangerous game she was playing.

"Cal, stop," pleaded the other soldier.

"Shut up, Luke."

"I think you should listen to your friend, Cal," hissed my sister.

"I bet you do. I'm gonna ask you one more time, and I'm not going to ask you again. You feel me?" Trina's legs both jerked and lifted right off the ground. Cal had yanked her off her feet by her shoulders. "Is . . . that . . . your . . . van?" he seethed. I could hear the bile in his voice. I think he was the kind of guy who liked to hit girls.

"Yes," whispered my sister through clenched teeth. "I stole a minivan."

Cal laughed.

"That's a federal offense, missy." He dragged Trina right over the counter. I heard her land with a thud on the other side.

"Ow," she yelped.

"Shut up," he yelled at her. "Where did you come from?"

I didn't hear her say anything, and I got really scared. I chanced a peek through the glass and saw one of the soldiers, I'm guessing Cal, bent down in front of Trina. He grabbed her hair and knotted it into his hands before leaning in so his face was right in hers.

"Where?" he snarled.

"Am . . . Amherst," she sniffed. Then she let the waterworks flow. I swear it was like watching an Oscar winning performance, because apart from her little meltdown on top of Mount Sugarloaf, Trina wasn't one to cry. This was a total fabrication. She was buying time. I'm just not exactly sure what she wanted me to do.

"Damn it, Cal. Now look what you gone and done?"

Luke, the other soldier, came over and pushed Cal out of the way. He squatted down on his knees and let Trina get a good, old cry on while he patiently waited for her to stop.

Cal stood up and slung the huge gun over his shoulder.

"I'm not watching this. Bring her or leave her, I don't give a crap. Diana said she wants survivors. She's a survivor. Just 'cause the whole world shut down don't mean it's time to stop obeying orders because of a pretty face. That ain't the army I signed up for." He clomped to the front of the store, right out the door, and down the steps.

"You okay?" Luke said to Trina after Cal stomped off like a little kid on a playground who didn't want to share his ball anymore.

"I . . . I don't feel good," she whimpered. "I think I need a doctor."

Ah, that's the Trina I knew and loved. Hopefully needing a doctor would get Thing One and Thing Two to lead us right to Mom and Dad.

"Don't feel good . . . where?"

Trina tentatively clutched her stomach.

"I've been puking for a week. I was going to go to the doctor on campus, but . . . but . . . everything happened."

"Damn, girl. You telling me you in the family way?"

Trina let loose with the waterworks again. "He . . . he said he loved me."

Two Oscars—definitely two Oscars—one for best actress in a horror film and one for best actress in a comedy.

"They all say that," said Luke. He stood up and held out his hand to Trina. At first she didn't take it. She shot a quick glance my way. I'm not sure if she knew I was watching or not. Finally, she gave her hand to Luke, and he took it and hauled her up.

That's when her knee connected to that place on a guy you're never, ever supposed to knee, well, except if you're Prianka.

She dropped him like a dead llama.

61

"SO NOW WHAT?" I said as I finished wrapping the duct tape I found behind the counter around Luke's legs.

His arms were easy. He was so doubled over in pain he didn't even know what was happening. Trina pulled her shoe and sock off and crammed the white cotton ball of smelliness in his mouth. He kicked a lot with his legs, so Trina sat on his chest, and I sat on his knees while I wound the silver tape around and around his calves until he couldn't move.

Finally, I wrapped a piece of tape around his head to secure the sock in place. Gross? Yes. A necessity? You betcha.

After making sure Bullseye stayed put, we dragged Luke to the back of the store, frantically looking for any place to hide while we had a chance to stop and think.

There was a bathroom there. We shoved Luke inside and scrambled in after him. I left the door slightly ajar and peeked through the crack. I could still see out the front door. Cal was leaning up against the jeep and smoking a cigarette. Well, if Poxers didn't kill him, I knew what would.

I turned to my sister. "That was really stupid, you know?"

Trina snorted. "I couldn't think of anything else. It doesn't matter. The point is they know where Mom and Dad are. They're being held by some psychopath named Diana. I could have just let them take me there, but what good would that have done? We don't need to be taken there. We just need to know where 'there' is."

"I guess," I whispered. "What about Sargent Micro Brain out there?"

"I don't know," she whispered. "I don't know."

Luke stared at the two of us with venom in his eyes.

"Your buddy likes to hit girls, doesn't he?" I said. "Not cool, man. So not cool."

Trina started biting her fingernails. If she had a bag of potato chips handy, she would be sinking her paws elbow deep into all that greasiness and shoveling them, double fisted, into her mouth.

"Are you okay?" I asked her.

"No. I'm totally not okay. We just, well, I think we just committed treason or something. Isn't assaulting someone in the Army like assaulting a cop?"

One wasn't much better than the other. Trina chomped away at her fingernails at a record clip.

I peeked out the door again and saw that Bullseye had crawled out from underneath the counter and was trying to make his way back to us. I kept shaking my head no, but he plastered on a grimace of determination and began belly crawling in our direction.

Outside, Cal flicked his cigarette into the wind, shouldered his mega-gun, and headed back up the stairs to the shoppe.

Bullseye heard the door open and froze. My heart started beating faster and faster. Now what were we going to do?

"Yo, Luke. What's the deal?" Cal stopped and looked around the store. "Yo. Where is everybody?"

That's when Bullseye started crying again. What was he thinking, leaving his hidey hole behind the counter? Now he was really screwed and maybe me and Trina along with him.

He wasn't even just crying—he was sobbing—awful, snot filled heaves that wracked his body in spasms. He didn't even attempt to hide. He just collapsed on his stomach and lay there, wailing and blubbering like an absolute lunatic.

"We're so screwed," I whispered.

"What the . . ." Cal stood there for a moment not sure what to do. On one hand, Luke and Trina were gone. On the other, there was a little kid in front of him, very much alive and having a major nuclear meltdown.

I guess he wasn't all bad, because he made his way through the store and hunkered down next to Bullseye.

"Hey, Buddy?" he said. "It's okay. I'm with the Army. Everything will be okay now."

Bullseye wailed louder and louder.

"Jeez," said Cal and took his gun off his shoulder and put it down next to him. "Come on, Little Guy. I ain't gonna hurt you. Honest." Cal reached over and gently put his big, meaty hand on Bullseye's shoulder and turned him over.

What he found was the muzzle of the pistol Bullseye had tucked into his pants, pointing right in his face.

"I wish I could say the same," seethed Bullseye through gritted teeth. "Now put your arms over your head before I blow your ugly nose off your ugly puss."

"Um . . . uh . . ."

"Do it," he screamed and shot off a bullet that whizzed right by Cal's ear and hit the wall on the opposite side of the store.

Trina and I burst out of the bathroom and ran to Bullseye.

"What the hell is this?" barked Cal.

"This is us saving ourselves and you letting a twelve year old get the drop on you," said Trina. "I guess basic training was a lot more basic than they let on."

"Did I do good?" asked Bullseye as he leveled his gun right between Cal's eyes.

"Good?" I exclaimed. "Are you kidding me?" I stared back and forth between him and Cal. The soldier's face was in the process of turning roughly the color of a tomato. Bullseye's hands were steady on the gun. "Good is an understatement. You did awesome."

62

EVERYTHING SHOULD have been easy, right? All they had to do was tell us where our parents were and we'd drop them some place nice and safe with no poxers around and a fighting chance to get back to wherever they came from?

No dice. If nothing else, both Luke and Cal were military micro-brains through and through. We put them in the middle of the gun shoppe, sitting in chairs facing the three of us. We had duct taped them so tightly to their seats that a fart couldn't squeeze out.

I knew we had to eventually cut them loose, but watching Trina, I wasn't so sure that was part of her game plan.

Without warning, she cracked Cal across the face with her open palm.

"That was for hitting me," she said. She made like she was going to turn away, but instead she back handed him across the face again. "And that was because I wanted to, you dumb ape."

Cal grunted because he couldn't talk with duct tape over his mouth. His eyes, however, burned with anger. I could see he was boiling inside.

I stepped forward and put my hands on Trina's shoulders.

"My turn," I said and reached around the back of Luke's head and peeled away the tape that was covering his mouth.

"Don't say a word," I breathed as I pulled my sister's smelly sock out of his mouth. He coughed and spat on the floor but said nothing.

Gross.

I moved over to Cal. His eyes bore into me. If I had to guess, I'd say that Cal was the scarier of the two. I could almost see the wheels inside his head churning. He wanted to get loose badly. He wanted to make us pay for what we did to him and his buddy. The fact that we were kids made no difference to him at all. Funny how you can read all that in a person's face.

I ripped the tape off his mouth, too, probably pulling some face stubble along with it. He glared at me but said nothing.

Trina spoke first.

"Here's the deal. You took two people who were coming to meet us," she said. "Those two people, the doctor and his wife, happen to be our parents."

Both soldiers stayed quiet.

"You're going to tell us where they are," I said. "Piece of cake. If you don't, well, there's no 'if you don't.' You're just going to tell us where they are, or we're going to make you."

I crossed my arms over my chest and tried to look as menacing as I could. Trina put her arms on her hips. Bullseye stood behind her with his pistol at his side.

Cal lifted his chin and looked directly ahead to an invisible spot on the wall behind us.

"Private Calvin Pooler," he said in a very clear voice. "North Carolina Unit 118, 9719021."

"What?" said Trina.

"Private Calvin Pooler," he said again, not looking at either of us. North Carolina Unit 118, 9719021."

I shook my head. I couldn't believe what I was hearing.

"Private Lucas Longo," said Luke. He also looked straight ahead. "North Carolina Unit 118, 2688417."

"What the hell?" barked Trina.

"Unbelievable," I said.

"What?"

"Name, rank, and serial number. They're actually giving us their name, rank, and serial number."

That's how it went for the next ten minutes. Anything we asked, any way we begged, they refused to say anything but the same old tired line.

Finally Bullseye offered to shoot one of them.

"NO," we both yelped in unison.

"Why not? That's what would happen in the movies."

"Because," I said. "Despite the fact that the world has turned into one great, big pile of crap, we don't have the right to shoot anybody." I looked at Trina because I wasn't quite sure I was speaking for both of us. "Right? Trina? Right?"

Trina licked her lips.

"Why not?" she said without any feeling in her voice at all. "Frankly, if we shoot one of them, the other one might talk."

She held out her hand for Bullseye's gun. He stared at her, clearly ready to puff out his prepubescent chest and stand his ground. Instead, he just scuffed the floor with his foot and handed the butt over to her. She weighed the gun in her hand before turning to face the soldiers.

"Sorry, Calvin," she said and pointed the gun at his face. "I just plain don't like you."

A bead of sweat dripped down from his closely cropped hair and traveled along the bridge of his nose. His eyes still registered off-the-charts hatred, or he had to pee in the worst way. I wasn't sure.

"She's going to ask you one more time," I said very slowly and deliberately. "After that I take no responsibility for my sister's actions. She wants our parents. We both do."

Trina cocked the gun, and I prepared for the worst. I'm not sure she'd really shoot, but at the moment, all bets were off. Besides, a bruise was starting to turn dark green where Calvin Pooler, North Caroline Unit 118, 9719021, had smacked my sister. If she had a chance to catch a glimpse of her reflection, I think she'd be pointing that gun between his legs not between his eyes.

Long seconds passed. Finally Bullseye cracked.

"Wait," he cried.

"For what? Trina snapped.

"Just, just wait."

"For what?" she demanded again.

"You . . . you don't get to decide this. You just don't."

"He's right," I said. "You don't just get to decide this. They're not poxers. They're people."

"Barely," she hissed. She juggled the gun in her hands. I was positive it was going to go off by accident. "So what do you want me to do?"

"First, give the gun back. I don't want you holding it."

"Fine," she muttered and handed the gun back to Bullseye. "Now what?"

I took a deep breath. "We bring them with us and let the others help decide."

The words came out of my mouth before I knew what I was saying. What was I thinking? I didn't want to expose Prianka to this. What about Jimmy? What about Sanjay?

Still, in the end, that's exactly what we did.

63

DUMB AND DUMBER had packed their jeep full with guns and ammunition from the Purgatory Chasm Gun Shoppe. There were also several cartons of cigarettes, a case of lighter fluid, a few other scary looking Army things, and groceries. A green cloth shopping bag printed with the words 'Save the Planet—Recycle' looked totally out of place next to the rest of their gear.

I guess, in the end, everyone was trying to do their part to reduce their carbon footprint.

We decided to take their jeep with us. Extra supplies were always a good thing. None of us were into unpacking the jeep and repacking Stella's minivan. We just wanted to get back to Aunt Ella's and figure out how to get Cal and Luke to talk. Besides, if they had friends, I didn't want to leave a trace of them anywhere.

No way.

Before we left, I ran across the street to a small drugstore. Inside, I found two rolls of ace bandages. We wrapped them around the soldiers' heads, making sure to cover their eyes. Then we taped them in place.

"What are you doing?" Cal muttered in that raspy, nasty voice of his.

"Making sure you don't know where we're going," snipped Trina. "Honestly, have you ever read a book or watched TV?"

"You better hope I don't get loose, little girl. You're in for a world of hurt when I do."

"Shut up," Trina said and duct taped his mouth again.

When she went to tape Luke's mouth, he said, "I'm good. I'll keep my trap shut."

"You do that," she told him and left the duct tape off his mouth.

Trina had learned to drive on a stick, and I really sucked at the whole clutch and pedal method, so we decided that she would take the jeep along with Bullseye and I would take the minivan with our guests.

We had a hard time loading them in because there was no way we were going to untape them, but damn, they were heavy. I put the seats down, and together, Trina, Bullseye, and I slid them in on their backs, chairs and all.

Then we left Purgatory Chasm and wound our way back up to the

Trail.

"I got to hand it to you guys," I said as I passed the Romance Rendezvous and spun the wheel of the minivan back the way we came. "I mean, seriously, less than a week ago you were the go-to guys if us civilian types ever needed help."

Nothing.

"How important is this Diana lady to make you want to beat on a teenage girl and kidnap her?"

"I didn't beat on no one," Luke muttered. Cal growled beneath all that duct tape, but he couldn't tell his pal to shut up. I was banking on that.

"No. No you didn't. Bully for you—you got a leg up on the dirt bag lying next to you."

Up ahead, a poxer dressed all in blue was dragging himself across the road. I slowed the van down and stopped. Trina pulled up next to me, and I lowered the window.

"I was thinking," I said. "I bet that dead thing up ahead is pretty hungry, and we don't really need both of these guys."

"Please don't," whispered Luke. "Cal's my friend."

"Who said I was talking about Cal?"

"Is he talking?" bellowed Trina. "Who said he could talk? I should have taped his damn mouth shut when I had the chance."

I winked at my sister and silently mouthed 'one of them will crack.' She nodded.

"Do whatever the hell you want," she said, loud enough for both men to hear. "Leave one of them for all I care. Hell, leave both of them. If they can't tell us anything, they're useless."

Again, another shining Oscar moment for my sister. She took off ahead of us in the jeep, taking a wide berth around the poxer.

"She's right," I said. "If you can't tell us anything, you're probably going to end up zombie chow."

"I . . . I can't tell you where your parents are," rasped Luke.

"Why not?"

"Because I don't wanna die," he said. *Cryptic much?*

"Why will you die if you tell me where my parents are?"

Luke was silent for a long, long time. I watched as the poxer, a mailman, slowly realized we were there and turned toward us. There was something wrong with him. I couldn't tell for sure, but maybe one of his legs was broken or mangled or something.

"She'll kill me," he said.

Cal's muffled cries came in waves.

"If you don't tell me where my parents are, I might just let that zombie up ahead kill you." Talk about working the dead letter room. This guy was perfect for the job.

"Better than her," he cried. "Damn. You don't know. You just don't know."

As the poxer got closer I realized the reason he looked so funny was that he was missing a major part of his leg. A jagged edge of bone stuck out of his thigh.

"You're going to tell me," I said. "Eventually, you both are going to talk, or we'll feed you to the dead ones without batting an eye. You get me?"

Nothing—again.

I pressed my foot on the gas and swerved around the pitiful thing in the road. Mr. Postman made a vague attempt to grab at the minivan.

Would I really do it? If they didn't tell me where my parents were, would I really feed them to the poxers?

I waited a whole ten seconds while I thought long and hard about exactly what I was capable of doing—just ten seconds. That's about as long as I needed to ponder the thought.

Yeah, I'd let the poxers have them.

I'd let the poxers have them in a heartbeat.

64

JIMMY WAS LEANING on the porch steps with Newfie. He was out of his chair with his shirt off and his head back, soaking up the last of the late afternoon sun. I swear if the guy got any more rays his freckles would have freckles.

Newfie didn't bark when we pulled into the driveway. He just stood and watched as I stopped in front of the barn and Trina slid the jeep in next to me. He did lower his head a little and push his ears back when he saw what she was driving.

I knew he was a good judge of character.

"Cool ride," said Jimmy as Trina hopped out of the Army-mobile. "I like girls in jeeps."

"I like boys who like girls in jeeps," she said and kissed him hello just long enough to make Bullseye groan and roll his eyes.

"You've missed some excitement while you were gone," said Jimmy nonchalantly as he pulled himself back into his chair.

"What do you mean?" I asked. "I'm sure what went on here can't be any more exciting than our little road trip."

"Yeah?" said Jimmy. "Wanna bet?" He pointed his thumb behind him to the front door. There was a large, red star painted over the white wood—obviously still wet. A few crimson lines dribbled slowly toward the floor. A crude circle was painted around the star.

I scratched my head.

"Um . . . are we Jewish now?"

Trina snickered. "That's six points, you idiot. This one's only five."

"Five meaning what?"

"Patriotic if you're a flag," said Jimmy.

I stared at the crude handiwork. Something about the blood red paintjob stuck me as familiar. Then I remembered why. The star was on the front cover of one of Aunt Ella's books that Sanjay had been reading. It was called a penta something.

"Pentragram." The word came to me out of the part of my brain that stores all my creepy movie imagery.

"Who's the artist?" asked Trina. "If Aunt Ella ever comes back home she's going to kill whoever did that."

As for me, I already knew who the culprit was. The knowledge sat in the pit of my stomach, in that hollow spot reserved specifically for realizing particularly unpleasant things. You know—the place that releases queasy little butterflies into your gut that flutter around like bats gone mad?

"Oh no," I muttered. "You can't be serious?"

"You ain't seen nothing yet," said Jimmy. He spun around in his chair and reached for the door knob. "By the way—the jeep—that's not Army, is it?"

"One story at a time," I said and pushed past him into the house.

I wasn't prepared. I think that whatever came out of my mouth was along the lines of something my parents were definitely not cool with me saying out loud.

Someone had redecorated the walls everywhere in bloody, red symbols and diagrams. The floors were covered, too. Everywhere I looked were pentagrams, squiggles, and lines that looked like they might have meant something to someone who rides a broom.

"No way," gasped Bullseye.

"Way," said Trina.

I whirled around with clenched fists and shot eye-daggers at Jimmy.

"You know, you're supposed to be the adult here."

"Tell that to your girlfriend's brother," he said. "He's a whole new level of something, man—a whole new level."

"Girlfriend," giggled Bullseye, like a twelve-year-old. Oh, yeah. He *was* a twelve-year-old. I punched him in the arm anyway.

I found Prianka in the library surrounded by all the books that Sanjay had been reading. She looked up at me. I could tell she had been crying. I wanted to say something but didn't know what to say. Instead, I sat down next to her. She had her finger in the middle of one of the hard covers called 'Spells of the Old Ones.' She held the volume out to me. The chapter she was on was called 'Protecting the Home.'

"None of this mumbo jumbo is real," I whispered to her. "It's just junk people make up to sell to gullible people who believe in this crap."

She nodded like she understood, but she still looked overwhelmed. I guess in her world, she was used to Sanjay's eccentricities. This, however? This was something new.

"When did he start?"

"Right after you left," she said. "He found the paint in the basement. I couldn't get him to stop. It's like he's vomiting up everything he's read right on to the walls."

I tentatively put my arm around her. I wasn't sure if we were at that stage yet, but it seemed like it's what she would have wanted me to do. She leaned her head against my shoulder and just sat there. Finally, she sniffed and wiped her eyes.

"I guess if any of these spells are for real, we're really, really protected," she chuckled halfheartedly.

"Or he's going to open up a gate to some other dimension that doesn't have poxers."

"Nah," she said. "Everyone would probably have three eyes or look like Chuck Peterson or something." She squeezed me tightly before pulling away. It was only for a moment, but it felt nice. I really wanted to have more of those moments sometime when we didn't have a child from Slytherin wandering the house and two Army guys held hostage in the back of Stella's minivan.

"Where's Sanjay now?" I asked her as I stood up, extending my hand to help her to her feet.

"I just left him upstairs a little while ago. Andrew's watching him."

I looked at her and laughed.

"You're autistic brother's babysitter is a crow. You do know how nuts that sounds, right?"

"What was I supposed to do? Jimmy gave up and went outside, and I really wanted to understand what Sanjay was painting. I came back here and found these books. I suppose I should be comforted knowing that he's trying to protect the house instead of summoning a demon from Hell."

"Hell is high school."

"Not for me," she sighed and dropped the book in the pile with the rest of them. "So how was your little adventure off the ranch?"

"Adventuresome," I said as I held my hand out for hers. "Really, really adventuresome."

65

WHEN WE GOT Luke and Cal on the porch, I unwound the ace bandages we had wrapped around their heads and pulled the tape free from Cal's mouth.

Luke's eyes grew wide when he saw the pentagram on the front door.

"What's this?" he whimpered.

"Shut up," barked Trina. "Did I say you could talk? I don't remember me saying you could talk."

Cal's eyes burned a hole in her head right where he'd probably shoot her if he could. All I could imagine was him picturing smoke coming out of that hole.

"You got something to say?" she snapped at Cal.

He sneered at her through a fog of hate.

"Private Calvin Pooler, North Carolina Unit 118, 9719021."

She lunged at him with her fist raised, but Jimmy caught her wrist.

"Chill," he said. "Private Calvin Pooler is going to tell us where your parents are, and my guess is he's going to tell us sooner rather than later."

Cal said nothing. I really, really was starting to seriously hate this guy.

Luke's face, on the other hand, was starting to turn an unhealthy shade of white. He couldn't take his eyes off the pentagram on the door. I caught that. So did Jimmy and Trina, and we all shared a knowing glance.

I patted the tacky paint.

"Look familiar?" I asked Luke.

"That's the Devil's sign, ain't it?" His voice began to warble. I knew that sound—the sound of fear.

"Look who gets a gold, five-pointed star."

"What . . . what . . . are you guys Satan worshippers?"

I didn't say anything. None of us did. We all just plastered smug, superior looks on our faces, but all the while I could tell each of us was thinking the same thing. If Luke was freaking out at one silly, little star on a door, what would he do when he got inside?

I think I was dying to find out.

"Enough with the questions," Trina snapped.

"Yeah," I said. "You're in the Master's house now." Trina and Jimmy looked at me like I had three heads. Hey, I was improvising. So sue me.

Luke, however, bought it all—hook, line and sinker.

"The . . . the . . . Master?"

The door opened, and Luke almost jumped out of his skin. Prianka and Bullseye stepped out on to the porch. Bullseye was holding Newfie by the collar. Maybe our big, black monster sensed what was going on or that none of us were pleased with Luke and Cal. Newfie didn't seem to need more reason than that to join the game. A long, low snarl came out of his mouth. He curled his lips and showed teeth for added effect.

"Lucifer—DOWN," I snapped.

Was that too much?

"You gotta dog named Lucifer?" muttered Cal, almost to himself. Those were the first words he said, other than his name, rank, and serial number. I could feel that little thing called his will beginning to crumble.

Good.

"Don't say his name," screeched Trina. "Don't you dare say his name."

"He . . . he . . . he's sorry," stammered Luke.

Jimmy wheeled forward. The muscles on his arms bulged as he slowly pushed on the wheels of his chair. Cal's icy gaze, now with the slightest hint of worry, shifted to him. Luke pushed himself back in his chair, trying to somehow hide.

"This is our world now," said Jimmy in a silky, smooth voice. "In our world you play by our rules." Newfie growled again, but Bullseye held him tight. "How about we go inside for a real chat? Maybe, if you're lucky, and you tell us what we want to know, things might go good for you. If not, well, Lucifer sometimes demands fresh meat. Who's to say?"

Luke began to whimper.

"Lucifer the dog . . . or . . . or . . . Lucifer . . . uh . . ."

Not such a stretch, really. We were living in a world of poxers now. Who's to say other things didn't exist? Demons, ghosts, any freaky thing you could imagine.

The only thing I knew for sure was that all of us needed to be on the same page if we were going to pull off this bluff and scare them into telling us where Mom and Dad were being held. Besides, I didn't like what I saw in Trina's eyes. Our sham needed to work because I didn't like where she was headed if it didn't.

Prianka caught on in record time—she didn't miss a beat. She stepped forward, taking over where Jimmy left off. When she was just a foot away from Cal she lunged out with her arm and grabbed his face in her hand. She squeezed tightly, turning his head first one way then the other as if searching for something in his ugly puss. He said nothing and neither did Prianka.

Finally, she let go and moved over to Luke.

"Don't," he whimpered.

"Don't. Stop. No," she mocked. "Is that what the doctor and his wife said when you took them?"

"Orders," stammered Luke. "We was just following orders."

"We follow orders, too," she hissed. "The orders we follow demand blood."

Prianka whirled around with dramatic flair and raised her arms above her head with her palms up.

"Take them both," she ordered the rest of us. "Take them both inside."

That's exactly what we did—dragging them in through the front door of Aunt Ella's house, the legs of the chairs they were taped to scratching against the floor and straining under their weight.

66

WELCOME TO THE Light and Dark house of horrors. We've spared no expense. Bloody, red demonic imagery everywhere and, to boot, a llama haltered and tethered to the coffee table in the living room.

We picked a black, watery-eyed one that liked to give kisses. She lay on a big mound of hay bedding, munching away. Newfie padded up to her and sat down—the lion with the lamb. For all I knew, since Aunt Ella used Newfie as a guard dog in the llama pen, they were probably friends.

After our parade down the hallway with pentagrams and strange symbols assaulting their eyeballs, Luke was fairly close to a mental breakdown. He was as white as a ghost. Whatever bible-thumping background he came from probably included juggling rattle snakes and speaking in tongues. If we were really lucky, he watched horror movies like I did, too.

Lucky? Hell, I was banking on it.

"What is that thing?" gasped Cal, staring wide-eyed at the llama. Wow! Not the brightest bulb on the porch. Ever hear of a zoo? In any event, his strong, no-nonsense name-rank-and-serial-number broken record was starting to crumble.

"A sacrifice," said Bullseye in a deadly serious voice. The words were prefect coming out of his mouth. There's nothing scarier than a creepy kid. Nothing.

"I'm telling them," yelped Luke to Cal.

"Soldier, shut your pie hole."

Trina threatened to backhand Cal again, and he flinched. "Scared yet?" she purred. "Good. The Master feeds on fear."

I think that was the icing on the cake. I'm not sure where Trina pulled that line from, but it was priceless. Luke started to cry—big, raspy, man-sized wails. What a wimp.

"I ain't going out in no demon ritual. Not like this. Not like this."

"Then tell me where my parents are," Trina bellowed.

Cal's voice cracked. "Don't you tell, Luke. Don't you dare."

Trina ripped off a length of duct tape and plastered it over Cal's mouth.

"I'm sick to death of hearing you talk," she said. "So don't."

"Speaking of death," Prianka began in a lilting, eerie voice, "I think it's time we get to the good part, don't you? Wait here." She glided out of the living room toward the kitchen. I followed her, leaving Jimmy, Trina, and Bullseye behind.

"What are you doing?" I whispered when we were out of earshot.

"I don't know. Making it up as I go along."

"You're doing a good job."

In the kitchen, Prianka pulled open one of the drawers and fished around inside. She opened two more before she found what she was looking for. She reached in, grasped the dark, wooden handle of a steak knife, and slid the blade free.

"What are you going to do with that?"

"I'm not sure."

"Don't let Trina near that thing."

"Why?"

"She might actually stab that Cal guy. He's a major tool."

"I know," she said. "But both of those idiots have to believe we mean business." She held the knife up in front of her eyes and licked her lips. "They have to really believe. Luke's the one who's going to cave first. As long as we can keep Cal quiet, Luke will tell us where your parents are. I know he will."

"I hope so," I said. "I really do."

Back in the living room, Luke renewed his sobbing when he saw the knife in Prianka's grip.

"I can't," he blubbered and snorted. "No way, no how. Either Diana will kill me or you will. Lordy, lordy, help me. I should have up and died with everyone else."

Jimmy leaned forward in his chair. "Who's everyone else?"

"The other units," he sobbed. "Us and the other units. We was doing maneuvers up in the mountains when everything happened. We was called in, but by then there was only a few of us soldiers left."

"Called in where?" pressed Jimmy.

Cal began to rock in his chair, his fists opening and closing and straining against the tape. A muffled roar came from beneath his blocked mouth. Jimmy ignored him and pushed Luke again.

"Luke. Called in where?"

I swear, Luke was about to crack. He opened his mouth to speak, but before anything came out, his voice caught in his throat, and his eyes bulged out of his head. A strangled, gurgling noise was all that he could produce. He was staring at the entrance to the living room, so we all followed his gaze.

Sanjay had come in.

Saying our mouths dropped open would have been a bit of an understatement. Sanjay was stripped down to his underwear. His bare feet slapped against the hardwood floor. He was decorated from head to toe in red paint. Strange symbols and words covered his skinny arms, his chest, and legs. In the middle of his forehead was a pentagram like the one painted on the door to the house. To top it all off, Andrew perched on his shoulder, his wings outstretched as Sanjay walked.

"He's here," I shouted because I really didn't know what else to do. I dropped to my knees and bowed my head. Jimmy caught on first. He lowered himself out of his chair and bowed his head, too. Prianka, Triana, and Bullseye did the same. Finally, Newfie got up and slowly walked over to Sanjay and stood by his side.

Now what? I caught Trina's eye, and she looked desperately at me then back to the floor.

"Oh mighty Master," I yelled before I could even stop the words from pouring out of my mouth. "What is thou willist?"

"What is thy will?" Prianka repeated. Even in dire circumstances she had to point out that she was smarter than me. Okay, so I wasn't that hot in Ye Olde English.

The room was deathly quiet. All we could hear was the sound of the llama chewing on her bed of hay. The rhythmic chomp, chomp, chomp was eerie.

Finally, Andrew cackled, "Thy will. Thy will," flapped his wings, and the oddest thing happened.

Sanjay spoke.

They weren't quite the words we were expecting him to break his silence with—but he spoke, nevertheless.

"I invoke thee, dark lord," he began in a booming voice. "Enter my circle. I call you on this dire hour to aid me in my foul deeds. Help me to perform the evil that I must do. Come at once and crawl inside my enemies' head."

He walked forward toward Luke and Cal, Andrew squeaking and squawking like a demonic, black chicken. Luke became hysterical and squirmed so much he toppled his chair over backwards and hit his head on the floor. Thankfully, he didn't boink his noggin hard enough to knock himself out.

"Oh, lordy, lordy, lordy," he wailed. "I ain't never done nothing to deserve this. I ain't never."

We all stayed crouched with our heads bowed, not sure what was going to happen next. Frankly, I was prepared for Sanjay to start spouting nicknames or directions. If he did that, we'd really be screwed.

Sanjay walked around the fallen soldier, stepped over him, and made a beeline right for Cal. He reached forward and ripped the tape from his mouth.

"I invoke thee, dark lord," he chanted again with his face scant inches away from Cal's. "Enter my circle. I call you on this dire hour to aid me in my foul deeds. Help me to perform the evil that I must do. Come at once, and crawl inside my enemies' head."

Andrew squawked, "Enemies' head".

Cal didn't miss a beat.

"They're at the McDuffy Estate up the road about twenty minutes past Purgatory Chasm."

That was easy. Why are grownups so damn stubborn sometimes?

"Are they hurt in any way?" asked Jimmy.

"No."

"How many others?"

"A couple soldiers, Diana and her people, the doc and his wife, and some folks I ain't never seen."

"Lordy, lordy, lordy," cried Luke again. I think we had broken something inside his head.

We all stood up a little relieved and more than a bit confused about Sanjay. Prianka moved forward, gently reached out, and tentatively touched her little brother's shoulder. He turned and let Prianka slowly guide him out of the living room and down the hall to the library.

We followed them, leaving Luke a blubbering mess and Cal probably wondering what he had just done.

When we were all inside the library, I closed the door.

"What the hell was that?" I gasped.

Prianka bent down in front of Sanjay and Andrew. The crow repositioned himself closer to Sanjay's ear and ran his beak through the boy's black curls.

"Sanjay?" she said, searching his dark eyes for any sign he was somewhere inside.

"The Gate, page forty-three," he whispered, his eyes still glazed. "Andrew said so."

We all shifted our gaze to the crow.

"Andrew said what?" Prianka whispered.

"Andrew's smart," said Sanjay, as though he was talking about Poopy Puppy instead of Jimmy's flying rat. His eyes grew less distant. He seemed to be coming out of his stupor. "Andrew's very smart. He told me to scare the tatti out of those two men."

The crow ruffled his feathers and chirped, "Tatti."

"He told me to scare the tatti out of them," said Sanjay in a quiet voice. "So I did."

67

THERE ARE SO MANY stupid arguments I could have come up with. I thought about it for a long time, but each one sounded worse than the one before. In the end, I didn't say anything at all. I just slipped away because I thought that was the best thing to do. It may not have been the brightest idea, but to me, it was the best.

Trina had left the jeep keys on the kitchen counter, and I already had the keys to Stella's minivan. While no one was paying attention, I took both sets of keys. Quietly, I tiptoed into the living room and held a small knife to Cal's throat. I whispered something particularly nasty in his ear and pressed down just hard enough for him to catch my drift.

He told me the McDuffy Estate was down a dirt road about a hundred yards past a big rock ledge covered with graffiti that loomed over the Trail.

That was good enough for me. I doubted he was lying. Sanjay's little display had probably knocked the lying gene out of his head.

The others were in the library. I mumbled something to them about going out for some fresh air and headed for the front door.

I underestimated Jimmy, though. He was smart—like Poopy Puppy smart—like Andrew smart.

"Hey wait up," he called after me. "I need a breather, too."

"Um, okay," I muttered as I walked on to the porch and sat down on the front steps. Twilight was coming, and the sky was painted with streaks of pink and orange.

Jimmy wheeled up next to me and stared into the fading light. "Red sky at morning, sailor take warning. Red sky at night is a sailor's delight."

"What?"

"That's what my foster mom used to always say. When the sky looks like this, expect smooth sailing."

"Who's sailing?"

"Seems to me you're about to," he said. "Pretty swift of you to take both sets of car keys so no one can follow."

"I don't know what you're talking about."

He folded his hands in front of him and bent forward. I could feel his eyes boring into the side of my head.

"So let me take a crack at this, and you tell me how I'm doing," he began. "I'm guessing you're thinking that Prianka's got Sanjay, Bullseye's too little, and Trina is so fired up about those two guys that she's likely to do something stupid. And me? Well you think I'm a cripple. How did I do?"

I couldn't look him straight in the face.

"You're pretty smart for a cripple."

"Sticks and stones, my friend. Sticks and stones."

I chewed on the inside of my lip. "I'm getting my parents. I don't expect you to help me, and I don't want anyone here to get hurt. This is my problem, Jimmy. Not yours."

"You're pretty damn stubborn for a spoiled rich kid from the burbs, you know that?"

"Yeah, whatever—I was born with a silver spoon in my mouth."

Jimmy chuckled. "Well I was born with a spork in mine. Same dif. We're both still alive, and I'm coming with."

Jimmy lowered himself out of his chair and scooted down the three porch steps to the ground. He motioned for me to grab his wheels. When I did, he climbed back in his chair and stared at me like he was Sprinkles and I had just asked her if she wanted to take a 'rideinthecar.'

"Is this right? Leaving them alone?" I whispered because I didn't want anyone to know what we were about to do.

"Tripp, man. Have you seen our girls? I think they handle themselves better than we do. Bullseye's a crackerjack shot, and our little shaman animal whisperer probably has more tricks up his sleeve than all of us combined."

He was right.

"What about all the guns and the ammunition?"

"The jeep's still loaded, right? We'll leave that for them and take the minivan. All we need is a handgun and some matches and maybe a little lighter fluid."

I agreed. We'd leave all the weapons and ammunition with them in case we didn't make it back. "Fine. We'll take the minivan and hope we have a plan by the time we get there."

Jimmy rubbed the red stubble on his face. "I'm working on it," he said. "I'm working on it."

I blew air out of my nose. "Okay. What about the elephant in the room?"

"We're outside, and there aren't any elephants here—only llamas."

"You know what I mean." I didn't want to have to say *you're handicapped!*

"No, Tripp. I really don't know what you mean." Jimmy licked his lips.

"I've spent my whole life looking straight ahead and not down at my legs. I'm not about to start now. I don't have a problem with being differently-abled. Frankly, besides running a race, I'm sure I can take you in pretty much everything. For that matter, between my wheels and your legs, I'd bet on me."

The sky was turning purple, and night was coming fast. I was thankful that he couldn't really see my face in the fading light, because my cheeks burned red.

"I'm sorry," I said. "I'm an idiot."

"Sometimes."

"A jackass, even."

"Keep going," he said. Nah—that was all the self-deprication Jimmy James was going to get out of me. Besides, we had a job to do.

"I'm good," I said. "Let's do this."

"Alrighty."

We both turned and looked at the farm house. They were all going to expel us from our little group when they realized what we did.

Expel us? Hell, they'd have to catch us and eat us first.

"One more thing," whispered Jimmy. He wheeled over to the jeep, quietly opened the front door, and leaned forward with his arm outstretched so he could reach all the wires under the steering wheel. He grabbed a handful and yanked as hard as he could. They came out in his fist, along with some spark plugs.

"What was that for?"

"You think taking the keys will stop any of them from following us?"

"Why not?"

Jimmy shook his head. "Because Sanjay read through every one of Stella's survival books," he said as he jammed the wires into the pocket of his jeans. "He could hot wire this thing in his sleep."

68

AS JIMMY AND I started the minivan and backed out of the long driveway, we both caught a glimpse of the front door slamming open. Prianka and Trina shouted after us in the darkness.

"Damn you," I heard one of them yell as I backed into the road, threw the minivan in drive, and took off without looking back.

"We are totally screwed," I said to Jimmy.

"No we're not."

"How you figure?"

"Because we're going to come back with your parents," he said. "Trina and Pri might be righteously miffed right now, but when we bring your mom and dad back home, we're going to get some mighty fine appreciation."

"I hope you're right," I said, "Because in case you haven't noticed, Prianka can turn a sunny day into a blizzard."

"Nope—hadn't noticed. I've been too fixated on someone else, Dude."

"Enough, okay?" I glared at him. "I'm still processing."

"Hey, just passing the time with a little conver—*Watch out!*"

A deer was frozen in the middle of the road. Its eyes were bright red in the reflection of the minivan's headlights. I stomped on the breaks and swerved sideways. The squeal of the tires was enough to spook her, and she jumped off the road into the trees. Seeing that deer reminded me of a line from a poem I memorized for ninth grade English. *The woods are lovely, dark and deep. But I have promises to keep, and miles to go before I sleep.* The words finally made sense. They were about life and death and how sometimes giving up and dying seems easier than doing what needs doing.

Yeah, maybe giving up would be easier, but not for me. That was someone else's solution. Mine was to get my parents back and make sure that my sister, Prianka, Sanjay, Bullseye, Andrew, and Newfie remained safe.

Jimmy, too.

He reached into the back seat and picked up one of the two handguns that we had taken out of the jeep.

"You think we're going to have to use that?" I asked as I turned on the high beams and saw two poxers come into view on the side of the road.

"I'm hoping not," he said as he pointed it at the two middle-aged things and pretended to blow them away. "I don't think I have the stomach to shoot something I know still has a brain left in its head."

I thought about Luke and Cal and wondered if they counted, because between both of them, they had just about two brain cells fighting for territory. Still, if someone got in the way of me getting my mom and dad, I'd shoot—wouldn't I?

We rode in silence for a while. The road made a quick jog and a curve, and we were back at the Trail. My high beams caught a glimpse of the poxers in the parking lot across the street. There were less of them than before. Maybe they decided that the doors weren't ever going to open, so they moved on in search of food. Who knows?

I gripped the steering wheel with both hands and scanned the dark road up ahead as I drove. Every once in a while we passed a poxer crawling along the tar.

Right before the Romance Rendezvous, I saw a poxer kid bent over on the side of the road with his face in a bloated, furry roadkill.

"That's nasty," said Jimmy.

"That's survival," I said. "Just the luck of the draw—one hundred to one. Ninety nine other times that would have been you out there licking up dead skunk."

"Raccoon," he said.

"Whatever."

A little further up the road was another car accident. I had to slow down and carefully inch my way around the twisted metal because the pavement was starting to get narrow. Ten minutes later, rock walls started to climb either side of the Trail, and the road got even narrower. I prayed that we didn't run across any more accidents. I wasn't sure I would be able to get the van around anything stuck in the road.

Just about the time I thought our little rescue mission couldn't get any bleaker, we turned a curve, and the high beams lit up a big, jagged cliff looming over the Trail. The rock face was covered with graffiti. What caught my eye most was a rainbow colored peace sign and a big heart that said *Jeremy and Amanda*.

Maybe if we ever got through all this, I'd come back here and spray paint *Tripp and Prianka* on a huge slab of granite. Girls are supposed to like crap like that.

I think.

"We're turning off just past here," I said to Jimmy. "How's that plan coming along?"

"The one I've been working on with no help from you?"

"Yeah, that one."

"I'll let you know," he murmured as he cradled the handgun in his lap.

About a quarter mile later I saw the dirt road that Cal described. I took a deep breath and pulled Stella's minivan about fifty feet down the dark gravel, eased over, and parked on one side. Branches scraped against the roof. Ahead of us, the dirt road disappeared into the night. Somewhere down there some really bad people were keeping my parents, and I had no idea how I was going to get them back.

"Turn off the lights," said Jimmy.

"Good idea."

"I'm filled with them, man."

"Good," I said. "Because I'm still waiting on that killer idea that's gonna get my parents out of this place with all of us still in one piece."

"Wait for it," Jimmy said as the darkness engulfed us. "Just wait for it."

69

I STARTED RUNNING last year. Not that I had plans on joining track—I just thought I needed to be fit. I also had some dumbbells in my room, nothing serious, just something to keep my arms from looking like they belonged on an old lady. I was really glad I was semi-religious about using them, too, because Jimmy's plan involved us leaving his wheelchair behind and me carrying him down that scary road and up to the iron gates of the McDuffy Estate. Let me tell you, he was heavy. Lugging his muscle-bound butt was one serious workout.

Neither of us were surprised that the whole place was lit up like a beacon on a light house. I'm not sure where the electricity was coming from, but I had to guess that anyone who had a place this far out probably relied on a generator or three.

I considered dropping Jimmy on the ground, but I noticed a video camera mounted on a ten-foot-high brick wall that extended off in both directions as far as I could see. Good for keeping poxers out. Good for keeping people in.

"We're being watched," I whispered under my breath. "Be a good cripple and play dead."

"I am so going to beat the crap out of you when we're done with all this."

"No you won't. You're too much of a pacifist. You'll get Trina to do it."

"True."

"Now shut up." The video camera whirred, pivoted, and pointed directly at us.

I lowered Jimmy slowly to the ground. He lay there, sprawled out like he was dead. We both agreed that we needed to look helpless—helpless and weak. Jimmy also told me to act a little slow. After all, we were in the hill towns of Massachusetts where everyone was missing at least one tooth and probably only got as far as the eighth grade. Slow was believable.

Still, I wasn't as good an actor as Trina. 'Slow' wasn't part of my repertoire.

"Help," I screamed at the camera. "If anyone's there, HELP!"

Jimmy moaned for effect. I bent down and felt his forehead before looking back up at the camera with the biggest, saddest puppy-dog eyes I could muster.

"Please," I sobbed and wiped fake tears from my eyes with my sleeve. "My friend's hurt. I . . . I . . . I don't have anybody else."

The camera pointed down toward me. I could see the dark, soulless lens, spinning round and round. I felt like I was being examined by a Cyclops.

Suddenly, a spotlight exploded into life and bathed the whole front of the estate in daylight. I put my hand over my eyes and squinted. We were being judged. I had to make the most out of our little ruse, because I wasn't leaving this place without my parents.

I grabbed Jimmy by his shoulders and pulled him up to a sitting position.

"See that, Jimmy," I wailed. "They're still good peoples left in the world."

Jimmy feebly hugged me, moaning the whole time. When his mouth was right next to my ear he whispered: "You suck at acting. You wouldn't even make it on daytime soaps."

"Bite me, Special Olympics."

Jimmy swooned and threw himself to the ground again.

"NO," I wailed. "Don't die, Jimmy. There're people here who can maybe help us. Just hold on a little longer."

A hint of a smile crossed Jimmy's face as he lay on the ground. He was trying hard not to crack up. His smile disappeared when we heard a grinding noise followed by a metallic ping. The gate had been unlocked. I didn't turn when I heard footsteps running through the yard on the other side of the gate—I just hoped they didn't belong to more soldiers with more guns. I had my fill of both.

"Is your friend hurt or dead?" yelled a voice from the other side of the gate—not deep enough to be a guy but not quite high enough to belong to a girl.

"He's hurt. He fell off his bike. I don't think he can move his legs."

I saw the silhouette of the person with the weird voice as he/she/it opened the gate and trotted over to us. When the figure came close enough, I narrowed the possibilities to she or she/it.

A little troll of a woman bent down next to me. She was wearing a dark t-shirt and fatigues. Dog tags hung from her neck. I couldn't tell if she was in the Army or making a fashion statement.

"Call me Cheryl," she said in a voice that sounded like she'd been screaming at a concert for twenty-four hours straight.

"I'm Andy," I sobbed. Jimmy and I had decided that we couldn't chance using my real name. We didn't know why, but it seemed like a bad idea if Diana, whoever she was, knew I was the doctor's son.

"My friend's hurt. The soldier men said you could help."

"Soldier men?"

"Yeah. The ones that talked funny. They said they were heading to North Carolina. They told us that there was food and water here but that they weren't staying."

Cheryl the It knitted her brow. "Damn deserters," she growled, and her face darkened. "What's your friend's name?"

"His name's Jimmy. We ran into each other a couple of days ago. He's the only friend I got left."

"Andy?" Jimmy moaned. "I can't feel my legs. Andy?"

Cheryl the It reached down and heaved Jimmy over her shoulder like he was a sack of potatoes. His eyes flew open, and he mouthed a silent *Yikes* as she jostled him around, flexed her squat, little troll legs, and began marching back toward the gate.

"Follow me," she grunted as she marched into the light. "Don't want to be caught out here without nothing to protect yourself." She spat on the ground, and Jimmy and I both almost hurled.

We were exactly where we planned to be. Still, as we walked through the gates of the McDuffy Estate, I somehow felt as though I was heading directly into the sun, and things that fly into the sun have brief but spectacular deaths.

70

"WE HAVE A medical doc," said Cheryl the It, as we passed through a big brick archway. "He'll take a look at your friend, kid. Probably just pinched a nerve or something."

When we reached the front door she banged on the dark wood with her tiny fist, which I had no doubt could pummel me senseless. "Open up, dammit," she growled.

She shifted her little legs from one to the other under the weight of Jimmy. The two of them looked funny because he was easily twice her size. Still, in arm wrestling I'd bet money on her against Jimmy any day.

I heard the door unlock and watched as it creaked open with a sound that was lifted right out of one of the ridiculous horror movies I used to devour. On the other side was a greasy looking guy in a lab coat with a comb-over, trimmed moustache, and goatee.

"What have we here?"

"This one needs to see the doc," said Cheryl the It to Dr. Greasy.

"The Doctor might not be so compliant today, Cheryl." The words slithered off his tongue. The guy was seriously gross.

"We'll see about that," she huffed. The muscles on her neck bulged under the weight of Jimmy. She stormed past the guy like he was nothing but empty air.

"Jimmy," I cried like a four-year-old. "Don't take Jimmy." I was completely serious. Jimmy's plan seemed easy enough—fake sick and get to see the doctor. There just wasn't a provision in our plan for the two us to get separated.

"He's in good hands, kid," growled Cheryl the It, and she disappeared down a corridor to the left.

We watched them go. Finally, Dr. Greasy snorted, closed the door, turned, and stared at me from head to toe.

"Where—where are you taking Jimmy?"

Dr. Greasy just sneered. I felt like a frog in Biology class. Jimmy told me to act slow, but I almost didn't need to act. I had no idea what was going on, and this whole place scared the tatti out of me. I knitted my brow, pouted, and put every mental effort I could muster into squeezing out a tear. Let me tell you, crying on cue is a special talent.

I'm not that talented—so I did the first thing that popped into my head. I threw myself to the floor and buried my face in my hands.

"I want Jimmy," I choked out through my splayed fingers.

Dr. Greasy just stood there waiting for me to finish. I gave him a little bit of a show before quieting down. Finally, after what seemed like eons, he cleared his throat, bent down next to me, and lightly put his hand on my shoulder.

"Your friend will be fine," he said. "How about some cookies and milk?"

I shook my head. Really? Cookies and milk? You got to be kidding me. He tried again.

"What's your name?"

"Andy Caron," I whimpered. Andy Caron was a kid at school who always had a booger hanging out of his nose. Nice enough, I guess, except for the booger. He was probably eating someone else's nose, boogers and all, right about now.

"Well, Andy Caron. My name is Dr. Marks, but you can just call me . . . well . . . you can just call me Dr. Marks."

Big of him—this was the kind of guy who demanded to be called Steven instead of Steve or Howard instead of Howie even though both names seriously sucked balls. This was the kind of guy who had absolutely no friends—ever.

"Uh huh," I managed.

"So how about those cookies?"

I shook my head fiercely and started to blubber, again. I was stalling, mostly because the idea of eating those cookies and drinking that milk sounded an awful lot like downing special Kool-Aid.

He curled his lip in disgust. Without warning, he shot his hand out and grabbed hold of my hair.

"Ow," I yelped.

Dr. Marks dragged me to my feet. This time there really were tears dropping on to my cheeks.

"Shut up," he hissed and let go of a fistful of my scalp, only to replace his hold on me with an iron grip around my arm. "I don't have time for this. I don't have time for sniveling halfwits, you . . . you . . . halfwit."

"Owee, owee," I cried again. That's what Trina used to say when she got a 'boo boo' when we were younger.

He dragged me down a central corridor past paintings of old people who looked like they had to be sitting on broom handles to make them pose so seriously. At the end of the hallway we came to a door with a card slot underneath the handle—the kind you see in hotels. He pulled a plastic card out of his lab coat pocket and inserted it into the slot.

The door clicked open.

We pushed through into another corridor, but this one was all white, like in a hospital. Dr. Marks pulled me along, his fingers digging into my bicep.

"Leggo," I yelped.

He squeezed even harder.

"You listen to me, Andy Caron, and you listen to me good. I am bringing you for some milk and cookies. When you're done eating them, and trust me, you will eat every last one, you're going to meet some nice people. Got me?"

"But . . . but what about Jimmy? What about the doctor?"

"After your snack," he snarled. His grip tightened even more. I prayed that Jimmy was being handled better by Cheryl the It. Actually, what I really prayed for was that Jimmy was being brought to my father. Dad would know what to do. With his help, we would blow this popcorn stand and leave these freaky people to whatever they were doing out here in the middle of nowhere.

We made a turn and found ourselves in front of another door. Again, Dr. Marks inserted his card and the door unlocked. I made a mental note that I had to get me one of those cards if we ever had a prayer of getting out of this place. We stepped into a great room in the back of the house. Everything was deep, dark wood with shiny surfaces, the kind adults don't let kids near until they are legally responsible to pay for damages. At the back of the room, a great glass wall separated us from the darkness outside. All we needed was a bunch of pretty vampires with sparkly diamond skin to make the picture complete.

Barf.

I counted six people in the great room besides us. There was another solider sitting sideways in a big, leather chair. He barely acknowledged us as he flipped through a magazine, clearly bored out of his gourd. In front of a bank of computer monitors sat some guys in lab coats and three librarian-esque women also wearing the fashion *du jour* and sporting granny glasses. The women's hair was so tightly pinned up that the skin on their faces was stretched tight.

The weird thing was that all of them, the guys and the ladies, looked a little too perfect—like robots or clones or people from Hollywood.

Black and white pictures danced across the monitor screens.

One showed the front of the house where Jimmy and I had enacted our premiere performance. Another showcased a room filled with people sitting on beds and talking, and a third showed another room filled with poxers. They were jammed in like sardines. A fourth monitor showed an empty room except for a young guy banging his head against the wall. I could tell he was a poxer without even seeing his face. The way he moved and his dirty hair—that's what gave it away.

Besides the soldier, who was engrossed in whatever rag he was reading, the rest of the 'pretty' people were watching the monitors with interest. Some of them stroked their chins or crossed their arms over their chests. One of the women had a pen wedged between her manicured fingers and kept pointing at the monitors filled with the living and the other one on channel dead.

Although I didn't hear their words, I knew what they were talking about.

They were experimenting—the question was, for what?

71

DR. MARKS DEPOSITED me in a room adjacent to the great room. He called it The Library. I rubbed my arm when he finally let me go.

"I'm getting your snack," he grumbled as he eyeballed me again—like I was the biggest delinquent he had ever met. "Don't touch anything."

He closed the door a little too roughly as he left. I heard the tumbler click into place.

I was locked in.

"Well that just sucks," I whispered under my breath. I looked around the room. I suppose The Library was pretty remarkable, if you were Sherlock Holmes or some other old, dead guy. Hard covered, leather bound volumes lined the walls in ten-foot-tall bookcases. There was also a ladder attached to a metal track about three-quarters of the way up that circled the room. I'd never really seen one of those before. It was classy, I guess—if you were impressed by that sort of thing.

I wasn't impressed.

In the center of the room was a big, mahogany desk topped with a neatly stacked pile of folders. There were also a couple of dainty, hard-backed chairs and a little table between them. An empty plate and glass sat on the table. I guess someone else had been offered cookies and milk before me. Maybe that person was now premiering on one of those monitors.

I went to the desk and starting rifling through the folders. I wasn't sure what I was looking for or what I would do with any information that I found, but Dr. Marks said don't touch anything.

That meant touch everything.

Some of the folders had weird titles on the tabs like 'Patient zero' and 'Exposure rate.'

I opened one and skimmed a few pages before my eyes stopped on a highlighted sentence that read, *'Current trending data estimates an immune response ratio of 1/132.'*

A few pages further I found another highlighted section that said, *'We are still somewhat confused about the nature of the Necropoxy organism. Although synthesized with a turn-off switch at the molecular level, rapid mutation has eradicated all forms of said switch.'*

I read a little more before turning a page and finding another sentence circled in angry, red pen next to a small diagram of the world with arrows and numbers. It said, *'Prevailing conditions, barring any unforeseen severe weather anomalies, estimate global infestation to occur in slightly less than sixteen hours and 37 minutes from equator to both poles.'*

I felt like puking. I suppose I wasn't surprised, but seeing the words in black and white was still a bit of a shock.

The simple truth was that a bunch of eggheads killed the world. I read the comic books and the graphic novels. People have been writing about the zombie apocalypse for years, mostly because the idea was so freaking outlandish that the stories made for a good read without the real, live nightmares.

Oops. That would be a big, fat mistake on that one.

There was a bright, red folder in the middle of the pile. The tab read 'Site 37—Opal, Massachusetts.'

Inside, the corners of most of the pages were worn and tattered as though they had been read a zillion times. The very first sentence jumped out at me

'In the unlikely occurrence of an exposure event, each Site has been staffed by five male and five female medical professionals of appropriate age and health along with two senior non-productive staff, all of whom who have tested immune to the Necropoxy organism. Their sole mission is to . . .'

I heard the lock pop and watched the door swing open, and there I was, still standing at the desk with the red folder in my hands.

Caught—um—red handed.

This time, an old lady came into The Library. She looked like she was getting ready to play a game of golf or have afternoon tea. She was wearing khaki pants, a pink shirt, a tan blazer, and her hair looked stylized in that short, gym teacher sort of way. She wore glossy brown loafers that were so shiny I bet her pet soldier in the great room spent a good hour working on them.

Half rimmed librarian glasses perched on the end of her nose.

She stared over those glasses at me for a good, long time—long enough for me to notice I was still holding the folder. I carefully lowered my hand and let the folder rest back on the pile with all the others.

She smiled and closed the door.

"I like the color red," I stammered. "Is Dr. Marks bringing me cookies?"

"Not just yet," she said. "Your name, please."

"Andy."

"Yes?"

"Andy Caron."

"Hmmm—Andy, you say?" The old lady smirked as though she just caught me cheating on an Algebra test.

"Andy Caron," I repeated. Geez, was she old *and* deaf? "Where's Jimmy? We were on bikes. He was hurt. The soldier men told us that we could come here, and you could help us and . . ."

She threw her hand up in that universal way that meant 'shut up.'

"I am Diana," she said.

"And?" Quid pro quo with a little smartass thrown in for good measure. She raised her eyebrows.

"Diana Radcliffe," she said.

"Where's Jimmy?"

"I heard you the first time. First, come and sit down and let's have a little talk, shall we?"

She motioned for me to sit in one of the petite little chairs. We were like two wolves circling each other as I warily came around the desk and slowly sat down. Old lady Radcliffe sat facing me, her legs primly crossed. She regarded me again, long enough for me to want to squirm, but I didn't.

"Did you find anything interesting in those folders?"

"The red one's pretty," I said, but the words sounded hollow. Yeah, lady, I found your plan to wipe out our species. Bully for you.

She licked her lips and let silence fill the void between us. Finally, she said, "Is that all?"

"I was looking for pictures."

"Were you now?"

"Yes."

"Did you find any?"

"No."

I heard an electric sound, like static. Shortly, an intercom voice from somewhere overhead filled the room and made me jump.

"Is everything fine, Ma'am?"

"Yes, Dr. Marks. I'm quite fine. Our guest and I were just about to have a discussion."

"Would you like refreshments for you and the boy?"

She regarded me. "That won't be necessary. I don't think our Mr. Andy Caron is hungry or thirsty just now, correct?"

She waited, clearly expecting for me to reply.

"Um, yeah. Correct," I said.

"Very well, Ma'am." The intercom clicked off, and we were alone again.

"You're a very brave, young man to carry your injured friend down a dark road at night, alone, considering the monstrous plague that has befallen our . . . race."

"I guess. I thought you might have a doctor here."

Diana chuckled.

"We're all doctors, my dear, or we wouldn't have been chosen to be here. We're just not medical doctors, per se. We understand microorganisms and sociological behavior and such. Sadly, not one of us can properly use a band-aid."

I was a little confused but as long as she was willing to play, so was I.

"But that Cheryl lady said you have a medical doctor."

"Purely by accident," she said. "Although he's not as cooperative as we would like him to be." Diana leaned forward in her chair. "Could you venture a guess as to why?"

This time I didn't answer her. On the outside my face was blank. On the inside I was giving a big high five to my dad. Why would he want to cooperate with anyone who was holding him and Mom against their wills?

"Oh, come now, Andy Caron. I'm sure you must have some thoughts on the matter."

I looked at the old biddy straight in the eyes.

"Maybe he needs a nurse. Does the doctor have a . . . nurse with him?"

Diana threw her head back and laughed.

"What's so funny?" I whispered.

"Priceless," she cackled. "Absolutely priceless." Diana reached inside her blazer, like a guy on a detective show reaching for a gun, and pulled out a crumpled bit of something. She reached over and handed it to me.

The color drained from my face. I was looking at a picture of me and Trina with Mom and Dad, taken when the two of us were twelve at a beach on Cape Cod. I remembered the fat lady in the bikini who took the shot for us. Maybe that's why we all looked like we were giggling.

I turned the picture over. On the back of the photograph it said 'Molly, Doug, Tripp, and Trina—Provincetown, Massachusetts.'

"Yes, Tripp. Your mother is still alive, although my understanding is that she's a real-estate professional, not a nurse. My question is, where is your sister Trina?"

My blood began to boil "Dead," I lied.

Diana raised her eyebrows. Her shark-toothed smile turned into a frown.

"She's dead." I screamed at her. My hands never left the arms of the chair, but my knuckles turned white.

Her rock-hard face didn't move, but something flickered in her eyes—maybe disappointment—like she had just sat in line all night for concert tickets and they sold out one person in front of her.

I raised my voice even more.

"You people and your freaking science project are to blame." I bellowed. "You killed her. You killed my sister."

72

DIANA MOVED ME to the great room with the pretty eggheads and the monitors. They were all still watching the grainy images on screen. Mostly, they were interested in the middle one with the people. The poxer on one of the other monitors was still banging his head against the wall.

Greasy Dr. Marks watched me warily with his beady, little eyes but didn't have to vice-grip me this time. The soldier had his gun leveled at me, instead. You'd think that there would be some weird rule against pointing guns at kids, but if there was, Diana didn't know about it.

"Jimmy still needs help." I snapped at her.

"He's being tended to by your father," she said as she perched in a winged back chair. "We are not barbarians, you know."

Wanna bet?

At least I knew that Jimmy had found his way to my dad. By this time, I'm sure he had told him everything, and maybe they were even working on a plan on how we were all going to get out of here.

Or not.

Note to self: next time we break into an evil stronghold, we need an exit strategy not devised by the ginger in the wheelchair with a taste for tofu.

Also, I wasn't sure where my mom was. I had to find her, too. That's the weird thing about parents. They often come in pairs.

The red folder had called this place 'Site 37.' I wondered how many sites there were. Was Necropoxy just in Massachusetts? New England? The world? According to what I read, the disease spread everywhere in sixteen hours and thirty-seven minutes, more or less, and that deadline had passed days ago.

That meant 'game over.' We, meaning those of the living variety, lost.

I watched Diana as she poured herself a cup of tea from a porcelain teapot and dumped a boat load of sugar in the pristine, little cup. It would have been great if any of the morons in here had woken out of their lunacy and switched out her sugar bowl for rat poison, but I suppose that was just wishful thinking.

Diana stirred her tea with a delicate, silver spoon and her pinky up. Yup—I officially despised her.

"What I would like to know, my young Mr. Light, is where Mr. Pooler and Mr. Longo are. You obviously met them or you would never have found out about our little camp."

Camp? Alright, sure. I suppose some people would call this camping. I just never met any of them.

"And what I would like to know, you old bag, is where my parents are."

The soldier repositioned his rifle. "You should talk to the lady real nice, my friend."

"I'm not your friend."

"Got that right."

Diana sipped at her tea. "Your father is directly down the hall," she said. "We have our makeshift medical office there. What a wonderful and serendipitous coincidence that we found him, don't you think?"

I just stared at her.

"What about my mom?"

"Now that one's a little trickier," she purred. Her eyes moved to the monitors.

Cheryl the It appeared in the room with the people who were sitting on the beds and talking. She had a rifle out and was saying something to them.

In a loud, clear voice, Diana said, "Cheryl, dear? Can you please ask Mrs. Light to face the monitor?

Cheryl looked right at us through the screen.

"Sir, yes Sir," she growled and stepped off camera. When she returned she had my mother by the arm. Cheryl the It pushed her forward so that her face filled the monitor. A lump caught in my throat. One of my mom's eyes was swollen shut, and her lip was cracked.

Rage boiled in the pit of my stomach.

"Please," whimpered my mother. "Please let me see my husband. Please let us get our children. I know they're safe. I just know they are."

"That will be enough, Cheryl," ordered Diana. My mother was pulled away from the screen. Diana turned her gaze on me. I was literally shaking I was so angry. "I see a family resemblance between you and your father," she said. "He looked at me in just the same way when I told him what we do here."

"So?"

"So? Is that all you have to say for yourself? Come now, I'm sure there must be a little curiosity in there. Just a tad."

"Listen, you poor excuse for a dried up librarian, I don't give a rat's ass what you do here. I want my mom and my dad, and I want them now."

"Or what?"

Damn, I wish I was clever enough to come up with an answer to that one. I wasn't, so I just stood there, the anger dancing across my face like wind stirring up a dust devil in the desert.

Diana rolled her eyes, not far off from the same sort of expression I had seen on Prianka's face once or twice.

"Cheryl," she said in a commanding voice. "Have we injected Mrs. Bijur?"

"Not my job," she said through the monitor.

Diana moaned.

"Dr. Chapdelaine?" she said to one of the men consumed with the images on screen. He was a little, rat-faced excuse for a human being with a blank expression and a shaved head.

"Yes, yes," he twittered. He checked a clipboard he was holding in his hands. "At nineteen hundred hours."

"Very well," said Diana. "Cheryl? Dear?" The burly little woman appeared back on screen. "Mrs. Bijur, please."

I heard a commotion on screen. Diana lifted a remote control, pointed at the screen, and pressed a button. The sound went mute.

"Ok, I'll bite. What do you do here?"

She took another sip of tea.

"Isn't it obvious, Mr. Light?" Her eyes went back to the monitors.

The poxer who had been banging his head against the wall had stopped. His head leaned to one side like he was listening for something. The next thing I knew he was no longer alone. A terrified woman with mousy brown hair, wearing dress pants that my mother wouldn't be caught dead in, was with him.

It was terrible. Either he was too speedy or she was too tired to fight, because the poxer sank his teeth into her arm in seconds.

The eggheads pulled out timers and alternated watching the monitor and checking their stop watches.

I could feel my face turning red and my eyes burning. Diana watched me intently.

"Well, isn't it obvious?" she asked again.

I didn't answer her. Nothing was obvious about this. Everything was insane—completely and totally insane—and the queen of Insanity Land was sitting in front of me drinking tea.

She put her china cup down and slapped both hands down on her knees. A lunatic's smile bloomed on her face.

"We're going to save the world."

73

A DOOR SLAMMED open on the other side of the room, and my father stormed in. The soldier immediately transferred the gun from me to my dad. I guess they didn't think of me as much of a threat.

"Dad," I cried.

I could see that he wanted nothing more than to run to me, but soldier guy had the muzzle of the rifle leveled at him. Dad raised both his hands, but he had his angry face on. According to Diana, I was sporting the same expression.

"What the hell is this, Diana? That's my son. I don't quite know how he got here, but he's here."

"Yes he is," she said in that calm, even tone.

My dad looked directly at the soldier and slowly lowered his hands.

"Get that thing outta my face," he boomed. The sound echoed in the cavernous great room.

My dad's a big guy. He's all about fitness and eating right. If there wasn't a gun between him and that soldier, he probably would have taken him apart.

The soldier looked nervously to Diana. She rolled her eyes again in that very Prianka-like way and dismissively waved her hand.

The soldier lowered the gun, and my dad ran and engulfed me in a bear hug. The pretty eggheads barely noticed, but Dr. Marks and Diana watched us with bored, intellectual curiosity, as though they couldn't quite understand this odd thing called family.

Dad practically lifted me off the ground as he crushed me to him, his face right up against mine.

"Jimmy's in a facility wheelchair," he whispered into my ear. "He's got things covered."

I desperately clung to him and whispered back.

"Diana thinks Trina's dead. Go with it."

He hugged me even tighter. Finally, Dr. Marks had enough.

"Are we done with the family reunion?" he snapped, but my father wouldn't let me go. Soldier guy finally intervened, reaching between our tangled arms and forcing us apart.

"Where's my daughter?" Dad barked at Diana.

"We weren't able to retrieve your daughter," she said.

"You weren't able to retrieve me either," I laughed. "I came to you." I turned to my dad and made with the puppy dog eyes again. "Is Jimmy going to be okay?"

"I don't think so," he lied. "It may be his lower spine."

Dr. Marks stepped forward, the grease practically oozing out his skin. If he was any slimier he would make little squishy noises on the floor when he walked.

"So what are you saying?"

"Are you deaf, you creepy freak?" I screamed at him. "My sister's dead, and my friend's a cripple."

Right on cue, my dad dropped to his knees.

"Trina's dead? My little girl?" He put his face in his hands and began to sob, loudly, like I had never seen him do before. Come to think of it, I've never see him cry at all. He was doing a bang up job, considering he already knew that Trina was safe and sound at Aunt Ella's house.

I put my hand on his shoulder.

Dr. Marks completely ignored us. Instead, he turned to Diana.

"Well, if the boy can't walk, he can still be of use to us, don't you think?" He pointed his chin at the monitors where there were now two poxers in the room when just a little while ago there had only been one.

The pretty eggheads huddled and conferred with each other. One of the plastic-faced women said, "Infestation in just over a minute, Diana. We've improved on the change rate."

Diana poured herself another cup of tea—probably just to be pretentious, and left it sitting next to the teapot. She nodded her head once to the woman and trained her eyes back on us.

"Come now, Dr. Marks. Let's not show ourselves to be too insensitive. The good doctor here just found out about the death of his daughter. I think we owe him a moment or two, don't you?"

The man's nostrils flared. "Everyone's lost people."

"You're quite right," said Diana. "But not as special as Trina Light, or for that matter, her brother, who very conveniently walked right through our front door."

My dad stiffened and got to his feet.

"What do you mean?" I said.

My father put his hands up and shook his head. He wanted me to be quiet, which wasn't the easiest of tricks for me to master. Instead, he sort of positioned himself in front of me.

"You're not touching my son, Diana," he said.

She sighed, somewhere between annoyance and boredom. "We do what we do for the greater good."

Dr. Marks took a step toward me, but my father blocked his way.

"We just need a little bit of his blood, Dr. Light," he said. "It would be foolish to waste the whole boy all at once."

Who's blood? What blood?

"Over my dead body," growled my father.

"That could be arranged," snarled Dr. Marks.

"Wait a second," I said. "Could someone please tell me what's going on?"

Before anyone had a chance to answer me, the monitors went blank all in rapid succession. The pretty eggheads yelped, and all eyes immediately focused on the black screens.

Dr. Marks momentarily lost interest in me and swiveled around to stare at the dead monitors.

"Dad?" I whispered. "I don't understand."

"You're most likely immune," he whispered, "To everything—the airborne virus and the bite. You're the product of two people who are immune. That makes you super immune."

I never stopped to wonder why, but I guess the odds that two people who were immune, like my mom and dad, met and had kids, were like a million to one. Furthermore, the odds that any of those kids survived the poxer hordes for the past week were even more astronomical.

Trina and I could really be freaks—really, really lucky freaks.

Still, at the end of the day, one thing was perfectly clear. These people wanted to experiment on the freaks, and if we didn't get out of here soon, they were very likely going to get their chance.

74

"GET THOSE MONITORS up immediately," ordered Dr. Marks, but no one in the room moved. They were like a bunch of little kids who accidentally dropped a drinking glass and let it shatter beneath their feet. They all stood still with their fingers up their noses.

"Did anyone hear me?" he bellowed even louder. His face turned red, and little beads of sweat erupted on his forehead.

My father stood in front of me, blocking me from everyone.

"You're not touching him, Diana."

"We'll see about that," she said. "Right now we have more pressing concerns."

Diana left her tea on the table and stood up. "Cheryl? Can you hear me?"

Nothing.

"Great," yelled Dr. Marks. "That's just great. The com is down, too? Chapdelaine, Jacques, Walls, go see what's happening with Cheryl."

Two of the tightly wound women stared at each other like they had just been slapped in the face. Dr. Chapdelaine just looked nervous.

"What if the power is off in that part of the building?" he chirped.

"What if it is?"

"The doors could be open."

"So?"

"Doors with . . . things behind them."

Dr. Marks looked like he was going to tear his hair out. His face turned another two shades of red, and his sticky hair plastered itself to his head.

"Doctors," said Diana with such presence that her voice sounded as though she was speaking through a megaphone. "Please go check on the monitoring system. This equipment is vital to our continued work and safety."

The three of them looked from Dr. Marks to Diana then back to Dr. Marks. They were scared. I could almost smell waves of fear rolling off of them.

"Oh for God's sake," she snapped. "Private Norris. Please accompany the doctors to the medical wing." That got them moving, and in seconds they were gone, accompanied by soldier guy.

The two remaining white coats sat down at computer terminals and began madly typing. That just left me and my dad, Dr. Marks and Diana, staring at each other.

She focused on my father but cast a disapproving glance my way.

"Is his friend really unable to walk?" she asked him.

My dad didn't say anything at first. He was still tensed up like a prize fighter right before the bell goes off for the next round.

"Doctor Light, I asked you a question." She sounded like a kindergarten teacher scolding a naughty child. I wasn't used to anyone talking to my dad like that.

"His friend, Jimmy, is unable to walk," he said evenly. Diana visibly sighed with relief—so did Dr. Marks—but their relief was short-lived. "But I think he's just fine the way he is," added my dad. He looked back at me and smiled. "As a matter of fact. Jimmy is perfect."

Dr. Marks and Diana gaped, wide-eyed, at my father. I especially enjoyed the part when the dawning comprehension seemed to color their faces.

"Is he even ill?" she said thickly, like her tongue was swelling inside her mouth.

"Define ill," I said.

The four of us stood there, my dad still blocking me from Dr. Marks, who, along with Diana, was quietly going mad. I don't mean angry mad, because they were certainly that. They were descending into crazy mad, like their carefully constructed house of cards was about to tumble.

"Do you want to be responsible for the destruction of the human race?" Diana screamed. Her words echoed in the cavernous great room.

My dad stood his ground. "It seems to me that people like you have already accomplished that," he said.

"People like me are going to save it," she seethed.

"By experimenting on anyone who's left?"

"Yeah," I added from behind my dad's massive shoulders.

"No," she said as she pointed at me. "By experimenting on the rare few like your son who are immune."

"The hell you are," I said.

"We will find out whatever it is inside of him that protects him from Necropoxy, and we will synthesize it to rebuild our race for those who are worthy enough to call themselves a part of it. And I don't care if we cut him into teeny tiny bits to do it."

My father and I both didn't know what to say. I'm not sure which part of what came out of Diana's mouth scared me more—the fact that she wanted to draw and quarter me until I bled an antidote or the fact that she just indicated that not everyone left alive would be good enough to be administered a dose once it was created.

"You're nuckin' futz, lady." Sorry. It came out before I could stop myself. My dad snorted—just a little.

"How dare you," roared Dr. Marks, but he didn't have a chance to say anything else.

I never thought I would actually say this, but it was a welcome relief when I heard a loud crash followed by gunfire in another part of the building.

75

"WHAT ON EARTH?" gasped Diana.

Dr. Marks's world had obviously titled on its axis. He spun around in circles as though he didn't know quite what to do. Finally his eyes landed on the last two white coats typing away at their computers.

"You and you," he screamed, pointing his slimy finger at them.

"But . . ." said one of them.

"Did I ask you to speak?" he roared.

She stopped talking, her fingers frozen in place above the keyboard.

"You have exactly two minutes. Go find out what is going on and report back to Diana and myself."

They immediately stood and rushed out of the room. When they were gone, he turned back to us, his chest heaving up and down like he had just run a marathon.

"Now that wasn't very smart, Dr. Marks," said my father.

"No it wasn't," murmured Diana, nervously. The only people left in the great room were an old lady, my muscle-bound dad, his amazing son, and the grease-ball with the comb-over. Dr. Marks reached into his lab coat and pulled out a small pistol, the kind that ladies probably carry in their pocketbooks. "Don't worry, Diana," he said. "I have this."

My father picked up a candlestick that was sitting on one of the nicely polished, dark wood tables and whipped it at Dr. Marks with amazing accuracy. The gun popped out of his hand and went skidding across the floor. He yelped in pain.

"And now you don't," growled my father and charged him like a bull. Dr. Marks squealed in surprise but didn't have a chance to get out of the way. My father grabbed him around the waist and threw him to the ground.

"Where's my wife?" he screamed at him. "You lock me in this chamber of horrors and tell me I'll never see my wife again unless I get used to administering cold medicine and wiping your noses?" My father grabbed him by the shirt collar and shook him so hard that I thought his head was going to break off. "Just who in the hell do you people think you are?"

I even cringed a little when my dad started punching him in the head—over and over again.

I was so amazed at my dad's utter coolness that I didn't even realize that Diana had pulled out an equally tiny pistol from her perfectly pleated jacket and leveled it at him.

"Good show. Good show," she said. "But I'm afraid we've had enough." She pulled the trigger and winged my dad in the arm. I saw a little spray of blood spurt out. Some red splatter even landed on greasy Dr. Marks.

"No," I yelped.

"Hmmpppf," groaned my father but didn't stop his full on throttling of Dr. Marks.

"I said ENOUGH," Diana screeched and shot the gun again, but this time, she aimed straight up in the air. A few chips of plaster fell to the floor at her feet.

You would think a bullet in the arm would have been enough to stop my dad, but the second shot was the one that made him stop.

I ran to him. "Are you stupid?" I yelled. "I came all this way for my father. Not for a dead dad."

My father's back heaved up and down. There was almost a week's full of rage and hatred built up inside of him. I could tell he didn't want to stop. He wanted to smear Dr. Marks into the floor. Finally, he leaned back on his knees and absentmindedly looked at this arm.

"Dad?"

"It's just a scratch," he said.

"Like a tough guy scratch or a wussy scratch?"

"Wussy scratch," he said and winked at me, but his face turned deadly serious when he locked eyes with the old witch and her teeny tiny gun. She'd maneuvered into his line of vision.

"I was taught to dissuade with a gun, not, excuse the pun, disarm. I'm assuming, Dr. Light, that the bullet only grazed you?"

"You're a good shot," Dad said.

We all heard another few bullets fly from somewhere in the building. They seemed a lot closer this time.

"Get off me," ordered Dr. Marks. His face was bloodied, and I think his nose was broken. It looked awesome.

My father stood up and admired the devastation he rained down upon the greasy doctor. He smiled. I bet it felt good. I wish it had been me who pummeled the guy.

Diana spoke with a steady, even voice. "You will tend to yourself and your wound, after which you will tend to Dr. Marks. He is important to me."

"I won't," said my father. "Not until you let me see my wife."

"She's unharmed," said Diana.

"How do I know you're not lying?"

"Ask your clever boy," she said.

I nodded my head. "Before the monitors went, I saw her." My throat tightened. "Someone beat her up a little."

My dad half-smiled. "That happened when the solders took us on our way to find you," he said. "Never corner a Light woman. She'll come at you swinging."

I could only imagine what happened between my parents, Luke and Cal. If they treated my mom anyway like they treated Trina, she could have easily gotten hit once or twice. That would have been enough for my dad to put his hands in the air and surrender. If there's one thing I'm sure of, he would have done anything to make sure she didn't get hit a third time.

We heard gunfire again. This time it sounded as though the shooter was practically on us. The next thing I knew, the door flew open, and a blur of people came streaming in. They were led by Jimmy, who was madly pumping the wheels on an old wheelchair that had nothing on his sleek, tricked out, modern one.

"Poxers," he cried. "Right behind us."

His words didn't register—not at first. Instead, my eyes landed on one of the women running in behind him.

She was my mom.

76

"WE NEED TO CLOSE the door," she ordered. "Throw me a keycard."

Jimmy took one of those plastic doodads out of his pocket, just like the one I had seen Dr. Marks use to open doors, and tossed it to my mom. She pushed the door closed and swiped the card. There was an audible click, followed by sighs of relief from at least a dozen people who had come in with them.

Unfortunately, that was followed by loud banging as the poxers who had been on their heels, hit the door.

Been there, done that, but most everyone else started to squeal.

Amidst the chaos, my dad took a step forward.

"Molly?" he whispered. My mom turned and saw my dad and immediately rushed into his arms. Touching, right? My parents were cool like that. Jimmy flashed a grin and gave me two thumbs up. Then he saw bloody, bloody Dr. Marks and Diana, who still had her pistol in her hand. Her face had turned to granite. Jimmy's expression turned grim.

"Be quiet, people," she said, but no one even heard her.

My mother saw me and threw her arms around me. I was taller than her by more than a little, but it still felt great to be getting a hug from my mom.

"They think Trina's dead," I whispered to her. "She's fine. Don't let them think otherwise."

She nodded and hugged me again.

Crack. Diana let another bullet fly into the ceiling.

"I said, be quiet," she screamed. More plaster fell to the ground. Maybe, if we were lucky, the whole thing would rain down on her.

People settled down enough for me to notice that none of the doctors, the soldier, or Cheryl the It was with them.

"Where are our people?" barked Dr. Marks as he got to his feet.

"Hey, you," yelled a big guy with tattoos all over his arms. "You're the one who laced my cookies and milk."

I snorted when he said that because, well, it was sort of funny. What was even funnier was when Tattoo Guy stepped forward and punched Dr. Marks square in the face. He went stiff and fell straight back like a tree falling in the forest. The big guy shook his hand and grunted like he just got a boo boo.

I think it was worth it.

"Yo, Dude," barked Tattoo Guy. Your 'people' aren't even people anymore. With any luck, they're monsters, and they're on the other side of that door with the rest of the freaks you collected along the way."

Dr. Marks got to his feet again. He was definitely getting the well-deserved beating of his life.

The banging on the door became more insistent. Everyone started to panic, except for Diana, the queen of the dead. She still held her pretty little gun in her old lady hands.

Jimmy reached around his back and pulled out one of the handguns we had brought with us. He must have shoved the piece into his pants before we were let into this insane asylum. He pointed the muzzle straight at her.

"Hey, lady. I'm not the violent type, but if you don't let us out of here, and now, I think you're going to have a red hot mess on your hands." He cocked the gun. "Don't try me. I've been through worse crap than this in the past week. Knowing you are connected at all is reason enough."

She pointed her gun right at Jimmy.

"And why is there a possibility that my people are now among the afflicted?"

Jimmy's eyes narrowed. "Your midget soldier thought I wasn't as handi-capable as I am," he said. "I cried. She came to check on me. I took her swipe card, opened some doors, and the rest, as you say, is history."

I take back thinking that Cheryl the It had anything on Jimmy. He rocked.

The color in Dr. Marks's face drained as much as I could tell through his growing mass of purple and yellow bruises.

"You opened our holding cells?"

"I set human beings free," said Jimmy. "The zombies? Well, let's just say I may have opened a few wrong doors along the way."

Diana's face tightened. "I suppose we'll have to start over," she said, staring directly at Dr. Marks. He only nodded his swollen, bruised head. Then Diana brought her other hand up to steady her gun, which was aimed directly at Jimmy. "It's too bad you won't be here to help us."

The people in the room gasped. Someone yelped, "Hey lady. He's just a kid."

As for me, I did the only thing I could think of doing. I pulled away from my parents and stood directly in the middle of her line of fire. If she was going to shoot Jimmy, she'd have to shoot him through me, and she wasn't going to shoot me. If I understood everything correctly, she needed what was flowing through my veins, especially if she was going to, as she put it, rebuild.

"Move out of my way," she screeched at me.

"Put the gun down, you fossil."

"You have ruined everything."

"I've ruined everything?" I had to repeat it again because I was sort of shocked. "I've ruined everything? You people are the monsters. This is just Site 37. How many others are there?"

She didn't say anything. I could tell she wanted to shoot someone, but she couldn't shoot me, and she couldn't get a bead on Jimmy, because I was standing in front of him. I suppose she did what she thought was the next best thing.

She turned and leveled the gun at my parents.

77

DO YOU KNOW when everything slows down, like when you take a spill on your bicycle or you drop a bottle of pop? You know what's going to happen, but time just seems like forever to get there. That's how I felt when Diana pointed the gun at my parents. She didn't need my mother, and my dad was only a medical doctor, not a scientist. I was her Holy Grail. My parents were just pawns.

I could practically see Diana's brain coming to the same conclusion, and I didn't know what to do. The banging of the poxers was getting louder. The people in the room were understandably freaked, and as soon as that old biddy stitched the most likely scenario together in her head, she was going to shoot my mom, my dad, Jimmy, or all three—and everything was happening in slow motion.

Dad stepped in front of Mom, shielding her. My legs began to shake. My whole life had brought me to this moment, and in this single instance in time, everything could change.

Was I wrong to come here? Should I have just left my parents with Diana? Maybe she would have kept my mother alive as long as my father did what she asked. What was I thinking? I was just a kid—a stupid, reckless, pain-in-the-ass kid, and now I was going to get someone killed.

Everything was so senseless and the one that made the least sense of all was Diana.

My legs started shaking more. I could feel them way down deep, like a rumble coming straight through my feet and up my calves. The vibration hit my stomach, and I could even feel the trembling in my chest—but it wasn't coming from me—it was coming from somewhere outside, beyond the glass wall in the back of the great room. All of a sudden, the back yard lit up, and I could see everything through the windows—giant fir trees, and birch, and oak. The lawn was neatly trimmed, and the trees hugged the edge of the grass like great sentinels, protecting the forest.

People started screaming, and for the first time, Diana's hand faltered, but only a little.

"What . . ." began Dr. Marks. That was all he had time to say. The window grew impossibly bright and a loud, blaring horn cut through the night. The wall shattered in an explosive burst, and splinters of wood and glass flew everywhere. Out of the spray of debris came a giant, yellow monster with a grill-like mouth and big square eyes.

Everyone scrambled for cover except for me, Jimmy, my parents, and Diana. We were locked inside a bubble, and the chaos around us didn't exist.

What burst that bubble was the squeal of tires, the smell of diesel, and the twin voices of my Aunt Ella and Trina.

"Get away from our brothers, you bitch," they both bellowed at Diana in unison, as they leapt from the school bus they were driving and pointed impossibly large guns, courtesy of Luke and Cal, directly at Diana.

My dad couldn't help but smile as he saw his sister, my aunt, and my sister, his daughter, coming to the rescue.

Proud moment if everything wasn't so weird.

"You don't know what you're doing," sobbed Dr. Marks. "We can fix this. We can really fix this."

"Fix what?" barked Aunt Ella at the oh-so-bruised greasy guy. "I don't give a rat's ass what the hell you're trying to fix here." She pointed at me and my parents. "All I know is he's my brother, she's my sister-in-law, and he's my nephew. They're coming with me."

Trina stepped forward, never questioning for a second that the witch with the pistol was any other than the infamous Diana.

"You have my parents, my brother, and my boyfriend, Grandma. Drop your squirt gun, or I'll blow your head off your preppy shoulders."

Diana didn't drop her gun. She didn't move. Instead her eyes narrowed, and she studied Trina like she was a lab rat.

"Trina Light—back from the grave, I presume." She switched her gaze to me. "And I thought it was such a pity she was dead."

"Not dead," snapped Trina. "But if you don't drop that toy by the count of three, you will be."

The banging on the hallway door sounded like gun fire. The smell of fresh pine and fall in New England—mixed with gasoline—filled my nose.

"One."

Diana did nothing. The gun was still pointing at my parents.

"Two."

With a look that I could only describe as snakelike, she lowered her arm but didn't drop the gun.

"Three."

Diana hesitated for like a nanosecond before carefully bending down and placing the pistol next to her glossy loafers. Somehow the two didn't seem to go together.

"Tripp," hissed Tina. "Take that popgun from her."

I didn't want to get any closer to Diana than I had to, but my legs chose to narrow the gap for me. They automatically carried me forward until I was right in front of her. She stared at me with utter hatred—a lava sea boiling beneath an icy crust. As I bent down to pick up the pistol, she shot out her arm and caressed mine.

"This isn't over, boy."

"Give it a rest, lady."

"We'll find you," she whispered. "Both of you."

"You and what army?" I spread my arms out. "Your doctors are gone. Your soldiers are gone. The only ones left are you and Dr. Marks. Look at yourselves. He's seriously close to useless, and you, well, you're a wrinkled, old bag of bones."

A shark-like grin spread across her face.

"We're Site 37, my dear." The words poured from her mouth like sweet, milk chocolate. Her gaze passed over me to the rest of the people there—the gaze of a smug, superior, genocidal maniac. "We might have lost a few minor players here," she said. "But our numbers? Our numbers are legion."

78

TRINA GAVE JIMMY a ration of crap for all of about thirty seconds before hunkering down and sucking face with him in front of my parents.

My father grumbled something. My mother was amused.

"I take it Chuck Peterson's out of the picture?" she asked me.

"Kind of," I said. Well, most everyone is out of the picture. Let's just get out of here, and we'll explain everything."

I wasn't looking forward to facing Prianka. I didn't have high hopes for the same sort of quick scolding and enthusiastic reunion that Trina gave Jimmy. Besides, there was still the issue of what to do with Diana and Dr. Marks.

Some people wanted to shoot them. Others wanted to open the door and let the poxers have dinner. Finally, the guy with the tattoos told everyone to shut up.

"Listen. It's the kids she's after, so let them decide."

I'm a lot of things. I don't think 'kid' is one of them anymore. Actually, in the past week, I've been an arsonist, a kidnapper, a semi-boyfriend, and almost a murderer. Still, I wasn't going to pull the trigger on this one.

"Leave them," said Trina. "It's not easy out there, and as soon as those poxers get through that door, they aren't going to want to be here, either. Let them figure it out."

"One thing's for sure," I added. "They aren't coming with us."

There was a general murmur of approval among everyone. In short order, we had an agreement.

They were on their own.

Diana sat with her legs crossed and a slightly amused look on her face. Dr. Marks cradled his battered head in his hands. Between my dad and Tattoo Guy, they probably gave him a concussion.

"That's very humane of the two of you," purred Diana. She was solely focused on just me and Trina. It was weird. Like no one else was there. "But I will find you—whatever it takes. Wherever you go, I will find you. What you carry in your genes is far too precious."

"Shut up," Trina muttered and rolled her eyes. "You're over."

"My dear," said Diana. "You may think you have shut down Site 37, but everything that has happened in this room—every word—has been broadcast to every other site in our network." She pointed up to one corner of the room. A small video camera was mounted on the wall. "You can kill me. You can leave me. It's no matter. I'm not the important one. You and your brother are. Surely, there are a scant few others like the two of you out there—the product of two immune individuals. But for right now, you are the two we've found."

Dr. Marks lifted his bloody face to us.

"We never meant for the virus to be released just yet. That was an accident. No one constructs the annihilation of a species without an antidote." There were tears in his eyes. I almost felt sorry for him.

But . . . nah.

We heard a small crack. The door that the poxers were banging on began to splinter.

"Time to fly, duckies," said Aunt Ella and began ushering everyone on to the bus.

Diana and Dr. Marks just sat there. They didn't ask for mercy. They didn't ask to come with us. I was tired, and I didn't care. After we were all on board, Aunt Ella pulled the handle, and the door folded closed. She started the engine and backed the bus out of the mess she had made of the McDuffy Estate.

I turned my head away as we left. I didn't want to see Diana again. I didn't want to see Dr. Marks. I had my parents, and they were safe. That's what I had come to do, and that's what had been done.

When we got around the front of the building I realized what the great crash was that we had heard earlier. My aunt had driven the bus right through the iron-gate. The mangled metal hung on its hinges, a mass of twisted iron with chunks of stone lying on the ground.

At the end of the dirt road, Aunt Ella let me, Trina, and Jimmy out of the bus so we could take the minivan. Jimmy was all too happy to chuck the hospital wheelchair into the woods.

"I want my baby back," he said as he caressed his tricked out wheelchair, safely folded in the back seat.

"I thought I was your baby," said Trina.

"Aw, Trina—I've got room in my heart for two."

Aunt Ella beeped the bus. I started the minivan and did a three point turn with ease. Not that I was ever going to take a driving test, but, well, yippee for me!

As I pulled out of the dirt road and on to the Trail, Trina turned to me.

"Just so you know, Prianka is pissed," she said.

I didn't answer her. I figured as much, but I didn't care. I couldn't wait to see her.

79

AFTER AUNT ELLA had put Uncle Don in the front pasture, Newfie in the barn, left her note, and gone out into the world, she encountered horrors that were beyond her comprehension. She never figured out that poxers burned, so she ended up doing an awful lot of running and hiding.

What was most important to her was to find survivors.

She found two.

One was an ancient lady named Dorcas Duke, who drove the school bus for the county regional district. Dorcas was like a hundred years old but tough as leather. The first thing she did was show my aunt exactly how to drive the bus and how to work the shift—just in case something happened to her. Luckily, my aunt had driven big rigs for a while . . . seriously . . . so she took to driving the bus pretty easily.

The second was a little girl named Krystal. As near as Aunt Ella could tell, Krystal's entire family had been taken out by poxers while she hid under her bed. When Aunt Ella was finally able to make Krystal realize that she wasn't going to hurt her, she coaxed the details out of her along with her age.

She had said she was 'this many,' holding up her pudgy little hand.

'This many' turned out to be four.

Aunt Ella brought Dorcas and Krystal back to the farm, not long after Jimmy and I had left. There, she found the satanic verses written all over her walls, along with Trina, Newfie, two soldiers being held prisoner with duct tape, an autistic Indian kid with a crow on his shoulder, his hot sister . . . ahem . . . and a prepubescent boy with a taste for firearms.

Trina and Prianka frantically ratted me and Jimmy out in under a minute. After a quick powwow, they decided that my Aunt Ella and Trina were going to come after us.

Later, I found out while Aunt Ella and Trina were saving our asses, Newfie adopted Krystal, just like he had adopted Sanjay. She ended up falling asleep with her arms dug deep into his thick fur.

Dorcas, who longed for a shower, went out into the brisk fall night and dunked herself in the pond. When she came back in, she helped herself to some clean clothes out of my aunt's closet before falling asleep in her bedroom upstairs.

Sanjay performed another weird ritual in front of our prisoners with Andrew by his side. After, he crawled underneath the wheelbarrow and fell asleep with his feathered protector sitting on top of the boat and eyeballing our duct taped duo.

Bullseye and Prianka were persuaded by a frightened but desperate Cal and Luke, to be freed so they could use the bathroom. Either that, or everyone was going to have to deal with the stench of poopy pants, which neither Prianka or Bullseye felt like stomaching.

Amazingly, the soldiers dutifully waited for each other outside of the bathroom door at full attention. When they were through, they marched back into the living room and let themselves be taped into their chairs again. I suppose the fact that Bullseye had a gun trained on them the whole time helped.

Around midnight, Prianka went out on the front porch. She was worried out of her mind. About a half hour later, Bullseye joined her. He couldn't sleep and was more than a little worried about us. In the late September darkness, Prianka Patel and Ryan "Bullseye" McCormick, the sixth grader from Deer Meadow Elementary School, actually talked real talk, not adolescent, snarky, one-liners. For Prianka, an early maternal instinct kicked in, not unlike the responsibility she felt for Sanjay.

The motherly feeling for Ryan that bloomed that night never went away.

Uncle Don's watch read two when Aunt Ella and I finally pulled into the driveway with a school bus full of weary refugees from Site 37. As headlights swept across the house, I saw Prianka standing on the porch with Bullseye. They were both holding rifles tightly in their fists, because we could have been any vehicle, friendly or otherwise.

Aunt Ella pulled the bus up in front of the barn. I eased Stella's minivan up alongside it.

Even before I turned the keys and the engine rumbled to a halt, I could feel Prianka's eyes boring into my skull.

"Now or never, man," said Jimmy.

"I'll take door number two."

"Wimp," said Trina.

"I like my life," I said back.

They both got out of the car. Aunt Ella opened the bus door and let out sixteen weary people, including my mom and dad. I smiled when I saw my parents, arm in arm, walking slowly up to the porch. Prianka and Bullseye put down their guns and hugged my aunt when they saw her. Jimmy high-fived Bullseye, but got the cold shoulder from Prianka. He shrugged and wheeled his way into the candlelit house followed by Trina and Bullseye.

Aunt Ella stood on the porch and waved everyone into her home. When the last person was in, I watched her turn and say something to Prianka. Prianka shook her head and plopped down on the steps with the shotgun across her lap.

My aunt put her hands on her hips and stared out across the field where she had put Uncle Don. She stood there a moment, crossed her arms over her chest, and stared at her feet. About a minute later she uncrossed her arms, took a deep breath, said something to Prianka, and went inside the house.

All who was left was just me and her, and I was afraid. I was very afraid.

The moon was out so I could see well enough, although everything looked a little like the picture on an old black and white television. Prianka didn't move. She knew I was sitting in the van. What was I supposed to do?

"She has a gun," I said out loud to no one. Not that I think she would have really shot me, but who knew for sure? It stretched across her lap like a safety bar on a rollercoaster. There we sat—me in the minivan and Prianka on the steps. Gray, moonlit darkness stretched across the gulf between us.

Hell—it might as well have been the Grand Canyon.

I shut my eyes, mostly because I just didn't want to deal. I got my parents. My family was all right and alive. That's what I wanted, and that need was what lit the fire beneath me this past week and kept me going.

Suddenly, something went off in my head. It was like an explosion—like this great big ball of light that illuminated everything. In that moment, I understood. I really, truly understood.

My eyes flew open. I pulled the keys from the ignition and slid them into my pocket. They jangled against the jeep keys I had stolen so no one could follow me and Jimmy to the McDuffy Estate. I opened the door and stepped out into the night. The air was brisk, but it still wasn't that bone-biting cold that sometimes happens in the fall before the snow comes.

Without hesitating, I walked over to the porch, mounted the steps, turned, and sat down next to Prianka. She was staring out at the pasture, so I did, too.

"I found my parents," I said. "I had to. I knew they were alive. I knew way down deep. I didn't have a choice, and I didn't want to make anyone else here choose, either. This was mine to do, so I did it."

Prianka didn't say anything.

"But I've been stupid," I said. "This whole time I've been

monumentally stupid. Maybe it's because I'm a guy. Maybe it's because I'm just not as smart as you. I don't know."

She still didn't say anything, but I saw her bite on her lip a little and stare down at her lap.

"This whole time it's been about me—my parents—my needs." I looked down. "What an idiot I've been. You lost your parents, too. And you don't know where they are or if they're alive or if one is and one isn't. You just don't know. You will probably never know. What's more, you have Sanjay to worry about and that's a whole lot of worry."

A tear rolled down her cheek.

"Pri, you've been carrying his weight for so long you probably don't even realize how heavy he is. Well, you don't have to anymore."

"What do you mean?"

"You're not alone, Prianka," I said to her in the darkness. "I have parents, so now you have parents. I have a family, so now you have a family." I reached over and pulled the rifle off her lap and placed it down on the steps below us. "I have you, and you have me. You've probably had me since kindergarten."

I stopped talking. My words hung in the air between us, and I thought they were going to hang like that for a long time.

They didn't.

Her lips were on mine, and her arms were around me in seconds.

80

STORIES LIKE MINE don't tie up neatly in a bow. Maybe in fiction they do, but this isn't fiction. Chuck Peterson died. Uncle Don died. Mrs. Bhoola and Bullseye's family and Mr. Embry and that lady, Mrs. Bijur, who Diana murdered by throwing her in with that poxer—they all died. Most everyone I ever knew died. All the kids in my high school and all the people on my street and in my town and, well, everywhere—they're dead, too.

Just dead—a lot.

That next morning, after chowing down on a huge breakfast everyone pitched in to make, we all gathered in the living room and decided that we couldn't stay, because sooner or later, Diana would find me and Trina.

Some of the people who we rescued from Site 37 said they wanted nothing more than to go home and search for their loved ones. Diana wasn't a threat to them anymore, and now that they knew that people like her existed, they would be on the lookout for them.

They just wanted to go their own ways. I could understand that.

Of course, we also had to contend with Luke and Cal.

The soldiers actually asked if they could come with us. Do you believe that? My mother was the one who said no.

"We would never be able to trust you," she told them. "You hit me. You hit my daughter. You were stupid enough and mindless enough to follow the orders of that evil, evil woman. You were evil, yourselves. I'm sorry, but I'll never believe you can come back from that. You can't come with us."

Her words were harsh, but I respected her decision.

Aunt Ella, however, showed them a little mercy.

"Before we leave I'll set you free," she said. "You're welcome to my house. There are stores of food in the basement and if you run out, there are the turkeys and the llamas out in the pasture." Bullseye didn't understand what she meant by that, so I smacked my lips. His eyes brightened with comprehension. He wrinkled his nose and swallowed.

Finally, Aunt Ella made them promise that if they left the house for good, they would set the animals free so they would all have a fighting chance at survival.

Just like us.

WHEN ALL WAS said and done, eight people left us that morning. There were hugs and tears and goodbyes. Each one swore that if the subject ever came up in their travels, they never heard of Tripp and Trina Light, the immune twins. We saved them all, and they swore to protect us.

Of course there were questions about where we were going, but we didn't exactly know.

In front of the soldiers, my father said that we might be heading out Route 80 across the country and maybe down toward Arizona. Duh, even four-year-old Krystal was smart enough to know what he really meant was we weren't going in that direction at all.

Outside, and away from the prying ears of Luke and Cal, I told those who were leaving about the Wordsmith Used Book Emporium in Greenfield.

"It's a safe place," I said. They all thanked me.

The eight who left us set out on foot, loaded up with a lot of matches and paper. Aunt Ella told them that further down the road there was a small group of houses. They would find cars there and probably poxers, too. They promised to be careful. We all said our goodbyes and watched them walk down the driveway, along the fence, and out of sight.

As for me, I never saw any of them again. Sometimes, I think we should have tried to convince them to come with us. You know—safety in numbers and all that—but at the end of the day, you can't tell other people what to do. You can only be there for them and support them in their own decisions.

Gee. When did I get so smart?

BY NOONTIME WE had packed the bus with as many supplies as we thought we needed. Before we left, Sanjay and Bullseye went inside with Aunt Ella to cut Luke and Cal free—one of them for the creep factor and one for the gun.

Later, Aunt Ella confided in me that Sanjay drew a circle around them on the floor with a magic marker and chanted some words that she didn't understand. Either he was protecting them or cursing them. Sometimes, I wish he had cursed them, but then again, if it weren't for Luke and Cal, I don't think I would have ever found my parents.

I had to give them points for that.

Without even asking, me, Trina, Prianka, Jimmy, Sanjay, Bullseye, Andrew, and Newfie piled into the minivan. Aunt Ella, my parents, Dorcas, Krysal, and six others took the bus.

We pulled away from the farm and headed back down toward Greenfield. At the bottom of the Trail, we could see that the highway was still teeming with poxers. Somehow, they didn't scare me nearly as much, knowing that my parents were right behind us. We slowly drove through the underpass and back up the hill toward Greenfield center.

There were still poxers everywhere, but not nearly as many as our first time through town. In the distance, I saw Chuck Peterson's Hummer glowing in the crisp sunlight. In front of Stella's building we stopped the minivan. I got out and trotted over to the bus.

Aunt Ella pulled open the accordion door.

"We just have to say goodbye to someone," I said. "Follow the road out of town so you're away from the poxers. We'll meet you in an hour."

I thought my parents were going to object, but they just nodded their heads like they understood. Maybe they thought that their kids somehow miraculously aged in the past week or that we were old enough to make our own decisions.

I guess we were. That still didn't mean that we wouldn't always need our mom and dad. After all, we traveled through the land of the dead to rescue them.

Aunt Ella pulled the bus away, and I drove the minivan around the back of Stella's building and parked in the alley. After checking carefully to make sure there were no poxers around, we all got out of the car and went to the back door. I took the key that Stella had given us and slid it into the lock.

"Stella?" we called out to her when we were all safely inside. "Stella?"

Prianka pulled out a flashlight, and we all made our way through the back of the bookstore, up the spiral stair case, and through the reading loft. We heard the stomping of feet on the stairs behind the big door, followed by a click as it was unlocked and opened.

"My word," Stella exclaimed as the light poured out and bathed us in color.

"We did it," I told her. "We saved my parents."

She smothered us all in hugs and kisses. Andrew cawed and Newfie even jumped up and bathed her with his big, sloppy tongue, even though he had never met her before.

When we were all upstairs, we told Stella everything. How we made it through Greenfield to my aunt's place, about Purgatory Chasm, Site 37, my parents, everything.

"It's not safe to leave the survivor banner out," I said. "You can't trust who you may come across. We told some people about you. If they come to search you out, they're cool. Other than that, you never know."

"The world's a bad place now," said Jimmy. "No one knows how long it's going to stay that way."

Stella shook her head. There were tears in her eyes.

"Where will you go?" she asked.

"Away," said Trina. "Just away."

"There are people who want us now," I said. "Me and Trina. Somehow they think we're special. Completely immune." I rubbed my hands together. "We don't even know if they're right."

"Hopefully you'll never get bit to test that theory," added Prianka.

Sanjay hung back from the rest of us. He took up his regular position by the bookcase with a book in his lap. Newfie sat by his side, and Andrew on his shoulder. There was still some red paint on him from his mad ride through the world of the occult, but other than that he seemed fine.

"And my special boy?" she asked. "Is he doing well?"

We watched him flip through pages, his little brain absorbing everything like a high-tech computer.

"Better than the rest of us," said Jimmy. "Sanjay's the man."

"Oh!" cried Stella. "I almost forgot." She rushed over to the big table in her kitchen and grabbed a paper bag that was sitting there.

"Ryan, um, I mean Bullseye got this for me," she said. Bullseye blushed and stared at his feet.

I didn't understand. "Got what?"

"When you left here," she said. "Those monsters—I saw what happened." Stella stood and walked over to Sanjay. She knelt down by him. Newfie bent down and lapped her face again. Stella took the bag and gently pushed it toward Sanjay.

"For you, my dove," she whispered.

Sanjay pushed the book off of his lap, took the bag, and carefully opened it. He reached inside and pulled out the impossible.

It was Poopy Puppy.

Sanjay looked at the stuffed dog in wonder. He was sewn together with brightly colored stitches. His left arm was new. A smile spread across Sanjay's face.

"Hey, Buddy!" he exclaimed.

Prianka put her hand to her mouth. I put my arm around her, and she leaned her head against my shoulder.

Sanjay hugged Poopy Puppy tightly and rocked gently back and forth.

"Found you," he whispered softly to the stuffed dog. "Found you."

Andrew cawed. Sanjay pulled Poopy Puppy to his ear and listened like he always had.

"Yes," he said. "Uh huh." Sanjay nodded his head. He looked up and found Stella's eyes. "Poopy Puppy says he went to the hospital," said Sanjay. "He said Dr. Stella fixed him. He's all better now."

"Yes," said Stella. "He's all better now."

Sanjay took Poopy Puppy and held him up to Andrew. The bird sized up the stuffed dog with his little, black eyes before gently rubbing his beak against the soft fabric. Sanjay also showed Poopy Puppy to Newfie. The giant dog sniffed at him and woofed.

"Poopy Puppy, this is Andrew," said Sanjay. "And this is Newfie." He hugged the stuffed dog close to him once more. "We're a family now, okay? A family."

I looked around at my friends—every one of them. Sanjay was right. We were a family now.

A smile spread across my face. A family—I could live with that.

THE END

Acknowledgements

Although there are those who may think writing is a lonely process, it is far from that. It takes the support and dedication of many people to see a story come to life.

First and foremost, I would like to thank David Gilfor for reading over my shoulder, chapter after chapter, making sure that my voice, my characters, and their exploits remained convincing and engaging.

I would like to thank Shira Block McCormick for her friendship and support and for gushing so much over the first short story I handed her that I simply had to write more.

I would also like to thank my group of readers who were always honest and never afraid to point me in the right direction: Tamara Fricke, Krystal Glushien, Patti Fischer, Danny Eaton, Sheryl Odentz, and Lauren Levin.

I would like to thank my mother, Joline Odentz, for tirelessly proofreading my work because 'I kant spel' and shamelessly promoting my writing to anyone who will listen.

Finally I would like to give a special thanks to Lois Winston, Ashley Grayson, and the folks at Bell Bridge Books, and my phenomenal editor, Debra Dixon, for taking a chance on me. You're the best.

About Howard Odentz

Howard Odentz is a life-long resident of Western Massachusetts, where he divides his time between writing and tending a small farm. His love of animals, along with the lore of the region, often finds its way into his stories.

The supernatural plays a major role in Mr. Odentz's writing. He is endlessly fascinated by the psychological aspects of those who are thrown into otherworldly circumstances.

In addition to Dead (A Lot), he has penned two full length musical comedies. "In Good Spirits" is inspired by the real-life ghostly experiences of a community theatre group and their haunted stage. "Piecemeal" tells the backstory of Victor Frankenstein's Hollywood-created protégé, Igor.

"I like writing about the supernatural world," says Mr. Odentz. "I'm from Western Massachusetts. There's more than enough paranormal activity in these parts to keep me inspired for years to come."

Dead (A Lot) is Mr. Odentz's first full-length novel.